D1327680

NAUGHTY

A Novel by

MONTE SCHULZ

Fantagraphics Books,
7563 Lake City Way NE
Seattle, Washington, 98115

Editor: Gary Groth
Cover paintings: Debbie Faas
Cover Design: Emory Liu
Title Font Handlettering; Nomi Kane
Poem Handlettering: Nicole Starczak
Editorial Assistants: Kristy Valenti,
Tom Graham, Janice Lee, and Jack McKean
Associate Publisher: Eric Reynolds
Publishers: Gary Groth & Kim Thompson

To disappoint the soul is a fearful deed for a man.

— W.Q. Judge

CALIFORNIA, 1956

JOE KRUEGER CAME DOWN from Washington State in the middle of a cold autumn evening. He kept a thermos of warm coffee on the seat beside him in the old Studebaker wagon and listened to swing bands from radio stations out of Eugene and Medford, and concentrated on staying awake. It had rained all through central Oregon and along the coast highway where wind blew strong off the ocean, buffeting his automobile as he drove south into California.

He reached Ocean City just after midnight. Low on gas, and none of the filling stations open, Joe decided to try and find some place to stay for the night. The rain had quit and he had his window rolled down to clear fog off the glass. He smelled salt water and drove downhill. A damp ugly wind blew off the bay and Joe saw lights along the cold waterfront. Three blocks above the wharf, he turned onto a narrow side street of weathered old residences and found a vacancy sign on the front stairs of a tall frame house at the end of the block. A lamp was lit in the lobby, so Joe parked the Studebaker, buttoned up his jacket, grabbed his duffle, and went to investigate a room. Up on the porch, he knocked softly at the front door while peeking in through the curtain lace. The registration desk was empty, but there was a light on in the kitchen at the end of the hall. He rapped more firmly at the glass. The wind gusted. He saw a door open inside the kitchen and a young brunette in a smock came up from the basement, rubbing her eyes. She looked disturbed. Her smock was dusty and she wiped her hands on her apron as she came down the hall to let him in.

"Sorry to bother you," Joe told her as she opened the door. "I need a room and I saw your sign out there."

"Well, it's awfully late."

"Don't I know it."

She frowned, but let him inside and he followed her over to the front desk where she pulled out the ledger. With a trace of hillbilly accent, she told him there was a room on the second floor. "It's small, but nice and comfortable. We're asking twelve dollars for the week. Mother cooks oatmeal and toast and eggs for breakfast."

"I don't know that I'll be here a week. What're you charging for overnight?" Joe needed to get back to Watsonville the day after next if he hoped to keep his job at the nursery.

"Well, mister, I'm not supposed to let a room go for one night. It's not good business."

"My name's Joe, and I'll pay you four dollars. I can't afford more than that. Otherwise, I'll have to sleep in my car."

The girl's eyes softened. "Are you down on your luck, Joe? That won't last, I hope you know. In fact, if you give me a lock of your hair and tell me your birth date, I can predict what'll happen to you during your life."

"I don't need a haircut to know what'll happen to me in the next six hours if you don't hire me one of your rooms. I'll freeze my ass off in that car out there." He opened his billfold and drew out four dollars. It was twice what any room here was worth, but he was dead tired and what choice did he have? "So what do you say? Give a guy a break?"

Wind rattled at the windows and rain fell harder, soaking the porch. A cold draft swept into the lobby from back in the kitchen. She told him, "If Mother finds out, she'll absolutely have my hide. You won't tell her, will you?"

"Nope." Joe handed over his four dollars. In another few minutes, he'd be asleep on his feet.

"No, that's too much." She slid one dollar back across the walnut counter top. "We both know it wouldn't be fair. Father says I'm honest to a fault, and I can't disagree because I was just born that way. It's a funny thing how some don't mind cheating another, but I just never seen the sense in it."

"Thanks."

"My name's Ida."

"Glad to know you, Ida."

She fluttered her eyelashes like a starlet. "I'm pleased you're staying with us, Joe." She shut the ledger and put it under the countertop, then came back around to Joe's side of the desk. He noticed she had big blubbers and a pretty smile. There hadn't been any girls in Joe's life for a while now and it was about time he got kissed. She handed him a key. "Your room's 2B. That's on the second floor. It's got a nice view of the ocean."

"Thanks."

"Do you want me to show you up there?"

"Sure, that'd be swell."

She smiled. "I'll just be a minute. We're putting a new disposal drain in the basement and I been cleaning up down there. It's an awful chore, but I just taken the tarpaulins off and packed them away, so it's done when my parents get back from Fort Bragg tomorrow."

"I'm not too tired to give you a hand if you still want one. How about showing me what you need done?"

Joe started toward the kitchen. He didn't get two steps before Ida blocked his way. "You can't go down there, honey, because it's not right to have a guest do something I have no trouble at all doing myself. Mother would have a fit if she found out. Besides, like I said, it's taken care of now, and doesn't need nothing except the finishing touches and those are mine to do."

Joe saw that she had dust on her skin and eyebrows from laboring in the basement, and that didn't seem fair to him. Maybe if he hadn't liked her it wouldn't have mattered. "You can tell me to mind my own business, but I don't care to go up to bed knowing you'll be griming yourself down here all alone when all you had to do was say the word and I'd help you out and be happy to do it."

"Well, then I won't do no more tonight," she told him. "How would that be?"

He smiled as he picked up his duffle bag. "Well, I'd say show me that room upstairs."

"Just let me close the basement so a stray cat don't get caught in here. They're such a nuisance and we have a window broke behind the roses. I won't be a moment."

Satisfied that he'd been a gentleman, Joe watched Ida rush off down the hall and into the kitchen where she shut the basement door, locked it, and then switched off the light. She had her business figured out, all right.

"You can go on up," she told him. "It's the first door on the left. I want to get some fresh towels."

THE ROOM WAS SMALL with just a ratty blue rug, a highboy dresser, a nightstand and reading lamp, and a common iron bed across from the bathroom. A single window pointed out over the side yard, faded pink roses on the wallpaper floor to ceiling, a painting of a mountain lake in a simple wooden frame next to the door, and a tall brass standing lamp in a corner by the window. After emptying his duffle and taking a leak in the toilet, Joe stuffed a couple shirts and a clean pair of trousers into the oak dresser and shoved the duffle under the bed. He hung up his jacket in a closet by the door, slipped his shoes off, then sat on the bed and waited for Ida. The old springs squeaked and the mattress was lumpy. A steep and constant rain streaked down the glass behind a linen shade.

Joe fluffed the pillow and leaned back against the headboard and fought the urge to close his eyes. It had been a long weekend and he was awfully tired. If he showed up a day or two late to Watsonville, his boss might possibly stand for it. Who worked harder than Joe, anyhow? If that sonofabitch didn't like it, he could lump it. Joe had been knocking around for so long now, it was tough to feel much loyalty. The nursery hired packs of Mexicans to haul fertilizer and dig the rows. They'd labor in the fields all day long until they smelled so bad you couldn't be indoors with them. After nightfall, some smoked tea and went to town and started knife fights and got tossed into jail or shipped home to Guadalajara. Others collected together in cabins and sang songs and drank tequila. If you spoke a few words of Spanish, you could make friends with some of them and those you did treated you like a king. They'd do anything for you, except introduce their sisters who'd only marry a gringo if he had money enough to buy her a house and was willing to swear allegiance to the Pope. The more he thought about it, the more Joe realized that Watsonville was a nothing job. Even the wetback Mexicans had it better than he did because their sole ambition in life was to stir manure and water the growing fields so they could take a few dollars back down to Mexico with them when the work ran out. Joe's boss owned the business and didn't care for anything else. He had a big fancy house on fifty acres with a nice yard of grass and oak trees and a big barn and four automobiles. His wife ran some political committee in town. Last year, a pair of fellows came into the county talking union and Joe's boss told anyone who'd listen that those two were Red Jew fairies who wiped their asses with the flag every morning after shitting on a picture of Ike. Joe met them on the highway to Castroville and gave them a ride and thought what they had to say about how a regular guy in America these days being no better off than a dog in a ditch was pretty goddamned accurate. He let them off in front of a drugstore and they gave Joe a pamphlet to study when he got home and thanked him for the lift. A mile up the road, he threw it out the window and didn't look back. Joe hated politics.

Rain drizzled down the glass and the room grew cold in the dark. Joe lay flat on the bed and thought more about Ida. She had a good figure and her big blubbers were eye-catchers, all right. If he could stay long enough, he might be able to bed her down. To hell with Watsonville. His boss was a dog-ass and his boss's wife was a whore. Only a month or so after Joe got hired, Gladys was down to the nursery twice a day prancing about in frilly blouses that sold her jugs to whomever was looking and giving Joe the glad eye when he drove the truck. He thought positively they'd have a lay, even if it put him in a fix. One day she slipped a private note in with a list of supplies that told him to go to a vegetable stand just south of town. Coming back from his errands, he parked on the roadside and walked out back of the business where a small house and a dusty garage were half-hidden under a grove of shade trees. Joe was so jittery he had to chug a bottle of beer before he left the truck. Gladys was waiting for him under a ripe avocado tree by the backdoor. Her blouse was unbuttoned to her navel. When he got there, she kissed him hard on the mouth. He grabbed her tits and kissed her, too, and she slipped a hand down the front of his trousers and rubbed him hard. He almost went haywire. Then she licked his ear and said they ought to go inside and he asked if anyone was around and she said, how the hell should I know? Well, Joe was plenty steamed up and not too scared of fucking his boss's wife, but he had no taste for trespassing and told her so as he pinched her nipples. She asked if he was queer and he said no, so she went inside the house and he followed her to the door and saw her lying face down on a brass bed with her bare bottom hiked up to the sky. His fly was undone and he was about to have it when he heard Mexican voices coming in their direction. Probably he shouldn't have run off into the strawberry field without telling Gladys she was about to have company. Half a year went by before he saw her again. This time she was at a hardware store downtown scouting house paint and complaining about school integration with a couple of her committee friends. Joe was one aisle over and fairly certain she hadn't noticed him, until Gladys leaned around the corner and shot him a cold eye as she said to her pals, *"Not all niggers are colored."* After that, whenever they crossed paths at the nursery, Gladys pretended Joe was dead. She sure was hot stuff, though.

Joe heard a knock at the door and got up to answer it. Ida came in carrying an armload of towels. She put them on a shelf in the bathroom above the toilet.

"I don't know how I forgot to bring them up here this morning," Ida said quietly, "but I've been awfully tired lately. I get the most dreadful pains in my back at night and I can't sleep a wink without my pills."

"Why's that?" Joe wished he could lie back down on the bed, but thought it would be rude.

She told him, "Well, you see, I had a serious accident last year. I was stepping off a curb downtown just when a bus driver let off on his brake and I was knocked back onto the sidewalk. My witnesses to the insurance company said I was almost killed, and when you're as close to God as I've been now and then, you know heaven's always a step away and when your hour comes, luck's got nothing to do with it. I just said a prayer in the ambulance and a doctor held my hand and told me I'd be fine. Besides, it paid fifteen hundred dollars. Can you imagine? All for not keeping my eye on where I was going."

"That's awful." Joe had never suffered a bad back and had no idea how it felt, though his dad wore a brace one summer when Joe was a kid and had to eat standing up.

"Yes, it is, but I'll survive. I'm stronger than I look." She smiled at him. "You just watch. I always make the best of things."

She sat on the bed with her arms braced behind her and hummed a tune Joe didn't recognize. He didn't know what to say. He felt jittery, but he liked her being in the room with him. Sitting down, too, he told Ida, "You got a nice voice."

"I have my inspirations," she replied, fixing him with a steady gaze. Then she slid over so close beside him, Joe could smell the lemon in her hair. She took his hand in hers and gave it a warm squeeze. "Do you think I'm fast?"

"I know I don't mind being around you," he stammered. "I think you're pretty swell, if that's what you're asking." He thought he should kiss her, but didn't dare. What if she thought he was being fresh and got scared and ran out?

"You don't miss much, do you, Joe?"

"Huh?"

"I couldn't say no if I tried." Then she gently kissed him on the lips.

Nothing in Joe's experience prepared him for how he felt after that. His fate was sealed. In this world, the brain is servant to the heart.

Ida kissed him tenderly once more, then pulled back. "I have strict ethics, you know."

Joe's hands were shaking. He hoped to kiss her again, so he told her, "I've been thinking about staying over another day or so, maybe going to the picture show tomorrow night." Joe drew a nervous breath. "How about it?"

"Aren't you sweet?" Ida offered a dreamy smile. "You always say the right thing, don't you? You better look out, or I might say yes."

A toilet flushed in a room at the end of the hall and Joe heard someone whistling tunelessly as a door closed.

Ida's gaze still fixed on him, she asked, "Would you really take me to the movies? Honest? It's Jerry Lewis at the Rialto."

"Sure I would."

"Then it's a date."

Ida kissed Joe again. She let him embrace her as she gave him one more titillating kiss, and then broke free. "I'm happy you're so sweet to me, but we both better go to sleep, honey. There's so much to do tomorrow. I'll let you help me, if you like."

"Just name it."

Ida kissed his cheek. "Good night, Joe."

Then she left.

After brushing his teeth, Joe turned off the lights and lay down again and thought about Ida and how much he liked her. She sure was a darling. He didn't intend to leave until he figured out what to do about her. Would she have him to bed? She sure kissed like she meant it and no girl had taken to him like that in quite a while. Maybe he loved her, and maybe not. Ida was no Doris Day, but she'd given him the go signal and what else did he have to do if he wasn't driving back to

Watsonville tomorrow? He heard a radio playing faintly upstairs and someone pacing about. Otherwise, the old house was dark and quiet for the night. From Joe's experience, most boardinghouses weren't very lively. Taking a room in one ordinarily meant you weren't too prosperous, and most tenants Joe had known didn't work much except for odd jobs about town. If you met them on the street you might guess they were vagrant or invalid. Nobody bragged about hiring a room in a boardinghouse.

Anyhow, Joe had a lot of thinking to do, decisions to make, things to consider no matter where he went. He'd come down to Ocean City that night from a reunion at Moses Lake with some of his old Army Air Corps buddies. They had hired a wing of rooms at a motor court near downtown Wenatchee with air conditioning in each unit and a steak joint next door, and went around together in a pack for one long weekend as they had during ground crew training before shipping out to New Guinea. Unfortunately, it rained every day so they mostly stayed indoors telling dirty jokes and playing cards, then getting drunk after dinner when they went out to the bars or the pool hall across the street.

Friday night, Joe bought the first round of drinks and gave a toast to old times, but as the reunion played out, Joe began to have a tough time remembering what he'd liked about these fellows he'd gone halfway around the world with during the War. Stebbins worked for Chevrolet with a dealership at Sacramento and spoke like a hopped-up car salesman, cocky and full of himself. Joe hated salesmen of any sort and wanted to tell Stebbins to shove it. At New Guinea, Stebbins would get a few guys together every couple of weeks to steal canned goods from the mess hall and sell them to the Aussies, which could get you five to thirty at Leavenworth. Not getting caught made Stebbins act like Douglas MacArthur. He'd been an idiot during the War, and he was still one. All weekend long he needled Joe for driving a

Studebaker. Why did he care what anyone drove? What did it matter? Well, Stebbins was just one of those guys who puffed himself up by running everyone else down.

Then you had Rutherford, the randiest fellow Joe ever knew in the service. His eyes would bug out if he didn't have a fresh lay at every stop, and he kept a scorecard on each conquest from March Field to Manila Bay, reciting them aloud from his bunk at night like batting averages, most of which were figments of his sexed-up imagination. Of course, since girls were scarce during the War, some guys would do nearly anything to get their mitts on one. In New Guinea, the native girls were so ugly only Rutherford and a couple of squirrel shooters from Tennessee would admit to putting the boots to them. One evening at Leyte near the end of the War, a scrawny Filipino brought his pregnant wife to the air base, offering her free to the troops because he said he couldn't handle her anymore. Nobody was surprised to see Rutherford shove his way to the front of the line. After dinner at the steak house Friday night, Joe went downstairs and scribbled Rutherford's phone number in a toilet stall across the cartoonish sketch of a crude sex act. He laid off what Stebbins said or did because he figured everyone hated car salesmen, anyhow.

Bill Hastings was a different story. He'd been one of Joe's closest pals at Moses Lake and Joe had gotten to know him pretty well. In the service, he was about the worst goldbrick of all time. Out in New Guinea, Hastings was always falling asleep standing guard under a shade palm and weaseling out of counting munitions in the bomb dump and not doing much of anything on KP duty. Late in the afternoon that Saturday at Wenatchee, when the others were getting drunk at Doyle's saloon, Joe and Hastings drove out to the Columbia River and parked the Studebaker under a dripping cottonwood and drank a couple of beers. That's where Hastings explained to Joe how he'd finally gotten on track. *"See, you can't be a goldbrick your whole life, Joe, and expect to get anywhere.*" He had a wife now named Audrey and a little boy in Cub Scouts and a good job managing a Western Auto store. He told Joe about going to college on the G.I. Bill and meeting his best girl on campus and how goddamned hard he'd tried to prove himself to her by driving a taxi cab after school five days a week, and still earning his degree. Then Hastings asked, *"So what about you, Joe? Blow anyone up lately?"*

At Wakde Island off the northern shore of New Guinea, Joe had been part of a detail that loaded bombs onto attack aircraft, one of which was piloted by a nice lieutenant named Crosley who actually associated with non-coms. He and Joe played cards together a few times, and once Crosley even showed Joe a picture of his wife, Mona, who looked like Anne Baxter's twin sister. They hadn't been married a month before Crosley shipped out to the Pacific, but she wrote to him every day to say she loved him and to come home safely. One balmy afternoon, with the engine cowl blocking his view, Crosley zigzagged his P-47 down a runway that extended the length of the island, carrying a load of bombs Joe had supervised himself. Crosley didn't get more than a thousand yards out over the blue ocean before his plane disintegrated in a massive fireball. He'd just given Joe and his crew a thumb's up before he got airborne, then he was blown to bits from one of the bombs detonating. Joe felt badly enough without guys ribbing him for the duration. Maybe if he'd captured some Jap officers or saved his platoon from a banzai charge, things might have been different. But that's just how his life seemed to go.

Once he was out of the service, Joe went home and slept in his old bedroom while he decided what to do next. Rather than looking for work, he'd borrow his dad's old auto and go driving after supper. It was summer, so there was still light for a few hours and the roads were mostly empty. He had a route he liked that took him past Miller's dairy and along the dusty apple orchards where new homes were being built for young men just like himself. Each one had a nice gravel driveway and a garage and a TV antenna on the roof. Joe drove up and down the narrow country roads pretending he was scouting property or coming home from his big job in the city. After sundown, he'd go into town and buy a hamburger and go to the movies or the bowling alley. Now and then he'd bump into someone he knew from school, tell a couple of war stories, and skip out the first chance he got. For a couple of months, his dad tried to sell him on a job at a cannery where he'd start by answering phones and ordering supplies. Instead, Joe packed up his duffle bag and took a bus down to San Francisco where he worked about half a year driving a newspaper delivery truck for the *Examiner* and shared a room at the back of his uncle's house with a housepainter who turned out to be queer. It was cold in the city and flooded with foreigners and Joe didn't make any friends, so he quit his job and rode a train down to Long Beach and talked his way into flipping hamburgers at a lunchwagon by the shore. He did this through the next summer and fall when the weather was gorgeous and there were girls all over the beach. He took a room above the garage of a house six blocks from the ocean where he was able to walk to work and pretend he had lived there his whole life. He bought the same swim trunks other fellows wore and dove into the surf like Johnny Weismuller.

Everything was going just great until he got the idea of looking up Crosley's widow, who lived with her folks a few miles away at San Pedro. Joe wanted to tell her how sorry he was about her husband getting killed, and after a month or so of mulling it over, he worked up the courage to telephone. She had a nice voice and seemed happy he called and invited him over the next evening for supper. He bought a new tie and a bouquet of daisies and rang her doorbell promptly at six o'clock. She looked even better than Anne Baxter. Mona had dimples and a good figure and a French hairdo. She told Joe he was the only one from Crosley's squadron who had ever called. He didn't bother to explain how he and Crosley were really from different outfits; they'd only known each other at Wakde where Crosley had died. But Mona's parents had gone to Coronado Island for the weekend, so she was alone that evening and happy to have company. She brought out a small scrapbook of Crosley's photographs and clippings, and Joe did his best to keep her spirits up by telling her a couple of funny stories involving Stebbins and some Army Air Corps guys who traded stolen gasoline cans for primitive wood carvings with a tribe of New Guinea pygmies. She said she liked how Joe laughed and asked if he wouldn't mind going out to eat and he thought that was a swell idea. Since he didn't have a car, they borrowed her mother's Ford and drove downtown for a steak dinner. Afterward, they went to a Gary Cooper movie at the Warner Theater. She held his hand for part of the show and he began to forget how they'd met. Back at her parents' house again, Mona invited Joe inside for a cup of coffee and offered him the use of their guestroom so he wouldn't have to take a taxi back to Long Beach, but Joe told her he had to work in the morning and called for a cab. Mona hugged him at the door before he left and kissed his cheek and he was pretty sure she had a tear in her eye. He felt rotten when he went to bed that night.

The next day, Mona telephoned to the hamburger joint. She wanted to see Joe when he got off work. Could he come over again? Sure, he could. Joe took a taxicab back up to San Pedro later that afternoon. Mona greeted him at the door with another little kiss and they cooked hamburgers on her father's backyard barbecue and talked about the future. Mona hoped to get married again one day and have a house of her own with a yard and a swimming pool and a family with lots of children. Joe agreed that was something to look forward to. After eating, Mona fixed daiquiris for them both and played a couple of Artie Shaw records in the living room. They danced for a while, then

Mona excused herself and went into the back of the house where she called for him after a few minutes. Joe followed her voice to the end of the hallway and found Mona in her bedroom wearing only a bra and panties. Shadows from a walnut tree just outside the window hid her face as she asked him to sit beside her on the bed. His hands trembled, but he did as she asked and she kissed him and unbuttoned his shirt and lay back on her pillow as he undressed. Later he would remember how softly she breathed, and the rosy scent of her hair. After dark, Mona fell asleep and Joe dressed again and walked out to the kitchen for a glass of water. Then he called a taxi and left without waking her. He wasn't ready for a wife, and certainly not Crosley's. Early that week, without telling his boss he was quitting or giving any notice to the owner of the garage apartment, Joe got on a bus in the middle of the night and left town.

He went to Modesto and lucked into a bed at a roominghouse and took a job cleaning up at a drive-in theater. It wasn't a bad situation at all. He didn't care how noisy things got or if the girls were homely and rarely paid him any notice. He bought some books on getting ahead in life and read them all cover to cover, but couldn't see how much of it applied to him. Most of the fellows they talked about seemed empty-headed, and the others were lazy do-nothings. Besides, Joe didn't want to run General Motors; he just needed something that would earn him a few dollars and buy him a steak now and then. The real problem was that Joe didn't have any ideas about what he ought to do. In the service, most of his thinking was done for him. He cleaned latrines, loaded bombs, got on and off boats, stood guard duty, serviced aircraft, and waited for the War to get over with. But everything was so complicated and difficult in civilian life. Maybe if he were smarter he'd be able to figure out how other guys got ahead. Some nights he'd lie in bed and worry that he was retarded and nobody had told him.

Joe's father had been a draughtsman and when Joe's mother was alive she made paintings of birds. Their home was full of books and artwork. When Joe was young, he was always asked if he loved to draw like his parents, but he had no talent for art and he read slowly, too. He enjoyed the funny papers and radio shows and riding his bike in the afternoon. As a kid, Joe was given an allowance of fifteen cents a week that he earned by sweeping the back porch of pine needles and leaves, and washing his dad's white Chrysler once a month. He might've had a paper route, except they lived out in the country on a quiet lane of maybe half a dozen families, and the newspaper didn't see fit to take him on. His mother thought that was silly, anyhow, because before she died, he used to help her pick raspberries in the woods and rake the yard each autumn. But back then, his schoolmates had real chores that kept them home when they wanted to play and thought Walter Krueger was about the best dad in the world because he didn't force Joe to take a real job. Every so often, though, Joe wondered if his dad really loved him, or just felt sorry for little Joey because he knew his son would never make anything of himself.

During his last year or so in Modesto, Joe worked as a janitor at a small elementary school. He'd read somewhere that the future is a mystery interpreted best by where we've been. Joe saw his own past as a futile mediocrity. He didn't need to be a millionaire; he just desired a modest success, some source of pride in accomplishment to lift him out of bed each day. But nothing went right. One cold November morning, when the children were in class, Joe decided he needed a cigarette, so he went to the janitor's closet, shut himself in, and lighted up. He was sick that day, vexed by a miserable fever. Dazed in the dark, he banged his forehead against a shelf and lost the cigarette into a bucket of lacquered rags he was supposed to have thrown out. He nearly burned down the school. They printed his picture in the evening newspaper and Joe's father telephoned to call him a goddamned fool. An hour later, he telephoned back, this time to apologize, reminding Joe that we all have to watch ourselves in order to do better for everyone's sake.

The next day Joe got fired.

When Stebbins telephoned about the reunion at Moses Lake, Joe was working for a nursery down in Watsonville, hauling plants and fertilizer and driving a truck. He'd quit smoking, rarely drank except for a few beers on the weekends, kept mostly to the clean and narrow, and his boss liked him. Why not? Nobody labored longer hours than Joe. He showed up at dawn and went home after dark. Most of his paycheck went into a savings account at a downtown bank. He was thirty years old and lived in the back room of a field shack and read Perry Mason novels and old issues of the pulp magazines *Stolen Sweets, Spicy Mystery Stories, Weird Tales*, and *Star Detective* in bed after supper. Sometimes he listened to the radio when it helped him sleep. He hadn't bedded a girl since Mona Crosley.

Sunday evening at Wenatchee, Joe and his three old buddies sat in a bar watching a cold hard rain drench the highway outside. Stebbins and Rutherford were both drunk and fighting over the phone number of their leggy redheaded waitress, while Hastings tried to recall the name of the ammunition ship they'd seen vaporized by a kamikaze attack off Mindoro in the Sulu Sea. Joe remembered how Jap planes would hide behind the sun-bright mountains, then attack out of nowhere, diving straight down the big smokestacks, terrorizing everyone on the oily blue water. Some guys got blown up and a lot of others lucked out. But a week before the Bomb was dropped, a fellow told Joe at Manila Bay that there was never any reason to worry; you'd either go home, or pass the clouds. Either way, it was all settled. Get rid of vanity and fear; life is the outcome of survival, and any future is the best reward. As evening rain fell at Wenatchee, Joe stood on the muddy roadside waving to his old pals as they drove off to sell automobiles, chase skirts, build backyard barbecues, and buy diapers for another newborn, scared as hell that he had outlived those traumatic days from Moses Lake to New Guinea and the Sea of Japan just so he could spread manure at Watsonville.

JOE WOKE SHIVERING in the dark room. The shade flapped at the window and he saw the frame was open a crack to the damp night air. He'd forgotten to close it when he put out the light. Rolling out of bed to shut the window, he heard a soft knock at his door. The knocking had awakened him, not the cold. Going to the door, he found Ida in a cotton nightgown standing alone in the dim hall. She was weeping.

"Something so awful's happened, Joe, I can hardly believe it."

He rubbed his eyes. "Huh?"

"A highway patrolman came over here to tell me in person, because that's how they do it in these cases. Oh, honey, I don't know what I'm going to do. They got killed, Joe, my parents, in a motor accident earlier tonight. They went upside down into the ocean, eight miles south of here. He said the Ford was crushed on the rocks and their bodies were washed away. He told me there won't be nothing to bury."

She collapsed into his arms.

Joe helped her to his bed in the dark and laid her down, then closed the door and rushed to sit beside her and hold her hand as she wept.

"God help me, I'm an orphan now, Joe. How am I going to live? What'll I do?"

He was shocked almost speechless. What could he say? "I'm so sorry. I wish there was something I could do for you. It's awful."

"Do you really? Oh gosh, I'm so sorry to drag you into this, Joe. It's not your fault. It's nobody's fault. I just didn't know who else to turn to, and you were so sweet tonight, offering to help me out in the basement.

And now this awful thing has happened, and everything's just gone black, black, black, except for you, Joe. Except for you."

Then Ida began crying again, and Joe put his arms around her and held her tight as she was wracked with sobs. He brushed her hair with his fingers, patted her shoulder, and kissed her forehead. What else do you do? When his own mother died of liver cancer, Joe had been stationed at Leyte and read about her passing in a letter from his father. He'd sat on a bunk by himself and cried and nobody had said a word. Now, Joe kept hugging Ida until her tears slowed and she quit shaking.

After a while, she sighed with a sniffle. "It's just so strange."

"What's that?"

"Well, how I knew somehow this would happen tonight, and yet I was taken by surprise, too." Ida sat up in bed, took a pillow, puffed it up at the headboard. Joe slid over next to her. "See, I'd finished straightening up downstairs, then fixed myself a bath. My back's been sore as the devil all day long and I couldn't wait to get into bed, even though I hadn't any hope to sleep. I felt so troubled all evening, like some strange supernatural warning in my bones that I knew was my gift telling me something was terribly wrong. Mother had me read her palm before they left to Fort Bragg and all I saw were happy signs, so I believed absolutely nothing could happen to them. Instead, I woke suddenly with a terrible chill and thought I'd left a window open, and I positively hadn't. Well, I got out of bed and went to the window, for some reason I can't explain, and saw a strange green light out on the ocean, like a heavenly star floating on the waves, and I experienced the most awful pain in my chest, because I'm positively sure that was a sign and once I saw it, that's all there was left of my parents, and that's when I heard the doorbell ringing downstairs."

Joe didn't really know what she was talking about, but he loved holding her hand. If she needed him to, he could sit with her like this all night long. He liked her and he liked this room. The bed was comfortable and was plenty big enough and he had a nice view of the ocean and a toilet that didn't flood. It was pretty swell, all right, especially with Ida here beside him. Too bad her folks were dead, but, like she said, that wasn't his fault.

Ida squeezed his fingers. "Oh, Joe, you won't run out on me tomorrow, will you? I don't think I could stand being here alone. How could I manage it? We've only got five tenants now, besides you, and who knows how long they'll be with us? Two of them are the sorts of fellows who blow about with the wind, and old Mrs. Pomeroy in 3D can hardly get out of bed anymore. But you know what? I bet you and me could make a go of it together, just the two of us. Don't you think? Oh, I'm so scared, Joe. Mother and Father are dead. I keep saying those words over and over in my head, and I just can't seem to get a hold of it. It's just so awful, so hopeless. I'm an orphan, Joe. A stupid little orphan. You'll stay here and help me, won't you? Please? I don't think I can ever do it without you."

What could he say? "Sure I will, honey. Whatever you need. I'll make it all better for you. I swear I will."

He drew Ida close to comfort her, when suddenly she kissed his lips. So he kissed her back, even as her tears wet both their cheeks. They kissed again and Joe didn't want to stop. Was this shameful? Loving her up in this hour of tragedy? What sort of fellow did that? Ida clung to him fiercely, her honey scent clouding his resolve to be moral amidst this horrible tragedy. They kissed for a long while, then, torrid and scandalously. Joe felt a thrill he hadn't known in years. Ida rubbed her cheek on his face and kissed his ear, then his neck, and shifted her body to spoon so closely Joe could feel Ida's heart thumping beneath her breast. The floorboards creaked as someone passed in the hall outside his door. Joe clung to Ida and shushed her breathing and noticed she'd unbuttoned his shirt. A warm, trembling hand slipped under his clothing and rubbed his belly. Ida whispered in his ear, "Honey, I don't want us to be angels. Not tonight."

Then Joe became frantic with desire. He dared to lift his hand and cup her bosom, but Ida squirmed free and put a finger on Joe's lips, then rose to her knees and hoisted her nightgown, revealing her Lady Jane cotton undergarments. In the lamplight, her skin was a smooth and pasty white. Joe kicked off his shoes. Ida leaned down over him, letting her brown curls fall free, hiding her face. She kissed him fiercely on the lips and slid her tongue into his mouth. Her breath was bitter with orange tea. She wrestled Joe out of his shirt and tossed it onto the floor, then removed her union suit, slipping it off her shoulders onto the bedspread. Then Ida leaned forward above the pillow and rubbed her ballooning breasts across Joe's face. She hummed tunelessly as she swayed back and forth, letting Joe lick at her nipples, taut and flushed. His brow was sweaty, his breath ragged. Joe's brain was spinning so wildly now, he felt feverish and mean. He grabbed her bottom and urged her downward to his groin. She rubbed her sex against his own and shook the bed, but the squeaking of the iron frame might have been in the house next door for all Joe heard of it. He shoved his pelvis up between her fleshy thighs and grunted like a dog, while struggling to lower his zipper. Ida helped him. She unfastened the waist button and unzipped him and tugged until she had his trousers down by his ankles. She was panting and her pale skin glistened, smelling of beauty powder and sweat. Her brown hair was clotted and damp. Joe shook off his trousers. In the glow of the corner streetlight, Ida's eyes gleamed with lust as she tossed away his shorts, too. Bare-naked on the bed, Joe was red-hot and scared to death he'd pop any second. He watched Ida quietly slip off the bed and remove her own frilly underwear. She wiggled like jelly. Joe's mouth was dry, his hands shaking. He thought she was gorgeous. Looking him dead in the eye, she put a finger to her lips, faintly smiling, and then eased onto the bed. When Ida crawled on top of him and shoved his peter up between her puffy wet thighs, Joe Krueger believed he was truly blessed.

A MEMORIAL SERVICE WAS HELD for William and Rosaline Macaulay a week later at Arcadia Cemetery on the forested high ground above Ocean City. Joe walked with Ida up to the chosen plot and stood with her in a cold wind. Several people offered eulogies to a fine, upstanding couple Joe had never met. Dressed in black, head to toe, Ida waited stone-faced as the others spoke, and when her turn came, she read a prayer apparently favored by her mother and father:

"The joys and tears and coilings of mankind are those of God in miniature. But within them is a secret door. Open it when you will, for it reveals your own immortal soul. Be still, and hear the whisper that reaches out to you in silent places. In one thrilling, breathless moment, the Light will filter through that golden door and awaken you to immortality before spring flowers bloom again."

Then Ida expressed her love for them, how eternally grateful she would always be to Our Heavenly Father for allowing her to be their proud daughter. She told a story about a peach basket half-full of ripened fruit on the front porch outside the house one summer morning, a filling for her mother's prize cobbler, and a raggedy vagrant wandering past with a hungry eye. Mother and daughter alike witnessed his furtive act of theft; they watched him sneak off with his goods, and then followed him down to his hiding place behind a plank fence in a patch of golden sunflowers. Mother confronted him with his crime and ordered him to follow them back to the house where she sat the wary vagrant down in her kitchen and baked a warm peach cobbler for him.

Lastly, Ida recited a poem she had written, inspired by her mother's gracious example:

"God might encompass our world
Enfolding each of us in love
To know the truth, a home above
Awaits thee, trusting soul who sees
That our creator protects the
Least of us, even infidels
Who walked lonely roads
Might see."

At the wake, many neighbors and acquaintances alike remarked how saddened they were by Bill and Rosie's death, and how composed Ida appeared through it all. Joe didn't know any of these people, and did his best to keep out of the way. Since he'd never known the deceased, he didn't know what to say, anyhow. After an hour or so, Ida went upstairs to have a bath and stay to herself. Except for old Ethel Pomeroy, the other tenants went out for the evening, too awkward in Bill and Rosie's absence to offer more than condolences to Ida. Also, they were clearly fearful of their own futures. Who would run the boardinghouse? Would it shut down? If so, where would they go? Mitch Brudvik, the furniture salesman in 2D, had tried cornering Joe in the kitchen to see if he could offer any hints regarding the disposition of the business.

"It's dead open and shut, the way I see it," he told Joe. "They were already hanging on by the skin of their teeth, and Bill had a good head on his shoulders. His kid's sweet, but she's behind the eight ball now, don't you think?"

"How would I know?"

"Well, do you think she'll skip?"

"No."

"What makes you say that?"

"She'll get help," Joe replied, annoyed at Mitch's attitude, as if he were hoping the place would fail. "Nobody expects her to do this on her own. It wouldn't be right. She deserves better than that."

"If you say so, but business is business, and this dump's been going down the toilet ever since I've been here, and I can't see how she's going to turn it around any time soon."

"Well, maybe you ought to move out," Joe suggested. "Isn't that what rats do? Desert a sinking ship?"

Then Joe walked off.

At dusk, he sat in the parlor window seat, staring out through the curtain lace to the quiet street and the gray ocean beyond. White caps thrived in the cold wind. Gulls sailed here and there. Lights came on along the waterfront. Upstairs, the old pipes shuddered as Ida drained the bathtub. Joe heard her singing.

A **WEEK OR SO** after the funeral, Joe sat with Ida in the kitchen going over stacks of paperwork on the house. They'd emptied out Bill and Rosie's file cabinet to try and get a fix on the state of the business. Two large apartments upstairs were available, one on the second floor and one on the third, both at the front of the house. The room on the second floor had been sitting empty since last spring, and the one on the third belonged to Ida's parents, a marvelous suite with its own bathroom. Joe naturally assumed Ida would take over that suite, but she argued how much smarter they'd be to keep it for hire. She had torn through their room like a cyclone, drawer by drawer and in and out of the closets, sorting jewelry and expensive knick-knacks from old letters and photographs, clothes, keepsakes, toiletries, tired odds and ends. Joe offered to help, but all she'd allow him to do was cart away bags of trash for the backyard incinerator. Ida stacked all of the framed photographs in a cardboard box and took it up to the attic with a pile of record albums, books, and an old steamer trunk of Rosie's clothes, combs, and brushes; Bill's possessions went to the Goodwill store downtown. Rosie's blue velvet-lined jewel box — pearls, rings, necklaces, earrings, pins — disappeared into a secret drawer within Ida's vanity. All of the quaint pictures that had hung on the wall were either hauled up to the attic or out to the garage where Ida offered them for sale one Saturday afternoon along with a couple of floor lamps and a Philco tabletop radio, three clocks, two gilt-framed mirrors, lambrequins, drapes, bed linen, and a big rug. They earned Ida $725 and change. A week later, she traded her parents' entire old walnut and mahogany furniture suite — bed, twin nightstands, vanity, armoire, and a highboy dresser — for the most up-to-date equivalent at Lehman's, with Mitch getting the commission. Ida found some war bonds with the title papers and a folder of important house and appliance receipts and warranties and had Joe drive her to the bank where she deposited them into her safe deposit box. After a week and a half, not a trace of her parents remained upstairs. The room was scrubbed clean and ready to rent.

"I don't just want to be successful, Joe," Ida told him at the kitchen table that afternoon, "I want to be a shot in this game. Someone to reckon with."

She suggested they put advertisements in the papers from Fort Bragg to Redding. Calling attention to the business was indispensable to success. What good was it to have a sign in front if nobody outside of Ocean City knew who they were? In her fondest vision of the future, she and Joe would remodel the old place and make it a posh old-fashioned hotel welcoming tourists from all over the state. Ida told Joe, "I suppose when people rode horseback, this house used to be pretty high class. It's a turkey now, but I really believe we can make it a winner again if we absolutely put our minds to it. I've just got that feeling, and I know I'm right. My intuition tells me that all it needs is a good facelift and some word of mouth. We ought to stand the expense, Joe, to put it right on the best track again. It's positively a money-maker, I just know it is."

Optimistically, he agreed. "I think it'd be a knockout."

ACTUALLY, THE PROPERTY WAS SUFFERING from decades of neglect and sagged eastward from a settling foundation. Joe found dry rot in the front and rear porches and each of the porch columns. Some double-hung windows high up on the front of the house were shorn of paint by ocean wind and rain, decaying the sills and the old redwood frames. In the backyard, a quarter of the fence posts had rotted and fallen over, and some of the pickets had been kicked in by kids or angry drunks. He scribbled a quick list of necessary tools and supplies and went indoors where the problems were worse yet. Up on the third floor, Ethel Pomeroy's pull-chain toilet had been leaking for years and had rotted out the floor beneath the tiles. He also noticed the roof had been leaking around the chimney and most of the downspouts on the gutters were cracked and rusted out. There were thousands of rat turds in the attic where the little bastards had gotten in through one of the rotten fascia boards. Digging around some, Joe discovered that the wiring under the floor had been chewed clean through, leaving him a roasted rat carcass for a souvenir. Taking up the attic floorboards to solve the rodent problem revealed a dried-up old rat's nest of treasures: a silver doll shoe, a pair of eyeglasses, thimbles and yarn, a five dollar bill, and a skeleton key that didn't fit any lock in the house. Downstairs, the water heater off the kitchen was full of silt and was only heating ten gallons or so of water and would have to be replaced. Naturally, the basement, too, had been leaking for years, and Joe figured it needed a French drain. He assumed that once he got into these repairs, he'd find even more to do, because that's how it seemed to go with old houses. He expected a lot of work, but he had gotten on a construction detail at Moses Lake during the War that repaired some old barracks and built a new one for the nurses, so he was ready for it. The question was how Ida would react, because she possessed a cold little eye when it came to money.

When Joe unfolded his list, she gave her usual sigh. "That's too much, Joey. I have to say I didn't count on us needing that much work done. We've got expenses I haven't even wrote out, yet. I've only got what was left me through my inheritance, and that's nobody's fortune."

"Well, I got some money we can use. I figure that's only fair. It's what I saved up from Watsonville and that's not a whole lot, but it's something. Maybe I'll cover the lumber if you can chip in another three hundred or so."

Ida shook her head. "In that case, you better count me out, Joey. I tell you, we just haven't got that kind of money to throw around."

"How about a loan? Banks love getting folks on the dole, don't they?"

"We're already into them for ten times that much. If it wasn't for our reputation, I expect they'd have closed us out long ago."

"Well, I'll think of something else, then. Don't worry. We're not going to let this place fall down on our heads. I promise you that."

"Thanks, Joey. You really do got some gumption. I knew it when we met. My intuition told me there's a fellow I can count on, and I was positively right."

Joe had a savings account with Bank of America that he'd kept as a fall-back for when he'd gotten tired of working and wanted to lay off for a while. He had about fifteen hundred dollars in cash available at any time, excepting five thousand dollars in war bonds his father had given him after Joe came back from the Pacific. Not too keen on cashing out his own nest egg on repairs to Ida's house, he'd hoped she'd try taking out another loan. The biggest trouble for Joe was that since he'd been to bed with his true love, he was finding it tougher and tougher to separate her situation from his own. What worried her, worried him, too. He saw her spirit sag whenever the subject of money arose, and that saddened him. Lovers share the heart's smallest ebb. We rise and fall with our darling's hopes and fears. Considering all the good he might do with it, Joe decided that subtracting a few dollars from his bank account was his only true choice.

The next month was the busiest of his life since the War. Joe took a drive down the coast to a lumberyard near Ferndale where he found everything he needed for the porches, windowsills, and back fence. The next day, he began removing all the boards from the front porch. In a day and a half, working morning to dark, he replaced several of the joists, including the mudsill, and put in new flooring. Doing so, Joe discovered the columns were rotted at the bottom. To fix them, he propped up the porch roof and sawed off the lowest six inches of the posts and replaced each one with new redwood. Then he went out to the backyard and pulled up all the old fence posts, dug new holes, bought new posts, poured concrete, anchored them in, and rebuilt the fence. A week later, with the porch and fence work completed, Joe took a ladder to the roof and found it was leaking around the chimney, so he had to have new flashing made by a sheet metal shop across town. Working between rainstorms took more than a month, but once that was done, he patched in the roof around the flashings and went to work on the front windows. Not one of them had been painted for years and the sills were rotting, so he spent two days removing four on the ocean side of the house and replacing them with new redwood from the lumberyard. While doing that, Joe came across a number of places up on the third floor where the siding had cracked and honeybees had built a hive in the side of the house. He had to smoke them out, then replace the rotted boards and weave new siding in with the old. Indoors was another problem. That leaking toilet across from Mrs. Pomeroy's room required Joe to remove the subfloor of the bathroom, repair two floor joists, and put in a new subfloor. Afterward, he had to re-tile the floor and re-install the toilet. Finishing there, he went back out onto the roof to take care of the rusted downspouts by repairing the fascia and soffits and putting in new gutters all around. At the end of the job, Joe shelled out a couple hundred bucks for a local electrician to install new wiring in the attic while he dug up part of Rosie Macaulay's flower garden beside the front porch for a French drain to keep water out of the basement. Then he decided he ought to paint the whole house, which required hiring two high school kids from town to help him with a month of prep work, having to sand and scrape the entire surface, then re-painting top to bottom in a couple shades of olive green.

By springtime, Joe's repairs and renovations had taken about four months and ran just under fifty-five hundred dollars. It also cost the boardinghouse a couple tenants when Stan Janes in 2A decided the dust Joe was kicking up all over the place was dangerous to his health. He gave Ida two weeks' notice, then left for a room across town with a fellow he knew at the radio store. As summer arrived, Mitch Brudvik began talking about getting a place somewhere out of town. He'd met a woman from Lancaster who dressed like Gypsy Rose Lee and drove a foreign convertible. She came up for a weekend and took one look at Ocean City and told Mitch he either had to move or find a new girlfriend. He rode her over to Reno and put them both up in a suite at a downtown casino and when they came back, Mitch told Joe he'd be giving up his room as soon as escrow closed on a house he had found in Sparks. That really put Ida in a bind and Joe felt it whenever they were in bed together at the end of the evening. She seemed restless and talked on and off about insurance on the boardinghouse and losing the business to the bank.

"They're absolutely going to come get me, Joe. I know that because I positively seen it in my sleep."

Then she would roll over and weep for a few minutes and Joe would let her be, not quite knowing how to put things square. He'd lie just off her shoulder and stare out the window at the clouds crossing the bay and count stars on the night sky and listen to auto traffic to see if he could tell a Chevy from a Ford. After a while, Ida would perk up and kiss Joe on the neck and undress and get all sexed up until they were both sweaty and worn out. Then she'd cuddle up beside him and act as if nothing in the world mattered but that she and Joe were there together and to hell with everyone else.

"WE OUGHT TO GET MARRIED, JOE."

Late that summer, Ida cornered him in the basement where Joe was puttering around the furnace, trying to decide if it needed to be retired in favor of a new one. She told him, "We're pretty good together, you and me, don't you think? I never met a man I could trust like I trust you, honey. And it's a pretty big risk for a girl like me with this house, and all I've got going here. You hear girls saying all the time how boys have only one thing on their minds and it's always a dirty thought, and that's no more true than a lie that says all girls want is a husband who lets them sit on a sofa all day. I'd have a sore back by Sunday and an itchy foot, because I never minded work one iota, and that's the honest truth. Joey dear, you know I hate being alone. I just can't stand it. Sure, I keep myself occupied with work that needs doing, but when I'm in bed at the end of the day, I want someone to keep me company. Ever since my folks came here, I imagined sharing a bed in this house with a man like you. It's a heck of deal, don't you think? Us two running this business side by side?"

"Do you really think we ought to get married? You got a good thing going here on your own. Why would you want to mess it up by dragging me along?"

She kissed him. "I love you, Joey. I'm not happy when you go off on your errands all day. I stop whatever it is I'm doing and listen for you, and when you're not there, I feel so blue I can hardly stand up. If I had one wish for my life now, I'd ask for you to stay with me forever.

Is that so terrible, Joey, being with me? I have to tell you something. Last night, after we were together, and you fell asleep and I went back to bed, I did a reading in the Book of Fate, and do you know what it told me? It said, 'The treasure thou wilt find, will be a partner, whose affectionate heart will share thy happiness, and sympathize in all thy sorrows.' Isn't that something?"

Well, Joe knew he wasn't the greatest catch in the world. Lots of girls had told him over the years that he was a peach, but Joe never thought of himself as much better than passing in a crowd: not a lemon, but no dreamboat, either. Maybe if he looked in the mirror he'd see someone who didn't deserve to have a girl telling him everything Ida had just said. Nothing had ever seemed fair to Joe before, nothing important went right for him, until this moment with this girl. So he told her, "I love you, too, sweetheart, and I can't for the life of me think of anything that'd make me happier than to marry you."

Persuading an old friend of Rosie's to look after the boardinghouse for a few days, Joe and Ida went to Reno on a recommendation from Mitch Brudvik who knew about a quaint little chapel only a mile from downtown that married young couples for ten dollars a pop and tossed in a bouquet of fresh red roses and a vanilla cake for nothing extra. Mitch stood up as Joe's best man and his girlfriend Holly acted as maid-of-honor. The ceremony lasted ten minutes and Ida wept like a baby and Joe shed a tear, too, then all four of them went out to a casino and celebrated until four in the morning. Joe hired a honeymoon suite for the night and made love to Ida at daybreak and nine hours later, they were driving south to see Hoover Dam and the Grand Canyon. They spent one night at a roadside motel that looked like a camp of wigwams and two more at a resort with a swimming pool and a dude ranch next door. Joe and Ida went for a dip at a hot springs one morning and the following afternoon took a mule ride back into the mountains where fortune hunters wandered in search of uranium. They met another couple of newlyweds from Ogden named Cathy and Dave Michaelis who collected Katchina dolls and talked about the Second Coming, which they insisted was just around the corner.

"Sputnik's one of the first signs," Dave announced as they sat at a cowboy restaurant outdoors for dinner. "It's the star called Wormwood that falls from heaven and brings on the end of times. Look it up."

Ida argued back, "I haven't seen no such thing in astrology and my charts absolutely foretold those fellows trying to shoot Truman."

Cathy warned, "The Bible tells us to beware of false prophecy."

"Well, dear, it's not false if it comes true, and that positively did."

Joe listened with pride as his new bride showed them how. Later on, when he and Dave were out in the parking lot getting the autos, Michaelis said to him, "That girl of yours sure is a talker, isn't she? I don't know that I could put up with my wife fighting me on every little thing I say."

Joe smiled. "Well, that's just it, isn't it, Dave? She was fighting you, and you couldn't take it. I wasn't worried a bit. Fact is, we get along pretty swell, her and me. I'm just glad I didn't marry a mouse like you did."

The next day, Joe and Ida drove out to see Hoover Dam. A fierce wind blew across the desert like a banshee, kicking dust up everywhere but at the dam itself where tons of polished concrete stood high in the hot sun. It was the most magnificent thing Joe had ever seen. His father had known Oskar Hansen, who designed the birdmen and star map on the promenade atop the dam. He'd received photographs and sketches of the dam and its sculptures in progress and talked about them for days. One afternoon before the War, Walter told Joe, *"A thing like that dam sticks in the soul of a man, pointing him up. Each of us needs something like it in our lives. Find one of your own, Joey, and you'll see I'm right."* Back then, Joe had only the vaguest idea of what his father meant. He had no aspirations that he knew of, no plans for anything greater than earning a few dollars at work and getting a girl from school going in the back seat of his dad's Chrysler on a Saturday night. At the dam, though, Joe put an arm around his new wife and something awfully big welled up inside him and he began to cry and hid his face from her and felt a glory wash over him that he had no way of expressing in words.

After another hour, Ida told Joe that looking down the face of the dam into the Colorado River made her dizzy, so they got back into the car and headed east to the Grand Canyon where they rode a burro and bought an Indian blanket. Then they went home.

FOR A MONTH AND A HALF, Joe thought he was living a dream. Ida took over the double room on the second floor and fixed it up for the two of them. She called it their wedding suite and kept fresh gardenias in a vase on her dressing table next to the window where the scent would carry to their bedside each evening. Joe took her shopping downtown for new curtains and sheets and pillowcases. "Something so up-to-the-minute, Joey," she told him, "that our guests'll see how well we're doing and give us referrals. You just can't underestimate the value of appearances. Dad and Mom taught me that. We don't need to spend a lot of money, either. I taken some out of the savings account and clipped a couple dozen coupons to cover a few other expenses, but I want our room to look nice. I owe it to you, honey. I really do."

One morning, he found a sweet little poem from Ida on his pillow:

But a Rose!

What you are like?
You are like an angel from the Heavens —
Your like the little stars above
Your like the beautiful moon sent down from Heaven —
Oh! just made for me to love!
Your like the little flowers that grows —
Your sweeter than any heavenly Rose!
Your like the Raindrops that fall on my window pane
Your like god's Reflection that shines in the window
on everything

Your like the little birds that sing in Spring
And each tear drop I shed is for you in vain —
Your like the little blue birds that sing in Spring.
Your all that I can say or do
So ask the little fairy to come along, and climb up,
and paint the moon —
So I'll send you a Rosebud as a token to show you
I sincerely love you —

Joe had never felt so adored. At night with the house put to bed, he lay in the dark beside his sweet Ida and wondered what he had done to earn this much happiness. Ida drew up a list of his favorite foods at breakfast, lunch, and dinner, and cooked each just how he liked it. She kept their room neat and clean and made the bed when he was in the shower every morning. Whenever they crossed paths, whether outdoors or in, she gave him a kiss. Those days, Joe worked dawn to dusk, keeping up on the repairs he'd done, running errands for Ida in and out of Ocean City, doing his best to promote new business — something that was mostly a failure. They had taken in two new tenants only a week after getting back from their honeymoon, a couple of men from Marin County who told Ida they were decorative painters. She thought that was wonderful because the interior always needed touching up here and there. She gave them Mitch's old room on the second floor and fixed it up nicely with some lovely blue drapes and a new calico bedspread. After four days, Joe smelled something funny in the hall outside their room and gave a knock and when the door opened, he was greeted by one of the men in a Chinese silk dressing gown and cold cream on his face. Peeking inside, Joe saw the other fellow lying on the bed stark naked with a drink in one hand, his engorged privates in the other. In the middle of the room stood a canvas and easel and drawn on it was a nude fellow grasping a phallus the size of a gourd.

A marijuana cigarette smoldered in an ashtray on the nightstand. Joe declined an invitation to join them for a smoke. That night, when he told Ida all about it, she claimed she had nothing against people of any persuasion, but still tossed them out. A couple of days later, Joe advertised the room at a reduced rate in the newspaper.

JOE'S TROUBLES BEGAN a few months after their honeymoon. Ida had gone downtown to the market for fresh vegetables and a roast, and asked Joe to clean the upstairs where Ethel Pomeroy was the only tenant left. For more than a year now, Ethel had kept to her room, enthralled with her television set and a new phonograph on which she played Eddie Cantor records, day and night. Joe hated going upstairs because she always seemed to know he was there and would begin calling for him to get rid of her food tray or fetch her medication or move the soiled pillow under her powdered bottom. Her bedroom stunk to high heaven and she always kept the shades drawn, so it was gloomy and sordid. Now and then, she'd even have stripped off her clothes and lay there naked and exposed, and if she caught him in the least glance, she'd grab a flabby pink tit and wiggle it for him and laugh like a lunatic. Before leaving, Ida reminded Joe to look in on Ethel to see that she had taken her pills, so there was no skipping out of it. God, he hoped she wasn't nude.

A glorious early spring afternoon permitted all the windows in the big old house to be thrown open to the ocean air. Curtain lace upstairs and down flapped in a breeze off the blue bay. The house was quiet, which usually meant Ethel was napping. Joe finished scrubbing the tub on the second floor, then put away the wash bucket and went upstairs. He trod lightly on the carpet runner as he ascended. The hall was drafty from a toilet window left open in the bathroom across from Ethel. With each step he took, Joe kept expecting to hear her call his name, but she didn't, and when he arrived at her door, he found the room to be exceptionally quiet. With anyone else, he would have knocked lightly to announce his presence, but sneaking up on Ethel was a better tactic. He twisted the knob and nudged the door open and had a peek and saw her propped up in bed, a framed photograph on her lap, eyes open.

"Ethel."

She didn't look at him.

The room reeked of antiseptic and wet bed linen and Joe guessed she'd pissed herself, but he had no intention of washing her off. That wasn't his job. He went to the washstand to fetch her heart medication and hoped she wouldn't fight with him. The last time he had been in charge of dosing her, she'd spat up all over him. Coming back to her bed, Joe saw she hadn't moved a muscle. "I got your pills."

She didn't even blink.

"Ethel."

Then he saw a fly on her nose. When she didn't brush it off, Joe knew she was dead.

Ida called the mortuary and made all the arrangements for Ethel's funeral. Rather than finding her a plot up at the Arcadia Cemetery, and having no idea how to contact any living relatives Ethel might have had, Ida decided to get Ethel cremated. Joe and Ida stood in as family at the services. Afterward, they picked through her belongings for anything needful and gave most of it away to Goodwill; the rest went to the dump. Then Ida scrubbed and painted, re-arranged the furniture, and Joe posted a new "Room Available" in the newspaper. The very next day, a nice middle-aged fellow named Theodore Haskins who sold Electrolux vacuum cleaners door-to-door took it off the market. He worked the region from Ukiah to Redding, so he was gone most of the month, a perfect tenant. They were thrilled.

A week later, Ethel's latest pension check arrived. For the past few years, Ida had been taking these checks to the Bank of America for

Ethel, putting part into the boardinghouse account to pay her rent, and cashing the rest for Ethel's living expenses.

On Friday, Ida took the latest check to the bank just like normal.

Joe didn't know about it until supper when Ida told him.

"Frankly, I'm awfully surprised," she admitted, ladling a spoonful of scalloped potatoes onto his plate. "I didn't guess that'd be permitted. I naturally assumed that when she passed on, that'd be it."

"Well, maybe they don't know."

"I suppose you're right. It's true that she didn't give notice to heaven," Ida giggled, "and nobody's come knocking to see if she's still kicking."

Joe took a drink of milk. "They probably didn't care to hear from her any more than the rest of us. She was a pain in the ass, if you ask me."

"Do you think it was a mistake?"

"Them sending the check, or us cashing it?"

"Well, them sending it. Though, honestly, I don't see nothing wrong at all with us cashing it. I did it under Macaulay, like I do all our house business, because that's how they know me. And Ethel was absolutely a mess and we could've taken a powder on her when my mother and father died, but we didn't because that was something we needed to keep on track, and Ethel knew it, too, positively. So, I don't see the least thing wrong with any of this."

Buttering his cornbread, Joe said, "Look, you know we can't fiddle around with the pension board every month. If they come knocking, I don't see how we'd explain cashing checks on a corpse."

"Oh, I guess I'm just tired of living these dollar days, Joey. Nobody's giving us a break and we work real hard to give our tenants a decent place to live. Don't you agree that counts for something? It's just got to because otherwise we're licked."

"Sure I do, but is it ever going to let up?" He chewed on a piece of cornbread and stared out the window to a sun-slicked ocean.

"How do you mean, honey?"

Joe swallowed the cornbread. "Well, we're getting down to nickels and dimes now and pretty soon something's got to give. Take that check you just cashed: if we were doing a top-drawer business, it'd be nothing to turn it back to the pension board and tell them, 'Thanks for the memories, now good-bye.' We haven't done that because we need those four hundred dollars. I agree with you there. We'd be strapped somewhere this month without it. Ethel's been here so long, we just kind of got used to having that little extra each month to help us out. We expected it. I guess that's the trouble. It's not hard getting used to lacking something you never had, but losing what you count on having is pretty tough."

Ida had a sip of water. "That's just my point, Joey. We're licked now without it."

"No, we're not. Maybe if you were a different kind of girl, that'd be so, but I've never seen anybody work harder to make a go of something than you since your folks died. You've given me more faith in this place than I ever had, not because it's got potential, though I suppose it might, but because of you being here to push it along. It's not Ethel's pension check that'll make or break us, honey. It's whether you want this place to work or not. Simple as that."

"I do, honey. You know I do, that's why I cashed Ethel's check, and why I think we ought to keep cashing them for as long as we can. Fact is, we absolutely deserve it, both of us. You know we do." Ida stretched across the table and took Joe's hand. She smiled. "I love you, Joey. It's on account of you that I rush about like I do. Why, if I was here alone, I'd taken this dump and thrown it in the ocean long ago."

"We could get in a load of trouble, you know."

"No, we won't," she told him. "My astrology tells me it's all clear sailing ahead, and I've never been wrong, not even once."

The next month, when Ethel's pension check arrived, Ida took it to the bank and cashed it.

O NE AFTERNOON IN MAY, Joe was cutting the lawn out front when a red Cadillac Eldorado convertible pulled over to the curb and a thin, smartly dressed fellow with an oily black ducktail haircut got out. He hurried around to the passenger side of his auto and opened the door for a young woman in a lovely red polka dot dress. She finished smoking a cigarette and flicked it away into the street, then primped her own frizzy black hair while checking her makeup in the rearview mirror. The man called up to Joe, "Say, pal, you got any rooms for hire? We just need one tonight."

Like Ida had told Joe when he first drove into Ocean City, renting day to day wasn't good business, but seeing as how they had five rooms gathering dust upstairs, if one night was all he could get out of these folks, that'd have to be all right. Besides, this was one of those lovely brisk spring afternoons of blue ocean waters and a pleasant breeze in the rooms of the old boardinghouse, a good advertisement for the place. Word of mouth went a long way.

So Joe said, "Sure, come on up and I'll show you what we got."

"Honey, get the bags."

"Sit on this, Frankie," the girl said, holding her thumb out, then went back to freshening her ruby-red lipstick.

"Well, suit yourself, but a joint like here ain't got a bellhop."

"Do you need help with your luggage?" Joe offered, trying to be agreeable in a business way.

"Naw, Vera's just being unsociable. Don't pay her any attention. She's had a long day. You know how it is with dames."

"All right."

When he reached the top step, the guy held out his hand. "Name's Spagnolini. Frank Spagnolini."

"Joe Krueger."

"Glad to meet you, Joe. Nice town you got here."

"What brings you out this way?" Joe asked, guiding Frank into the lobby.

"Nothing special. Just seeing some of the country. My wife likes getting around."

Joe went over to the desk and grabbed the registration ledger. "Well, this is a good time of year for that sort of thing. I always hate having to go somewhere when it's raining, and up here there's a lot of that."

Frank took out a cigarette. "Anything to do after dark?"

"Depends what you like."

"Vera likes to go dancing," Frank said, lighting up.

Joe scribbled the date onto the ledger and slid it over for Frank to fill out. "I guess the Blue Oasis out on Murdoch Road is the only thing to fit that bill. They say it gets pretty wild."

"Thanks. We'll give it a try."

"That'll be ten dollars," Joe said, as Frank slid the ledger back across the desk. "One night, right? I'm going to put you in 3B. It's one of our suites. You'll like it. I think it's the best room in the house."

"Hell, in that case, give us two nights. I can't tell you from day to day what Vera gets in her mind to do, but I need the rest." He pulled a couple of tens from his billfold and gave them to Joe.

Vera came through the front door, lugging two suitcases. "Thanks for nothing, Frankie."

Spagnolini laughed. "Hey, sweetheart, glad you could join us."

She dropped the suitcases and sat on one of them. "You're such a rat."

Frank grinned at Joe. "Check and double check."

"Finally, we've got some guests with spunk, Joey," Ida said, fussing at the kitchen table. Joe had introduced her to the Spagnolinis before Frank and Vera headed out to the Blue Oasis for dinner. "You did good, letting them have the room on a short term. My sense tells me they'll stay a while. Just you wait and see. I'm positive about this."

"Sure, honey."

"I tell you, we need something new in our lives, people to do things with."

"Oh yeah? What sorts of things?" Joe pulled up a chair at the table and sat down. It was dark out now, about an hour past a blue dusk. The light in the kitchen felt dim.

"Well, I've been reading about bridge parties. It seems everyone's hosting them these days. It's something to bring a little zing into the house."

Joe watched the moths flapping at the backdoor light and thought about putting a screen on the door for when the evenings became warmer. He hated getting bitten by mosquitoes while he was eating supper.

"Are you listening to me, Joey? I'm fed up with sitting home every evening. All I do is clean and go to bed."

"You don't like cards," Joe replied, wondering where this complaint of Ida's had come from. "You told me so yourself when we met."

"Well, maybe I've changed." Ida ran her dishrag under the faucet. "Besides, it's not that I hold any great enthusiasm for stunts of any kind. That's not my point. All I meant was that we're stuck in a rut and we need to get out of it. Sooner, the better."

"I guess so."

"By the way, you got this in the mail." Ida handed Joe a sealed envelope with a return address to Santa Fe, New Mexico, where his father had moved about six months after Joe took the nursery job at Watsonville. Joe had sent him a telegram the week he married Ida and got one back that said only: CONGRATULATIONS. Joe figured his dad was probably upset that he hadn't been invited to the wedding, but he hated to travel and Joe knew he wouldn't have come, anyway.

"What is it?"

"How should I know? Have a look."

Joe tore it open and found a letter tied in with a stack of real estate documents.

May 3, 1958

Dear Joey,

What on earth are you doing up there? I hope you're not planning to get into logging. I just read a story in "Western States" that listed timber as the second most deadly industry to its employees, right after fire departments. It won't pay to saw your leg off.

Did you know your Uncle Bill passed away last month? Chuck Henry says Bill had a stroke at the racetrack and couldn't be revived. He probably never knew what hit him. Well, your uncle left us the house on Ellington Avenue, and I've decided to give it to you. Maybe you can use it as a rental. Chuck went through the house after the funeral and said it looked pretty ship-shape. I thought you could take care of any fixing up it might need. Anyhow, it's yours to do with however you decide. I just want you to have it. It's something to sink your feet into. This'll be your first house, Joey. Make it something you'll never forget.

Love, Dad

Joe showed the letter to Ida, who read it quickly then handed it back to him.

She said, "We positively ought to go see your new house as soon as possible."

"Well, it's nothing special, I ought to tell you right now. Just an upstairs and a basement garage. The bottom floor of this place is bigger than that whole house and there's not much of a backyard at all."

"That's your tale, Joey. San Francisco's a big step up from here, and I want to see it. Don't spoil yourself by playing alone. We're here together and don't you forget it."

"Well, if you're that anxious, maybe we ought to go down there next weekend. Your friend Joan can come over and look after things overnight."

"I'll talk to her tomorrow morning because I know how you let things slip your mind when you don't care to remember them."

"Suit yourself."

Once Ida had left for one of her astrology meetings across town, Joe went upstairs to watch Jackie Gleason on the Philco set. When the show ended, he felt restless and decided to walk down to the bowling alley on Union Street. Joe didn't have any real friends in town, except for a couple guys from the paint store who liked ten pins and Joe didn't mind rolling a few games with them every so often. He found Carl Weygand there tonight with a hotsy-hipped cutie whose platinum blonde hairdo was bigger than Ida's head. Every ball in the rack reeked of her perfume. Her name was Suzy and she was visiting Carl from Salinas, where the two of them had met at a big artichoke festival a few months back. Joe watched her throw nine gutter balls in a row, then bought himself a beer and rolled a one-ninety, beating Carl, who blamed Suzy for distracting him by bouncing her tits in his line of sight. They bowled three more games and Joe won two of them, then Carl decided to quit for the evening and went back to the lounge where he bought cocktails for the three of them.

When Joe got back to the house at half past eleven, he heard Ida's voice up on the third floor where he'd put the Spagnolinis. She was singing "Bibbidi-Bobbidi-Boo" at the top of her lungs. Joe stopped in his own room to use the toilet, then washed his face, put on a clean shirt, and went upstairs to see what was doing. Outside the door to 3B, he could hear them dancing and whooping it up. Vera sounded sloppy drunk and Frank was talking loud enough to be lit to the gills himself.

"Give it to me, baby," he laughed, *"and I don't mean maybe!"*

"Sure as shootin', sugar!"

Did Ida know how much noise they were making? You could probably hear them out on the sidewalk.

"You're my sugar pie!" Frank sang in a hoarse voice.

"And you can eat me right up," Vera sang back.

What kind of people had Joe hired a room to? And why was Ida joining in? She was lucky Haskins was out for the night, or their last monthly tenant might be packing his bags.

Ida sang, *"Salagadoola mechicka boola bibbidi-bobbidi-boo. Put 'em together and what have you got? Bibbidi-bobbidi-boo."*

God, Joe hated that song. Was Ida drinking, too? He could hear her clapping and stamping her foot like a hillbilly to that stupid tune. Vera cackled. Joe heard the window open, then Frank's voice shouting to a car on the street outside. That was enough for Joe. He knocked at the door.

Frank answered, "Welcome to the Ritz!" He smelled like cooked fish. Behind him on the green stuffed sofa, her legs splayed wide in black fishnets, lay Vera, a smoldering cigarette in hand. Her face was painted up like a gypsy, rouge smeared across her lips, violet eye shadow, black hair fussy and wild, like she'd just stepped out of a cement mixer.

She was completely stewed, while Ida waltzed about, singing, "Salaga-doola means mechicka booleroo, but the thingmabob that does the job is bibbidi-bobbidi-boo."

Seeing Joe, Ida burped, and then giggled. "Hiya, sweetie. What brings you up this way?"

Frank stepped in. "Your wife's a knockout, Joe. She really is."

"Oh yeah?" Joe had never seen Ida so batty.

"Vera thinks so, too. Don't you, dear?"

Vera nodded. "She's a queen bee, Frankie, if I ever seen one." She pursed her lips and winked.

Joe didn't know what the hell to think. This whole party upstairs was a masquerade of liquor and eye chatter. Worse, Ida was part of it, and not by accident. Joe guessed she'd come upstairs straight from her astrology meeting once she heard the peppy music. Ida had strict ethics about certain things, but she was no puritan. Joe found that out once they began bedding down together. She liked sex and even acted dirty now and then, so maybe none of this was a surprise.

"Show 'em your steps, Joey," Ida teased, dancing across the room toward him. "I got the heebie-jeebies."

"Your little lady's saturated," Frank told him, lighting up another cigarette.

"Oh, I haven't had a drop," Ida said, grabbing Joe around the waist. "And I don't need any to get close to my Joey. He makes me quiver with a look, and that's the truth." She nuzzled his neck and licked his ear.

Joe was mortified. A month ago, Ida would've gone on and on about how immoral people like this were, how ungodly, and likely tossed them out on their heads. Now what? The room was thick with cigarette smoke and booze and the music was playing too loud and Frank was staring at Ida's bottom like it was a New York steak.

Joe leaned forward to speak in Ida's ear. "We ought to go back down to bed, honey."

She giggled. "I've been waiting for you to say that." Then she grabbed his bottom and gave it a squeeze. Frank laughed and Vera narrowed her eyes at Joe and blew him a kiss before taking another drink of bourbon.

Joe lowered his voice. "I mean, it's late, honey. We ought to go downstairs."

"Don't try to skip out," Frank spoke up, a jump ahead of Joe. He switched radio stations until he found Eddie Fisher. "We're just getting oiled up here. Vera's going to put on her act for us and you don't want to miss that. I tell you, it's really something."

"He used to be my manager," Vera said, "until he tried to take out his ten percent in trade."

"Yeah," Frank said, "but I never did have a noodle for business."

"You think with your noodle," Vera laughed. "That's your trouble."

"What fellow doesn't?" Frank said, blowing a smoke ring out the window. "Ain't that so, Joe?"

Shuddering in Ida's arms, Joe blushed.

"Joe's got no use for his noodle that I'm not familiar with," Ida said. "So long as I feed him up every so often, he'll keep it straight as an arrow."

Joe frowned. "Cut it out."

He felt like the fatted calf.

"Hush, dear." Ida put a finger to his lips. "We're all pals here. Aren't we, Frank?"

"Vera?" Frank turned to his own wife who was washed now across the length of the sofa like a drowsy cat. "Don't poop out on us. Did you hear what Ida just said?"

"Sure, Frankie," Vera slurred, barely able to raise her head. "She's a sweetheart, all right. I bet Joe can't keep his mitts off her. And I wouldn't mind getting confidential, neither, if you bring me a sandwich and another bourbon."

"How about a slice of lemon meringue pie?" Ida asked Vera, as she twirled Joe about in a half-circle. "I just baked it this afternoon. It's awfully good. You can ask Joe. Isn't it good, dear?"

"Sure."

"Can Joe feed it to me?" Vera asked, trying in vain to prop up on her elbow. "I bet he knows which piece I'd like best."

"Don't tempt him, honey," Frank told her. He snuffed out his cigarette and flicked the butt out the window. "Can't you see he's trying to keep fit? He's probably got Charles Atlas in his sock drawer, don't you, Joe? What do you weigh? One-sixty?"

Joe shrugged, still figuring out his escape. "I don't know."

"He's lots skinnier than you are, Frank," Vera added. "And you know I like 'em skinny."

Frank said, "That's because you're on a diet of men, sweetheart. It's in all the papers."

"Joey's got some meat on his bones, believe you me, " Ida told them both. "I should know because he's positively better off than when we met. Why, I thought he looked like a beanpole back then." She gave Joe a pinch in his ribs and a little kiss.

Joe swore he saw Vera dip a hand between her thighs and wink at him. Frank had a wry smile on his sloppy mouth. He knew Vera was flirting and he egged her on. "If you had Joe pinned in the sack, honey, would you hurt him?"

Vera cackled. "I'd wrap him up like a stick of gum, and spit him out in the morning."

Ida said, "Joe doesn't chew gum."

"He'd chew me," Vera insisted, readjusting her position on the sofa. She raised one leg, hiking up her skirt just long enough to give Joe a shot at her panties, which were black and didn't hide much.

"Would you, dear?" Ida asked Joe, tickling his rib. "Would you chew her up in nothing flat?"

Frank went over to the toilet and closed the door behind him.

"Don't fall in!" Vera called after him. Then she smiled at Ida. "He's clumsy that way. Get him a little fuzzy and he'll pee all over the toilet, then plug the bowl with his head. My Frankie."

"Mine hardly drinks at all, do you, Joey?" Ida remarked, trying to get him to take a dance step to her lead. "He gets the heartburn and can't sleep afterward."

Joe shrugged. "Beer won't go to your gut like most liquor, but I'd rather not drink much before bed."

"You're a sensible fellow, aren't you?" Vera asked, smoothing the skirt down between her thighs. She pursed her lips and blew Joe a nasty little kiss. "I bet you don't do nothing wrong that Ida can spank you for. Isn't that so?"

"Joe never lets me spank him," Ida said. "He's got a soft bottom."

Despite Perry Como singing out on the radio, Joe heard Frank fart loudly. Vera giggled.

Then the toilet flushed and Frank reappeared, frazzled and red-faced. "All right, who's game for a swim?"

THE NEXT DAY, Joe was out in the backyard just after lunch, raking leaves from the flowerbeds, when Frank popped his head through the open window on the third floor. "Say, how's about a pow-wow?"

"Pardon?"

"Vera's off to the beauty parlor and I thought me and you could grab a beer and grind our brains over a couple thoughts I had this morning."

"What kind of thoughts?"

"Meet me out front and I'll tell you."

"All right," Joe replied, tired of raking, anyhow. "I'll be there in a minute."

Ida had taped a note onto the refrigerator saying that she'd gone downtown to see Harvey Brunner at the real estate office and wouldn't be back for a couple of hours or so, leaving Joe on his own for the afternoon. She'd still been acting peculiar when they got up in the morning, humming that idiotic tune she sang for the Spagnolinis last night. She licked Joe's ear to wake him and grabbed his peter when he rolled over. Ida wasn't much for sex before breakfast, yet now she was putting the make on him and he hadn't even brushed his teeth. Joe knew Frank and Vera were responsible for the change in Ida and wasn't sure how he felt about it. There was something suspicious about those two that troubled him. What were they doing here? Who can afford to drive around the country in a fancy car and still need to stay the night in a two-bit boardinghouse? Vera played the part of a vamp and Frank built up her game, both of them acting loose and dirty. Joe enjoyed sex as much as any other guy, but mushing up in a crowd felt nasty and crude. Because they'd already put it over on Ida, Joe decided what he had to do was try and size up these two sex-nuts to see if they were on the up-and-up or trying to pull a stunt of some sort.

Joe met Frank out on the front porch and they decided to take a stroll down to the waterfront where Frank could watch the fishing boats go out.

"If I didn't get the wee-wows like I do," Frank said, walking out onto the pier, "I'da joined the Navy."

"Everybody gets 'em sooner or later," Joe told him as a cold wind kicked up across the bay. He remembered puking his guts during a card game on the troop ship and getting sent up on deck to air out.

"Ida says you went to sea, huh? Fought the Japs?"

Joe nodded. "Army Air Corps in New Guinea."

Frank took out a cigarette. "See some action?"

"Got bombed now and then."

"Pretty hairy, huh?"

"Sure it was."

Frank lit up and tossed the burnt match into the harbor. "Well, I wished to hell I could've gone over there and helped you fellows out. Goddamned draft board said I had a bad stomach and sent me off to radar school with the eggheads. I always had a pretty good feel for electronics, so they stuck me on a workbench in front of a gizmo that wound up helping our bombers find Nazi targets in the dark. The swell thing was that it gave me a pretty feasible idea about an electronic gyro for atmospheric navigation that I took a patent on after the War and wound up selling to Grumman for a fairly hefty profit. Big nest egg, to tell the truth." Frank exhaled smoke into the salt breeze and laughed. "Fact is, I haven't had to work a day since. Can you feature that?"

Joe shook his head, though he'd certainly heard of guys gaining the advantage of military details that translated into careers outside of the service. Too bad there hadn't been any fortune to be made in loading bombs and digging trenches. Otherwise, he might be another Rockefeller.

Frank told him, "Well, one of these days I'll probably have to put my nose down and think of something else even niftier if I want to keep off the time clock. Vera likes getting around, seeing things. That's how we met, incidentally. She'd just ducked out on a job punching tickets at the El Cortez in Vegas and I was on my last day of a month-long holiday after cashing my first royalty check from Grumman. I saw this sweetie pie march out of the casino, bawling like a baby, so I stepped up and spilled a drink on the bricks to slow her down. When she landed in my lap, I knew I was set for life."

Joe smiled. "That's a swell story."

Staring off at the ocean, Frank took another drag off his cigarette. "You said it, pal. Having the right dame in your corner makes all the difference in the world. I used to be a pretty nervous guy, if you know what I mean. I guess I wasn't cut out for sitting in a bar making a play for every skirt that comes along. What's the use in that? You buy 'em a few drinks, go back to your room, hump till you keel over, then wish you'd gone bowling when they start telling you their dress size, and you know you can't stand 'em with their clothes on, anyhow. Don't get me wrong, I like noodling as much as the next guy, but once I met Vera, well, she put me out of the game, and I tell you I don't miss it one bit."

The wind rose off the water and gulls circled over the cold bay. There were boats coming in now from the north, and others headed out. Joe almost wished he were onboard one of the outbound vessels.

Frank asked, "So, what's the story with you and Ida? Still sweet on her, or dragging an anchor? I mean, I think she's really something, you know, how she was swinging it last night."

"We get along just swell, if that's what you're asking." Joe was reluctant to share too many details of his private life. Whose business was it, anyhow, whether he and Ida went dancing at night, or stayed home to watch Sid Caesar?

Frank flicked his cigarette into the tide. "I don't mean to be nosy."

"Okay."

"Vera says you're the kind of nifty proposition she had her eye out for when she met me. What do you think of that?"

"Oh yeah?"

The cool breeze swirled off the water and Frank started walking down the pier. "Think I'm pulling your leg?"

Joe followed along. "Are you?"

Frank laughed. "Hell no! I asked Vera if that meant she was about to tie a kite to her ass and take the wind and she blew smoke in my face. Then she got all sentimental, so I guess she's still soft on me, after all."

A stink of fish billowed toward them on the draft from the trawlers moored farther ahead. Frank watched the fishing boats, too. He told Joe about a cousin of his who owned a houseboat at Key Largo that capsized in a hurricane, nearly killing the whole family. "Now he's running charters for sword-fishing out in the Gulf and doesn't think twice of it. Me, I'd wear water wings in the tub if they fit."

"Does Vera know that?" Joe asked, unable to resist.

"Sure." Frank grinned. "Only one of us needs to get wet in this family."

In the kitchen at twilight, Ida asked Frank and Vera if they'd care to dine out. Coming late to the conversation from a shower upstairs, Joe didn't get to share his opinion.

"That's okey-doke by me," Frank agreed, "so long as I'm springing for it."

"Not on your life," Ida said. "Joe and me got no alibis for our business, but we know how to treat our guests. Besides, it's nice to get out of doors now and again."

"Well, how's about letting me buy some champagne for dessert? We can do our celebrating upstairs when we get back. What do you say?"

"Oh, that'd be nice."

Frank grabbed his hat. "Well, I'll go get it right now."

"How about if we all go together?" Ida suggested, taking her purse. "Joey?"

"Sure," Joe replied, getting up from the parlor sofa.

Frank shook his head. "No, let the poor dope stay here with Vera. I think these two ought to have a chance to get to know each other."

Ida smiled at Joe. "Is that all right, dear? We won't be gone long."

"Sure." He was glad to be rid of Frank, anyhow.

Vera mashed her cigarette into the ashtray by Ida's brass table lamp. "I'll keep an eye on him for you, honey. Trust me."

"You just be sure that's all you keep your eye on," Frank chided, zipping up his jacket.

Ida blew Joe a kiss as she led Frank out the door. "So long, dear."

After Frank and Ida had driven off, Joe went into the parlor and sat in his easychair. The street outside was empty. A cold fog swelled over the harbor. Following behind him, Vera lit another cigarette and sat down on the blue sofa. She looked sexy as hell. If Joe weren't married, he thought he'd lay her before his shirt hit the floor.

"Do you want to come over and keep me warm?" Vera asked, patting her skirt. "I got a spot saved right here on my lap." She gave him the glad eye and he could tell she meant it.

"I don't want to get punched in the nose," Joe replied, feeling a little nervous. He didn't trust Vera. What sort of woman gets fresh when her husband's only a few blocks away?

"Aw, Frankie's a pussycat. Believe me. He's never rumbled in his life. That's half his trouble. He gets his jollies sitting in the front row more than being on the field, if you get my drift."

"Is that so?" Joe was dubious about why Frank had left them alone. Didn't he know his wife was sexed up like this?

"Absolutely," Vera said. "He gets the jitters and can't swing his bat. I bet you don't have that problem, do you, honey?"

"Does Frank know you're talking like this?"

She smiled. "Oh, sure he does. In fact, I'll bet you a dollar he's got your honeypie singing her best song on his zipper right now. If you ask me, those two have it for each other, though I don't see why Ida needs to be that way when she's got a smoothie like you at home. Of course, I noticed she's a little waspish, if I'm being honest."

Joe glared at her. "Lay off the personal remarks, will you? I don't want to hear any more about that."

Vera rose from the sofa and walked over so close the gardenia perfume she wore bloomed in Joe's nostrils. "How's about we go upstairs, just you and me, and play house for a little bit?" She licked his neck, which gave him the shivers.

"Don't do that."

Vera purred, "Why not? Don't you like girls?"

"I got one already," Joe replied, anxious as hell for Ida and Frank to get back before things with Vera got crazy.

"So you're a one-horse fellow, huh?"

"That's right," Joe told her, maybe a little more self-righteously than he knew to be true. "And don't forget it."

Vera slipped her arm about his waist. "Well, I don't believe you. I think you like me." She nuzzled his neck. "And I sure like you."

The telephone rang in the office and Joe shot away from Vera like a rocket to catch it.

"Hey, what's your hurry?"

He shut the door behind him. "Hello?"

"Joey?"

It was Ida.

"Yeah?"

"Frank thinks we ought to have a shore dinner, so how about if you meet us at Leon's Seaside Café. He's hungry right now, so hurry along. Can you do that? Frank and me'll get a table for the four of us."

When Joe came out of the office, Vera was freshening her lipstick.

He told her, "We're meeting Ida and Frank for seafood."

"Oh, I love lobster. You're a peach, Joey!"

"It was Ida's idea."

What the hell had he gotten into, Joe wondered, hiring that suite to those two? Vera was a flirt like nobody's business. He grabbed the keys to the Studebaker and headed for the backdoor, Vera right on his heels.

Out by the garage, she said, "My uncle had one of these autos when I was a little girl. You ought to look into something more up-to-the-minute, don't you think?"

"This suits me just fine," Joe told her, firing up the motor. "I don't need a new car, and we can't afford one, anyhow." She climbed in beside him and he backed out of the driveway.

"That's not what Ida says," Vera remarked. "She told me she feels like Daisy Mae in this heap and can't see why you won't look into something classy like our Cadillac or one of those neat white Thunderbirds. She says it's not an issue of money, but that you're too stubborn to try on a new pair of shoes until you wear a hole in your old ones."

"She said that, huh?"

"Sure she did."

Joe pulled out onto the street and headed toward town. He rolled down his window to let some air into the car and then gassed the Studebaker along Ocean Street to downtown. Lots of people were out on the sidewalks this evening, window-shopping and popping into the Chinese restaurant or the Odeon movie house on the corner of Fifth Street to see the new John Wayne picture.

"Honey, I think you're a pipperoo," Vera said, sliding close to Joe. She put her fingers on his collar. "Isn't that all that matters?"

"What's wrong with Frank?"

She toyed with the top button of Joe's shirt. "Not a thing, if you don't mind a fellow with low voltage in his do-dads."

Joe dodged a pair of jaywalking teens and shrugged Vera's hand off his shirt.

She pouted. "You're not a square, are you, Joe? I hate squares."

Joe gripped the wheel, his eyes fixed ahead. "I'm not a square."

"I'm glad, because I want to have fun, Joe. Let's have some fun, me and you. What do you say?" Her hand fell to his trousers where she grabbed his peter and fondled it as they passed the Goodyear tire store near the end of downtown. Joe brushed her hand away, but she hooked her fingers under his belt and wormed her hand inside. Then it felt so good, he quit discouraging her and drove on for another three miles with Vera rubbing him almost to squirting his shorts before he spotted the winking blue neon sign of Leon's Seaside Café.

Ida and Frank were seated at a corner booth next to a broad plate-glass window that looked out on the gray evening bay. The low dining room ceiling lights were a dim amber and bottled candles flickered at every table. Cigarette smoke and a smell of liquor clouded the room. Joe followed Vera to the red leatherette booth. Out in the parking lot, she'd goosed his ass from the Studebaker to the front door.

Frank slid out of the booth to let Vera in beside him. "Don't tell me what kept you. It's none of my business."

"You know I don't kiss and tell, Frankie."

"Joey doesn't, either," Ida said. "He's a perfect gentleman that way."

Joe sat down next to Ida and gave her a peck on the cheek. She took his hand under the table and gave it a gentle squeeze. He felt sick to his stomach for what he'd let Vera do to him in the Studebaker. What the hell had come over him?

Ida had ordered a couple bottles of sparkling rosé, one of which was half-empty, and Frank already had a cranberry eye. Ida seemed sort of tipsy, too, and she rarely drank at supper. Straight off, Vera grabbed the closest bottle and poured herself a glass of wine.

"Will you have some, too, honey?" Ida asked Joe. "It's awfully tasty." She put her fingers to her lips, suppressing a burp.

Frank laughed out loud. "Your wife's a kick, Joe. I can see why you keep her around."

"It's more like she keeps me," Joe replied, trying to be congenial. He took the bottle of rosé and poured himself half a glass. The wine glimmered in the limp candlelight.

Frank raised his own glass to make a toast. "Here's hearts and flowers!"

Joe clinked his glass to Ida's, but felt as if he were at someone else's party. A waitress came over and passed out the menus and Vera took ten minutes to decide on what sort of fish to get.

"How the hell do I know where they caught it?" Frank asked, when his wife worried if the halibut had fallen off a truck. "If it don't stink, eat it."

"I haven't ate oysters since I was a little girl," Ida remarked, skimming the menu. "Do you think they're filling?"

"Depends how many you eat," Joe said, worried about bad fish himself. Nothing had gotten him sicker than a swordfish steak one night at Long Beach that set his boiler off like a rocket. He decided on a lobster plate.

Once they'd all ordered, Frank told Joe, "Ida thinks we ought to rendezvous down at San Francisco some weekend for a crab dinner at Fisherman's Wharf."

"That sounds swell to me," Vera said, cracking a breadstick in half and dipping it in her wine. "I hear there's a million shops on Union Square." She fastened her gaze on Joe as she licked the tip of it.

"I've never ridden a cable car," Ida remarked. "Do lots of people fall off?"

"That was swell of your pop to give you that house down there," Frank said to Joe. "Ida told us all about it. You got a sweet deal there, pal. Property values are flying through the roof in the Bay Area. I'd give an arm and a leg to get a place like that. It's a nice investment."

Joe shrugged. "There's just a couple of rooms upstairs, a garage below. I thought about fixing up the downstairs, making a rumpus room out of the garage, or maybe turning it into a little apartment and renting it out to someone."

"Would you allow pets?" Vera interjected, gulping down a swig of rosé. "Frank says I can get a dog if we settle somewhere."

"She wants a Pekinese," Frank said, shaking his head. "I asked her, why have a dog that ain't no bigger than a cat?"

Once dinner arrived, they ate heartily, Joe with his lobster plate and steamed potatoes, Ida slurping her oysters on the half-shell. Frank had ordered a combination platter of scallops, shrimp, and crab, while Vera picked apart a salmon steak with a side of lima beans. They killed both bottles of wine and ordered a third. By now, both Frank and Vera had a distinct glow on and became that much more affable and forthcoming regarding the profit Frank earned from his aeronautic gyro deal with Grumman.

"I wouldn't call it a soak 'em price," Frank explained, "but we stepped it up enough that I won't have to be working on time payments when my hair goes gray. The big cats tried to shade me a grand at every turn, but I let 'em know I wasn't some dry land sucker making a blind swap. I knew what I had, so I was able to cut a pretty mean deal with those fellows. Every month I get a fat check in the mail, and Vera gets a new pair of shoes."

Vera told Ida, "Frankie's got most of it stashed away somewhere even I don't know about."

"Oh yeah?"

Frank smiled. "Check and double check."

Joe said, "I never could save much money. Whenever I got enough to be dangerous, it always burned a hole in my pocket."

"Until he met me," Ida said, taking Joe's hand. "I put him on the straight and narrow once I did a reading and absolutely saw that he had good intentions and only needed someone to point him in the right direction."

"Did you hear that, Frankie?" Vera chimed in. "All it takes is a good woman to help you fellows figure it out. So why won't you let me dress you in the morning?"

"Vera can't polish my shoes without getting ink all over herself," Frank said, spearing a chunk of shrimp with his fork, "but she's a champ with the lights out."

Vera grabbed Frank's face and kissed him square on the lips. "Ain't that the truth, sweetie?"

Ida laughed. "She's nutty for you, Frank, I promise you that. I think you're positively lucky to have her, just like me and Joey."

Frank filled himself a glass of rosé. "I'd say that rates another toast." He raised his glass. "To holy bedlock!"

After the toast, Vera and Ida got up to go to powder room. Once they'd left, Frank said, "I think we got a pretty swell deal cooking between the four of us, wouldn't you say?"

Joe picked over the remains of his lobster shell. "Yeah? How's that?"

Frank smiled. "I almost hate to admit it, but anyone can see that Vera's stuck on you."

"Why do you keep talking like that?" Joe said, damned uncomfortable with this whole circumstance. It just seemed unnatural, how they were all behaving, like those cheap paperbacks he used to read. He felt dirty just discussing it.

Frank took out a shiny Ronson lighter and lit a cigarette. "Talking like what?"

"You and her are married." Joe spoke firmly, while keeping his voice down. "So are me and Ida. I'm not out there fishing for something new. Sorry if it looks like that, but it's not so."

"Hey, there's no reason to get your back up," Frank told him, leaning closer. "We're all grown-ups here, right? Look, me and Vera've been riding around for the past couple years or so, and it's just hell trying to make friends. Well, last night she told me she's tired of doing all this for laughs. She says she wants a place of her own and someone she really likes to go shopping with, and that you and Ida are about the swellest people we've ever met and maybe we ought to chase you two down to 'Frisco, partner up in that house of yours. Ida tells me there'd be plenty of room with you two upstairs and us in the basement. If we made a decent apartment of the downstairs, all four of us'd be cozy together. She thinks we really ought to look into making a case this week for doing just that. I had no argument with her. What do you think?"

"I don't know," Joe replied, wondering who came up with that lamebrain scheme. Sharing his goddamned house? Who says so? "It's a pretty small place, I got to tell you."

"Well, I don't mind a tight fit so long as it's warm, if you get my meaning."

Joe nibbled on a bite of potato while Frank drank another glass of sparkling wine and grew more and more sentimental about the necessity of the four of them sticking together. Joe repeatedly dodged the subject. It was noisy in the café, people at the bar gabbing louder by the minute as the bartender kept his customers oiled with cocktails and beer. Out on the bay, moonlight flickered across the cold water and a wind came up, flapping through the colored flags on the night shoreline.

Then Ida and Vera returned from the ladies room, more excited than a couple of kids on Christmas morning. Peering over his drink, Frank asked, "What's gotten into these two?"

"I don't know." Joe couldn't recall the last time he'd seen Ida so delirious.

The women slipped into their seats, tittering like dingbats. Neither spoke. Joe had no idea what was going on. Frank put down his drink with a frown, then said, "So? Spill it, girls."

Vera announced, "We want to go for a drive."

Frank exhaled a puff of cigarette smoke. "What's the punch line?"

"We're getting stale here, me and Ida," she told him. "We gotta let loose."

Ida added, "We'll be going in your beautiful Cadillac, Frankie. It'll be the best time ever."

"Says who?"

"Says me and Ida," Vera replied. "And when we're good and ready, we'll come back to our room and fix you up with a party, maybe reward you with something extra special."

"Oh yeah?" Frank turned again to Joe. "Does that sound like your idea of a good time? Riding around in the middle of the night with a couple of worn-out dames?"

Vera slapped Frank on the wrist with a spoon. "Who are you calling worn out, Mister Poopy-Peter? Why, me and Ida can run rings around you two fellows any night of the week, can't we, honey?"

"You betcha," Ida agreed, nudging Joe with her elbow. She grabbed his hand under the table and gave his fingers a healthy squeeze.

"What if we don't want to go?" Frank asked. "Maybe me and my pal Joe here got some plans of our own cooked up that don't include hot-rodding."

"Well, then, me and Ida ought to take a powder on you right now," Vera warned. She nodded at Ida who reached into her purse and took out Frank's car keys, jingling them for effect. "What do you say, dearie? Should we just get the Caddy ourselves and ditch these two bozos, maybe find us a couple of real cannonballs?"

Ida snuggled up against Joe, nuzzling his ear. "I still want my Joey to come with us so we can go all over tonight. The whole gang of us. What do you say, sweetheart? Won't you, please?"

"Sure, " Joe told her, resigned to the idea now. How else could he keep his eye on her? "Let's go whoop it up."

"Gee, thanks, Joe," Frank said, draining his last drop of rosé. "Wait'll you see what you got us into."

Speeding north up the highway toward Crescent City, Joe was sitting behind the wheel of Spagnolini's red Cadillac Eldorado with Frank on the seat beside him. Both women huddled in back, scarves tied over their heads against the cold ocean air.

"See how she handles that turn?" Frank pointed out as Joe angled out of a curve on the winding coast road. "Like a dream, huh?"

"Yeah," Joe said, steering the convertible through another tight bend. This car was lots bigger and more powerful than his Studebaker. He was scared to death about crashing it, but Frank had insisted he take the wheel back at the restaurant, probably because Joe was the most sober of the group. Ida agreed, badgering him into popping over to the driver's side as they climbed in.

"Nothing like it on the road today," Frank added with pride as Joe motored on. "Vera wants one of her own in aquamarine." He peeked back over his shoulder where Vera was teary-eyed with laughter over something. "Say, what're you two yakking about back there?"

"It's just girl-talk, sweetie! Don't pay us any mind."

With the old highway empty, Joe gave it more gas. Grass swept back on the roadside shoulder as they shot past fields of clustered oaks and old fence lines and steep dark bluffs above the flat gray ocean. Frank spoke in his ear. "Do you ever get the feeling these dames'd rather taken the car out by themselves? I don't think they need us."

Joe braked awkwardly approaching a tight turn and had to jerk the wheel hard over to keep the auto out of the ditch. There was a squeal from the backseat as Ida half-tumbled across Vera's lap.

"Hey! Watch out! Trying to get us killed back here?"

"Sorry!"

"Easy, tiger," Frank said, grabbing the wheel. "A light touch is all she needs. Like Vera's bottom."

"Shove it, Frankie!"

"Where?"

For the next hour or so, Joe did his best to keep focused on the road ahead while his drunken passengers played charades and sang along to jazz tunes on the radio. Frank brought a flask out of his jacket and shared it with everyone but Joe, who was egged on by his new pal to give the Caddy more gas, "really let 'er out." He scared himself on a few straight-aways and almost ran it into a ditch, swinging through a steep curve, and didn't really slow down until the girls started yelling at him. All in all, he actually enjoyed driving around, even with this carload of inebriates. Just like Frank said, the Cadillac was a dream. Joe wondered if he could swing the bank to buy one on credit. His Studebaker was almost played out and Ida was right: only a third-rater drove one of them these days. If he had any self-respect, he'd dump it. Maybe some high school kid would take the thing off his hands for a fair deal. Why not? The motor was strong and the suspension still held up. He'd hate to see his old wagon go, but these convertibles were pretty nifty.

Back in Ocean City, Joe drove the Cadillac over to the restaurant to pick up his Studebaker and then followed Frank and Vera across town to the boardinghouse, where Frank wheeled the Cadillac to the curb out front and shut off the motor while Joe parked up by the garage. Ida slid out of the Studebaker and hurried up the steps to unlock the front door.

"I'm freezing my monkey off, Frankie," Vera complained, unbundling herself as she got out of the Cadillac. "Did you have to drive so fast?"

Frank chased Ida up the front stairs. Wind raced off the bay and chilled the night air. Joe had no feeling in his face, and his ears hurt as he got out of the car. It was a little after ten o'clock, and the plan was for the whole gang to go up to Spagnolini's suite for a nightcap. Ida called to Frank from somewhere down the hall on the second floor and he shouted back that he was heading up to his room. Joe felt almost left out and went to the downstairs toilet to relieve himself. The long ride had left his bladder aching.

"Are you okay, Joe?" Vera spoke just outside the toilet. "Frank wants me upstairs, but I'll wait here for you if you like."

"No," he told her through the door as he did his business. She was becoming a habit Joe needed to crack. "You go on ahead. Tell Ida I'll be there in a minute. I got to clean up first."

"We won't start our party without you, honey. I promise."

"Thanks."

Joe waited for her to leave before flushing the toilet. Once he heard Vera's footfall on the stairs, he washed his hands, then came out. Up on the third floor, Frank's radio was already piping Perry Como loud enough to be heard out in the street. Joe figured he was giving Ida a rush before the party began. He went to the office and locked the door for the night and switched off the downstairs lights. Then he went up to his bedroom and changed shirts and shoes and washed his face. Despite being called repeatedly from up above, Joe didn't hurry. What was there to look forward to? More boozing? His head was sore enough. Also, he was pretty tired from the drive and could've gone to bed if he wasn't obligated to join Ida and those two blockheads. Inviting them down to San Francisco to live in his own house was outrageous. Standing at the bedroom window, gazing out toward the cold and windy bay, Joe tried to decide where he'd gone derelict in his duty to Ida. Didn't he fluff up her pillow on those nights when she came out of the shower begging him to go to work on her? What had she ever asked of him that he hadn't done? He combed his hair and went upstairs.

Arriving in the third floor hallway, Joe heard Vera having a mouth fight with Frank over a trip to a resort in Arizona she wanted to take and he didn't, claiming a case of insufficient funds.

"Oh, Frankie, that's a load of crap," she complained. *"The rooms weren't more than ten dollars and you have more than that in your billfold right now. Let's all sing like the birdies sing, 'Cheap, cheap, cheap.'"*

Frank laughed as Joe knocked on the door. *"Honey, our cat sings better than that."*

"We don't have a cat."

"Well, then, let's get one."

Frank greeted Joe with a cross-eyed grin. "What kept you?"

"I had to clean up."

Joe saw Ida standing by the window with a glass of champagne in her hand, facing out toward the gray moon-lit ocean.

"What for?" said Frank, who'd tossed his own jacket onto a mahogany plant stand that used to hold a fern Ida bought for the room. His dress shirt was unbuttoned at the collar and wrinkled to his waist.

"Leave him alone, Frankie," Vera snarled from the sofa. She tapped ash off her cigarette into a porcelain teacup. "At least he's gentleman enough to wash his hands."

"I'll take a bath, if you like," Frank told her. "Soon as we're through here."

"Thank goodness," Vera said, "though it won't be any too soon for me. I don't know how Ida could stand you on the ride to the restaurant."

"Same as Joe could cuddle with you and keep his nose clean."

"Shut up."

Frank went over to the short walnut bookcase on the closet wall where he kept his assortment of liquor bottles, a cocktail shaker, and some glasses. He poured himself a couple shots of gin, then raised a toast. "Here's to my lovely wife! Ain't she a package?"

"Quit giving me the razz, Frankie." She sniffed her underarms. "I mean it."

"Check and double check." Frank drained his drink, and strolled back through the open curtain into his bedroom where clothes were strewn across the bed, sheets rumpled and fussy, four old cotton pillows stuffed up against the headboard. Actually, the whole suite was a mess. That sofa Vera stretched out on cost sixty-five dollars at the furniture store last month, and Joe already noticed a couple of fresh coffee stains on the cushions, courtesy of the Spagnolinis.

Sitting down on the sofa, he remarked, "I can just see how swell we'd get along in San Francisco. Whose hot idea was that, anyhow?"

"Be nice, Joey," Ida advised, strolling over now to wrap her arm around him. "We're all grown-ups here, aren't we?"

From the bedroom, Frank called out to Ida, "You bet we are, sweetheart, and I'll prove it to you if you come over here and let me give you a rush."

Whistling along to the radio, Ida went to help Frank straighten up the bed. Vera snuffed out her cigarette and slid over next to Joe, wrapping her arms around his waist, blocking his view of anything except her face. Her perfume bloomed. "I can't stand to stare at Frank's puss another second. You won't make me, will you?"

Joe felt as if a big joke was being played on him. There was just something fishy about all this. Out of the corner of his eye, he saw

Ida set her glass of champagne on Frank's nightstand. Perry Como finished singing *"I Wonder Who's Kissing Her Now,"* and Joe heard the springs squeak as Frank climbed into bed.

Vera kissed Joe on the nose. "Would you like me to fix you a drink, sweetie?"

"No, thanks. I'm going easy."

"You don't like to drink?"

"I like it all right," he told her, rising to catch sight of Ida. She was next to Frank on the bed now, her shiny black shoes kicked off. "I guess that wine was enough for me tonight."

Vera tugged Joe back down beside her onto the green stuffed sofa. "Take a load off, honey. I'm lonely."

When the song ended, Joe heard Ida and Frank mumbling puppy love on the bed. He tried to sit up again for a look, but Vera wouldn't let him. Instead, she kissed Joe on the lips. Her breath was scalding and wet, tasting of gin and stale lipstick. Joe felt his face flush. The radio came back on in the bedroom, spilling jazz into the humid air. Ida was humming along with the Stan Getz Quartet playing "This Can't Be Love."

"Are you nervous, Joe?" Vera breathed in his ear. "You seem nervous."

"This is nuts," he murmured, still trying to see over Vera's shoulder.

Ida squealed back in the bedroom.

Unbuttoning the top of Joe's shirt, Vera slipped a hand inside and rubbed her fingers over a nipple until Joe gasped, and Frank began laughing like a hyena over something Ida had just told him. Again, Joe tried to peek over the sofa to see what his wife was up to, but Vera grabbed him. "Don't you want to discover me, Joe?"

"Huh?"

Vera kissed him hard on the mouth as she pressed her breasts against Joe's chest, pinning him to the sofa back. She drew open her silk blouse and Joe stiffened in his shorts. Her bra rubbed against his chest and felt pointier than Ida's old cowcatchers. Vera fumbled with Joe's zipper and his head swam like he'd been boozing since supper. His peter felt ready to punch a hole in his trousers when Vera began rubbing her bottom on him. What the hell was she doing? He squirmed underneath her, trying to get up.

"Am I crushing you, honey?" She leaned back, drew down his zipper, and stuffed her fingers inside his shorts, grabbing hold of his do-dad. "Here, let me straighten you out."

Joe panicked. "Hey!"

"What?"

"Don't do that."

"Do what?" Vera giggled.

Joe heard the bedsprings romping and noises that Ida only uttered in the throes of hot passion. "Let me up!"

Vera laughed as Joe tried to squirm out from under her. "Joey, don't quit on me now. Haven't you ever been on a ball?"

Frank let out a groan as the iron bedstead rammed the wall behind it.

Joe gave Vera a shove to the side and slid a leg out from under her, jerking her hand free of his pants. "Just let me up, all right?"

"How's about this?" Vera undid the clasp on her bra, freeing her tits not six inches from Joe's face. She'd dabbed perfume between both breasts and Joe's nostrils filled with the luscious scent of gardenia. Her aureoles were bigger than a silver dollar and coffee-dark, her nipples thick. She rubbed one of them across his lips, murmuring, "Make me happy, Joe."

Joe's head swam with lust, his trousers bulged, but he could hear Frank panting like a dog and imagined the expression on Ida's face, her mouth open wide enough to stuff a peach into. "Get off me."

"Wait!"

Joe shoved Vera off balance and slid out from under her legs. Then he stared into the bedroom and his stomach flip-flopped. There was

Frank on his knees naked as a baby and Ida bare, too, her mottled haunches raised, her pink face sideways on the pillow, Frank humping her like a hound dog.

Vera popped the button on Joe's trousers. "Don't watch them, Joe. Let's have our own party. I want you all the way."

Seeing his wife go the limit with another fellow right before Joe's eyes was shocking. As June Christy sang "Something Cool" on the radio, he watched Frank thrust enthusiastically into Ida, over and over again, making the bed squeak like a flivver.

"Don't watch them, Joe," Vera said, rubbing her tits on his arms. "Let's raise the devil ourselves. Just you and me. Really do it up big. What do you say?"

Suddenly this third floor suite that had seemed like a damned fine room a couple days ago became horrid and cheap. Listening to Ida get the business from a clown like Frank just made it that much worse. He blamed Frank and Ida both, but he might just as well have faulted himself since it was he who hired out the room.

"Come on, Joe," Vera moaned, grabbing his balls. "Love me up."

A breeze fluttered the curtains at the window, fanning the odor of liquor and cigarettes throughout the suite. Frank quit hammering at Ida. He reached over to the walnut nightstand and took a cigarette in one hand, then grabbed his lighter and fired it up. Joe watched Ida shift around beneath Frank, so that she was on her back. Her eyes met Joe's and she smiled as Frank took a long drag off the cigarette and stuck it into the glass ashtray on the nightstand, and lowered himself back onto her. Ida grabbed Frank's face in her hands, parted her thighs, and kissed him square on the mouth, and he mounted her again.

"Joe!" Vera quit stroking him. She wore a pout on her face. He had no idea what she was unhappy about and didn't much care. In fact, despite how stiff he'd gotten, Joe had a lot less desire for sex now than he'd had three minutes ago. He felt disgusted. If he were a real man, he'd climb off the sofa and go paste Frank a good one in the mouth. He'd like to see how good Frank was in bed with half his teeth knocked out.

"Don't you want me, Joe? Ain't I luscious?" Vera asked. "We can have loads of fun. What do you want I should do? Just tell me and I'll do it."

Joe wanted to tell her to go to hell, but instead he shoved her back down. Wasn't that the point of a big dirty flesh session? Treat 'em rough?

"Get ready."

"Yeah?"

"And take off your bottoms. Let's quit fooling around. What're we here for anyhow?"

In the bedroom, Ida was panting like crazy now. Her puffy face was beet-red, her eyes shut tight, fingernails scratching Frank's bare back. Seeing that was enough to make Joe sick to his stomach, and Vera wasn't doing much more now than giving his own peter some lame tugs.

"Well?"

"What?" Her eyes glistened in the smoky lamplight and she smelled oily.

"Let's get down to business," Joe told her, anger rising. "Isn't that what you want? Or are you just here to watch Frank fucking my wife?"

She sat up and narrowed her eyes. "Don't you like me, Joe? I thought for sure you were one of those slick fellows when we first met. I could tell you had the eye for me straight away. Wasn't I right?"

"Are you going to fuck me or not?"

Vera rubbed him harder, glancing briefly over to the bedroom where Frank was arching high over Ida, his brow almost banging the headboard. After all that sexed-up urging, Vera still hadn't made the slightest move toward lying back on the sofa.

"Well?" Joe's patience with this entire fiasco was waning quickly.

Vera kept pulling on him like crazy, seeming more desperate than passionate. "I can't."

"Huh?"

She dropped her voice. "The curse."

Joe couldn't believe his ears. "You're on the rag?"

Vera nodded.

"That's swell. What was all that about going the limit?"

She jerked his rod with a dirty grin, but it came off half-baked. "Doesn't this feel good?"

Just then, across the suite, Frank grunted once like a hog and collapsed happily on top of Ida.

Joe jumped up off the sofa and left the room.

MOONLIGHT LIT THE WALL next to his bed where Joe lay woozy and despondent. What a miserable experience. Ida had come downstairs a couple hours after Joe left, all giddy from liquor and stinking of Frank. When she discovered how Joe hadn't shared her enthusiasm for that stupid party, she pretended to be mortified.

"Well, didn't you enjoy yourself at all? The rest of us did, and if you didn't, I can't imagine the reason why not. We were all in it together. Vera sure thinks so."

"To hell with her, too."

"I thought you liked her."

"Well, I don't. She's every bit as rotten as Frank. They're both rats in my book."

"Well, Frank thinks you're swell, and so does Vera. They're honest about that, I can tell. Frank knows you're jealous of those checks he gets from his gyro invention, so he doesn't take these personal slights of yours to heart. I think that's commendable."

"Well, maybe he ought to," Joe said, "because I hate his guts, and I have since the day we met. I didn't trust him then, and I never will now. He's a lousy little rat. I don't care how much dough he's got in the bank, if he's even being square about that."

"Well, he is, in fact, because I saw his check for the month. It's two thousand dollars. He showed it to me when we were downtown. I didn't really trust him, either, until I saw it, even though my astrology told me he was on the level."

"Well, I still don't trust him, and I don't like him, at all. He's a gutter rat."

"You already said that, Joey."

"Well, it's true. And you know why."

Joe put his back to Ida. Seeing her thumping the bedframe up in Frank's room nauseated him. Nobody was innocent, himself included, but Joe decided that Ida and Frank had conspired with Vera to run up the pressure on him so they wouldn't feel guilty over screwing each other.

"Well, I won't say he forced me," Ida confessed, rising to go to the toilet. She ran water in the sink and mopped her face with a damp washrag while Joe stared at the pale half-moon through the curtain lace, a sky dark blue over the night ocean. A single automobile drove slowly past on the street below. Joe listened to Ida undress and come back to bed. The mattress sagged as she climbed onto it. She fluffed her lacy pillow and gently lay down facing his back. Joe felt like Ida had kicked him in the groin. He thought maybe he ought to pack up his suitcase and beat it out of town tomorrow. The old Studebaker had a full tank of gas and four new Goodyears. That'd get him far enough to make any apology of hers a long distance call. Of course, what he'd done with Vera was just as dirty. Had Vera stripped to the buff and laid down for him on the sofa, he'd have done to her like Frank did Ida. That jazz on the radio Frank played certainly contributed. Ida liked hearing music all day and night, while Joe preferred it quiet when he was in his bedroom. Whenever Ida wanted to listen to one of her radio programs, Joe made her go down the hall to 2C, a room that had poor morning light and was never hired out. He reasoned that Frank knew about this and deliberately bought a radio to seduce Ida. Also, Frank got her drunk. Normally, Ida didn't touch liquor unless she had a special occasion and wanted to get into the spirit. Weeks and weeks might pass between drinks. Unlike people who imbibed alcohol as part of their common activities, Ida rarely mentioned liquor when she wasn't drinking, except to comment on the extent to which others abused it. She applauded Joe for the restraint he showed with beer. Why quarrel over a habit that doesn't exist? Now they had more trouble than a few too many drinks, thanks to Frank the Rat.

Lying quietly on his side, Joe listened to the Spagnolinis moving around up on the third floor and the radio still singing in the walls. Didn't they ever go to sleep?

"Joey?"

Ida nudged him in the ribs.

"Yeah?"

"Are you awake?"

"Sure I am."

Ida sat up. "I went downtown to see Harvey this afternoon, did you know that?"

"No." Joe kept his back to her, his eyes on the window where he could see the moon through the curtain lace, glowing behind the clouds over the bay.

"Well, it's positively the smartest decision I ever made since we taken over this house. Harvey thinks so, too. That's absolutely what he told me and he ought to know, don't you agree?"

"Don't tell me it's another mortgage, because then I wouldn't agree with you or Harvey. We don't need to get any more over-run on this dump than we already are."

"Well, I'm selling, Joey. The whole property. Lock, stock, and barrel. We're getting out of here, and I don't mind telling you, it's not soon enough. It's just no good for us anymore. We work too hard and don't get nothing out of it except a sore back and stack of bills we can hardly manage. I positively thought we could make a go of it with the two of us working together, I really did. And you've been a dear, Joey, with all you done here. But we're wearing ourselves out for nothing, and I say this ought to be the finish. So I went downtown and told Harvey we wanted out and he told me 'It's about time, Ida. Everyone in Ocean City's expecting this and you'll get a terrific deal for the property because the lot's worth twice what the house is, and there won't be any shortage of big offers. Just you wait and see.' So we drew up the papers and put out a notice and I expect it won't be long before someone hands us a check and lets us go."

Joe rolled over in bed to face Ida. She sat propped up against her pillow now, pale moonshine on her face. "Where're we going to go?"

Ida smiled. "Down to San Francisco, Joey, to that darling house of yours. If you don't mind sharing it with your little wife, I think we can absolutely do something big down there. I saw it in my reading last week when you were out to the movies and it really gave me a start because it was so unexpected, but sometimes that's how heaven comes to us."

"How're we going to pay the bills? I'd have to get a steady job down there, and that won't be easy, you know. Good work isn't so available you can just waltz in and pick up a paycheck. It might take a while to find something. I won't shovel shit somewhere just to get out from under this place."

"Joey, we been on our knees since we taken over this turkey, and I say enough is enough. Do you see that beautiful moonshine on the bay? Well, that's God's reflection shining through the window on everything we do. Can you feel it on your face? I can. It warms my soul and promises that our time here is up, and we're supposed to go down the road to our new lives and never look back. So that's what we're doing, and once it's decided, there's positively no use in putting it off. Believe me, sweetheart, this is all for the best."

WHEN JOE GOT UP the next morning, the house was empty, so he ate breakfast by himself in the kitchen. Afterward, he tossed some clothes into his duffel, left a note for Ida, and drove the Studebaker down to San Francisco. He made one stop at Ukiah for lunch and another in Novato, late in the afternoon, where he telephoned Chuck Henry to arrange for the house key. Fog chilled the bay when Joe crossed the Golden Gate Bridge at sundown. He bought a crab plate at Fisherman's Wharf, and then went out Van Ness and Mission to South San Francisco where he drove around for almost half an hour before locating the small house on Ellington Avenue. Joe parked in the driveway and got the key out from under the staircase. He let himself in through the front door upstairs and switched on the lights. Most of his uncle's furniture remained, including the Philco TV set. Only the fat leather easychair was gone, a gift to Chuck for looking after the house since Uncle Bill passed away. Joe had a look at the back bedrooms and the bathroom and went into the kitchen and thought the house wasn't half bad. The carpets smelled worn out and he'd have to replace the linoleum in the bathroom, but he could stand that expense if he did the work himself. Uncle Bill had been a bachelor his whole life, so there wasn't much to the decorating, just some wildlife prints and faded wallpapers that he probably inherited when he bought the place during the 1930s. Ida could probably fix it all up to suit them both. She had a good eye for that. Down in the basement, Joe saw space for a couple of small rooms if he put in a cement slab and framed up another wall. It used to be a garage, but the big door was replaced by a regular one with a lock that didn't take Joe's key.

He telephoned up to Ocean City to let Ida know he had arrived okay and when no one answered, Joe drove back to Van Ness for a steak dinner and went to a movie afterward. He spent the night in his uncle's bedroom, and the next morning he ate breakfast in Daly City and paid a visit to the utilities office to have the gas and electricity switched over to his name. Then he went back to the house to nose around some more. Joe almost cracked himself in the head drawing down the ceiling ladder to the attic. There were a couple trunks full of shirts and trousers, some cardboard boxes stuffed with letters and old magazines, a shoe rack with four pairs of spats, and a set of rusty golf clubs. He kicked over a dried up rat's nest, then went back down again to look over the bedrooms. The back room Joe had shared four years ago with the fruity painter had two single beds and a closet full of more junk. The chest of drawers was packed with old clothes. Uncle Bill's bedroom was still ship-shape except for more clothes in the highboy dresser and shoes on the closet floor that Joe tossed out onto the carpet. He found two size-sixteen satin evening dresses tucked away in a garment bag behind Bill's coats with a swallowtail tuxedo and a postal uniform. They joined the pile of discards. Once he finished cleaning out the drawers in both bedrooms, Joe telephoned Goodwill to arrange for a truck to come out later that afternoon and take away the junk from the spare closet, his uncle's clothes, a lamp stand in the living room with a busted socket, and a set of flamingo embroidered towels that Joe hated. He left the stuff in the attic for another visit.

At lunch, Joe got burned up again over Ida and Frank. His imagination ran crazy as he pictured all sorts of dirty scenarios in 3B. Thinking about it made him feel like puking up his hamburger, and he swore to put an end to all that the minute he got back to Ocean City. Just after the Goodwill truck drove off, a plumber came out to Ellington Avenue and Joe took him down into the basement to have a look at a leaky pipe. While it got fixed, Joe tried telephoning Ida once again. When no one answered, he was sure that she and Frank were fooling around, and Joe considered staying in the city. Why not? He had his own house now. Who needs a wife that beds another man? At sunset, he drove out to North Beach and ate a plate of meatballs at Vanessi's, then went up to Finnochio's for a drink, where the queers dressed like women and put on a goofy cabaret show. After a lisping brunette sat in his lap, Joe ran out and went back to Ellington and fell asleep with the radio on. When he woke up in the middle of the night, he decided he ought to go home, after all.

Heading back to Ocean City the next morning, Joe ate pancakes on the waterfront in Sausalito and watched the gulls shit on the railings while he worked out a speech to Ida. Sunlight rippled across the waters of San Francisco Bay, and the early breeze wasn't as cold as yesterday. If he and Ida moved to Ellington Avenue, there had to be some agreement about how she behaved. Also, that rat bastard Frank and his stupid wife were to stay away for keeps. Joe watched a gull fly off with someone's toast. After breakfast, he found a pay phone up the street and telephoned the house again. This time, a fellow answered whose voice Joe didn't recognize.

"Hello?"

"Who's this?"

"Gary."

"I'm Joe Krueger. Is Ida there?"

"Nope, she went downtown with Frank."

"What're you doing there?"

"Digging a hole in her basement."

"What for?"

"She says a disposal drain."

"How come you're answering the phone?"

"She paid me three dollars."

Joe hung up.

THE HOUSE WAS QUIET as a morgue when Joe finally reached home after dark. The kitchen door was ajar and he took a peek into the backyard before pulling it shut. Frank's Cadillac was parked at the end of the driveway in front of the garage and the top was up. Joe took a beer out of the refrigerator and drank it, then headed down to the basement for a look at the job Ida hired. The old wooden steps were a hazard. Somebody was going to break his neck on them one day. At the bottom, he flicked on the lights. Just ahead of the stairs, the concrete had been torn up with a jackhammer and a fairly decent hole dug, roughly four feet deep by three feet wide by four or five feet long. It looked big enough to lay in a new disposal unit or whatever Ida wanted. There were three sacks of cement over to one side of the basement, a couple of water buckets, a shovel and pickax, a big canvas tarpaulin, and a wheelbarrow for mixing the cement to seal the floor once the plumbers came to finish their part of the job.

After Joe came back up into the kitchen, he went to find Ida. Stopping at their bedroom to lay off his duffel and wash his face, Joe heard someone walking around on the third floor. He went to the foot of the stairs and listened for half a minute. Frank's radio was playing Woody Herman and Joe bet Ida was up there having a party. Goddamned sonofabitches. He wanted to throw Frank out a window. Back in high school, Joe's girlfriend Tammy cheated on him with Vernon Deaver from shop class. When Tammy saw Joe punch Vernon in the head out behind the gymnasium, she told Joe to get lost, so he stopped calling on her. Later on, he decided his mistake had been hitting Vernon with Tammy there to see it.

Joe crept upstairs to the third floor hallway and had a listen at the door to 3B. He heard jazz on the radio, but no voices or bedsprings squeaking. A small truck drove past on the street outside.

Then the door opened and Ida was right in front of him.

"Joe!" She clapped a hand over her mouth. "My goodness, you scared the daylights out of me!" She looked flustered. Her blue daisy print dress was rumpled, her eyes glossy and pale, face flushed and shiny with perspiration. "I was just coming downstairs. Did you eat supper yet? I'll fix something for you, if you like."

"No, I ate at Fort Bragg."

"Was it a long drive?"

"Thirteen hours, not counting stops for gas and such."

Ida stepped forward and embraced him with a good warm hug and a kiss. "I missed you, Joey."

He tried looking past her into the room. "Where's Frank and Vera?"

"Honey, you couldn't imagine what Harvey told me when I asked for a reduction on our last mortgage, because we positively need to fix a fair price for this place without pitching ourselves into the poorhouse."

"Did Frank tell you to hire that new disposal drain in the basement?"

Ida frowned. "Honey, it's not right of you to second-guess me on what ought to be done before the buyers come out for a look-see."

"It's not right what you did with Frank."

"Do you hate me, Joey? Do you wish I was dead? Because I can see that disgust in your eyes as if you were wearing a sign that says so."

"I don't know."

"Why, I bet you thought I've been looking for a new heart, didn't you?"

"I didn't think anything at all."

"You believe I love him, don't you?"

"Do you?"

Ida sniffled. "Why, I hate his guts, Joey. I honestly do. He's nothing to me but a rotten pervert. I let him have his way with me so we could get a few things that we need, and no other reason. I did it for you, honey, bless your heart." She forced a smile.

Joe felt agitated, ready for a showdown. "Where's Frank now?"

"In the room."

"And Vera?"

"She's there, too."

"Were you wrestling with Frank again tonight?"

"He's been peeping on me, Joey, right from the get-go. Did you know that? When you went bowling Tuesday night, he waltzed in and saw me undressed and didn't make any excuse about it."

"I guess I'm not up with the times," Joe said, not surprised to hear that Frank was a peeper. That sort of thing suited a rat like him. "What else did he do?"

"You know, honey, from the day I first put my hair up, one fellow or another has tried to make me a mother. It's what a girl expects. Frank's nothing special in that regard."

"Well, he didn't need to peep when I was up here before," Joe said, getting mad again. "You made sure of that."

Ida scowled. "I won't fight with you about any of this, dear, because I know my own faults better than anyone else. I admit I've done some things that positively shame me, and only God can put off my sins, and I accept that, absolutely. But it's also mine to make straight as a die."

"And how the hell do you expect to do that? Haven't we had trouble enough without you paying the interest? And why in God's name did you invite those sonsabitches down to my house at Ellington, anyhow? Why all these goddamned shenanigans?"

"Do you really care to know? Because I can't tell you, dear, if you're going to be hot with me." Ida put on that phony pout of hers that Joe found annoying. Besides, he was debating whether or not to settle up with Frank right now and be done with it.

"Go ahead, spring it on me."

"Well, you ought to know that I wouldn't any more have talked those two into moving down with us than pitched pennies with a monkey — unless I had a good reason. Which I did."

"And what's that?"

"Not ten hours ago, I persuaded Frank to put in his mail-forwarding address to 490 Ellington Avenue, San Francisco, California, which'll mean two thousand dollars a month coming straight to our doorstep, free as the air."

"Oh, for Pete's sake, Ida! Do you think I'm a nitwit? That's his money, not ours. What're you going to do, flop him on the bed every month? And what about Vera? All she talks about is Union Square. Did you nag her, too, to take an early retirement?"

"I didn't need to."

Ida stepped aside to let Joe into 3B.

Vera was out cold on the green sofa, clutching a box of Fig Newtons, where just the other night she and Joe had cuddled up. Back in the bedroom, "Mona Lisa" played out of the radio on the nightstand next to Frank, who was shirtless and stretched out on his belly, face buried in a pillow. The curtains on each window were drawn shut and a fire crackled in the front room hearth.

Scared of waking them, Joe stopped just across the threshold and hissed at Ida. "What is this?"

She spoke plainly. "I slipped them a Mickey Finn."

"Pardon?"

"I put knock-out drops in a bottle of Frank's bourbon. It did the job."

"What for?"

"They'd have fought me, otherwise. It was easier than hiding behind a door and cracking them on the head.

Joe stared at Vera and back to Frank again, not quite believing his eyes. He walked over close to Vera and discovered she wasn't breathing. The shock almost knocked him over.

"She's good and dead, Joey. Both of them are. I smothered them with a pillow after they went unconscious from the dope."

His voice trembled. "You're being funny, right?"

"What had to come, had to come, " Ida explained calmly. She went to the closet and grabbed Frank's wardrobe off a wire hanger.

Joe stared at Vera. "You killed them?"

Ida laid Frank's wardrobe onto the carpet. "Their souls are flown to the seat of God's eternal blessing. I checked my astrology before I drugged them to be sure of that. Heaven knows what's right."

"For godsakes, Ida, you must've snapped your cap!"

"On the contrary, Joey, I gave all of this quite a lot of sane consideration. Last night, before I came upstairs from the kitchen, I did a reading that told me there weren't any fateful signs ahead of us whatsoever if I chose this course of action — but I know you don't put much faith in my gift."

Joe wanted to grab a bottle of Frank's bourbon. "That's not it, at all. I'm just scared crazy for both of us. You and me together."

"Are you sure?" Ida sounded dubious. "I say that because, strictly speaking, you don't have any blame for what just happened up here, and nobody could prove you did, although appearances alone positively wouldn't help any of our reputations."

"Well, I'm not going to do any run-out, if that's your worry."

"Are you sure?"

"Yeah, I'm sure."

He wasn't sure, but he felt he ought to say so, just the same.

"Well, I'm not concerned, Joey. I trust you like a husband who loves me more than the oath he took on our wedding day."

Feeling lightheaded, Joe sat down in the chair by the window. He was terrified now. How did all this happen? What was he supposed to do? His wife just murdered their tenants. Was she insane?

Ida gave a sigh and went over to hold his hand. "Darling, they were the worst heels I ever knew, and you can't dispute that. We were in very bad here with that filth these two people persuaded us to do, like ten times poison and Gomorrah, Joey, and it would've only gotten worse unless I put a stop to it. And it was up to me, honey, because Frank had no great fondness for you at all, and would've had his eye out for just this sort of trick unless I put it over on him this way tonight, and that's the simple fact of the matter."

"Why not just throw 'em the hell out of here? Tell 'em to get lost?"

Ida peeked briefly through the curtains. "Because people like them just don't ever go away, Joey, no matter what you tell them. They're not reasonable like me and you. Would you want them sitting on our doorstep six months from now, waiting for us to change our minds? I couldn't tolerate that."

She went back over to the wardrobe and pulled out the last of Frank's clothes and laid them on the floor next to the sofa. Joe wondered how Ida could act so ordinary. He'd seen her more worked up over spring cleaning.

"Well, what do you have in mind we should do?"

"Honey, that's the simple part. We'll take these two down to the basement and put them in the hole that fellow dug today. I'll call the plumber tomorrow morning to tell him we changed our mind about the new waterlines, that we couldn't afford it and just have to make do with what we have already. He won't question that because it's none of his business and we're saving him all sorts of work he didn't want to do, anyhow. I tell you, that was the laziest fellow we've ever had out here."

Joe had a black thought. "Did you know you were going to do this when you hired the job in the first place?"

Ida put on her most earnest expression. "Now, Joey, you know we positively needed that drain installed and I hired the job in good faith. Honest to goodness, I didn't know any of this would happen until I found out just what thoroughly nasty human beings Frank and Vera really were. I hope you don't think I'm the sort who could take another life without considerations. Planning to kill somebody is an awful deed, believe you me. I wrestled with this all last night and hardly slept a wink from fretting over it. Joey, please don't despise me for what's gone on in this house since those two arrived. Not in my wildest imagination could I ever have seen myself doing what I've done these past couple of days. It almost feels as if I've been dreaming something dark and terrible and nobody's been able to shake me awake. I suppose you and me ought to have gone off alone and really had a set-to about what was happening, but we didn't and I got to feeling very alone and responsible for ridding our lives of this trouble we did nothing to ask for. Now, I don't blame you for not helping me. How could you have seen around the corner? My own divine gift hardly helped and even then I wasn't sure what it was telling me, only that nothing good was going to come from any of this, but if I sat on my hands, we'd both be in terrible, terrible trouble. So I did the only thing that seemed to make any sense at all. If it's the wrong thing, well then, I'll be the one to pay. And that's how it should be."

Joe sighed. Unfortunately, he agreed with her, and he sure didn't want to go to jail. No matter how wrong it was, how despicable and immoral, Frank and Vera had to be dumped into that hole in the basement and forgotten about.

Ida added, "We've both been erratic, honey, and there's no trying to dispose of our responsibility, but common decency forbids our pretending it doesn't exist. Heaven excuses all earthly sins save one: denying heaven and our Lord above. Put evil behind you, the Bible says, and speak no more thereof."

"Isn't there a lake of fire in there somewhere?" Joe said, feeling awfully cold. Nothing he'd done wrong in his whole sorry life compared to this.

"Only for the two-time loser," Ida replied. "And we'll absolutely never make this mistake again, Joey. I promise you that."

JOE DRAGGED FRANK'S BODY down to the basement while Ida hurried about the suite, collecting all of the Spagnolini's possessions. After sneaking a glance into the backyard to be sure nobody was spying, Joe wedged Frank's shoulders into the basement door to keep it open until he could reach inside to get the light on. Then he gave Frank a push and let his body tumble to the bottom. Joe left him where he landed and went back upstairs for Vera.

Ida was a human hurricane, sweeping everything out of 3B that belonged to Frank and Vera. She had a pile of clothes and other paraphernalia on the old rug in the middle of the suite. Folding a cotton sweater into Vera's suitcase, she told Joe, "I suppose I might've purchased some quick-lime to dissolve the bodies, but once I decided what had to be done, it was too late. Buying it this afternoon would look suspicious after we make these two disappear. You know, people up here aren't dummies, so we can't be too careful."

"Are you going to turn off the radio?" From the bedroom, Jerry Vale was singing "Innamorata," another dago song Joe hated. Why not listen to Nat King Cole or Jo Stafford? Someone with class.

"No," Ida replied, trying to pack a peach silk slip next to the sweater. "If anyone's listening out of doors, I'd like them to think our guests are still here. Besides, music makes me happy. Mother used to say she was saddest when she sang, and I saw those tears she shed much too often, but music makes my own heart glow, Joey. Isn't that beautiful?"

"Sure."

Next, Ida dumped the contents of a rhinestone cosmetic case out onto the rug while Joe went over to Vera. He had no idea how to pick her up. He liberated the box of Fig Newtons and shoved the coffee table back with his foot to give himself more room. Since she was lying on her right side, he slipped one arm under her waist and grabbed her left arm at the bicep and tugged her upward, then danced Vera like a department store mannequin out into the hallway.

Down in the basement again, Joe flopped Frank on top of Vera like Jack and Jill. Straightaway he could see the hole needed to be dug a lot deeper. He was tired from driving all day and wanted to lie down. But he grabbed a pickax and dropped into the pit and started hacking away. After extending the length of the hole another eight inches, Joe carved away at the sides of the hole, widening it so he'd have more room to maneuver when he got to digging out the bottom. He had done a lot of digging on Wakde Island. Everyone did. You dug holes to stay alive. Or at least that was the drill. Every night there, a single Jap bomber came over to drop its ordnance on the three-mile-long air strip where Joe worked, then flew off again. One day, the CO wanted the revetments made higher to do a better job of protecting the aircraft, work that didn't get finished by early evening, so he ordered a couple of young privates from Pennsylvania to complete it in the dark by flashlight. Of course, they were scared of getting blown up and wanted at least to wait until the bomber came and went, but some idiot told them, *"Don't worry about a thing, boys, 'cause the little bastards can't see."* Naturally, one of the Jap bombs landed square on the kids' bulldozer. After that, everyone dug a little faster.

Joe slaved for an hour, then climbed out of the hole and traded places with Frank and Vera. He began shoveling concrete rubble onto the bodies until Ida called down from the kitchen for him to quit. He heard her dragging a suitcase across the linoleum floor to the basement stairs. Joe stepped aside as the suitcase tumbled to the bottom.

"Don't bury them yet, Joey," Ida told him, "because I have some other things to put in there." Then she hurried back upstairs.

Joe presumed Ida intended to burn Frank and Vera's clothes, so he went to the furnace and cranked it up. Then he went to fill a big bucket of water from the kitchen sink for mixing the cement he'd need for resurfacing the basement floor. Joe kicked some more rubble into the grave while he tried to figure out what to do with the dirt that wouldn't fit in the hole. Once it was cemented over, maybe he'd fill the wheelbarrow, and then dump what was left in a corner under the windows where he had been piling junk all year.

A short while later, Ida arrived with the last suitcase and Vera's purse stuffed full of her cosmetics and jewelry. "All the clothes go into the furnace," she told Joe, "and both suitcases, but we need to pry off the latches because they won't burn and it wouldn't do to have someone sifting through the ashes and turn them up. They'd ask why we burned a suitcase instead of taking it to the dump, and there won't be a good answer."

"All right, I'll get a pair of pliers."

He went back upstairs to the closet off the kitchen where he kept a shelf of small household tools. While Ida fed Vera and Frank's clothing into the flames by the armful, Joe pried all the hardware off the suitcases and tossed the pieces into the hole. Then he jammed both suitcases into the furnace and shut the iron door. Ida stood over the hole with Vera's jewelry box, a sequined purse, and her rhinestone cosmetic case. As she tossed them into the grave, she said flatly, "We're not thieves, you know."

Ida took a shovel and helped Joe bury Frank and Vera Spagnolini. Once they were finished, she went upstairs while Joe mixed the cement and laid down the new floor. A chill ran up his back every so often as he labored to do a decent job of it. With the furnace blazing and the windows closed up tight, working on the floor gave him a bad sweat and he had to stop twice to go up into the kitchen for a drink of water. After Joe finished smoothing off the concrete, he filled the wheelbarrow with the dirt displaced by Spagnolini's grave and dumped it in a corner under the window beside the furnace to keep it as far from the new concrete as possible. Then he grabbed the old canvas tarpaulin and laid it across the fresh section of floor.

Joe found Ida upstairs at the bedroom window, staring out at the cold windy bay. She sounded melancholy as she came away from the window, her face weary and gray.

She told him, "Honey, we need to get rid of Frank's automobile. It's too suspicious to leave sitting out back in our driveway and them gone for good. Who'd believe someone leaving such a nice car outdoors like that? It needs to get out of town, Joey. We might stall for a week or so, giving out a tale how Frank and Vera took a bus holiday, but what do we say afterwards? And besides, we've already done the mail forwarding to San Francisco, so that's where they'll be expected, and that means their car, too. So, I don't see anything but that we hide it somewhere and pretend it's none of our concern where they went."

"How are we supposed to do that? Roll it off a cliff?"

"No, I want you to drive up to Crescent City and dump it there. You can take the bus back."

"All right," Joe agreed, glad that Ida had thought most of this out for him. He couldn't do it on his own. Not tonight, at least. His brain was too scrambled.

"But don't park at the bus depot. That red Cadillac's too hot a number for one small parking lot. Nobody in his right mind would ever leave a car like that parked for longer than a couple of hours. But if you dropped it along a side street two or three blocks from the bus depot, I doubt anyone'd pay it much notice. I'm sure they'd assume the owner was coming back any minute."

"What're you going to be doing?" Joe knew he couldn't afford to be cut out of the details when things were this serious. Ida always had a way of doing business to suit herself best of all.

"I've got to finish cleaning up the suite and give the room a good polish for tomorrow in case we get someone stopping by to look it over." She took the keys to Frank's Cadillac out of her smock and gave them to Joe. "Here, you better get going."

J OE GRABBED HIS OVERCOAT from the closet and doused the back
porch light. The night sky was cloudy now, so he didn't worry
about being seen as he crossed the yard to the driveway where the
red Cadillac was parked. He drove north out of town, keeping safely
below the speed limit. A thick damp fog had settled over the coast and
he only saw one other automobile on the road. He had the radio on
for a mile or two, but switched it off when he became afraid someone
might hear it as he drove by. Hiding a murder was complicated. One
slip-up meant a ticket to the gas chamber. Joe thought that Ida must
have gone into mental bankruptcy when she decided to kill those two.

Two hours later, Joe skirted the center of Crescent City in favor of the
waterfront where the bus terminal was just across the street from a park.
He followed the alphabet-lettered streets into a small neighborhood of
old frame houses and eased the Cadillac over to the curb between two
other automobiles he hoped were parked for the night. After checking to
see the street was empty, Joe got out and locked the car. He kept his hat
low on his forehead as he walked down E Street and back along the sidewalk to the bus terminal, where he bought a couple of magazines and
a one-way ticket to Ocean City. He found a wooden bench near a telephone booth and put his back to the rest of the crowd. People came and
went, occasionally giving him the once-over. Nobody stopped to talk. An
hour or so after buying his ticket, Joe saw a pair of cops arrive outdoors
on the sidewalk. Panicked, he got up and went to the washroom and
parked himself on a toilet where he stayed until he heard a bus arrive at
the terminal. By then, it was half past three in the morning.

JUST BEFORE DAWN, Joe's bus pulled up to the Pacific Avenue terminal at Ocean City. He took the old alleyway behind Front Street so nobody would see him. Not two blocks from downtown, Joe saw the glow of flames on the foggy sky. When the breeze shifted at Third Street, he smelled smoke and saw a gang of kids hurrying in the direction of a fire. A siren shrieked and a police car roared by one street below Joe's alley. He cut through a grassy field to Front Street where he saw three city fire engines in front of Ida's boardinghouse. Nothing was left from the top half of the old building. Fire had consumed all of the attic and the third floor, collapsing the bottom half into incandescent rubble, millions of sparks blowing free into the gloomy night. Firemen set a cordon about the house, keeping a big crowd down on the sidewalk. Joe watched as fallen timbers crackled and groaned while the fire consumed room after room on the lower floors. Every corner on the ocean side of the house was aflame. The fire department punched holes in the weakened siding, knocking out glass and shearing off blackened roof tiles for the hoses. More fiery sparks exploded out of the wreckage. A water truck from down on the street showered the frame house next door and police cars filled the street on the downtown side.

Joe found Ida down the block, standing with a small crowd by a telephone pole. She had wrapped herself in a cotton shawl, her eyes fixed on the raging flames as another section of the damaged frame collapsed, crushing the burning fretwork on the east side of the house. Her smock black with soot, Ida didn't even flinch as her belovéd rosebushes ignited in the rubble of the crumbled porch.

"Ida."

"Oh, Joey!" Her face lit up when she saw him. "Those awful people burned down our house tonight. They burned it down, and skipped town just like you predicted they would. You were absolutely right about what rats they were, Joey, and I admit I ought to've listened to you, because look what they did to us."

"What are you talking about?"

Ida's eyes welled with tears. "I told the marshal that we have no idea what we did to deserve this, Joey, we absolutely don't, because we showed those two strangers every possible kindness, but when we put our backs to that smut they were peddling, this is how we were repaid. By burning us out. Those sonsabitches positively did us in, and it's not exaggeration. I don't know why we ever let them through the door."

Another blast of heat singed Joe's face. "What do you mean they burned us up?"

Ida grabbed Joe by the arm and hustled him down the sidewalk away from the fire engines and noisy crowds of spectators. His Studebaker was parked at the curb near the Marina. Ida unlocked the car and got inside with Joe.

Once both doors were closed, she told him, "I've had a terrible time getting all this straight in my mind since you left. We couldn't leave a trail to those two skunks, and I just plainly didn't trust myself to get everything cleaned up and hid away. What if we forgot something little that became the clue that led both us to jail? So I decided it all had to go, every last shred of it, and I didn't take that judgment on lightly. My parents left me this house and it means the world to me, Joey, you ought to know that. But what happened earlier tonight just can't be forgotten, because no matter how hard we tried to put it behind us, whenever we went down into the basement we'd know what a terrible mistake we made letting those people into our lives. That's why I sent you off to dump that car to make it look like they'd skipped out on us after starting the fire. I tipped a bottle of Frank's gin into the fireplace and set a match to it and poured another bottle onto the rug under the sofa and lit that, too. You should've seen it go up. My oh my! Then I went down to the basement and opened the furnace and shoveled some sparks onto those old linseed oil rags and paint cans you had stored out in the shed, then ran for the hills. The fire shot up through the vents like a rocket, Joey. I had no idea it'd go off so good. It happened awfully quick. I almost didn't make it out myself. You should've been here, honey. It was really something."

Joe nearly keeled over. "You burned the goddamned house down? Are you nuts? For godsakes, Ida, it's practically all we own in the world!"

"Oh, it's all insured, Joey. Don't let that bother you. Harvey'll see to it that we get a fair price for the lot. It's why I went to see him yesterday and the day before that, too. We drew up the papers to sell and whether the house is here or knocked to the ground, we get our fair market value. And I kept the name under Macaulay, too, like I always did everything, Joey, so now we can begin a new life and nobody'll follow us out of here. That's the deal I struck. This fire doesn't change one iota of that contract."

Joe stared back to the flames, horrified as the structure burned through to the bottom floor. "Everything inside's gone, too. You burned us both out! Good grief!"

Ida grabbed him. "No, Joey, you're wrong about that, too. We absolutely didn't lose anything personal. Before I struck a single match, I packed us up: your duffle and my trunk and two suitcases full of every dear little thing my mother and father left me. It's all in back of this car here right now, just waiting for us. Why, we can leave tonight, if you want. Maybe we ought to. We could stay the night at Rio Dell and drive on to San Francisco tomorrow afternoon."

But Joe felt as if he'd stepped overboard in mid-ocean from the transport ship to New Guinea and nobody had noticed. He was swimming alone through the dark, a thousand miles from shore. "You're crazy, Ida. You're out of your goddamned mind."

"No, I'm not, Joey." Ida grabbed his chin. "Look here, I know you're tired, and maybe none of this makes sense right now, because it hardly does to me, either. To think that just last week I was planning a rhubarb patch out back and saving up for a new parlor sofa. Isn't that funny? But then those horrible people came into our lives, and just like that, when I came home this evening, between doing the last thing and the next, I was just absolutely washed up. So I took care of us the only way I know how. Truth is, Joey, I simply refuse to be served to this place, any longer. No matter what we did tonight, our lives have to go on. That's all we can do now. It's time to start over."

THREE YEARS LATER

PICTURE A LONG DUSTY STREET of filling stations, car dealerships, insurance offices, bowling alleys, tire shops, taverns, and motels. Lots of motels, where nobody was getting rich because business these days on Rose Boulevard was not good. Most looked rundown and vandalized, occupied by tenants who were locals down on their luck or tourists on a budget, apathetic to the dilapidated surroundings.

Muriel Knutsen owned the Rose City Motor Court and wanted out. When she'd bought the motel, the business had been failing and Muriel had never lost a dime on real estate in her life. Since quitting the nursing profession back in 1938, she'd found a golden touch for boosting value in rundown properties, mostly up in Washington State where her family lived. With a cash settlement from her first husband, who'd chased a buxom young switchboard operator out to Florida, Muriel purchased a swampy waterfront lot at Westport and financed twelve cabins on the site that became the Dock Cabin Motor Court. Her investment of one thousand dollars earned out enough in a couple of years after the War to let her buy up a derelict roller-skating rink and a livery stable on a rundown block in Tacoma. She sold one to a supermarket chain and the other to a big appliance store. Both investments paid out like a ransom, more than forty grand in eight years. So Muriel went south to California and got married again.

Lonnie Knutsen was a former major in the Army who was gassed at the Argonne during the First World War. He was a tall, dignified fellow who had earned a degree in geology and worked as a newspaper editor at San Diego for twenty-three years until Parkinson's disease dumped him into a convalescent hospital. While scouting real estate down around Oceanside, Muriel hired out as a temporary nurse helping with the most hopeless cases at the same hospital and met Lonnie outside the cafeteria one afternoon. The old Major had slipped on a patch of spilled coffee and needed rescuing. A month later, Muriel married Lonnie to get him out of the sanitarium. Then she got sick herself and decided marriage to a permanent invalid was impossible, so she divorced Lonnie and placed him in a temporary bed at a convalescent home in San Diego until she became well enough to improve both their situations. The Rose City Motor Court arose out of that circumstance.

Six months after recovering from her bout with meningitis, Muriel received a notice in the mail regarding a motel up north in Santa Rosa that had come up for sale at a bargain basement price, just a thousand dollars for all nine cabins and the land they occupied. The last owners had lost their shirts and needed the cash to pay off creditors. Muriel took the motel off their hands for eight hundred dollars. The owners of the Bluebonnet Motel next door told her she had just made a shrewd deal and were eager to see the place improved, anticipating that a decent business across the parking lot would inflate the value of their own property. How could she go wrong? Santa Rosa was anticipating a boom and Muriel fully expected to reap the benefits. She rented a small house a mile from the motel, then brought Lonnie up to live in the cabin next to the front office so she could look after him until his family decided where he ought to live out what days remained him.

Now two years had elapsed since she took ownership of the Rose City, and business was still rotten. A freeway extension to Highway 101 bypassed Rose Boulevard, leaving everyone along that mile of dusty sidewalks high and dry. On a good weekend, she might have a couple of cabins hired out in addition to one she was renting month to month to a family of apple pickers from Bakersfield. Muriel advertised in the local papers and bought one thirty-second spot a week on the radio, all money flushed away with no benefit derived. She became depressed and wanted out, writing to her sister Agnes how she was unhappy with the property and glad she hadn't sunk more money into it. Worse yet, the Major had deteriorated to where he drooled when he spoke, and Muriel resented having to care for him. What was becoming of her life? She worried about money and the atom bomb. If the Russians attacked, everyone in America would be killed, mostly from fallout. The very thought terrified her. She had dreams of flying off to South America. After reading in a financial journal that anyone with a few thousand dollars in cold cash could make a million dollars down in Brazil, Muriel began spending her evenings poring over maps of plantation land and river properties on the Amazon. A thousand acres could be hers with tenant farmers and a big house of tall curtained windows and a second floor gallery, perhaps a boat landing so she could navigate the dark waterways to distant river towns for needful supplies, or have her own airstrip cut into the sugar cane fields with a seaplane she would learn to fly down to Rio de Janeiro on weekends where she might meet a man who would make love to her in a woven hammock under the banana trees in his walled garden. All she needed was to get rid of the Rose City Motor Court for enough money up front to buy a plane ticket and fund her South American expenses for six months.

As luck would have it, her buyer strolled across the parking lot one afternoon from the Bluebonnet Motel. Mrs. Long had been a nurse like Muriel and owned a couple of apartment buildings down in San Jose, a big ranch in Colorado, percentage in some oil wells, and stocks and bonds worth hundreds of thousands of dollars. She and her husband had just come up to Santa Rosa from San Francisco for a short-term business opportunity in agriculture on the outskirts of town. When Muriel remarked about wanting to travel down to Brazil, Mrs. Long told her, "Why, that's such a funny thing, because we've also been looking for more investment properties, especially in South America. We hear that's absolutely the place to make money these days."

That afternoon they became friends, and Mrs. Long even began helping out around the Rose City Motor Court because she liked to keep busy. She confessed to Muriel how her star charts showed that she needed a change in her life and was convinced that operating a motel would do the trick.

"I don't mind work one iota," she told Muriel, while mopping out the bathroom in Cabin Six. "Better to wear out than to rust out, I've always said."

What Muriel hoped to do was persuade Mrs. Long to run the motel while she went down to Brazil. A good business arrangement benefits both parties. If Mrs. Long wanted to get her feet wet in the motel game, why not here?

The next evening, Muriel agreed to do an astrology reading with Mrs. Long in her living room after supper. They sat across from each other at a coffee table and shared a bottle of wine while Mrs. Long studied her charts.

"Do you see this here?" Mrs. Long explained as she revealed her findings. "You're now entering a period when everything you do will go well for you. You must seize the opportunity. Invest your money in new ventures. Act boldly."

Ordinarily, Muriel didn't go in for hocus-pocus like that, but with a big success being foretold for her personally, Muriel could scarcely contain her glee. "Well, that certainly does seem definitive. Can it be true?"

"Oh, it's positively true," Mrs. Long assured her with great confidence. "And with the stars in your favor, there'd be absolutely no risk."

A few days later, Muriel wrote home to her mother in Port Townsend that she had found a woman with a great deal of money to take the motel off her hands. Lonnie would be fine. He received monthly disability checks from the government and Mrs. Long promised to see to his care while Muriel was gone. Once she had earned enough from her investments down in South America, she intended to place Lonnie in a good convalescent home. It would all be wonderful.

ACROSS THE PARKING LOT at the Bluebonnet Motel, Joe Krueger read the September issue of *Popular Mechanic* and listened to a ballgame on the radio. It was half past eight and still warm out and Joe had the air conditioning unit ramped up to full blast to kill the odor of his cabin. These units weren't much for frills. A living room with a kitchenette. A bathroom that had a toilet, shower, and sink. A bedroom in back with twin nightstands, a chair, and a dresser. The wall-to-wall carpet was brown and stained with oil tracked in from the carport. A stink of cigarettes and mold pervaded.

Ida had been gone for a couple hours to see her new friend Muriel next door. She had been buttering that woman up all week while Joe paced about the motel grounds, bored to tears. He hated Santa Rosa and thought the people were blockheads. One evening after eating supper down the street at the Rancho Tavern, Joe had caught a thirteen-year-old juvenile delinquent from the motor court trying to sneak into his room through the bathroom window by cutting a big hole in the screen with a Scout knife. When Joe grabbed him by the seat of his pants, the kid jabbed back at Joe with the blade and cut his shirtsleeve, whereupon Joe smacked the kid on the side of his head, knocking him out cold. Police came and did some yelling and copied statements from witnesses, one of whom, an old lady across the driveway at the Rose City Motor Court, claimed to see the whole episode, naming Joe as the assailant. A few nights later, Joe thanked her by scooping a dog turd off the sidewalk and dropping it on her doormat with a note from Lassie.

Joe put his magazine down and went outdoors where the air was cooler. A light breeze redolent of dust and dry grass drifted across the late summer twilight. He heard radios and phonographs playing in rooms across the motor court, and a TV set glowed blue behind the linen shades at the manager's office on the corner. Joe went back indoors for a beer and took a peek out the window toward the Rose City Motor Court. What the hell was Ida cooking up over there? She just raved about how smart Muriel had been with her real estate investments, and Ida admired rich people. Muriel wasn't quite rich yet, but she was better off than they were. Joe's bank statements proved that, but he also understood it's no good being afraid. Something needs doing at every hour of the day and the trick is to get noticed. That means being willing to do what's asked of you without making excuses. Joe Krueger had a bad back and a sore knee that refused to quit him, but nothing kept him in bed past seven in the morning. He had too much pride for that. Work keeps the heart fit. Nothing in life was truer than that.

Just past nine o'clock, Joe was watching Red Skelton on TV when he heard the front door open and then Ida singing at the refrigerator as she fiddled with her tomato juice bottles. Muriel had put her on to that nonsense. The day they said hello, Ida began drinking tomato juice and counting calories. Not that Joe thought she was too plump. Sure, her bottom wiggled like jelly when she crossed a room these days, but if reducing meant those blubbers of hers had to shrink, too, then Joe's vote was for Ida to quit measuring her waistline.

A gasoline commercial ran on the TV set as Ida strolled into the room, a giddy grin on her face.

"Joey? Are you awake?"

He rolled over onto his shoulder. "Sure."

"I thought you fell asleep with your westerns on again."

"Nope."

"Well, I've been over helping Muriel plan her trip. Soon as she gets a buyer for the motel, she's packing up. We spent all night working out where she ought to go first. She said Rio de Janeiro, but I told her to go inland where the land's cheaper and there's gold if you know where to look."

"Oh yeah?"

"Muriel says I'm the smartest woman she's ever met. How do you like that?"

"I wish someone said it about me."

Ida stared at him, then added, "This motel game has a lot going for it, Joey, more than meets the eye. People don't want to share a house. They want a cabin of their own. Muriel bought the Rose City when it wasn't worth much more than the dirt it's piled on, and now she's got every bank in town trying to loan her money on it so she can invest in more properties. She says real estate in South America is the next big boom, so that's where she wants to go now. And do you know what?"

"No, what?"

"She's asked me to go along with her. What do you think of that?"

Ida had a look on her face that meant Joe had better start worrying. Confidence grew in Ida a devil-may-care attitude that led her to taking chances most people wouldn't ordinarily consider. Joe was naturally conservative, maybe to a fault, but his darling wife couldn't let her piggy bank alone more than a month or two before she just had to crack it open and buy a new air conditioner or an electric coffee pot.

Joe sat up. "Why the hell would you want to do that? I wouldn't go."

"Well, it'd be just her and me, anyhow. I knew you wouldn't want to go down there with us girls. Besides, if Muriel can't get the Major admitted back into a convalescent hospital, she'll need someone to look after him until she does."

"Good luck."

Joe scoffed at that idea. Lonnie Knutsen was hard pressed to wipe his own ass these days. He dribbled and tripped over his own feet when he walked and nobody but Muriel could understand more than half of what he said. Joe felt sorry for the old guy, but not enough to be his nursemaid.

A car pulled into the driveway just outdoors. Joe heard a woman's voice call to someone across the motor court. A horn honked and someone yelled back. The motel was noisy every night.

"Muriel thinks we're millionaires," Ida remarked, dialing down the volume on the TV set. "It's the funniest thing, too, when she suggests that, and I doubt she means it as flattery since she's done very well for herself since the War."

"Is that what you told her?"

Ida had a way of exaggerating herself to people that bordered on deceit. By now, Joe had gotten so used to hearing her stories that he became skeptical of nearly everything that came out of her mouth.

She smoothed the bedspread and sat at the foot of the bed. "If you knew Muriel like I do, you'd see she's nobody's fool. I simply remarked that we've done quite well with real estate ourselves, which was one of the reasons we came up from the city this month. And that's the truth, because if José hadn't been so stingy with that farm of his, who knows where we'd be tonight?"

"He never said a word about sharing any of his business with us, and I warned you not to pop your mouth off about that. You just didn't listen to me."

"That's your tale, honey. I spoke with Maria when you and José were outdoors stacking those crates and she assured me they've been desperate to keep that farm away from the bank. It's ten acres, you know, which is a lot of work for two people and no help to count on. With all four of us pitching in, we could've made a go of it."

"If you say so."

Ida got to her feet and went to switch on the bathroom light. Checking her hair in the mirror, she told Joe, "Honey, the simple fact of the matter is that Muriel's getting out whether I go with her or not, and someone's going to take that motel of hers because she showed me the books tonight and my astrology agreed that it's absolutely a profitable business with the right person at the front desk. And after talking with the Crandalls here, I positively decided that it ought to be us if we really hope to make something of ourselves."

"Well, gee whiz, honey, I'm sorry if we aren't having it easy these days, but I don't worry too much about that myself anymore, because I got a job, remember? And that's worth a lot in my book."

"Nonsense! Del Crandall tells me the motel business is a sure-fire way to make a good living without overstraining yourself. Mabel and him have been at it for almost eleven years now and aren't the least worn out, and they don't have any debt to speak of, either, so I'd say that's a pretty fair endorsement."

"Sure it is, if your best ambition is to work a motel. I'd rather boil up some other ideas myself."

"Well, I don't want to be a ninety-day wonder."

"Who says you have to?"

"Don't dispute me, Joey, because I absolutely don't have the patience for it tonight."

"Look here, I don't want to operate any goddamned motel, and that's all there is to it. You go ahead and do what you like, because you sure don't need my opinion on the subject, but just count me out."

"Well, then, I will."

Ida shut the bathroom door.

JOE THOUGHT THE PROBLEM with Ida was that she believed everyone was out to get her. Most of that first year in San Francisco,
she had her eye on every patrol car driving by the house on Ellington
Avenue. Their new phone number was unlisted. Using a fake name,
Ida telephoned to the real estate office in Ocean City and discovered
that her property had been sold for commercial real estate. She'd been
smart, after all, to keep going by Macaulay up there, so they didn't
leave a trail out of town. Eventually, a new hotel with a restaurant and
gift shops occupied the whole block and the old boardinghouse was
forgotten. Nobody ever dug up her basement.

For the first couple of years, Joe took work at painting houses in
the Fillmore district and welding boilers at the shipyards. He joined a
union and found steady construction work along the waterfront from
Fisherman's Wharf to the Bay Bridge. Working day labor in San Francisco was a headache and paid a Chinaman's wage, but at least Joe
had a reason to get out of bed in the morning. He met some fellows
he liked and went out for a beer with them after work most afternoons.

Ida had her own ways of keeping busy. She found a Rosicrucian
church and attended meetings on Tuesday nights and subscribed to a
handful of astrology magazines she studied before bedtime. She hired
herself twice a week to a nursing position in a convalescent hospital
near San Bruno, and volunteered as a den mother with a neighborhood Cub Scout troop. The other mothers invited her because she was
friendly with all the kids in the neighborhood and gave birthday parties and baked cupcakes for the little ones. Every Wednesday evening,

unless it rained, she drilled her Cub Scouts up and down Ellington Avenue, barking at them like a non-com. Ida even voted in her first election. Joe liked Ike all right, but he wouldn't vote for that shifty Nixon sonofabitch; Ida didn't want a Catholic in the White House taking orders from the "Poop." Then she saw Jackie on television and asked Joe if she ought to buy a pillbox hat. Ocean City seemed ages ago.

After Joe went off to work each morning, Ida spent most of her time doing housework and running errands. She took pride in her housekeeping and kept the linen fresh and ironed, the floors swept and waxed, and both bedrooms neat as a pin. On her days off from nursing, Ida would go shopping up on Mission or ride a bus to the Emporium at Market Street and Powell, and come back home late in the afternoon laden with packages. Those first couple years in the city, Ida had plenty of money to spend, because Frank Spagnolini's invention checks came to the house once a month and Ida forged his signature before depositing them in her own bank account. She offered five hundred to Joe each month, but he didn't want any of that money and told her so. "It's a lot of trouble, Ida, and we ought to forget about it. I got a job that pays a fair salary now and we don't need anyone else's money."

"That's your tale, honey. I'm still washing the floor on my hands and knees."

"Then get a mop."

But Ida kept cashing Spagnolini's checks, until one day they just stopped coming. Ida waited a couple of weeks, then went down to the post office and asked if Frank's mail had gotten lost and nobody had any answer because his magazines were still arriving. So Ida waited another month, then typed a letter to the federal agency that issued the checks and signed Frank's name to it. When she didn't get a response, Ida told Joe to telephone to the agency that issued the checks and pretend to be Frank Spagnolini and ask what happened to the money.

Joe refused.

"Are you out of your mind?" he said, still trying to forget Ocean City. "The next thing you know, one of those government fellows will ring the doorbell and we'll have to explain where Frank's gone off to and pretty soon they'll have us taking Chessman's seat in the gas chamber."

"This is not a funny situation, Joey. I worked it out in my books and it's positively the best thing for us to do because we can't get by without that money."

"Well, I can get by just fine and I'm not going to do it, and that's that."

So Ida made the call herself. She said she was Vera Spagnolini and that Frank had suffered a car accident and couldn't come to the phone but needed the money to pay his medical bills and couldn't they just hurry up and send his check? She was told that Frank's contract had elapsed and there wouldn't be any further payment. Ida threw the telephone down and left the house.

Reducing their income by two thousand dollars each month would have been a blow if Joe hadn't gotten his union card. Ida counted on Frank's check more than he did, so when the money stopped coming, Joe just saw it as one less headache. He wanted to forget everything about Ocean City, and quitting Frank's money helped. Except for a new Philco television set she bought on sale, a lot of it had gone out to racetracks at Bay Meadows and Golden Gate Fields, anyhow. Thanks to a nice fellow Joe met at work named José Hernandez, Ida had discovered horse racing. A group of them had driven to the track one Saturday afternoon and Ida put some money down on a horse she had a hunch about and won forty dollars. Joe couldn't get her to stay away after that. A couple of times a week she took the bus out to Bay Meadows and placed bets on horses she had investigated through her astrology charts the night before. She won the daily double on four occasions and a Trifecta. After that, all sorts of people started listening to her. She became the Star Lady and went around the tracks sharing tips on future races. Joe thought betting on horses was a waste of money and Ida used to swear that gambling was a sin, but now she argued that her predictions were based on sound astrological interpretations, so chance had nothing to do with her picks. In the kitchen one evening, with her charts spread out across the table, she explained, "Astrology can't be used for any purposes except good, and gambling is evil. If I wasn't winning, I'd know positively I was going against God's best intentions and that wouldn't do me any good."

"Well, I still think it's a racket."

"Then maybe I won't share my profits with you."

"Who's asking you to?"

Joe Krueger didn't care about luck. He had a house of his own and a union hod carrier job two blocks up from the Ferry Building where he could look out across San Francisco Bay from the rooftop at lunch and smell the salt air and not worry about anything except working hard and staying out of trouble. Ida thought hod carrier was an awful job and said he ought to quit it. Joe told her she had some funny ideas about getting ahead.

Then Ida got knocked out of a jitney on Mission Street.

She had just stepped onboard for a ride up to Union Square when a fellow trying to make a U-turn slammed square into the back of the jitney, throwing Ida out onto the sidewalk. She was almost killed. Joe got a call at work and took a cab to San Francisco General where he found Ida with a cast on her leg and mad as a hornet. "I tell you, Joey, that man absolutely tried to murder me. He said he was just trying to keep it in the road, but if I hadn't gotten hold of the lamp post when I flew out of that jitney, I would've cracked my head open and been done with it. But I'm still here, and someone's going to pay."

The next week, Ida took a taxicab up to Melvin Belli's office on Montgomery Street in North Beach and hired a lawyer by the name of Seymour Elrod to handle her complaint. She had Elrod file a personal injury lawsuit for $100,000. Joe thought that was a big mistake, but Ida wouldn't hear a word of it.

"Don't fool with those insurance fellows," Joe warned, as she limped out the door. "It'll be more trouble than it's worth."

But Ida wanted the money. Since that rainy night at Ocean City, Joe had learned that his wife had a bright eye for profit. Ida would butter up one of the Cub Scout mothers on the block by baking her a pie, then borrow twenty dollars and forget to pay it back; or collect money for a den raffle that somehow never came off. She was a card, all right. Joe didn't even know half the people she talked about. Ida had astrology friends and gamblers from the racetrack and nurses she knew from the hospital. On evenings when she invited her Rosicrucians over for a meeting, he'd go bowling out in Daly City, or ride a bus up to Turk Murphy's for a drink with some fellows from the waterfront who all seemed more content with their lives than did Joe. His pal José Hernandez bragged about a small farm he owned up north, and a young bricklayer they both liked named Lester Collins had a boat he sailed down to Baja every year and a fifteen-year-old Mexican girlfriend. This world belonged to people who got out of bed every morning with an eye on that bright day after tomorrow. Joe wasn't one of them, but Ida was, although you had to wonder if she didn't purposely defy her own instincts.

Each evening after the accident, Ida would drag herself about the house on Ellington, complaining about her leg and a pain in her spine and the fierce headache she was sure was about to split open her skull. She would wander from one room to another, ranting about the doctors who refused to believe how seriously she had been injured and threatening to sue the whole bunch of them. Dissatisfied with the progress of her lawsuit, Ida began going to Melvin Belli's office every afternoon. Elrod tried to be helpful, but he told Ida she was asking for a lot of money and the insurance company was doing a study of her injuries. Soon afterward, Joe noticed a couple of fellows in gray flannel suits parking across the street at odd hours. That's what really led to all the trouble that followed. One of the neighbors told him they were insurance men investigating Ida's jitney accident. They had a camera pointed at Joe's living room window whenever Ida was home, which meant the curtains had to be closed and the lights turned off. It drove Joe crazy. One evening, he crossed the street with a fat egg salad sandwich and pasted it onto the camera lens before the fellow saw it coming. They almost got into a fistfight right there on the sidewalk until the other fellow got out of the car and put a stop to it and the insurance men drove off and didn't return for almost two weeks.

Ida's mood deteriorated daily and she began acting out of sorts. Joe came home from work and saw her marching her Cub Scout troop up the block in parade formation. Hut two-three-four, hut two-three-four! Her voice echoed above the din of his bus driving off. Some of the boys were crying. One of them lost count and fell out of step and she began screaming at him. People came out of their houses to watch. The parade of Cub Scouts fell apart and Ida left them on the sidewalk and went home. A day later, the troop's parents accused her of being dictatorial and fired her. Ida became so enraged that she tried to get Belli's office to sue them.

Joe stayed longer after work every day.

Then Ida told Joe she was sick with leukemia. "It's not a simple thing to admit, honey, even when I know absolutely how serious this is, but you're my husband and I love you and if my blood kills me I don't know how I can ever take care of you."

"Who says you're sick?"

"Doctor Bloch, and I believe him because leukemia runs in my family and I positively need transfusions just to make it up the sidewalk these days."

"Transfusions? What the hell does that cost? Are you sure you need them?"

"Joey, if you paid any notice to me lately, you'd see I'm in awful condition. Doctor Bloch insists I'd be in the grave without new blood in my system and I'd say eighty dollars a week is a fair price for keeping me on my feet, wouldn't you?"

Joe thought she was exaggerating about her leukemia, but the money was serious. "Eighty dollars a week? Are you out of your mind? Who's got that kind of money, Ida? We'll be broke by Christmas."

"Nonsense! I win more than that at the track on Saturdays and Mr. Elrod tells me I'll be seeing a check for five thousand dollars pretty soon, so long as we can keep those insurance men off our backs. Why, I had one of those fellows chase me down to the bus stop last week and I had to call the police to get him to stop it. Joey, we're going to have to do something about this situation and I mean soon. Insurance companies make a game out of not paying up and they'll use every trick in the book to catch me in a misstep so they can cancel us all together."

Later on, after everything that happened up in Santa Rosa, Joe came to see how it all began with some idiot smashing into Ida's jitney. Without that stupid traffic accident, there wouldn't have been any lawsuit, no insurance men stalking Ida day and night to see if she was faking her injury, and no reason to pack up and leave Ellington Avenue for a few months and end up at that goddamned motel. But that's just what Joe and Ida did. One nice spring evening, José Hernandez had them both to supper to meet his wife Maria, and over a game of cards he explained all about his ten acres of corn and vegetables and how swell things were up north in the farm lands. With the new job on Clay Street not scheduled to begin for another six weeks, José told Joe that he and Maria would be at their farm starting on the weekend, and that Joe and Ida were welcome to come visit. His farmhouse had only one bedroom, but there were motels a mile or so away and José could meet them at the bus stop when they arrived in town.

That night in bed, Ida told Joe, "I'm sick and tired of those insurance fellows giving me the evil eye when they seen me wear that cast for three weeks, and my spine is twisted up like a pretzel. I want to get rid of them, Joey. Maybe we ought to go into strawberry farming. Maria said you could grow anything on that land and she never farmed before in her life. Wouldn't you like to own a piece of land, honey? We could find a nice piece of property and go into business like José and Maria. I've always wanted to grow strawberries."

"What would we buy it with? Our good looks?"

Joe was tired of moving around. Anyhow, why should he? Those insurance fellows weren't chasing after him. That was her problem.

Ida said, "We could take a mortgage on this house, Joey. The banks pay out enough to keep us going here in the city and up there, too."

"I don't care to be picking strawberries like a Mexican. You go do it, if you like, but count me out. I've smelled enough manure in my time."

Just the same, two weeks later Joe boarded a Greyhound bus with his old Army duffel and took a seat beside Ida for the ride up to Santa Rosa. His life took odd turns and often he felt as if he were zooming around on a whirly-gig, barely able to hang on. The afternoon sun beat on his face as the bus ran north up the highway. He tried to come to grips with everything he had done since getting out of the service and saw it all as unrelenting trauma. Where were the blue skies?

JOSÉ AND MARIA HERNANDEZ owned a nice little house on a flat ten-acre property about six miles south of town. The fellow next door had chickens and milk cows and a tire swing for his kids next to a barn with some fruit trees and a couple of old automobiles parked under a live oak. It looked like a decent life. The less you need, Joe thought, the better off you are. Greed is what kills you. It nags and nags until you do something stupid.

Sitting in the kitchen after supper, José told Joe and Ida, "When I worked for Thorpe down on Mission, I had a hard time getting out of bed in the morning. I'm retiring this year so me and the missus can stay up here year around and keep the farm going."

"Growing's a good business proposition," Ida agreed. "Especially if you grow something people eat a lot of. Strawberries, for instance. I thought me and Joe would buy some land and grow strawberries for the local hotels and restaurants."

"I don't know nothing about strawberries," José said, "but we're just farming for us these days. I bought this place so I didn't have to work for no one else."

"I've never had a boss in my life," Ida remarked, folding her arms and sitting back in her chair. "I'm a nurse."

Maria said, innocently, "Aren't the doctors your boss?"

Joe almost laughed, but Ida had that look on her face.

She told Maria, "I do what I know is best, and that's how it is. Nobody tells me otherwise."

Joe agreed. "Ida hates to be crossed. She'll box your ears if you catch her at the wrong time of day."

Ida smiled. "I've never done nothing of the kind. If some don't agree with me, that's fine. I won't fight. I prefer to be peaceful. I learned that from my mother. And she loved strawberries and never got tired of planting."

"Farming's damned hard work," José said, getting up for another cup of coffee. Maria had baked a fresh apple pie for dessert that sat on the table. "If you got a bad back, you can just forget it. Hoeing the rows'll kill you."

"Well, I've got a good strong back," Ida remarked. "and I've probably dug a mile of rows in my time."

Joe turned to José. "You won't catch me with a garden hoe for anything. I hate farming and I'm not that big a fan of strawberries, either."

Ida scoffed, "Oh, there's nothing to it."

"Is that so?" Joe said, suddenly irritated with her boasting. "How about we go outdoors right now, honey, and you show us how it's done?"

Maria disagreed. "I think we should eat this pie before it gets cold." She removed the cloth from the pie plate. The warm spicy aroma filled the small kitchen.

"No, we ought to let Ida do some digging while it's still light out," José said, putting down his cup of coffee on the kitchen counter. "Maybe she'll teach us a thing or two. The pie'll wait."

Maria frowned. "Be polite, cariño. She's our guest."

Ida set her napkin beside her plate and stood up. "Honey, that pie of yours looks positively delicious and I'll have a big slice just as soon as I prove what a woman can do when she chooses to put her mind to something." She looked José in the eye. "Show me the way."

Joe got up next to her. "Ida, what are you trying to prove?"

"Don't say another word, Joey. I've got no quarrel with either of you that can't be settled in a plot of dirt."

They all stepped outdoors into a pleasant twilight where a soft breeze crossed the yard. Next door, José's neighbor fiddled with one of his autos and two small boys sat on the back porch step reading comic books. José took a hoe out of the garden shed and gave it to Ida who waited by the vegetable patch. "Don't wear yourself out."

"Thank you." Ida grabbed the hoe and marched off down the rows to a spot that needed a fresh furrow. Joe followed. José walked closer and Joe worried that Ida might slug him with the hoe. Maria stood by the back door, hands on her hips. José had met her at a fiesta near Fresno about four years ago and married her after a month. She was sixteen years younger than him and wanted children, but José told her she had to wait until he retired. That's how he got her to agree to buying this farm and growing vegetables. Maybe if José bought a tractor one day, farming wouldn't be so tough. Joe had driven the tractor at Watsonville on those afternoons his foreman had the day off, because his boss didn't trust any Mexicans behind the wheel, but if he ever needed to drive a tractor again to earn a living, he hoped somebody would slam him in the head with a shovel.

Just like that, Ida quit digging and dropped the hoe without saying a word and walked back through the yard shadows to the house. Maria let her indoors. José picked up the hoe and returned it to his shed, and Joe helped him stack a pile of fruit crates out back of the garage. Then he and José went back inside to eat some apple pie.

Later that night, after José had let them off at the Bluebonnet Motel on Rose Boulevard where Maria had found them a room, Ida told Joe, "You can twist a dollar six ways to Sunday, but selling strawberries by the roadside isn't the way to make a go of it these days. Maria's trouble is that she lets José give her the runaround because she wants to have a baby, and I think she's making a big mistake there. She's too cautious. She ought to tell José that he needs to keep working those jobs in the city if he wants her to stay with him. Farming's no more work than any other thing that gets you out of bed in the morning, but I just couldn't see breaking my back when there's no real money in it. We need to find another business."

L ATE ON A BLUSTERY DECEMBER AFTERNOON, Muriel Knutsen puttered about her bedroom, checking drawers for anything she might have forgotten to pack in her suitcase. It was horrid trying to remember everything that needed to be settled before she left to her evening flight for Mexico City. And that wasn't counting the paperwork she and Mrs. Long needed to register with a notary public for transferring ownership of the motel, nor stopping at the bank in San Francisco to collect her traveler's checks. It was all so terribly complicated. Thank heavens she had someone to help her manage this whirlwind of necessities.

Nervous about the hour, Muriel peeked out her window across the windy parking lot. Ida was due here at the motel any time now. She promised Muriel they would get down to the city before her bank closed, but the Greyhound bus wasn't fast and Muriel hated to be rushed. If there was rain, traffic would be worse and she might be late and need to do this all over again in the morning and then she'd worry about missing her connecting flight to Rio de Janeiro. If that happened, she'd have a fit. Too bad Muriel had to leave her Lincoln up here. She loved that car. Ida would hold onto the keys because she didn't drive and Muriel never let anyone behind the wheel. Maybe once she was settled in Brazil, the Lincoln could be shipped down to her. That was an idea. She'd look into it after she arrived.

Muriel opened her door and stared out across the parking lot to the Bluebonnet Motel. Where was Ida? Had she forgotten about seeing the notary? Good gracious! Muriel considered Ida Long smart, but not educated. She spoke like a hillbilly and had some outlandish beliefs. When they first discussed South America, Ida seemed to think Brazil was next door to Mexico and told Muriel she had driven there one weekend with a friend from Oceanside. But then she also knew how far Rio de Janeiro was from São Paulo and where gold was discovered on the Madeira River near Porto Velho, so she was no dummy, either. In any case, all that mattered was Ida intended to buy the motel, because Muriel's bags were packed and she had an airplane ticket in her purse. Lonnie knew she was leaving and acted as if the world were ending. Muriel told him repeatedly that he would be taken care of and not to worry. She wrote a letter to his son, Larry, down in San Diego to let him know she was on her way to Brazil and that a convalescent home would probably be best for Lonnie now. Larry wired back to let Muriel know neither he nor his brothers would be able to afford a rest home for at least half a year and that Muriel had better make arrangements for Lonnie to remain at the motel until circumstances improved. Fortunately, Mrs. Long came to the rescue once again.

"Honey, it's absolutely a shame that some of us can't see fit to take care of our neighbors, but that's the only way I know how to live. Me and Joe would be glad to look after Lonnie, and he'll be happy here knowing you're on your way to a better life."

Muriel purchased Lonnie a good television set and a new table with a built-in tray so he could eat his supper and watch his favorite shows without having to get up and move around. She also bought him a fresh suit and six pairs of cotton shirts and some trousers with easy zippers. Although he was no longer her husband, Muriel acknowledged her moral responsibility to him by lending Mrs. Long five hundred dollars toward expenses for Lonnie's medical care and well-being. After that, his family would need to bear the burden of his health and future care, because Muriel expected to be in South America for quite a long while — if she even came back at all.

Muriel checked her watch as a truck roared by on Rose Boulevard. She wanted to stop at the Emporium on Market Street to buy some new handkerchiefs. Travel was exciting. She looked out the window again. Where on earth was Ida?

66 I **TELL YOU, HONEY,** I had my pocketbook on that table not ten minutes ago and now it's gone, and I haven't a clue where it could've gotten off to."

Ida blew about the kitchen like a tornado, dipping into drawers and cabinets, and came into the living room where Joe sat in his easy chair reading *Life* magazine.

"It's positively got to be here somewhere because I never go any place without it and I remember telling myself to put some fresh tissues in my purse on top of the pocketbook in case my nose starts running in the car. Did I tell you I've caught cold? I'm sure I got it next door when Mabel practically sneezed in my face. That woman pretends to know something about everything, yet she's got the manners of a cow."

Joe didn't bother looking up from the article he was studying on America's Jupiter rockets and those monkeys shot off into space. He had no interest in girl gossip. For a while there, Ida and Mabel would watch *As The World Turns* together nearly every afternoon and go shopping all over town in Mabel's sedan, but now that Ida had hitched herself to Muriel's dump next door, they couldn't stand the sight of each other.

Ida ran into the bedroom and Joe heard the closet doors swing open. She was about to throw a fit again. The dresser drawers slammed shut and Ida went into the bathroom and closed the door. Joe put aside the magazine and got up and had a beer from the refrigerator and went out onto the porch. A shiny Chrysler convertible drove into the parking lot and stopped by the office. Some fellow wearing a straw hat and a wrinkled Aloha shirt got out. Joe noticed a couple of kids on the passenger side flipping yo-yos. When one hit the other in the head, they both started screeching like peacocks. Joe hoped Crandall didn't give those people a room next door. He might have to kill them.

The toilet flushed and Ida came out of the bathroom. "You know, honey, it wouldn't be the awfullest thing in the world if you helped to find my pocketbook. Muriel's waiting for me and we've got to get to the notary to sign the papers. Are you absolutely sure you don't want me to put your name on the deed? I'm still willing to do so, even though you haven't lifted a finger to help me buy her place."

"You go right ahead and be queen of the motel," Joe said, still watching the kids in the Chrysler. They were both crawling into the backseat now. "I told you, I don't want any part of it. That place is a dump."

"Honey, it's no joy trying to explain something you have no enthusiasm for. I'll write my name on the bottom line and pretend you never heard of me and that'll be all of it. But when I make a success of the business, I'll share the profit because you're my husband and it won't cost you nothing but a kiss now and then."

"Do what you like."

Ida nudged Joe at the door and showed him the black purse. "Look here! It was in the bathroom sink. I can't imagine how it got there. Sometimes I wonder if I'm not right in my head."

A cold wind blew across the motel parking lot as Joe watched the straw-hat fellow come out of Crandall's office and get back into his Chrysler and put the top up. The sky was cloudy now. His kids were still screaming at each other as he drove off.

"Aren't you going to kiss me, honey? I won't see you until tomorrow morning."

Ida waited beside him, her red lips puckered.

Joe gave her a nice warm kiss and told her, "Be sure Muriel drives safely. There's a lot of nuts on the road."

Ida shook her head. "Joey, sometimes I wonder if you need a hearing aid."

"Come again?"

"I told you half a dozen times today that we bought tickets on the Greyhound to the city tonight. Muriel's leaving the Lincoln here with us and I'll ride the bus back tomorrow."

"I can't keep up with all your plans."

"Well, you don't need to, honey." She kissed his cheek. "I've already worked everything out on my own."

HOURS PAST DARK, Joe stood outdoors by the parking lot in a cold breeze staring up at the electric sign above the front office that said "VAC N Y" because Muriel hadn't paid to fix the burned-out letters. Who would want to stop here? People don't care for a place that's rundown. They think of bugs and rodents and soiled mattresses under old sheets. Roadside businesses have to try hard to get customers to pull in, and if light bulbs are burned out or screens fallen off a window or two, that can cost you. Motels are a tough proposition. Del Crandall had told Joe that when they spoke about Ida buying out Muriel's interest in the Rose City Motor Court.

"I think your wife's making a big mistake."

"Ida thinks there's about ten thousand dollars equity in the place. I guess she got that figure from Muriel."

"She's wrong."

"Well, what would you pay for it?"

"As little as possible," Crandall said. "It's a dump. If the wind blows, it'll fall down."

But Ida assumed ownership of Muriel's motel a week later.

Then she begged Joe to help her clean it up. He told her he'd rather burn it to the ground. Instead, Ida gave him a couple of kids from the Bluebonnet next door who helped cart out the trash from Muriel's apartment and the other cabins, including Lonnie's room next to the front office. Joe brought in some oilcans to use for incinerators and also cleared space at the back of the parking lot for a trash heap of old furniture and fixtures that needed to be junked. Meanwhile, Ida went through Muriel's apartment, drawer by drawer. She called Joe down to see what she had pulled out of a wooden box in Muriel's bedroom: some yellow envelopes filled with powder and a hypodermic syringe that Ida told Joe was used for dope.

"I knew that woman was sick somehow. She just didn't seem right in the head. That's what dope does to a person. And I'll tell you something else, Joey: that busybody Mabel knew about this, too. She was here snooping not ten minutes ago when I found this stuff and she tried to tell me it wasn't anything unusual because Muriel was a nurse. I asked her, 'What sort of nurse keeps dope in a dresser drawer?' Well, you should've seen the look on that woman's face when I picked up the telephone and rang the sheriff's office and told them all about Muriel's dope. They told me to break the syringe and flush the powder down the toilet, so that's what I'm going to do, although Mabel wants me to wait and show it to her husband. Why would I do that? There's something funny about those two, as well. It positively wouldn't surprise me if they were fixing each other up with Muriel's dope. They're probably all hopheads."

Joe went back to burning garbage. His helpers, fourteen-year-old Mary Baker and her little brother Eddie, stacked more than fifty issues of *National Geographic* with copies of *Look* and *Time* and *Life & Health* magazine outside of Muriel's old cabin. Ida had gotten permission to dump anything Muriel had left behind, except for Lonnie who sat in a green lawn chair outside of his own door and seemed unclear about what was going on. Poor fellow. Joe nodded to him each time he passed by with another load of junk for the oilcans. Lonnie just blinked.

Joe burned trash for three days until the neighbors complained and Ida ran out of excuses and told Joe to put the fires out. Ida paid the kids five dollars and gave the girl a canary as a thank-you present, then told them to stay away until the motel re-opened. Only two of the cabins were fit to be occupied, and Ida needed to get tenants in there right away to help defray some of the cost of her repairs. By doing most of the work himself, Joe had saved hundreds of dollars, but he warned Ida not to expect him to stay on the job much longer. She had already gone out and bought a neon sign that renamed her motel "El Sombrero" and put up a new awning for the front office and hired a painter to re-do the look out front. She also hired a week's worth of labor to renovate two of the cabins that Joe told her were already in fair condition for a motel of this sort. He just thought she was flushing dollars down the toilet.

"I tell you this place still isn't fit for hogs and I've done everything I can. You ought to give some thought to what you throw money at. For godsakes, Ida, don't get yourself in a hole over this dump. It's not worth it."

"Well, I have my own bank account, sweetheart, and my own worries that don't concern you unless you want them to. Muriel signed the deed to this motel over to me because she had faith that I could make something of the business and I positively wouldn't have taken on the cost and responsibility if I'd had the slightest doubt. I never expected you to stay here by my side, honey, and I'm grateful for all the help you've been. You needn't feel guilty."

"I don't."

THE WEEK BEFORE CHRISTMAS, Joe was outdoors on a cold, breezy afternoon fixing a leaky faucet behind the front office when he noticed a fellow in a dark blue business suit snooping through the weeds by one of the back cabins. Ida had gone holiday shopping in the city, so Joe put his wrench down and went over to point the guy to the sidewalk. Motels attracted bums and fleas together. You needed bug spray indoors and out to keep the pests away. This one's story was that he had been hired to install a water softener at the motel.

"Who says?"

"The owner. She knows the water quality of this place is pretty rotten. We're going to fix it up once and for all."

"And who are you?"

"Bert Wilson. Wildew Water Conditioning."

He offered a hand and Joe took it. "Joe Long."

"Oh, the husband!" Wilson grinned as they shook. "Glad to know you. That wife of yours is a darned smart lady. Ordinarily I have to come out and sell my customers on a water softening system, show them why it's important and saves money in the long run. But she came to me, said what she needed, and asked me to come out and install it. I was impressed, let me tell you."

"I'll bet you were." Joe realized Wilson here was probably a bedbug who did more business under the sheets than on the porch. Evidently, milkmen weren't the only happy fellows these days.

Wilson nodded toward the motel. "This place really has some potential. Could be a gold mine in the right hands."

"Oh yeah?" Joe thought he sounded like a phony. At least Ida didn't talk about getting rich here. Some guys will say anything to get a sale, and they're a menace to your bank account.

"Sure," Wilson cheerfully explained, "because one day Rose Boulevard'll be an important thoroughfare again, and when it is, all these properties'll go through the roof. Just you wait and see."

"Well, I'll have to take your word for that." Joe hated people telling him what was coming tomorrow or the day after next. "Once I finish helping my wife clean up this dump, I'm leaving and hope to God I won't be back."

Wilson's smile didn't budge. "Well, to each his own, but we'll put in your water softener and see if that won't perk things up a little bit."

"What's the charge for that?"

"Oh, I worked it out with your wife," Wilson enthused. "She preferred an installment plan and I thought that was just fine. We went over to the Bank of America last week and I served as a credit reference so she could borrow five thousand dollars. Your wife gave me three hundred bucks for doing that and I agreed to let her have a six-thousand-dollar water softener for forty-nine hundred with a thousand down, and the rest by March. I threw in the labor at no extra charge."

"She gave you three hundred bucks for holding her hand at the bank?"

"I stood up for her to get that loan and your wife's no nickel hugger. I did her a favor and she paid me back."

"I'll bet she did."

Wilson frowned. "What are you driving at?"

A cold gust of wind rippled through the weeds along the motel wall. The morning weather report called for rain by supper and Joe still had a load of work to do. He wanted Wilson to take a hike. Besides, Joe hadn't known this guy ten minutes and he hated him already. "Just don't butt into our business. We can take care of ourselves."

Wilson gave the motel another good long look. "I can see that." Then he smiled. "Let Ida know I was by, won't you?"

THAT EVENING AFTER SUPPER, Ida came into the bedroom when Joe was watching Rawhide. She had a AAA road map in her hand and a scheme drummed up that almost made him fall off the mattress. It had to do with one of Muriel Knutsen's out-of-state properties, another sad-sack motel going to pot.

Sitting down on the bed, Ida told him, "It's called the Dock Cabin Motor Court, and since Muriel plans to sell it off, she said I was absolutely free to go up to Westport and take whatever fixtures or furniture I wanted."

"Where the hell's Westport?"

"Up in Washington State at Grays Harbor on the coast, by Aberdeen. Muriel says it's beautiful."

"Sure it is," Joe told her, "if you like rain. No wonder she's selling. Everything's waterlogged up there."

"Honey, we need to refurbish this motel and I positively can't afford to go out and buy fresh furniture for every cabin and replace all the old fixtures that are broke."

"Who says you need to? It's a goddamned motel, not the Fairmont. What do you expect?"

"Joey, people who hire a room in a motel know what they're paying for or they wouldn't have stopped by. But that doesn't mean they want towels that are gray, or a toilet that leaks, or a saggy mattress. Then they feel cheap and go away unhappy and won't come back again."

Joe gave up. "So what do you want from me?"

She folded open the road map. "I need you to drive us up to West-port tomorrow morning. Muriel told me I can use her Lincoln if it's an emergency or a special circumstance and this positively fits that since I've already hired a moving van at Westport to load up everything we take out of that motel there. Juanita's coming, too. That way if your back goes out on you, we won't be slowed down. I'm paying her a hundred dollars, so she'll work hard."

Joe took a look at the AAA map. "It's a long haul up there, Ida. It'll take all day and another one after that to come back again. Who's going to take care of this place while we're gone if that fat Mexican's coming with us? Lonnie?"

"Don't be funny. Mary's mother volunteered when I promised to baby-sit Eddie while she and her husband go to Monterey next weekend. I told her there's nothing to it, and she can look in on Lonnie while she's here."

"You're not paying her anything?"

"She didn't ask."

"Are you paying me?"

"Of course."

She leaned over and kissed him.

The next morning, Joe's alarm went off at five sharp and Ida had a pot of hot coffee and a couple of hardboiled eggs and toast waiting for him in the kitchen. Joe took a quick shower and got dressed. He heard Juanita clumping about out in the front room, humming the theme song to *Howdy Doody*. The girl was nuttier than Ida. Joe had met Juanita when Ida took the keys to the motel and hired her to help at the front desk. She was a Mexican, built like a tractor, with a puffy brown face she must've bought at a second-hand auction and a long black braid down her back. She smelled like pancakes. For some reason, Joe always felt like giving her a good shove. Why she and Ida got along so well was one of those conspiracies only another nut understands.

The morning air was cold and foggy when Joe Krueger finished his coffee and got behind the wheel of Muriel's white Lincoln. Ida told Juanita to sit up front next to Joe.

"I'll sit in back so I can keep my eye on you two. And don't drive too fast, Joey. I get sick to my stomach."

Six hours later, Joe stopped for gas and oil at Crescent City where they all got out to stretch their legs and buy some sandwiches and candy bars. Juanita and Ida both used the toilet and came out squabbling over paper towels. The station attendant asked Joe how long he had owned the Lincoln and Joe said not to tell anyone but that they had just stolen it for a joyride and were taking it back once he filled it up with gas. The attendant laughed and gave Joe a nice wave as they drove off.

By mid-afternoon, both Ida and Juanita were asleep and Joe listened to Benny Goodman and Harry James on the radio through Oregon and watched the clouds blacken to the east as the sun went down. He could hardly keep his own eyes open as he drove west out of Portland toward Highway 101 on the coast to Astoria where Ida wanted to take the ferry across into Washington State. But they arrived a quarter of an hour too late.

"We can go around," Ida told Joe, "because it's not even a hundred miles. You can see here on the map."

"Nope, I can't drive any farther tonight," he decided. "I'm too sleepy."

So they found a motel and stayed the night, then got up early the next morning and took the ferry across the Columbia and drove on to Westport after breakfast.

Muriel's Dock Cabin Motor Court was on the waterfront with a nice view of Grays Harbor and the Pacific Ocean. You could see the fishing boats at the marina, people laboring on the docks, white gulls drifting on the wind. Juanita got out of the Lincoln and went down to the water and waded in up to her knees while Ida took a set of keys from her purse and unlocked the building. The motel was closed for business, and the cabins were empty. Joe inhaled that strong marine scent of the ocean as he poked around the grounds for a few minutes, then went indoors to see what Ida was up to.

"I hired a Bekins van," she told him, coming out of the office. "It'll be here tomorrow morning at eight sharp and we can't waste any time loading up. Muriel had the power turned off when she closed the motel for the winter, so we'll be working in the dark if we take too long."

"Did you bring a flashlight?"

"No, honey, but we have kerosene lamps, if it comes to that. Where's Juanita?"

"Taking a swim."

"This isn't funny, Joey," Ida said, heading to the door. "I'm not paying that blubber-belly to fool around." She stepped out onto the porch and shouted angrily for Juanita at the top of her lungs. The next time Joe stuck his head out the door, he saw the Mexican on the stoop, daubing mud on her toe.

Joe asked her, "What happened?"

"She stepped on a bee," Ida told him as she crossed the grassy yard from the Lincoln. She had the trunk and the back doors open. Wind blew off the gray cloudy harbor. The sky smelled like rain.

Juanita explained, "I didn't see it in the sand."

"Well, that's not much excuse," Ida snapped, and went back indoors to begin stripping the linen, blankets, bedspreads off all the beds and loading them into the car. She told Joe to collect every one of the electric heaters and flatirons and wall panel heaters, too.

"I want all of it," Ida told him as she rushed about. "Don't let it go to waste if it's anything we can use."

"I can't get the heaters out of the wall without tools."

"Well, there's a Sears-Roebuck store over in Aberdeen. We'll go over there for lunch once we finish stripping the beds and you can get what you need. Just do what you can until then, all right, honey? We positively have to be through by tomorrow morning when the van arrives."

Juanita limped into the office and went to use the toilet. She smelled like a sewer. Ida yelled at her to hurry up.

Joe spent the next three hours taking everything that wasn't nailed down and stacking up a pile in the main building. Most of it seemed like a lot of junk to him. He was also uneasy about what they were doing, stripping Muriel's motel like that. It was a shady business and Joe knew it. Juanita also suspected this wasn't all on the up-and-up. She kept asking Ida what to say to the cops if they stopped by to see what was going on and finally Ida yelled at her that Muriel was a hopeless dopehead who had sold her the motel in Santa Rosa under bad circumstances, but that Ida had the papers to prove all of this belonged to her now, and she could do with it however she wanted and to quit worrying and get back to work.

They stopped for lunch at half past two. By then, the Lincoln was stuffed with assorted bed linen and blankets and bath towels. Ida locked up and Joe drove them north along the water to Aberdeen, where they bought a couple of wrenches, a set of screwdrivers, and a wrecking bar over at the Sears Roebuck store. Then they came back to Westport and had a fish dinner at Sourdough Lil's on Dock Street. While they ate, Juanita complained about her aching back and Ida said she could go sit in the car for the rest of the day if she needed to, but then she wouldn't get paid. Joe's own shoulders were sore and, since he wasn't earning a cent on this job, if it weren't for Ida giving him the bad eye, he'd go sit in the Lincoln himself.

Back at the motel, Ida led Joe on a tour of the cabins where she pointed out everything she wanted removed for the van in the morning:

beds, stoves, refrigerators, toilets, wash bowls, and shower connections. By then, the temperature had dropped and a damp wind was blowing hard off Grays Harbor. The cabins felt cold and drafty and Joe went to get his jacket. When he came back indoors, Ida and Juanita were going at it again in one of the bedrooms. He poked his head into the hornet's nest.

"Honey, it's going to take some really hard work here," Juanita complained, sitting on the bed. "Do you even know how to undo one of these?"

"Of course," Ida snapped back at her. "Do I look like an idiot? Besides, Joe's going to help, aren't you, dear?" She looked up at him, hopefully.

"Sure, honey."

It wasn't a big sweat. He just had to undo the screws that joined the beds to the wall, stack the mattresses and box springs, and haul them outdoors.

Ida said, "We're going to have to work all night if the van's coming at half past eight in the morning. We need to get everything out of here."

"Well, I can't stay up all night," Juanita said, taking a candy bar from her pocket. "I'm tired already."

"Then go to sleep," Ida told her, heading for the door. "Me and Joe'll finish the job. But you positively won't get a dime."

Juanita followed her out the door and Joe lit some candles and a couple of kerosene lanterns and spent the next seven hours taking the beds apart in a dozen cabins. He also pulled the plugs on all the refrigerators, unfastened the stoves and toilets and sinks, and undid the showerheads and handles, piling them up by the front door in each of the buildings. Halfway through the job, at two in the morning, he took a break and went to see what Ida was up to. If he caught her and Juanita sleeping on the job, he planned on driving the Lincoln back up to Aberdeen and hiring a room in a motel. He was cold as hell by then, and his hands were numb and raw and he felt exhausted.

Back at the main building, Ida had collected all the silverware together in a pillowcase and removed the doorknobs from each of the bathroom doors. She had unscrewed every light bulb from its fixture and wrapped them together in a bedspread. Working by candlelight and a single kerosene lamp, Ida went from room to room, unfastening the switch plates from the electric plug outlets and tossing them into another pillowcase she dragged around with her. When Joe came in, Ida was working alone.

"Where's Juanita?"

"I told her to go out to the car and have a nap. Her teeth were chattering and I absolutely couldn't work with her complaining about the cold. She's got a bean for a brain."

"Well, it's damned cold in here," Joe said, rubbing his hands.

"I know it is," Ida said. "That's why I'm working. I got to keep warm."

"Of course you do."

"Joey, I have something to tell you, and if you don't like it, there's nothing I can do but be honest with you like I always have been. Will you hear me out?"

Good grief, now what?

"All right, spill it."

"You know all this stuff we're loading out of here?"

"It's what we're talking about." Joe's stomach was growling from hunger.

"Well, honey, it's stolen goods that dopehead Muriel sold me and I just couldn't leave here in the morning and let someone else come to collect it all when we can't afford these things otherwise."

"You're joking me, right?"

Joe thought if his blood pressure went any higher, his ears would pop.

Glancing out the window into the dark, Ida told him, "Muriel bragged about how smart she was with her real estate investments, but she's the biggest thief that ever walked this earth. Maybe she was legal before the War and earned honest dollars when she was nursing, but once she got her dope habit, she's been a fiend about money and all her morals flew right out the window and she's gone crazy, stealing from everyone but the Pope to pay for her needles and powder. I don't know why I let her talk me into doing this, Joey, honest I don't. I guess I'm just that way about helping someone out of trouble. Do unto others as you would have them do unto you."

Joe decided he'd heard it all now. "For Christsakes, Ida, did you fall out of tree? If all this junk is stolen merchandise, then we're on the hook, too, for taking it out of her motel. Even if you're not right in the head, you can see that much, can't you?"

"It's not that simple, honey," Ida explained. "Muriel put my name on the deed for this motel when she left the country, so I'm involved whether I like it or not. She's a lot smarter than I am, I have to admit. We did a reading together in her kitchen and I never saw that side of her and my books positively ought to have revealed her evil, so I can't explain what went wrong, but it's an awful mess."

"You're damn right it is. We could go to jail."

Ida told Joe, "I'm sending the van down to a Bekins warehouse in San Rafael. It's not even under our name there, so nobody'll bother us. You worry too much, honey, and it's positively the wrong way to live."

Too angry to say another word, Joe left to finish stripping the back cabins. He passed Juanita as she came out of the dark from the Lincoln. She looked like a wreck. Joe ignored her.

He worked the rest of the night, unhooking a big water tank Ida wanted and slugging the last toilet out of the back cabin at sunrise. The indoors of the motel looked like a junkyard when he was finished.

At seven o'clock, dead on his feet, Joe drove the three of them through a cold gray drizzle to a breakfast café for coffee and eggs near the marina. When they returned to the motel, the Bekins van had arrived. Two fellows had come along to load everything and didn't want any help, so Joe, Ida, and Juanita slept in the Lincoln until the van was packed. A winter storm swept in off the ocean as Ida gave the driver instructions where to take everything, and they left Westport together by mid-afternoon. Joe ran out of gas after the ferry crossing at Astoria, and then had to fix a flat tire under Ida's umbrella three miles outside of Red Bluff on Highway 99. Rain poured steadily on the long dark drive back to Santa Rosa.

THEN IT REALLY RAINED LIKE HELL through the holidays. Ida paid Juanita a few dollars extra to take charge of the front desk so she and Joe could go down to San Francisco for a week. They bought a soaking wet fir tree at a corner lot in Daly City and decorated it in the living room at Ellington, and rode the Muni up to see the Ice Follies at Winterland. For her Christmas present, Joe gave Ida a pair of gloves from the Emporium and a gold-filled scarf pin, and she gave him mother-of-pearl cufflinks. On New Year's Eve, they ate dinner at the Golden Spike and hired a taxi to the Fillmore jazz club and drank a glass of champagne at midnight and went home afterward to love each other under the sheets. Ida was a trauma to Joe and he didn't trust her to tell him the day of the week, but she was his wife, too, and that still meant something to him. He refused to desert her over a second-rate motel, no matter what the threat.

The day he got back from San Francisco, Joe had to dig a drainage trench along the north side of the building to offset some flooding in a few of the cabins. With a pair of fellows from town, Joe excavated one hole in a carport and another couple on the west side of the motel until the whole property looked like a skirmish line. Del Crandall came over from next door to complain about the mess in the parking lot. Joe told him that the motel belonged to Ida and he ought to mind his own goddamned business.

"Well, it's noisy, too," Crandall said, "and Mabel can't take her nap in the afternoon with all that racket."

"I can't take a nap, either, when I'm working. Have her put a bucket over her head."

"You and Ida are going to run this place into the ground."

"Then it'll look like yours."

"Go to hell, Krueger."

"I'm burning my ass right here."

In fact, Joe Krueger's true hell started with a telephone call that Ida took about a month after the episode at Westport. When the phone rang at the front desk, Joe was busy tightening up a drainpipe in their bathroom. He heard Ida identify the El Sombrero and ask how she might be of help. Just that quickly, her tone changed and Joe could tell she wasn't happy talking to the caller.

"No, I've already told you she's gone. . . . Pardon? . . . Are you deaf? All of it belongs to me now! That's what ownership means and I have the deed to prove it. . . . Well, I don't appreciate being talked to this way, either. . . . That's your tale, honey, but I won't . . . Well, you can't blame me if she went off to Mexico with that dope peddler. . . . Yes, you heard me say it plain as day. Dope peddler! . . . Well, that's what he was, and maybe she is, too. . . . Hello? . . . How's that? . . . Same to you, honey!"

Ida slammed the phone down.

"Who was that?" Joe asked, coming into the front office.

"None of your concern," Ida replied. "That's who."

"Suit yourself."

"I will."

Then Ida grabbed her purse and walked out.

Ten minutes later, the telephone rang again. Joe answered. The voice belonged to an older woman who asked to speak with Mrs. Long.

"She's stepped out for a while. How can I help you?"

"My name is Lois Claiborne and I'm trying to reach my daughter, Muriel Knutsen. I've been informed she's sold her motel to you people there and left on a trip somewhere. I'm trying to find out where she might have gone. There's been no word from her in almost two months and it's just not like Muriel to go anywhere without writing to us."

"Well, what do you want me to do?" Joe asked, uncomfortable talking about Muriel. He hadn't cared for her when she was around and now that she'd gone off, he hadn't any opinion about the woman, one way or the other.

"You see, I just thought someone there might have some information regarding Muriel's whereabouts, something that could help us find her. It's not a lot to ask."

"It is if I don't know anything."

"May I ask whom I'm speaking with?"

"Joe Long."

"I thought so." Lois paused as if she were writing a note to herself. "My younger daughter Agnes called earlier and was put off in a very unpleasant manner. She's quite close to her sister and can't stand this mystery. Muriel's always been ambitious, but she loves her family, and has always been a very faithful correspondent. She simply wouldn't disappear without letting us know how to reach her. Maybe you can't understand that."

Joe felt irritated now, mostly with Ida, who'd gone out and left him to handle this mess. What the hell did he know about Muriel? If Ida were here, she'd put this lady straight and the phone would quit ringing. Then Joe could go bowling and forget all about this.

He said, "If I knew where she was, I'd say so. Last I heard, she was flying down to Brazil. So I guess that's where she is. I've never been there, but I hear it's a pretty big country. Maybe they don't have phones or a post office where she went. You never know. I was in the Pacific during the War and mail was pretty damned slow, let me tell you."

He hoped she'd hang up.

Lois said, "You're very smug, aren't you? I suppose that motel is all you think about these days, and Muriel's whereabouts aren't worth a nickel to you or Mrs. Long, but I'll have you know we're a very persistent family and we intend to get to the bottom of this, with or without your help. Thank you very much."

Then she did hang up.

And Joe went bowling.

DOWNTOWN THAT SAME AFTERNOON, Sheriff's Inspector Dan Ellison lit a cigarette and stared at the stack of reports on his desk. More juvenile delinquent disturbances. Domestic squabbles. Theft and burglary out on the Russian River. One stabbing. His office was cramped with four metal file cabinets, a couple of chairs, a hat rack, and a big oak desk he had bought in Modesto when he thought his days in law enforcement were over and real estate was the next big thing in his life. Ellison had the blinds closed all morning because he had a migraine after breakfast and threw up his coffee in the car.

His partner, Gordon Cochrane, poked his head inside the door. "Danny?"

"Yeah?"

"The sheriff wants you to go see the owner of a motel out on Rose Boulevard. We got a call about an hour ago from a lady up in the Seattle area who says her sister Muriel's missing and wants us to look into it. Apparently her sister used to own the motel and sold it to a Mrs. Long, who claims the sister ran off with a dope peddler to Mexico. The lady who telephoned says the Long woman sounded suspiciously bitter and she couldn't understand why that was so. She says the idea that Muriel ran off anywhere with a dope peddler is ridiculous. Also, there's a problem with another motel Muriel owns up in Westport, Washington. Apparently, when this lady and her friend went out there to see how the cabins had been withstanding the winter, they found all the cabins had been gone through, the furniture removed, wall siding stripped from the interior of the office, plumbing and fixtures taken out, doors pulled from their casings. I don't know why, but they seem to think Mrs. Long might have had something to do with it because Muriel's Lincoln was up there at the same time and a strange woman was seen loading laundry into it. Why don't you take a ride out there and see what you can find out. I told the lady we'd call her back this evening. Here's the information."

Cochrane handed him a sheet of paper and Ellison looked it over. The lady who telephoned was named Agnes Webber. Her sister was Muriel Knutsen, whose husband, Lonnie, still lived at the El Sombrero, which was operated now by a Mrs. Ida Long. Muriel was last seen six weeks ago by Del and Mabel Crandall, owners of the Bluebonnet Motel next door to the El Sombrero.

Cochrane told Ellison, "Find out what Mr. Knutsen has to say. He'll probably know where his wife went."

"Why didn't the Webber lady just ask him herself? She doesn't have a telephone?"

"She says this Knutsen fellow's got Parkinson's and his face is partially paralyzed, so he's hard to understand over the phone. Apparently he was an officer in World War One, and I guess he got gassed. She thinks it'd be easier for us to talk with him in person."

"All right, I'll take a run out there and see what I can find out." Ellison snuffed out his cigarette in a black San Francisco Giants ashtray. "Someone always knows where the wife's gone. If it's not her husband, I'll lay you ten-to-one it'll be a gal at the motel. Ladies gossip, you know? If her husband's a basket case, she probably wanted to get away from him, anyhow."

Most of the motels on Rose Boulevard were outside of Santa Rosa city limits, and that meant the sheriff's office rather than city police had jurisdiction. Ellison handled investigations from one end of the county to the other and spent half his day in a Ford sedan. He kept a thermos of coffee on the seat beside him and a pack of Camels in the glove box. Now and then he stopped to call his girlfriend who worked nights down in Novato and wanted Ellison to quit his job so they could get married. Ellison had no desire to marry a roadhouse stripper.

The El Sombrero was a dump by any standard. Ellison parked his Ford in a stall by the front office and had a look around. Motels generally depressed him and this one was pretty bad. Stucco peeling off the walls, dumpster full, palm trees haggard, sloppy yard work. Ellison went into the motel office and found a pudgy Mexican woman half-asleep at the front desk next to a hand-lettered placard that read: *Take a Siesta After the Fiesta*. When he identified himself and showed her his badge, she perked up. He asked, "Are you Mrs. Long?"

"No, she's gone for the afternoon. I'm minding the desk for her."

"What's your name?"

"Juanita Lopez."

Ellison scribbled that into his notebook. "Where can I find Lonnie Knutsen?"

"Next door over. Cabin Two. He's eating lunch."

"What do you know about the previous owner of this place, Muriel Knutsen?"

The woman shrugged; her eyes seemed glassy. Ellison assumed she'd had her own lunch out of a bottle today. "I don't know nothing about her except what Mrs. Long says, which is that Mrs. Knutsen took her money and went to Brazil. I only met her once when I was looking for work here and she was packing up to go. She told me her and Major Lonnie was getting out of the motel business and flying down south. I thought she meant Mexico, but Mrs. Long told me South America and that Mrs. Knutsen probably wouldn't be coming back."

Ellison wrote all that down, too, and asked if Juanita would mind introducing him to Knutsen. They went next door, where Juanita knocked once and let herself in. Ellison followed. Lonnie Knutsen sat in front of a TV tray table eating a plate of macaroni and cheese. He was gray and gaunt, dressed in a common red plaid shirt with gray slacks, his hair combed to one side, his skin mottled, blue eyes moist and lively. He greeted Juanita with a droopy smile and attempted to raise his fork but failed.

"Hi, Major," she said, patting him on his shoulder. "I've brought someone who'd like to ask you some questions about Muriel."

Ellison stepped forward. "Major Knutsen, I'm Dan Ellison, with the sheriff's office. How do you do?"

Lonnie spoke as if he had mud caught in his throat. Ellison had no idea what he said and looked to Juanita for help. She told him, "Lonnie says you're here about Muriel, aren't you?"

Ellison nodded. "Yes, sir, I am. Her sister Agnes telephoned our office to see if we might be of some help locating her. We hear she's left the country, but her family hasn't heard a word in almost a month and I guess they're worried. Is there anything you can tell us about where she went or how her family might get hold of her?"

The Major's face tightened and his eyes narrowed. He carefully laid his fork on the TV tray and rattled off a long answer that took a couple of minutes to finish. Once more, Ellison turned to Juanita for a translation. She said, "Lonnie doesn't know where Muriel went and he doesn't know why, either, except that she expected to take a trip to South America with Mrs. Long, who would pay for all her expenses, including arrangements for the Major to go back to a convalescent hospital in San Diego. But then Mrs. Long bought the motel from Muriel, and her and her husband Joe have been looking after Lonnie until Muriel comes back. Her Lincoln's still here and she loves that car more than anything in the world, and he says that if Muriel had planned on being gone for a long while, she'd have put the Lincoln into storage."

Then Ellison asked Lonnie if he wanted to make a formal missing-persons complaint. "Muriel's sister seems pretty worried, but since you're Muriel's husband, maybe you ought to be the one to get the ball rolling."

The Major grunted a reply with a shake of his head that Juanita translated as: "They're not married anymore, so he doesn't believe he can do anything about that. It's not his business."

"Maybe not," Ellison agreed. "By the way, do either of you know why Mrs. Long would tell Agnes that Muriel had run off with a dope dealer to Mexico?"

Juanita shrugged. "She can be pretty mean when she wants to."

"Is that so?"

Teary-eyed, Lonnie mumbled another few words and Juanita told Ellison, "Lonnie says he doesn't think he'll ever see Muriel again."

Anxious to finish up the investigation, Ellison stopped by the El Sombrero once more after supper and found Mrs. Long at the office reading the morning newspaper. She was dressed like a housewife in a simple rose-print dress and apron, her brown hair curly and unkempt. She looked as sloppy and tired out as the old motel itself.

After showing his badge, commenting on the nice evening weather, and lying about the general look of things about the motel grounds, Ellison took out his notepad and pencil. "So, how long have you owned this property?"

Mrs. Long shut her newspaper. "I recorded the deed on January 3rd. It's all legal, all properly signed and witnessed. What more do you want to know?"

She drummed her fingers on the desk, feigning impatience. Ellison ignored that. Nobody likes to be questioned on purpose or intent, particularly when it comes to ownership of anything valuable. He scribbled a notation about the calendar behind Mrs. Long that showed the wrong month and marked down a couple of dates that were circled. Next, he asked, "Well, I'd like to know where Mrs. Knutsen is right now."

She scowled. "Well, now, I don't think that's any of your business, and it's not anybody else's business, either, except Muriel's."

"She wrote her relatives that she was planning to go to South America."

"Maybe that's where she is."

"She said she was going with you."

"Yes, I hear that's what she told her family, but all she ever wanted from me was to buy the motel. I bought it and she left. If you want my opinion, I think she intended to go to South America with someone else besides me."

"Who?"

"I don't know, and I wouldn't tell you if I did. That's her business."

"How come you told her sister she'd run off with a dope peddler from Mexico?"

"I said they had no business meddling in Muriel's affairs. I hate people who meddle in other people's lives. When those crazy ladies kept calling, I told them that about the dope peddler to shake 'em up a little. I guess it paid off, didn't it?"

Leaving the motel, Ellison decided Mrs. Long was a screwball.

Cochrane was in his office an hour later when Ellison came back to headquarters with his report from the motel. There had been a fatal shooting out at a trailer park on the Russian River just after six p.m. and thirteen men were sitting in county jail, each one of them considered a suspect. Thanks to that, Cochrane had lost his enthusiasm for the missing persons case.

"So it's a dead end?" he asked, trying to ignore the vicious crime scene photographs of the shooting victim at the trailer park. A shotgun blast had taken off half the boy's head.

Ellison explained, "Muriel Knutsen's been gone more than a month now, maybe to Mexico or down to South America, maybe to investigate real estate opportunities, maybe on a tryst with someone nobody wants to talk about. That Long woman seems to know more than she's willing to tell, but she's a real sourpuss and it's pretty clear she won't tell us anything useful unless we can push her somehow."

"And the Major?"

"He's just a sick and confused old man. Why Muriel didn't put him back in a convalescent home before she took off, I can't figure. I don't think he knows, either, unless something came up pretty damned quick that caused her to run off overnight."

"It sounds like a mess."

Ellison reached into his shirt pocket and took out a cigarette and lit it with a match from a cup on Cochrane's desk. "Well, here's how I see it. Without a formal complaint, there's just not enough to base an investigation on, but we could take a closer look at the sale of the motel, how it came about and when. Check the paperwork, signatures, and dates. Maybe you could place a call back up to Washington and let Muriel's family know that without any further information, there's not much else we can do. If Muriel doesn't want to keep in touch with her family or let them know her whereabouts, that's her prerogative. Meanwhile, I'll pay a visit to the courthouse, see if I can turn something up."

The following morning, Ellison went to the county recorder's office and had the files on the Rose City Motor Court/El Sombrero pulled and found the deed filed just as Mrs. Long had said it was, with IRS stamps affixed for six dollars. There had been no price listed, but Federal law required a dollar and ten cents for each one thousand dollars, which meant that something over five thousand dollars had been paid for Muriel's interest in the motel. The buyer was designated Ida Long, a married woman, as her separate property. The deed and signature were witnessed by Nanette Farley, a local Notary Public, on January 3rd.

"So this was legal?" Ellison asked, trying to keep track of who signed what.

"Legal as can be," she told him, "although I can't swear to the signature of Mrs. Knutsen because Mrs. Long recorded the deed. But we can accept a signature when it's been notarized, as this one was."

"But you recognized Mrs. Knutsen?"

"I not only recognized her," she told Ellison, "I required her to provide additional proof of identity."

"And you're positive that it was Mrs. Knutsen, and not Mrs. Long, who requested you to notarize the signature?"

"You're kidding, of course, right? It's my duty to establish the identity of any person before attaching the notary seal."

WALLY HUSTON HAD GIRL TROUBLES. Peggy Milton had lots of sex appeal, but she also wanted a big spender and Wally was between jobs, renting a room at the Bluebonnet Motel to save what few dollars he had left in his pocket from installing a linoleum floor over the holidays. Peggy had her heart set on a millionaire and Wally didn't compare well to a gas station attendant. Probably they were headed for a crash.

So Wally was thankful to run across Ida Long when he did. He noticed some of the renovations on the El Sombrero and thought he could've done better. Working in construction since high school, Wally knew good work when he saw it and figured he was superior to most. One rainy afternoon in mid-January he walked into Mrs. Long's front office and volunteered his services. At first, she was cranky and told him to mind his own business. Then, an hour later, Ida Long knocked on his door to tell him about a job down by Daly City that needed doing right away.

"Me and my husband are making an apartment from our basement and we have to put in a garbage disposal. It used to be a garage, so the floor's cement and needs a hole dug and my plumber told me it'd be cheaper if someone else digs the hole. If you could do that for us tonight, I'd pay you fifteen dollars. What do you say?"

"How big a hole?"

"Well, I can only judge by what my plumber told me, but he positively said four feet by four feet, and maybe a little deeper. Can you do that?"

"Sure," he replied, "but why do you need it done so soon? That's pretty short notice."

"Well, one of my tenants, Lonnie Knutsen, has a medical appointment at Mt. Zion hospital this evening, and another tomorrow morning at seven sharp, and his doctor wants Lonnie fixed up with a room there tonight. Since him and I are going that way anyhow, I thought we might all ride down together after supper. If you drove us in my husband's Lincoln, we'd save on bus fare. Does that fit?"

Wally thought it fit like a big pain in the ass, but he wasn't about to talk his way out of a job. Her motel still needed a lot of work and he figured that maybe by digging her stupid drain hole, she might just give him a bigger job later on. So he told her, "It fits just fine."

"Come over at half past five and don't be late. I'll have Major Knutsen packed up. It's supposed to rain all day now and I hate to be driving fast when the roads are wet."

Wally telephoned over to Peggy's house on Wright Street and told her about the job. Just like he expected, she groaned. "Honey, you got no head for business at all. When she said fifteen dollars, you ought to have said you'd do it for thirty dollars. Then she'd probably say twenty-five, and that's what you'd agree to. She undercut you and you bought it. That's why you need someone like me in your life."

"What've I been telling you, darling? You really make it go for me."

"Maybe I'll ride down there, too. It'd be good for us to get away for a little while."

"I'm not sure she'd go for a party of four."

"Why not? Tell her we're a package. She won't make a fuss. You're doing that lady a favor. For fifteen bucks, you're doing her a big favor."

In fact, Mrs. Long didn't mind at all. She told Peggy how pretty she was and that Wally was lucky to have her. The white Lincoln was parked in the dark, rain-drenched courtyard, soiled with soot and wet leaves. Wally climbed in behind the steering wheel and started the engine to get the defroster running while Peggy and Ida saw to Major Knutsen, who needed help just getting out the door. Rain hissed in the trees over the motor court, gusts shook the palm leaves. The Major wore a broad-rimmed fedora and a gray overcoat, and Ida held a black umbrella over both herself and Peggy as they guided the Major to the car. Wally stepped out briefly to give them a hand.

Then Peggy slid into the front seat next to Wally, and Ida climbed in back with the Major as Wally switched on the headlights and drove off to San Francisco. Since he hadn't driven a big Lincoln before, and the evening highway was slick with rain, Wally drove with extra care and kept to the speed limit. Most of the trip, Ida discussed astrology with Peggy, who read horoscopes in the newspaper every morning and believed every word of them. Propped up like a mannequin in the backseat, the Major had little to say himself. He mumbled on and off in that slurry speech of his, barely audible to Wally. Ida seemed to understand him, patting his cheek off and on, chatting back to him as if he were an infant. Wally felt sorry for the old guy.

Ellington Avenue was bleak and cold. The rain cut back to a thick drizzle kicked about by occasional wind gusts off the evening bay. Wally parked the Lincoln at the curb in front of the small white house and helped the Major get out of the car while Peggy followed Ida up the stairs to hold open the door. The street was a plain neighborhood of average houses and simple working people. Wally sort of liked it. He also knew Peggy wouldn't live here for a million bucks.

On the front stoop, Wally shook the rainwater off his blue Dodgers cap, then wiped his shoes on the door mat and helped Ida get the Major out of his overcoat. They put him on the tattered sofa facing a cheap Philco TV set. The small living room smelled of cooking grease and mold. Stains marred the carpet and the furniture looked ready for a flea market, except for a mahogany record cabinet under the front window and a long, narrow oak bookcase filled with astrology volumes and stacks of old magazines. The walls had a handful of fine prints featuring mountain lakes and deer, but needed a fresh coat of white paint. Peggy had gone to the kitchen to wash her hands. She always washed her hands after a car ride. Wally kept his jacket zipped up because the house was chilly, no surprise for a dump like this. While Ida went to use the toilet down the hall, Wally kept his eye on the Major, who sat on the sofa with a goofy expression on his face. The old fellow really did look pathetic. If that's what Parkinson's does to you, Wally thought, I'd rather get hit by a truck.

The back toilet flushed and Ida hurried out. She opened the door to the basement and switched on the light. "Let's take the Major downstairs with us. There's a rumpus room he can wait in while you're digging."

Peggy came out from the kitchen and went to the basement stairs for a peek. She told Wally, "I don't want to go down there. It looks creepy. I think I'll wait up here."

Ida snapped at her. "No, you won't, honey. We have a tenant hiring our guest room in back and he needs his privacy. It's part of our rental agreement."

Peggy frowned. "Wally, you know I don't like basements."

"Close your eyes if you get scared. We won't be long."

The Major sat like a wax figure on the sofa. Both Ida and Wally were required to get him on his feet and down the basement stairs. Once they got him to the bottom, Ida led the Major off to a small room just off the main basement floor where she switched on another light. Wally heard her speaking to him in a soft, pleasant voice as Peggy called down from the top of the stairs.

"Wally?"

"Yeah?"

"Can't I stay up here?"

"No."

The basement was gloomy and dank, stinking of wood rot and mildew and damp earth. Who was going to rent a room down here? The space was narrow and the ceiling wasn't much more than seven feet high. Better for a garage than a basement apartment. He remembered Ida telling him something about planning to have a wood floor laid over the concrete and Wally thought that was a good idea. A nice polished wood floor with new walls and ceiling, some decent lighting, real furniture.

"Wally!"

"Get down here, Peg."

Wally looked around for the pick and shovel Ida told him were there. His work gloves were in his truck back at the motel. Bringing the Major out into the rain had distracted him. If digging gave him blisters, he'd be damned sorry tomorrow.

Ida came out of the small room and went to the bottom of the stairs and shouted up at Peggy. "Honey, come down here this instant! I can't have you disturbing my tenant."

"I don't see anybody."

"He's in his room sleeping. If you wake him up, there'll be trouble and I can't afford it. Don't stand there, honey. Shut the door behind you and come down."

"Wally?"

"Do as she says."

Peggy scowled as she came down the old stairs into the basement. Ida told Wally his tools were in the other room, so he went to get them. The Major was sitting on a small metal chair, propped up by a ratty pillow at the small of his back. This was more like a plywood box than a rumpus room. Peggy came in and sat on another metal chair across from the Major. She gave Wally the evil eye, so he took the tools and went back into the main basement with Ida.

"I want you to dig right here," she instructed him, pointing to a space near the stairs. "It ought to be roughly four feet on each side, kind of square, if you follow me."

"How deep?"

"Oh, at least five feet. The plumber told me he needed that much to work with, or he'd get fouled up with the pipes we're putting in."

The telephone rang upstairs, but she ignored it.

"All right."

"You better hurry," Ida instructed. "We can't be late for the Major's appointment."

"Well, I'll do my best."

"Thank you."

Once Ida went back into the other room with Peggy and the Major, Wally grabbed the pick and began slugging the cement floor where Ida indicated she wanted the hole. It was rough going. For half an hour, he hardly saw much progress at all besides smashing the old cement into chunks. With the basement so confined, his ears rang from the impact blows and fragments of concrete nicked his face. Eventually he found a rhythm and ripped through the old cement until the pickax struck earth and sank six inches deep. Then Wally grabbed the shovel and began digging the hole.

An hour or so later, Ida came out for a look. Now Wally was down to his ribs, filthy with dirt and sweat when Ida told him, "It's too small. That's not what I'm paying you for. It's got to be bigger than a sink."

"You didn't tell me nothing about a sink. You said four by four." Wally scraped the shovel across the hole, tagging both sides. "This might be a bit bigger, actually."

"Well, it's still too small. The Major's falling asleep and I'm afraid we'll be late to the hospital if you don't hurry up. Your lady friend's getting anxious, too."

Then she walked off.

The basement air smelled vaguely of dead rats and sewage. Wally wiped his brow and rolled the shovel over in his hands and began chopping at the walls, prying slabs of damp soil off, widening the basement hole on all four sides.

The telephone rang again upstairs, but nobody answered.

About twenty minutes later, Ida came out from her rumpus room. "I just got to thinking about it and maybe my plumber said five by five, but I disagreed with him because that's just too wide and I think he wanted to put in a larger unit than we need so I'd prefer you to keep it less than he wanted, but more than you got there."

Wally put down the shovel. "Tell you the truth, Mrs. Long, this is more than I counted on. I know we agreed to fifteen dollars, but digging a hole this big is a lot of work."

"That's your tale," Ida said, smoothing back her hair. She looked drowsy. "Fifteen's what we bargained on, and that's what I'll pay. I can't afford to have you clean me out."

"And I don't care to get taken, either. You specifically said four by four and that's what I dug. Size of a catch basin. Then you came back and told me that's too small, so I made it bigger. Now you want it bigger still, and that's more than we fixed a price to, but you won't kick in another few dollars. It's not fair."

Ida took account of her surroundings and the dirt hole. She stared at Wally, and huffed. "I'll pay you fifteen here and another five when we get back tonight, because fifteen is all I can pay out of what I've got in my purse and I'm not so rich to carry more than I need to spend. I've got too many bills to pay and people chasing me around, and if that's not good enough for you, then you can quit right now and take a train to Wall Street."

Wally had no idea what she meant by that. He said, "You'll pay me another five back at the motel?"

She nodded. "My husband's got that much in his wallet. I know because I gave it to him myself last week after I found Mrs. Crandall's dog and she paid me a reward."

"Well, how much more do you need me to dig?"

Ida came over to the hole. "Oh, just a little deeper. I guess the sides are okay. Can you do that?"

"Sure, I suppose so."

"Thanks, dear. I'm glad I hired you."

After she left, Wally hacked another six inches into the plumbing hole, flattened out the bottom, and skimmed the walls with the edge of the shovel. When he was done, Wally climbed out of the fresh hole, worn to the bone. Next time, he'd ask for twice what the job called for and let the cards fall on his side of the line.

Ida showed Wally where to wash up in the bathroom upstairs. Then they led the Major out of the basement through a door that opened onto the driveway and got back into the Lincoln and drove across the dark city in a cold miserable rain to Mt. Zion Hospital. Ida told him to park at the curb while she went to check on the Major's appointment.

"We're pretty late and I don't want to blame you," she said to Wally as she grabbed her umbrella, "but if his doctor's occupied, it's because your digging caused us to miss him and we might be here a while."

What the hell was she talking about? His fault? "That was a tough job."

"Well, I'm sure it was the best you could do." Ida shut the door and hurried off up the wet sidewalk.

"Did she pay you?" Peggy asked, once Ida had gone into the hospital. Rain began to fall harder now, flooding the driveway around the Lincoln, drizzling down the car windows.

"Not yet," Wally replied. "But don't worry. She will. We got her car."

The Major slurred something from the back seat that Wally didn't understand. "How's that, sir?"

Peggy translated. "He says this is Muriel's auto, not Ida's."

"Oh yeah?" Wally smiled at the Major. "It's a nifty car, sir. A real kick to drive."

Peggy said, "Me and the Major got to know each other while you were digging that hole. He's a pretty wild guy, once you get to know him. I think he's got a crush on me." She smiled at Lonnie. "Don't you, Major?"

"Is Mrs. Long taking good care of him?" Wally wondered who looked after the old guy all day while Ida was out. Her husband didn't seem the nursing type.

Peggy said, "Who knows? That woman's nuts. I don't trust her. You better be sure she pays you tonight."

"I will."

"Does she know you're broke?"

"I'm not broke."

"Darling, digging a hole in someone's basement at this time of the night for fifteen dollars says you're broke."

"To hell with you, too."

The rain softened in the lights of the hospital as Ida came out from the lobby, limping under her umbrella. When she got to the car, Ida told Wally how the Major's doctor was delayed, but they wanted her to bring him, anyhow. "They say the cold out here's not healthy for him, and if I bring him indoors, they'll keep him comfortable until his appointment."

"Are you sure?"

"Are you a doctor?"

"No."

"Then help me get him out of the car."

Wally climbed out into the rain and went around to help the Major up onto the sidewalk. The old guy was stiff as a board, barely able to slide out of the back seat. Wally put the Major's fedora on his head and made sure he was steady. Ida took him by the crook of his arm. She told Wally, "I'm going to wait for him until he's settled with the doctor and I don't know how long that'll be, so you and your young lady can just drive the Lincoln back home. We'll take a taxi cab to the bus depot."

"What about my money?"

"Do you expect the Major to wait here in the rain while I get it out of my purse? We'll be back tomorrow. I'll pay you, then."

"You promised me tonight."

Ida let go of the Major's arm to fish a coin pouch from her purse. She counted out three five-dollar bills and thrust them into Wally's hand. "Good-bye!"

Then Ida grabbed the Major once more and led him off through the drizzling rain toward the hospital stairs. She didn't look back. Wally got back into the Lincoln and started up the motor.

"How much did she pay you?" Peggy asked as Wally drove out into traffic on rainy Lombard Street.

"None of your business."

"You're such a sap, Wally."

JOE KRUEGER STOOD on the wet stoop of his cabin watching a handful of kids from across the motel court tossing a football back and forth in the rain. Kids didn't care about getting wet. Slip and fall, skin your knee, what of it? Nothing'll put you out of action. When Joe was a boy, they used to make a game of throwing rocks at each other in the apple orchards. Marty Gregori hit him once above his ear and knocked him cold. If Joe ever had a son, he'd teach him to duck. One of the kids overthrew his target and the football bounced off the windshield of a station wagon parked out front and rolled into the street. A passing driver laid on his horn as another kid ran out after it.

Joe went back indoors and took a beer from a refrigerator and sat down at the kitchen table. Ida had promised she would be home to cook tonight. It's lousy to eat by yourself. He finished the beer and went to get another. He'd about had enough of the motel and this sorry town and Ida's business. After she'd told him Lonnie's family had come to pick up the Major one night last week to put him into a convalescent home, Joe realized he had no more real day-to-day responsibility at the motel. He began thinking about staying down in San Francisco, where he had steady work and fellows to go around with who enjoyed his company. A marriage that didn't include both people wasn't worth much. Ida could be a neat wife when she remembered she had a husband. The telephone rang all day long with calls from men Joe had never heard of, asking for bills to get paid over work he didn't know anything about. That stupid water softener fellow was coming by every other day now and Ida's bank called over and over again. Ida had cut him out of her affairs since he refused to join her motel venture. No gripes about that. But since his decision, she didn't make love to him like before and wouldn't whisper in bed to him like she used to up at Ocean City before Spagnolini came along and ruined everything.

Joe went up to the office to look for Ida. He found it closed and the yellow neon El Sombrero sign switched off. He thought she might be down in the city with fat Juanita, so he telephoned to the house on Ellington. Ida had been all over the place with her lamebrain sidekick recently, coming and going, coming and going, only she knew where. Joe had quit asking after Westport.

He let the telephone ring a dozen times and hung up. He was hungry. Rather than walking half a mile down Rose Boulevard to the Wrangler Steakhouse, Joe went back to his cabin and took some hard-boiled eggs out of the refrigerator and ate them cold with a piece of toast and a glass of milk. He thought about telephoning his dad to see how he was doing. Joe gave some consideration to the idea of riding a bus out to New Mexico to visit him for a week. He'd been invited a lot and hadn't ever gone. Helping Ida had occupied too much of Joe's time and his dad gave him a warning about getting too involved with her motel business: *"Love's not the answer to everything, son. Just keep your thinking cap on, will you?"* Then he had gotten himself hired to that job on the wharf and this new one at Clay Street, and how was he supposed to get away? When Joe was on Wakde Island, he had written home once a week, sharing some war news about Japs his company had killed and lying about his own involvement with island combat operations. He never wrote a word about digging out airstrips or loading bombs. In fact, Joe really didn't write much at all that was true about the Army Air Corps in the South Pacific. He lied about New Guinea and Manila Bay and Leyte, and once he came back stateside again, he lied about Long Beach and Modesto and Watsonville and Ocean City. Ida lied to Joe and Joe lied to his dad. Honesty is the first casualty of bad choices. Lies collect like unpaid bills. You pay interest on them with the same sleeplessness and dread of being found out.

Joe didn't telephone to his dad that night. Instead he decided to tell Ida he'd help her at the motel one more month, but after that he was calling it quits.

ZELMA WILSON WAS A NAG. Get me a fur coat, take me to Vegas, buy me a new DeSoto, build us a swimming pool. When Bert went out bowling with the fellows, she'd telephone at ten sharp to make sure he was there. If not, she'd call Pelligrino's, and his Elk's lodge, then the police and report him missing. She pestered and pouted when he went down to San Francisco on a business call. Why couldn't she go along and see a movie at the Fox? If he really loved her, he'd take her shopping to Gump's on Union Square. Whenever he did run her about, he was always driving too fast or too slow. If he chose a Chinese restaurant, she wanted a steak. If he chose Italian, she'd rather eat chow mein. His ties were crooked, and his shoes needed polishing. Why couldn't he comb his hair to the left instead of the right? When would he take her to New York City like he'd promised when they were dating? Bert Wilson wasn't the sort who got a divorce. He had been brought up better than that. When her nagging became intolerable, he'd buy a bottle of Scotch and lock the door to his den. They hadn't made love in three years.

Which was how he excused his behavior with Ida Long. Any fellow who goes out on business calls is sure to run across his share of women. Thirty-four years with Zelma had given Bert a license to notice the opposite sex. Ida wasn't a bathing beauty by any stretch, but she had a good figure and a hot glint in her eye and pretty well knew how to get what she wanted. Bert could see that from the moment he laid eyes on her in the driveway of the El Sombrero. Ida was a worker, not some beauty shop honey who kicked and moaned over a drop of sweat. He found her alone, emptying out a metal trashcan in a plain peach housedress and a straw bonnet. She had telephoned his office that morning regarding a busted water softener for the motel the previous owner had installed and asked him to come out and let her know if he had anything better. That's how Bert Wilson did most of his business: face-to-face. Some fellows preferred sitting in their air-conditioned offices working deals on the telephone, but Bert found big flaws in that. How could you tell if a client was earnest over the phone? How could they tell you were on the level and interested in having their business? Once Bert saw the motel, he knew Ida was serious because the property was a wreck. Bert parked his Oldsmobile away from the entrance and got out and introduced himself. First thing she told him was that she wanted to modernize the motel to bring a better clientele than Rose Boulevard ordinarily attracted.

"Most of these motels are dumps," she told him, "and they're hiring out to bums. Better people don't want to associate with bums."

Ida led him on a tour of the motel grounds, cabin by cabin, up and down the dusty palm-shaded motor court. Those rooms she hadn't gotten around to renovating were just awful. The old iron bed frames in a couple of them were rusted and ready to fall apart. Showers were moldy and the floor pans cracked in places. Nearly all of the mirrors had gone cloudy, carpets reeked of mildew and cigarettes, drapes were threadworn and dingy. Ida told Bert that fixing the motel had strapped her for cash, but that she'd been in a terrible jitney accident in San Francisco a few months back and had a lawsuit pending and her insurance settlement, which would take care of most of her bills, and that the Bank of America downtown had generously offered her a loan to cover expenses until her insurance money came through. What would help, she told Bert, was if he'd let her put a thousand dollars down on the water conditioning unit and pay off the balance in three months once she was more settled financially. He told that it would be better for him if she could manage a quick loan for the full amount and she agreed to try.

Bert drove Ida downtown to the Bank of America and went in with her to see a loan officer named Cornwall who handled her accounts. Bert's offer to serve as a credit reference was all she needed to get her five-thousand-dollar loan. Once she came out of her meeting and went to the teller's window, he was shocked to hear Ida ask the girl to fill out a bank check to Wildew Water Conditioning Company for three hundred dollars. Bert tapped Ida on the shoulder. "That's not what we agreed on. You were supposed to pay me two thousand today."

She gently took his hand. "But that's not what this is for, honey. It's just a little payment for all the inconvenience I've put you through, running me across town and standing in for me with the loan department. I'll pay you for the water unit tomorrow. That's what I was talking to Mr. Cornwall about. My attorney telephoned this morning to let me know my insurance check is ready to be mailed here, so that's what I'll pay you with as soon as it arrives. He says he expects it tomorrow, or the day after, at the latest."

Bert felt like a king for the rest of the day. Most fellows in business tend to believe in their own abilities. Confidence breeds success, and success breeds optimism. The trouble was, Bert's good judgment had gone haywire once he laid eyes on Ida Long. Something about her tipped him overboard. Zelma noticed it, too. She drove over to the motel with him one afternoon when Ida telephoned to ask his opinion on a plumber for a new shower installation. Zelma became jealous after Bert gabbed on a little too long about all the swell work Ida had put into the motel. She went to go sit in the car, and when Bert came back to drive them home again, Zelma referred to Ida as a squinty-eyed pygmy and asked if Bert had a crush on her.

He acted shocked. "I don't know what you're talking about. Ida's a customer, and that's all she is."

"Customer my eye! That woman's a fake, I tell you. I know her type. If you get mixed up with her, she'll take you to the cleaners."

"Take me to the cleaners? Look who's talking!"

Anxious to get paid what Ida promised as a down payment on the water softening unit, Bert telephoned on and off for a couple of weeks until he realized she wasn't going to be calling him with news from her insurance company. Then he began dropping over. It took a couple of visits for Bert to catch her, but early one morning he saw Ida watering the potted plants by the front office and pulled into the driveway. Ida put up her story again, apologizing repeatedly for stalling him on the payment.

"It's not my fault, honey, although I take responsibility because I'm not the sort to welsh on a deal, but the bank lost the paperwork on that loan they gave me against my mortgage and they're the ones that promised me your two thousand dollars and they know you need it and told me they won't keep you waiting another week, so help us God. And I'm so sorry about all of this, Bertie, because I taken your unit and used it all this while for almost nothing and I know that, too. But I won't make you wait much longer than another week even if I have to take the money out of my own pocket to pay you and that's a fact."

"It's not that I don't trust you, Ida. You know I do. But I have bills to pay, and my creditors aren't as sympathetic as I am. So if you could telephone the bank and let them know I've come to collect on that unit, I'd sure appreciate it."

She put down the water pot. "All right, I'll do that right now."

Bert followed her indoors and sat down on the lobby sofa and lit a cigarette while Ida went into the back room to make the call. After ten minutes or so, Ida came out again and plopped herself down on the sofa next to Bert and told him, "The fellow who was handling my mortgage account just lost his uncle and had to go to Florida for the funeral.

Another fellow named Mr. Crawford tried to find my papers in their workbook and had no idea where they went, so I asked if there was any way at all to get some money out of them to pay you for what you're due and they told me that would have to be a new account and the manager for those just left for the day and won't be back until Monday because of a vacation he's had coming for a year and hasn't took."

"Why couldn't they just assign someone else to your account for this case? What he said doesn't make any sense."

"Well, I asked just that question myself, and you know what he told me? It's a matter of privacy for my own protection! Can you feature that? They're saving me from my own money." She laughed. "Isn't that funny?"

"It's ridiculous." Bert got up off the sofa. "In fact, I'm going to go down there myself right now and give them a piece of my mind, because it's not just your money they're talking about. It's mine, too, and they ought to be told."

Ida stood, too, and grabbed his arm. "Why, it's the first thing I says to them when they gave me the bad news. But it's just how they do business. Mr. Crawford told me it's a bank rule and there's no exception they can make that won't get them in trouble if they overlook it."

"Well, that's a lot of hooey." Bert took a nervous drag off his cigarette. "I hate to be a grump about this, Ida, but I need my money, and I need it now. Harold Stamos from the cement factory called me three times this morning already wanting to get paid for a job I hired out on Redwood Avenue last month. I've stalled him because I thought you'd come through with enough cash that I could pay what I owed and clean up my books. Now I don't know what to say. This is all a big mess."

"I'm sorry, honey," Ida said, touching Bert's hand. "I guess I have to blame myself for trusting those local bank folks like I did. What I ought to have done is had my lawyer advance me the money from his office in San Francisco. That would've been the easy fix."

"Why don't we just drive down there and get it? You could call and tell the guy we're on our way. That way this'll all be settled and we won't have to worry about it anymore. What do you say?"

She thought for a moment. "Well, so long as you don't mind the ride."

"Hell, I'll drive to Alaska if that's what it takes. Like I said, I got to get that money today."

An hour later they were crossing the Golden Gate Bridge, admiring the view over a windy San Francisco Bay, sailboats and seagulls out everywhere. Rushing on into the busy city along Lombard Street, Bert had no idea what was coming because he never could have predicted it in a million years. At Ida's attorney's office on Montgomery Street, he waited out in the corridor while Ida went in for her insurance check. When she came out of his office, tears had smeared her mascara and her hands were empty. Heading down the staircase to the street, she told Bert, "That fellow won't pay me a filthy cent until the case is settled and he won't work on the case until next month."

"So, you didn't get the money?"

"No, but we can still go to my bank here in the city because I put in for a loan last month and I'm positive it went through. Unless you'd rather go home and forget all about it."

"What sort of loan?"

"Twenty-thousand dollars. I applied for it so Joe and me could fix up the motel and establish ourselves down here, too, like Jews do, you know, borrowing from as many places as you can to get your credit rating. Once I showed them the papers from the motel, they told me it'd be a sure thing. Do you want to go?"

"Well, for christsakes, I ran you here to get that check from your lawyer, and now that you don't have it, I suppose there's no other choice, is there?"

Since Ida's leg was bothering her too much to walk, Bert drove them over to California Street and smoked a cigarette while Ida went to get the money. Half an hour later, she came out of the bank and told him that her loan wasn't redeemable today. She claimed she had ranted and raved, even threatening to withdraw her savings account, and when nobody budged, there wasn't anything left to do but go to her stock broker and sell the stocks she'd bought after the War.

She told Wilson, "It's not a smart thing financially to do, Bertie, but I believe that fair is fair and I want you to know I'm honest and if I have to sell some stocks to cover my debt, well, that's what has to be done."

Bert knew Ida was hoping he'd tell her to forget about it and pay him later, but he needed the money right now. So he started up the car and they drove another few blocks downtown and parked near the Pacific Coast Stock Exchange. She asked him once again to wait in the car while she went to do her business. Bert switched on the radio and listened to Faron Young and thought about Ida's figure. If it weren't for this damned money situation, he could blow her to dinner and have a good time. He knew she'd cuddle if he pressed the issue. Just thinking about her made him sharp. Lots of women flirted with him, but if he ever got Ida far enough away from town, he bet she'd go the limit. And nobody needed to know except the two of them.

Another quarter of an hour went by and Bert became bored of sitting in the Oldsmobile, so he got out and crossed the street to find Ida. He went into the stock exchange building and asked at the desk where she'd gone. The reception didn't recall seeing her at all. Irritated now, he went to use the toilet. After that, he smoked a cigarette, waited around for another ten minutes, then went upstairs and found her sitting on a bench, head in her hands.

"Ida?"

She looked worn out. "Bertie, they told me I couldn't sell the stock now, that it was listed under a domain I never heard of and that I'd take a bad penalty if I tried to, so I can't give you the money today, and that's just all there is to it. I'm so ashamed."

"Well, this is a hell of a deal, Ida. How can you be fixed up with a bank and a stockbroker that won't give up your money when you ask for it? I just can't understand that."

"I can't either," Ida said, taking Bert's hand and holding it to her teary cheek. "It's not fair at all. It's my money, not theirs."

"What can we do? My creditors'll fry my ass if I come back tomorrow with an empty pocketbook. It's not how any sane fellow does business if he expects to keep his head above water."

"What if I put up some of my Glickman stocks in your name? Say, five thousand dollars worth? Would that help? It's not cash, but it's practically as good. Then you could have a loan from your own bank in cash that'd cover those fellows chasing you around and we'd be square when my insurance check comes in."

Bert figured her stock security had to be worth twice the value of his water unit and he'd be cheating Ida if he let her give it to him, but he couldn't help himself. Money was money. "Well, I can't say that's a bad idea. If you think it's fair."

"I can't be complaining when it's your money that's owed and my promise of payment." Ida got up from the bench. "Let's find a phone so I can call my broker."

"Well, it's sure generous, even with what you owe me."

"I think it's only fair, honey. You've been so patient."

Bert relaxed on the bench and lit up another cigarette while Ida went off to phone her stockbroker. He felt a little guilty because, as a matter of fact, that water conditioning unit wasn't even a new one, not that he'd ever let on to Ida about that. It's how business was done. So long as the unit was working fine, where it came from wasn't much of an issue. Now, if the customer asked, then you went ahead and let her know the status of what she was buying. And if a problem with the unit arose, then it'd get fixed free of charge, and if that didn't pan out, you'd go ahead and install a new one. No harm, no foul. When Bert was new to the business, he thought the whole scheme smelled fishy, but once he saw how everyone was doing it as a normal course of the trade, well, he just went along with it. Now it seemed as normal as breathing. He'd even stuck an older unit into his sister's house.

After a few minutes, Ida came back down the hall with a sour expression on her face and mumbling to herself. When Bert got up, she told him, "Honey, they won't let me buy more stock until I've paid off what I've already ordered. When I tried to explain how you loaned me some money and the stocks were to help pay off my debt, they suggested I take out another loan to cover half of that, and if I did so, they'd advance me the rest. So I telephoned to my bank and they agreed to give me the money, but I can't get it until next week, and my stock broker won't let me have those shares for you unless I can cover it with a thousand dollars in cash, which I don't have right now and they know it. We positively ought to've stayed home and wrung this out over the telephone. Now we're stuck having to take a drive to Sacramento if you really need to get your money today."

"Sacramento? Good grief! Are you kidding? Why?"

"Well, I have a lock box up there from when me and Joe lived at Elk Grove before we came to San Francisco. I ought to have enough cash in it to trade for those Glickman shares, if you're willing to ride us up there."

This was nuts. Bert checked his watch. Half past ten. Well, if he and Ida left now, they could make Sacramento and still be home by five o'clock. Why not? Besides, he enjoyed her company. She smelled nice. Things could be worse.

They drove the Oldsmobile up to the state capitol past miles of agricultural fields and roadside fruit and vegetable stands. Ida chattered non-stop about her childhood in Germany and how she decided to become a nurse. Bert didn't even try to keep his eyes off her bosom. A couple of miles outside of Sacramento, Ida asked if they might stop so she could get something to eat at one of those drive-up restaurants just off the highway. Burt wasn't hungry, but he needed a cup of coffee to perk him up, so he swung the Oldsmobile into the parking lot and shut off the motor. Ida got out and went into the restaurant without waiting for Bert. He guessed she needed the toilet, so he locked the car and followed her inside. First thing he did was telephone home to tell Zelma he might be late for supper and not to wait for him. Naturally she wanted to know whom he was with. When he told her, she hit the roof and hung up.

Ida came out of the toilet and chose a seat at a booth near the front window facing the highway and ordered a grilled cheese sandwich from their young waitress. Bert asked for a cup of coffee with cream and sugar, and a jelly doughnut. He loosened his tie. Ida apologized once again for failing to pay off her debt on the water conditioning unit and Bert accepted her apology, explaining his own urgency with those fellows at the cement contractors. "They're sonsofbitches when it comes to credit, I tell you, but they do a hell of a job."

"I hate to be a bother," Ida said, her eye on the road outside, "but I hope you trust me."

"Sure I do," Bert told her, his own focus on the gentle curve of Ida's neck where a brown wisp of hair curled round her ear. She was cuter than Zelma. If he didn't quit looking, he'd have to kiss her. "This is just business. If I wasn't so fond of you, we wouldn't be up here. It's a pretty long haul today."

"Bertie?"

"Yeah?" He loved when she called him Bertie. It meant she had the hots for him, too.

"I don't have any money in a bank up here. That's nothing but a story I told you to see if you'd drive me here."

"Pardon?" He thought he heard her wrong.

Ida reached across the table and took his hand. "Honey, I positively needed to test you over how much you cared for me and my problems. I know it's not fair, but, you see, I've had fellows cheat me all my life, so it's hard to trust anyone besides my husband these days. That money I told you I had up here is out in Pine Meadows, Wyoming, and I'll take a bus there today and get what I owe you and we don't have to do no more business if that's your preference, but I like you too much to tell a lie and this is the truth, absolutely."

Bert was stunned. What could he say? A hundred miles on the road for nothing? "What about that stock broker fellow? That Glickman stock?"

Ida watched carefully as a couple of white Ford sedans cruised by outdoors, then told him, "Bertie, I'd make that trade in a second if I had the money to do it with. Honest, I would. That's why I'm going to take the bus to my lock box in Pine Meadows and get what I owe you. It's only fair."

"What's it doing out there?"

"We used to live there, me and Joe, for about a year or so after he got out of the service. His family's all around those parts and he opened a bank account we never touched with fifty thousand dollars, which is all we'd saved between the two of us before we married."

"And you'll go all the way there by yourself to get some of that money for me?"

"Sure I will, because it's only right with everything you've done to help me this month. I don't mind that one bit. I'm a fair person and I want you to know that."

Ida had the hook in him, all right, but what else could he do? Go back to town and call his creditors and tell them they wouldn't be getting any payment out of him today? He'd sound worse than Ida. No, in fact, when he thought about it, his only course of action was one Ida had just laid out for him. They'd climb back into the Oldsmobile and go get his money. It'd be one hell of a long trip, but once he came back from Wyoming and told those fellows how far he'd driven to settle his debts, they'd have a whole lot more respect for him than they did this morning.

"Tell you what," Bert said, picking up the tab for lunch. "Forget about taking a bus. I'll drive you there myself."

"Are you sure?" Ida said, grabbing her purse. "I must be awful to get you involved in my problems. You don't hate me, do you?"

"No, honey, I think you're just swell." Bert smiled as he got up from the booth. "And I like riding around with you. No reason we can't enjoy ourselves, is there?"

Back on the interstate, they headed northeast for Reno. Yesterday, Bert would have told Ida to take a bus and wire him the two thousand dollars when she arrived. Today was different. Somehow, he couldn't get himself rid of her and didn't mind the feeling. He knew this crazy excursion wasn't only about paying off a debt. If somehow things worked out where he ended up romping on her, well, that's what he really wanted, didn't he? Money wasn't everything.

They had a nice drive over the Sierra Nevada. Bert adored the view of the buttes across a hundred miles of ponderosa pines and the blue mountain sky sparkling on the cold waters of Donner Lake. The day was warm and he left the windows rolled down and hung his arm out into the auto draft while Ida talked non-stop about living in San Francisco and her Rosicrucian friends and how one day Bert ought to take a drive with her down to see the Healing Temple at the Oceanside Order. Every so often, he caught Ida looking back over her shoulder at the traffic behind them. Did she think someone was following them?

Stopping just once for gas and a visit to the toilet, they reached Reno in just under three hours. On the high desert across the Nevada state line, trees were few and the grassy hillsides were brown and rocky. The town was drab and homely, lots of small plain homes and a number of casinos, chintzy hotels, and whorehouses. One night in Reno was usually all Bert could stomach. He parked on a street outside one of the gambling houses and they went into the restaurant and ordered a steak dinner. Bert also had a couple of drinks, after which he decided to play some blackjack. Drinking always gave him the itch to gamble. Ida told him that gambling was a sin where she came from and she'd rather sit out in the Oldsmobile and read her astrology papers. After she left, Bert won about forty dollars, had some pie and coffee at the snack bar, and went back out to the car where he found Ida in the front seat, sleeping like a baby.

When Ida woke again just outside of Elko, she told Bert she was thirsty and asked if he could stop somewhere she could get a Coca-Cola. About ten miles ahead, he found a Richfield station. Pulling up to the pump, he told Ida, "You go have yourself a bottle of pop while I gas up."

"Don't use your credit card."

"Why not?"

"It'll leave a trail," Ida told him. "That's not smart."

"What do I care about being smart in the middle of the desert?"

"Think about your wife. Pay cash and don't use the card."

"I don't want to spend my cash."

"All right." Ida dipped into her purse and took out a fifty-dollar bill. "Save me the change."

Then she went off to the Coke machine, jangling a handful of coins from her purse. Bert broke the fifty to buy gas because she owed him that money, anyhow. If she wanted to pay for gas with his money out of her own pocket, that was fine with him, but why care about credit card receipts? He stood on the highway side watching a line of eighteen-wheelers roar past to the east, kicking up a long hot cloud of dust.

Ida drank half her Coke by the icebox and headed for the restroom. Her breasts jiggled under that sundress she wore. Zelma's titties were too small to jiggle. Curious about how Ida's bosom felt to squeeze, Bert got back into the Oldsmobile and fired up the motor. Maybe they could stop somewhere and he'd find out. Then Ida came out of the toilet and they drove back onto the dark highway toward Salt Lake City.

After a few miles, Bert spoke up. "That's a cute dress."

Ida sipped from the Coke bottle.

He added, "I really like it."

She smiled. "I know you do."

"Oh yeah?"

"Sure, you been staring at me all day now. A girl notices these things."

"A pretty damned good-looking girl, too," Bert told her, "if you don't mind my saying."

"I don't mind."

Bert felt a flush. "It's not like there's any law that says a fellow can't tell a girl she's a looker if he thinks she is, you know."

"I know it." She took another sip of her Coke.

"Well, you're a looker." His palms were sweaty on the steering wheel as he became aroused. Her perfume seemed to flood his brain.

"So are you," Ida's lips murmured into his ear. She kissed his neck, then slid back and took a long look down the highway at a couple of cars coming up behind them. "Maybe we ought to pull off the road."

"Huh?"

She tickled his ear. "Let's park."

"Yeah?"

"Don't you want to?"

"Sure." Bert steered the car off the road into the desert. He switched off the headlamps. "You're driving me crazy, Ida," he told her, as he shut off the engine. "I can't drive unless I kiss you."

"What're you waiting for," Ida giggled, "a telegram?"

"Nope," he said, then grabbed Ida and pulled her close and kissed her square on the mouth. They kissed and kissed. Bert thought he'd fly right out of his pants. Zelma hadn't kissed him like that in years. Ida ran her fingers in his hair and bit his earlobe and rubbed his chest with the palm of her hand. He spread his fingers wide and grabbed her breast and could hardly believe how soft it felt. Ida shrugged off her sweater and slipped her fingers inside his shirt and teased him. He pressed her deep into the seatback and tried to move on top of her, but there wasn't enough room.

"What do you say we get into the back?" he offered, so consumed by lust he was barely able to speak.

"How come?" She giggled again. "Are you sleepy?"

"I'm nuts for you, honey, that's why. What do you say?"

"Are you sure it's not the liquor making your proposal?"

He laughed. "Hell, no!"

"'Cause you're drunker than a hoot owl and I don't think it's funny."

"I'm not drunk."

"From where I'm sitting, you are, and that's not something to brag about."

"Who's bragging? I just want to kiss you again."

Ida sat back with a smirk on her face. "Do you know how many men have told me that?"

"Six?"

"There you go, smarty pants. Now I wouldn't kiss you for a thousand dollars."

"Well, you owe me twice that, so you better plan on more than kissing tonight."

Ida got out of the Oldsmobile. So did Wilson. A cool wind blew across the desert, kicking up dust. A pair of long trailer trucks rumbled past on the highway.

Ida told Bert, "No man's going to touch me. I'm married to my husband and no man ever — "

Before she could finish her sentence, Bert took her into his arms and kissed her hard on the mouth. She was right about the liquor and he knew it, but didn't care. "Let's get in the backseat, honey. I want you so bad I can't stand it."

She laughed. "Oh yeah? Like this?" She fingered her blouse, flicking a button loose, exposing more of her bosom.

He grabbed her for another kiss, jamming his tongue down her throat.

Ida squirmed free, wiping a hand across her mouth. She spat into the dirt. "Listen here, buster! You're crazier than a bedbug. You can't do this. You're a married man. What's wrong with you? You're drunk. I think you better straighten up and go back to driving."

"I can't drive another mile unless you make me happy, and that's all there is to it. Let's have a party. What do you say?"

"Out here in the middle of the desert? Are you trying to be funny?"

"Why? Who'd see us?" Bert's hands were shaking and his mouth was dry. He couldn't remember the last time he'd felt so sexed up for a woman.

"I would," Ida said, calmly, "and God would know, too. His rules keep my body for Joe and him alone. You ought to know that. I bet your wife does."

By now, Bert didn't much care about anyone's rules, much less Zelma's. He had driven Ida halfway across Nevada and wanted some payback for his trouble. He told her, "I don't want your body. I want to do something else."

He opened his pants.

Ida gasped. "What do you expect me to do with that?"

Bert brought himself close, nearly bumping into her. "Don't tell me you've never seen one before. Take a guess."

"Not out here where anyone can see, I won't. What do you take me for?"

Bert was going nuts now. "Well, let's get into the backseat."

"Are you going to force me?"

He frowned. What did she take him for? "Why do you say that? Do you want me to? Some girls like that kind of thing."

"Not me, but if you have a gun, I guess there's not much I can do out here alone, is there?"

He thought a faint trace of a smile crossed her lips, so he put a swagger into his voice. "Well, then I'll tell you I got a .38 in the glove box. Are you going to make me take it out? Because I will, if you don't start behaving. Believe me, I don't have a lot patience right now."

"What do you have a gun for? Are you a marshal?"

"Well — " Bert fumbled to pull out his wallet. Flipping it open, a couple of cards fell to the ground, one of which had a police shield stamped on it.

Ida's eyes popped wide open. "Oh, you're with the Revenue Department, huh? That's the FBI! I knew you weren't some ordinary fellow from that day we met."

Bert stuffed the cards back into his wallet. "Yeah, well, it's not something I'm supposed to spread around. We have rules about secrecy, you know."

What the hell was he telling her? That card came with an application to a cop magazine called *Officials & Revue*. Is this what it took to get under her skirt?

Ida backed up and opened the rear door of the Oldsmobile, keeping her eye on Wilson. She didn't seem scared or worried in the least. Some women liked sex more than men did, or so Bert had heard fellows say down at the bowling alley. Not that he'd ever met one of that crowd. Zelma acted like she was on a housewife's payroll whenever Bert mounted her. She'd pretend to be heaving with passion as Bert did his business on her, but any fool with half an eye for true passion could see she had less interest in sex than for vacuuming the den. There were sluts up and down Rose Boulevard of all ages on the weekends who knew more about sex than Bert did, mostly because they got more of it. Why was it so tough for a fellow to get a grin out of a girl once her clothes came off? Love was a god-damned mystery.

But Ida had a smile on her face when she planted herself on the rear seat of the Oldsmobile and hiked up her skirt.

"Sure you want me to touch you?" Bert asked huskily, as he stood over her. He stroked himself stiff. Another line of trucks roared by on the highway. Wind gusted across the cold desert night.

"Not with that," Ida warned. "I told you, my body's been given for Joe, and him alone."

"Well, then what do you mean?"

Ida looked Bert in the eye. "Use your finger."

"Yeah?"

She nodded. "I guess you know where to put it."

Now he grinned. "Sure, I do."

Then Bert nudged her panties aside and began diddling her like they were kids at a drive-in movie. That wasn't half bad. In fact, he got a kick out of it. She squirmed like a worm on a hook. Without the wind blowing, someone up on the road could've heard her moaning. Ida was louder than Zelma, who rarely peeped at all. Bert went at her like a fiend and she spread her legs wider yet. He worked three fingers inside of her and had plenty room for more. That's when she mentioned the Coke bottle.

"You serious?"

Her voice was dusky and wet. "I dropped it by the front seat and I can't think of anything nastier than that and if you try to use it I might scream, so you better be sure it's what you want to do."

"I've never done that before."

"Me neither and anyone can see why, but I'm not your wife and you can't do that other thing and I know which is worse tonight and you do, too."

That was the craziest thing a woman had ever asked Bert to do to her, but he did it, anyway, and decided it wasn't half bad, even if the idea was nasty. Ida took to it better than he hoped and closed her eyes mostly and made sounds he'd never heard from a woman after she told him where else to put his finger. Then they both got tired and Bert tossed the Coke bottle out into the desert, smashing it on a rock, and let her grab him for good and all, and that was that.

An hour later, they crossed the state border into Utah.

After that, Bert had enough of driving. He'd drunk six cups of coffee and still had a hard time keeping the car on the road. He woke Ida up and suggested to her that they hire a plane at Salt Lake and fly onto Wyoming. She agreed and they boarded the noon flight. Bert hadn't been this far east since his father had taken him fishing out to Coeur d'Alene when he was a kid. Sailing over the plains at twenty thousand feet aboard the DC-3, he could hardly recall seeing such beautiful country. His frustration at getting dragged all over the west melted away as they flew on through the clear blue skies. With just one stop halfway, the DC-3 circled down to land at a cold Cheyenne airfield two and a half hours after taking off from Salt Lake City.

"Soon as we get into the terminal," Bert told Ida as they disembarked, "you go to the telephone and call the bank and tell them we're coming. That way we can be in and out again before they close."

An icy wind blew across the tarmac as Bert followed Ida indoors. After sceing she had enough change for the telephone, he went to smoke a cigarette. Frustration burned his gut as he thought about this stupid bank problem and the money Ida owed him. Sure, he'd gone crazy with her out there in the desert, and maybe that hadn't been the best idea he'd ever had, but now he needed to get his goddamned money and go home.

Ida sat at a telephone beside the terminal coffee shop, speaking with the operator when Bert came up on her. She was scribbling a phone number onto the back of a map of Wyoming. "Yes, well, dear, that's the number I already tried and I was connected to a feed store...Huh? No, 3-2-3-8. Yes, that's the one... Are you positive?... Okay, because I'm not rich and I can't call every number in this state." She looked up at Bert. "They given me the wrong number twice so far and I don't believe they know what they're doing out here."

"Well, what's the name of the bank?"

"Pine Meadows Savings & Loan."

"Is that here in Cheyenne?"

Ida shook her head as she dialed another number. "Hello? Yes, I'm trying to reach the accounts department of your bank. Pardon? Well, what time did they close? I have half past three and most banks stay to business until four o'clock. . . . Yes, well, that won't help me, now will it? Well, same to you. And thanks for nothing."

She slammed down the phone.

Bert glared at her. "Let me guess: they're closed."

Ida stood up. "They told me to be there first thing in the morning and they'll pour us a cup of coffee and turn over the money, absolutely."

"So you say."

Bert was trapped and he knew it. After riding a bus up the highway to Pine Meadows, he and Ida found the Ranger Motel in a shelter of fir trees just off the highway and took a couple of rooms for appearance's sake. While Ida was outdoors sorting through her purse, Bert asked the motel operator to give them rooms as far apart as possible. He just thought he needed a break from Ida. But then they went out to dinner at a restaurant just across the road and, after a few drinks,

Bert became sentimental about her and invited Ida to the picture show when they finished eating.

"Not tonight, mister," Ida told him, cutting into her steak. "Who do you think you are? Rock Hudson? I know what you want to do in the dark."

Bert finished off his latest martini and left the olive. "Now that's a fine opinion you have of me, seeing as how we've just driven half way across the country together."

"Well, it's the truth, isn't it?" She laughed. "You know I've got the intuition and it positively tells me to go back to my room and lock the door. Besides, you're still drunk."

"No, I'm not."

"That's not soda water you're drinking, mister. I absolutely never seen a fellow put it down like you do."

"Well, I'm not drunk."

"That's your tale." She laughed loud enough to turn heads in the small lamp-lit dining room.

Bert felt like slugging her. Instead, he reached into his jacket and took out a bottle of white pills he'd gotten from Roger Halliday at the Elks Lodge last week.

"What're those?" Ida asked, as Bert popped a couple into his mouth.

"Do-it-yourself-sober-up," he told her. "So I don't need to hear anything else about my drinking from you. Now, do you want to go to a show or not?"

"Not with you, honey."

"What's with this hard-to-get routine all of a sudden? Aren't we friends anymore?"

"You're crazier than a bedbug. Maybe I ought to telephone my husband and tell him what you tried to do to me out there in the desert."

"Tried to do?"

Ida smiled. "How about buying me some pie à la mode?"

After dessert, Bert escorted Ida back across the highway to the motel, and went to have a word with the manager. There wasn't a clock in his room and Bert needed to be up by seven to shower and eat breakfast before driving over to the bank when it opened at nine. He didn't trust Ida to get him there on time. Something about that woman drove him crazy enough to ride beside her for eighteen hours and have a jump in the car like they did, but another thing made Bert ask the motel manager to keep an eye on her. She was beginning to spook him.

Bert watched television until the stations signed off one after another and he was left staring at a snowstorm of static, but couldn't sleep. Those funny pills he'd taken to fight the liquor gave him a buzz and kept him up. At half past two, he heard a knock on his door.

"Yeah?"

"It's me, Bertie. Put your pants on and open the door. I got something for you."

"What's that?"

"Open up and I'll show you."

Oh brother, now what? Bert got out of bed and retrieved his trousers from the chair. Zipping them up, he went to the door and propped it open with the chain still fastened.

Ida was holding a coffee pot and a couple of magazines. "Can't I come in?"

"Well, I'm pretty tired," Bert told her with a big yawn. "And it's kind of late. I guess it's probably better if you don't. We've got a lot to do in the morning."

Ida nodded at his television set flickering static. "By the way, I have more stations on the TV back in my room. Why don't you come and watch it with me?"

"Ida, we have the same antenna and the same frequency as the rest of the motel. Everything's the same."

"That's your tale. Come on over and take a look for yourself. It positively works better in my room." She gave him a smile. "I don't have cooties."

Bert couldn't quite put his finger on it, but something about Ida wasn't right and he didn't trust her. "Like I said, I'm dead tired and I've had a long hard day and I want to get rested up for tomorrow."

"Are you still drunk?"

"Huh?"

"My husband knew fellows in the service that drank so much they couldn't get to sleep unless they was passed out and I wonder if that's your trouble, too. You're alcoholic."

"Ida, you better go back to your room and leave me alone, all right? It's too late for this."

"How about if I run a bath for you in my cabin? When I was a little girl and had the shakes and couldn't sleep, Momma used to run a hot bath and make me soak till I was out in no time at all. It's worth a try, don't you think?"

Bert watched a Ford truck loaded with baling wire rumble past on the road out of town. A cold wind gusted in the motor court. "I'll see you in the morning, Ida."

"Well, if you had your wife all the way back in the woods where they put me, would you leave her there by herself? Tell me that."

"You're not my wife."

Ida scowled at him. "No, I'm not, and I'm glad of it, because I don't know that I could put up with everything you done to me since we left town. I have more self-respect than that."

"Good night, Ida."

Whatever worries Ida had left him with at night didn't carry over to morning, and Bert knocked on her door at eight o'clock after he had showered and shaved with a razor he borrowed from a fellow at the front desk. She didn't answer. Bert walked around to the back of the cabin to the bathroom window and listened for a shower running. When he didn't hear anything, he went up to the office to see if Ida had left any messages for him. The desk manager told Bert that a long distance call had come in for him from a Mrs. Long asking him to stay there until she finished some business she had to take care of at noon. She'd be back afterwards.

"That was it? That's all she said?"

"Yes."

"How'd she sound?"

"I don't know what you mean by that."

"Forget it," Bert said, heading for the office door. "I'll be back later on. If she calls again, let her know I'm still here."

Bert ate a leisurely breakfast of ham and eggs, toast and coffee, then found a bowling alley up the street from the bank and spent most of the morning rolling ten pins. A fellow from Billings in town on a business call had some drinks with him at lunch and they both shared horror stories about wives who weren't sympathetic to the real problems of earning a living these days. He also told Bert about a scrumptious lady in Grand Junction he'd been romping the past couple years. He said she was ugly as a mud fence, but knew fourteen good sexual positions. Bert didn't tell him anything about Ida. The less said about her, the better.

A little after one o'clock, Bert went back to the motel and knocked at Ida's door. When no one answered, he tried the office again and found a different manager on duty and had to explain his situation with Ida all over again.

"She was behaving sort of strange last night," Bert told him, "and since she's not answering the door, I thought maybe you could help me out."

"What do you want me to do?"

"Well, I'd like to have a look in her cabin."

The manager shook his head. "We're private here and folks know that."

"Look, I just want to be sure she's okay. Nothing else."

"All right, but if she won't come out to see you, we'll have no business asking her to do so."

Bert took out a cigarette and lighted up. "Sure."

At Ida's cabin, the manager rapped at the door. He waited a few seconds and tried again. "Mrs. Long?"

Bert went to the window, but Ida had her curtains drawn shut. The manager banged at the door. "Mrs. Long? This is Floyd from the office. Are you in there? Hello? Are you all right?"

Bert took a drag off his cigarette. "What did I tell you?"

"Are you sure she's in there?"

"No, and that's just it. See, I can't imagine where she'd go. We had a bank appointment today."

"And she didn't leave you a note or anything?"

"Nope."

"Because we don't ordinarily go into our guest cabins unless it's an emergency. People like their privacy."

"I'm sure they do."

"But you think she might be in some trouble or such, right?"

"Maybe." Bert shrugged, finishing his cigarette. "Like I said, she was acting a little crazy last night, so I can't tell you what she might be up to, only that we were supposed to meet for breakfast and then go over to her bank. Now she's not answering her door. That's all I know."

"All right." The manager took out his key ring and unlocked the door. "Mrs. Long? Are you in there?"

When he got no response, the manager went in, Bert trailing behind him. The room was empty. No purse, no clothes, some magazines strewn about. The bed looked as if Ida hadn't slept there at all.

Nothing in the bathroom, either. None of the towels had been used. Bert was shocked. He sat down on the bed. "Well, I'll be damned."

"You said you saw her last night?"

Confused, Bert nodded. "Yeah, she came to my room in the middle of the night and wanted to watch TV. She was acting sort of odd, so I said I was tired, and she left."

"Well, I don't know what to tell you, but she's not here now."

"I can see that."

Deciding to put Ida's story to the test, he went back up the highway to her bank and asked to see one of the account officers. He showed his identification and related most of the events of the past twenty-four hours, finishing with the simple question of whether or not Ida Long had been to the bank that day. He was told flatly that no one there had ever heard of her. That was all Bert needed to know. Within the hour, he telephoned to the airport to check on flights that evening to Salt Lake City and discovered a seat still available. He bought a bus ticket to Cheyenne and rode down the pine-shrouded highway after supper. Two hours later, Bert Wilson was heading home.

EMILIO SANCHEZ WAS ALSO HEADED WEST. He had gone out to Omaha to help his uncle build a bedroom addition on a new ranch house and then do a few weeks' work on a big construction site at a downtown hotel. He had planned on the hotel job paying his bills for a couple of months, but that went bust over a union dispute four days after he finished his uncle's addition. Now he was going home to his wife and daughters flat broke.

What Sanchez needed was gas money. Without that, he had no chance of driving any farther west than Salt Lake City. If he found someone to share the expense of the trip, he'd have some hope of getting home this month. So he got the idea of advertising at a bus depot. He drew up a sign that read: **San Francisco Bound — Need a Rider** and planned to hold it up next to the ticket counter and see what happened. He intended to try Cheyenne first, and if that didn't pan out, he'd go down to Denver where there were more people. Not everyone liked riding a bus.

Sanchez got lucky. Not much more than a couple of hours had passed at the Cheyenne bus depot before a short pasty-white brunette in a plain pink dress came up to him, introducing herself as Maria Cooper and telling him that she would buy gas for the car and pay him another fifteen dollars if he promised to drive straight through to San Francisco.

"My husband just passed away in Knoxville," she explained, "and I've been invited to stay with my sister in Daly City and babysit for her while I'm straightening out my affairs. I've had the awfullest backache sitting on that bus from Tennessee, so I'd be grateful to travel with you."

Apparently she only had a purse to carry because her suitcase had been taken to the wrong bus at St. Louis. Sanchez led her out of the depot to his Dodge and let her sit beside him as he drove up onto the highway. Most women were nervous traveling with a strange man, but Maria Cooper acted as if she and Sanchez had been schoolmates, chattering on for hours across the vast expanse of flat grass prairie earth. She was good company for Sanchez, who missed his wife and felt lonely so far from home. He had no need of wayward women or booze parties in city hotel rooms and told her so as the miles rolled on to the west. She seemed appreciative of that, affirming her own fidelity to the poor fellow she had just buried.

"Oscar had a cancer in his lungs from coal mining, yet I didn't hear one peep out of him until he couldn't breathe right and I taken him to the doctor who told Oscar he was finished. We never spent one week apart since the day we married and I can't get over the fact that it's you and not him sitting beside me just now. I suppose some of us don't believe we're meant to take our steps two by two, but I'd have a quarrel with anyone who thinks we're better off on our own. That's just how I'm made."

Sanchez drove all day without stopping, and he let Maria nap in the backseat when he noticed her nodding off outside of Salt Lake City. Then he took an hour himself under the shade tree of a roadside stand while Maria bought them cheese sandwiches and filled a thermos with hot coffee. She also offered a plan to help pay her way west. Passing through half a dozen small towns, Maria had Sanchez stop at the local Catholic churches, where she got out and went to borrow money, and left one church with a credit slip for a tank full of gasoline.

Climbing back into the old Dodge, she told Sanchez, "Charity is a blessing, honey, that some forget came from the mouth of our Lord. 'Though I have all faith, so that I could move mountains, and have not charity, I am nothing.'" She smiled sweetly. "I absolutely could see your generosity the instant I laid eyes on you. You're good as gold, and I'm so pleased we're helping one another. I tell you, it's a rare thing in the world these days."

Sanchez agreed as he wheeled his automobile out onto the road again. Maria Cooper offered to share half of the gas money she received from the church when they reached San Francisco if she had any left over, and he thanked her for that, too. She was quite a woman, all right. Quietly, Sanchez recited a prayer of divine gratitude his mother had taught him when he was a boy in San Antonio.

Then they drove on toward evening.

Maria crawled into the backseat and fell asleep again. Sanchez drank coffee from the thermos. About midnight, he steered the Dodge off the highway into a filling station at Carlin, Nevada. The gas needle was almost on empty. He shut the engine off and woke Maria when he honked for the station attendant. A light was on inside the garage, but nobody came out, so Sanchez went to see if the fellow was sleeping. He knocked on the door and waited. The road was quiet and empty. He knocked again and when nobody answered, Sanchez looked across the road to the filling station on the other side where he could hear a radio faintly playing in the office. Maria stepped out of the Dodge and patted down her dress. She looked dizzy.

Sanchez decided to go ask about gas at the other station in case the fellow here had gone to bed for the night. "Keep knocking," he told Maria, "in case he's sitting in the john. If he comes out, we'll buy the gas here. There's no reason to move the car if we don't have to."

"You better give me some money."

Sanchez frowned. "You told me you'd buy. That was our deal. I've done the driving."

"I don't remember no such thing, mister, and I don't have a dime to my name."

"You got money from those churches."

"That's your tale. They only gave me that gas slip you used."

"Why, you're a cheater! You told me you had money. I ought to let you out here for good."

"You won't do nothing of the kind, because I'll get the gas. Just you watch."

"You get the goddamned gas, lady, or you're walking!"

Furious, Sanchez crossed the road to the other filling station. There were car lights in the distance and a stiff wind rising through the dark trees on both sides of the narrow highway. He hoped to strike some sort of bargain for a tank of gas. That woman was a liar. He had half a mind to knock her down. Indoors, the radio clicked off and Sanchez heard someone shut a door. Then he saw a fellow walk into the office, so he rapped on the window and the fellow waved and came outdoors into the wind.

"How can I help you?"

"I need some gas."

"Is that your car over there?"

"Sure, but I guess the station's closed. I honked and nobody came out."

"Well, Jimmy's there now," the fellow said. "Is that your lady?"

Sanchez looked back across the road and saw Maria standing under the pole light at the garage door with a fellow in overalls. He was kneeling over Sanchez's box of tools. The trunk of the Dodge was open. Sanchez began yelling. Maria saw him coming and ran off into the thicket behind the filling station. That was that. The station attendant reported the incident to the police, but Emilio Sanchez never saw Maria Cooper again.

ELLISON HAD JUST COME into the office from the coffee shop across the street when Cochrane rang him to come upstairs.

"I got something for you on that missing persons case at the motel."

"What is it?"

"A telegram from Washington State."

"My back's killing me. Why don't you just bring it down here?"

"Tell you what," Cochrane offered. "I'll buy you lunch later on if you get up here in the next sixty seconds."

Cochrane switched off the Giants' game on the radio and handed Ellison a telegram when he came in. Muriel Knutsen's sister, Agnes, had wired a copy to the Sheriff's office that morning and followed it up with another pleading telephone call. Nobody seemed to know where Muriel was, and neither her sister nor her mother seemed to believe Mrs. Long's story about a trip to Brazil. They thought the very idea was ludicrous. *Where would she go? What would she do? What about Lonnie? What about us?* Something's awfully peculiar, they argued, but hadn't come up with any evidence of wrongdoing. It was a dead end. Until this telegram arrived:

Dear Agnes: I would like for you to keep your nose out of my affairs. Lonnie and I are all right. If you keep this up everyone will be upset. Tell mother not to worry. I was within 100 miles of you a couple of weeks ago, after I heard what I heard I stayed away. Would you please accept Lonnie's check at this address. I will write in two weeks so don't be upset. And please stay out of my affairs. Love, Muriel, Lonnie and Dave.

"Now, that's something."

Cochrane told Ellison, "Apparently it was telephoned to the Western Union office in Salinas from a pay phone, so there's no way of checking the exact origin of the call. But Agnes says it's a fraud."

"How so?"

"Well, for one thing, she has no idea who this 'Dave' fellow is, and neither does anyone else in her family. For another, she says Muriel always signed her letters 'Mimi.' And she mentions 'this address,' but doesn't tell what it is. They say the whole telegram is a fake. They're pretty adamant that it doesn't sound like Muriel at all and that something's happened to her. Also, they've contacted Lonnie's son down in San Diego and no one there had heard anything about this. They'd assumed the Major was still up at the motel."

"Well, I suppose it's possible someone could've impersonated Muriel, but what's the angle? The woman's already missing. Why draw more attention to her? I just don't think any of this makes much sense. For instance, why invent this 'Dave' fellow that nobody knows? If it was meant to throw her family off the track, it did just the opposite. Maybe Lonnie's sort of a different case because he was still there after Muriel left, but I don't think it's a set-up at all. I'll bet Muriel's taken off, probably Lonnie, too, and that's the end of it. I think it's a misunderstanding between her and her family. There's no crime here that I can see."

Cochrane said, "They have a lawyer flying down from Seattle next week. He's going straight to the motel and wants you to meet him there. He'd like to talk to Mrs. Long."

Ellison rolled his eyes. "God, I hate that lady. She's a nut."

"Then go out there with the lawyer and wrap it up," Cochrane told him. "The sheriff says he's tired of knocking around on this case."

O N JOE KRUEGER'S FINAL NIGHT at the El Sombrero, he lay stripped to the waist in bed listening to a pair of drunks arguing over a mutual love interest named Cherry. The thin lace curtains hiding the window screen washed in and out on the evening draft. Rose Boulevard was restless and so was Joe. He hadn't seen his wife in more than a week, not since he'd caught sight of her pushing a laundry cart out by the motel office while he was cleaning ants off the kitchen countertop. Earlier that same day, she had told Joe about a leaking waterline in the basement at Ellington, so he assumed she was down in the city lining up a plumber. That is, until one of his pals from work dropped over to check on the house a couple of days ago and found all the lights put out and the doors locked up tight. Joe felt like giving Ida a good swift kick for deserting him. At six o'clock this morning, Lonnie's son Larry had telephoned to ask where the Major was. When Joe told him that he heard Lonnie had gone to a convalescent home somewhere, Larry called him a goddamned liar and hung up. Then, later in the afternoon, that blockhead Wilson dropped by, claiming Ida had stolen a .38 revolver out of his glove box, which prompted Joe to ask just what the hell Ida was doing in his car, anyhow. If that wasn't enough, Mabel Crandall waltzed over from the Bluebonnet after supper with a bowl of tapioca pudding she'd cooked. Joe was pretty sure Mabel had her eye on him. She sat on his sofa with a goofy smile on her face for half an hour, talking his ear off about her book-of-the-month club and how swell Loretta Young tuned in with the new aerial on her motel roof. She only left when Joe told her he had diarrhea.

After going out to switch off the front porch light and lock up, Joe fixed himself a glass of warm milk and a plate of toast and went to bed with the television set on. He watched Jack Paar for half an hour or so, then undressed and brushed his teeth. Climbing back into bed with the latest issue of *Cavalcade*, Joe heard a key turn in the front door lock. He listened as Ida fiddled about with her purse in the dark. She was a good liar and he figured she had her story worked out already, so he didn't plan on giving her the third degree. What good would it do, except to get them both worked up? He heard her pour a glass of water and drink it with a loud hiccup.

Ida came down the hall, holding her shoes as she sneaked into the bedroom. Joe watched Ida open her purse and slip something under the silk undergarments in her bottom dresser drawer. He almost laughed, she was such a sneak. For some reason, Ida had a problem behaving like a normal person and sticking to the rules. During the War, there were nuts and malcontents who never wore socks or shorts, wouldn't stand up for an officer, stole any bit of loose change lying around, and lied to everyone in the South Pacific about where they came from or what they did before enlisting. In Joe's company, there was even a kid from Arkansas who had to be scrubbed with a G.I. brush once a month because he refused to wash himself. Ida kept a neat house and her kitchen clean, but she didn't pay much notice to what others thought of her besides how much money she earned and what properties she owned. She brought her own cheering section to every conversation and told anyone who would listen how she expected to be rich as all-get-out one day and live happily ever after. Back when they were first married, he and Ida used to lie down together in the afternoon with the radio on and talk about playing it all by ear, two by two. These days, however, Ida was simply incapable of keeping up her end of the bargain. Joe could see that now. She was only out for herself.

Ida tiptoed into the bathroom and closed the door. Joe slipped the magazine into his drawer on the nightstand. Rolling over in bed, he heard a dog barking across the motor court at the Bluebonnet as wind gusted through the ratty palms and a lady's voice called out for the dog to shut up. A pack of souped-up hot rods rumbled past on Rose Boulevard. This section of town was lousy with juvenile delinquents.

Ida tapped his shoulder and sat beside him. "Joey?"

She had stripped down to her slip, and smelled of camphor cream and rosewater.

"Huh?" He pretended he just woke up.

"I'm home."

"Yeah?"

She kissed his cheek. "I missed you. I had the worst time being away so long."

"Where were you?"

"If I tell you, Joey, you have to promise not to get mad because I'm too tired to fight with you and I can't do nothing about it, anyhow."

"Wilson came over here this afternoon looking for you. Says he wants his money and he's tired of waiting."

"Well, I told him to lay off until I went to the bank. I think he needs his ears cleaned out."

"He's says you stole a revolver from his glove box."

Ida stiffened. "I don't know anything about that, honey, no such thing. That man's crazier than a bedbug that ever lived."

"You are sure lying, Ida," Joe said, sitting up now. He was growing angry and couldn't help himself. "I know because I'm your husband and you can't deny that. So you better start telling the truth."

"Joey, I am telling you the only way I know how."

"Then, for godsakes, tell me the goddamned truth!"

Ida began to weep. She put her face in her hands and slumped over and sobbed. She did it to gain sympathy. Let her cry. She'd still need to tell him where she'd been all week and what she'd done.

People walked past on the sidewalk outdoors laughing. Joe heard the stale palms rustle overhead. The town was rude and homely. He despised being here. Tomorrow he intended to buy a bus ticket back to San Francisco and stay there for good.

Ida quit sobbing and raised her face to look at Joe. She wore a pitiful expression. "Honey, just let me explain my side of it. I had business to take care of in the city and I'm not ashamed to tell you I had a dispute with the bank and went down there with Wilson to clear it up. And that should've been the end of it because I told that Wilson we were through for the day and I wanted to go home and cook supper for my husband who works harder than any man I ever known. But he wouldn't let me. I asked him to drive us back home and he told me to hush up with the ugliest look I ever seen. He was hopped up on liquor and couldn't be reasoned with and I was afraid to jump out because he was driving like the devil by then. Honey, I know it's hard to believe, but Wilson kidnapped me clear to Utah and tried to make me one of his wives, like Brigham Young. I had to ride the bus back alone, and I was too ashamed to tell you, and only Juanita knows, which is why we hid out on Ellington for a couple of days until I settled down enough to see I couldn't hide any of this from you, anyhow. You're my husband and ought to know the truth."

Joe thought he'd heard everything now. "Ida, you're just not clicking. George Evans went by the house last night and didn't see any lights on. He's not a liar, either."

Ida scowled. "Well, think of that! Me and Juanita sleeping with the lights out! That sure is a funny thing!"

"Knock it off."

"Joey, those insurance fellows haven't quit, and they may not care if you show your face in that big picture window, but I tell you, I can't take chances like that. Last night, when we got back from my treatment at the hospital, Juanita parked the car on Whipple and we walked over to the house and let ourselves in through the basement. It was dark as pitch, but Juanita had a lighter and once we got to the stairs, we were fine. I had her close the drapes in the living room and we lit a candle over the toilet and she slept on the sofa and I put a blanket on the floor and it wasn't the best night's sleep I ever had, but we made do."

Joe didn't know what to believe anymore. Ida told so many lies she probably didn't know the difference. On the other hand, Wilson seemed just like the sort of sonofabitch who wouldn't have any trouble at all laying his hands on another fellow's wife. Trouble was, Ida liked to flirt, too, so it wasn't impossible to see the both of them driving off into the sunset together. It was Wilson's story about his .38 revolver that didn't make sense. So Joe asked Ida again, "What about stealing that gun?"

She gave a dramatic sigh. "Honey, I already told you, that's his tale and I don't know nothing of the kind because I never held a gun in my life and wouldn't know what to do with one if I did."

Now Joe knew she was lying. Who didn't know how to shoot a gun? He told her, "I don't know what the truth is here, but I'm quitting this place tomorrow. Me and George and some of the fellows are hired down on the Embarcadero next week and it pays a good wage, too, and it'll go all spring. Maybe into summer."

Ida's voice firmed up, just as Joe expected. "Honey, I told you I need you here to look after the place until I can hire someone to handle the front desk. Juanita doesn't have a brain in her body and this business positively needs someone to help me run it."

Joe shook his head. "And I'm telling you, honey, it's no soap. I didn't sign the papers to this dump. You did, so it's your concern, not mine.

I got my own job to look after. Someone needs to pay the bills in this family."

After that, Ida lay stone-still next to Joe and didn't speak another word. Soon she was snoring.

Joe took a couple of hours to fall asleep. He knew Ida was angry and that got him mad, too, and kept him awake thinking about all the nonsense she'd dropped on him since they first took a room across the court at the Bluebonnet. If that Muriel woman hadn't gotten friendly with Ida and talked her into taking over this stupid motel, he and Ida could have left town and gone somewhere down the coast, maybe Monterey, and found a cabin by the ocean and forgotten about those insurance cops all together. This whole business made his head ring like a bell. Once they were rid of it, maybe he and Ida could finally get straightened out and become husband and wife again. Joe hated frying his own eggs.

BERT WILSON heard the telephone ringing when he was in the toilet. His stomach was sore and he had a headache from fighting with a customer over on Fourth Street who tried to jigger his water softener to bypass some pipe into a homebrew unit he had wired up in his garage. The fellow wanted a full refund and Bert told him to go to hell. Doing business on days like this was a pain in the ass.

He heard Zelma answer the phone. "Hello? . . . Yes, whom may I say is calling? . . . Just a moment, please." Zelma's voice was flat and cold, which meant the person on the other end of the line wasn't someone she cared for. "Darling, it's for you."

Bert zipped up and flushed the toilet. "Who is it?"

"Your motel girlfriend. Ida Long."

"Oh, good grief." Now that capped his day. What the hell did *she* want? "All right, I'll take it in the office. And she's not my goddamned girlfriend."

Bert ran water in the sink, washed his hands, then quickly dried them on a towel. He hurried to grab the telephone. That idiotic trip out to Pine Meadows was the craziest thing he'd ever been involved with. All that driving and the pack of lies she'd told about her lock box and the bank. She was not only looney, he was beginning to suspect she might be some sort of crook, too, one of those confidence grifters. Worse still, he was pretty sure she'd copped his .38 revolver out of the glove box. He found it was missing after the trip and wanted it back before she used it on someone.

"All right, honey, I got it. You can hang up." He waited to hear the phone click down, then spoke softly into the receiver. Zelma didn't need to hear any of this. She already thought Bert had a hard-on for Ida. That had been true a month ago, but nothing about that woman made him stiff anymore. He thought she was nuts. "Yes?"

"Hi, Bertie."

"Don't call me that." Wilson stretched a leg out and kicked his office door shut. "What do you want?"

"Are you mad at me?"

Bert switched on his desk lamp and sat down. "Where's my money? That stunt you pulled put me up to my eyebrows with the bank. I had to take out another loan just to pay off what you owe me."

"I bet you thought I ran off, didn't you? Don't blame me for those Jews at the savings and loan. Someone cleaned me out and they absolutely won't say who."

"I'm sending a couple fellows over tomorrow to pull out that water unit. You've been conning me all along, and I've had enough."

"That's what I'm calling to tell you about. I sent a telegram to my lawyer this morning, and he wired me the cash, all two thousand dollars. And there's an extra hundred for all your trouble. Honest to God, I've got it right here at the motel. If you come over, I'll positively give you the money."

"Ida, I guess you think I'm a complete idiot, is that it? I chased that payment of yours halfway across the country and came home empty-handed. I wouldn't go outdoors now if you told me my house was on fire."

"Quit that, Bertie. You're the one run out on me, in case you forgot. You wouldn't believe the trouble I had getting back here. I thought I'd die."

"Sure you did."

Just hearing her voice got Bert angry. He was pretty sure he hated her guts now and if he didn't owe Stamos that cement money, he'd tell Ida to shove it and take her to small claims court. On the other hand, that two grand could pay half his bills this month, so he just couldn't afford to let her off the hook. Then again, a little voice in his ear was telling him that if he was stupid enough to drive over to that crappy motel again, he'd be sorry. But he sure as hell didn't want her coming to the house, either, even if she had the cash in her hat. Maybe riding over there was a good idea. If Ida actually had the money, he could settle up with her. And if she didn't, his boys could go ahead and take out the unit. God, this was unbelievable. He was just lucky Zelma didn't know what he'd been up to with Ida. She'd fry his hair.

"All right, Ida, look here: if you cross me this time, I'll go to the authorities and fix your wagon. Don't think I won't."

"Don't be rough, Bertie. I've got the money, honest I do. Just hurry over here. I took a sleeping pill and I hope to get to bed early tonight."

"I'll be there in fifteen minutes. Just be sure you've got it all waiting for me. In cash, like you said. No checks and no IOUs. I'm not going on any more of your wild goose chases."

"Don't worry about a thing, Bertie. It's all here."

"And don't call me Bertie."

Wilson hung up the phone and went out to the hall to get his coat. Zelma saw him from the kitchen. He told her he had to go downtown and he'd be back in an hour or so.

"In that case, I'm going with you," she said, taking up her purse. "I'm tired of staying home every night." She'd put on fresh lipstick and freshened her face makeup. She must have guessed he was going out.

"Zelma, I got business I need to take care of. This isn't a social visit."

Frowning, she went to the coat closet to fetch her new gabardine. "Fine! You can do your business, then take me to dinner. And I don't mean a hamburger at the bowling alley, either. I want to go to the Ponderosa and have a big steak. We haven't been out on the town in months, and I refuse to stay home one more night. I'm going with you, Bert, and that's all there is to it."

Arguing with her was a waste of time, so Wilson shrugged and grabbed his hat. "If you say so, dear."

They drove to the El Sombrero as the sun went down, Wilson rushing through traffic and skipping a red light four blocks from the motel on Rose Boulevard. He suspected Ida had another card up her sleeve, but he had no idea what it might be. Nor did he particularly care, because this was the last straw for him. If she didn't pony up with the cash, then by noon tomorrow Wilson intended to send Eddie and Dave over to snatch out the water conditioning unit.

"Look at this," Zelma remarked as Wilson swung his Oldsmobile into the dusty courtyard of the El Sombrero. "I thought you said she'd fixed things up. It looks as dreadful as ever."

Trash spilled out of the garbage cans on the side of the motel. Paper littered the driveway. All the trees and foliage were sick. That whole section of property on the boulevard looked sloppy and pathetic.

Wilson shut off the motor. Curiously, he found himself defending Ida. "Oh, she did all right. You can't make a monkey do the waltz without some help and most of this she's done herself." He opened his door and got out. "Now, look, dear. Just stay put until I get back. It should only take a couple of minutes."

"Why can't I come in?"

Wilson went around to her side of the automobile. "Because I want you to stay here with the car. Do you understand? We'll go dancing after dinner, if you like. Just do as I say."

She smiled, warily. "Do you promise?"

Wilson leaned in and gave her a kiss. "Sure."

"All right, then, I'll stay right here till you get back, but don't be long."

"I won't."

Wilson left Zelma and decided to take a peek at the back of the motel before seeing Ida Long. He needed to determine how difficult it would be to take out the unit, and what condition it was in. Wind rattled the motel blinds. Traffic rumbled past on the boulevard, and some young toughs yelled back and forth at each other across the road. Not a chance in hell would Wilson hire a room in a dump like this. No wonder Ida had such a hard time making a go of it.

A glow from the streetlamps provided enough illumination for Wilson to see what he needed to behind the El Sombrero, where his water unit had been installed back of Cabin Eight, tucked beneath a stunted old palm tree. But now all he found was an empty spot of flattened grass.

"Sonofabitch!"

His water unit was gone, snatched clean off the wall. Wilson kicked at the palm in disgust. How could he be such a sap? He should've known Ida might take it out herself. That conniving little thief! Well, that was that. Now he'd *really* give her a piece of his mind. They were going straight to court, where she'd fork over every last penny owed him if it was the last thing she ever did.

Wilson was boiling over by the time he reached the door to the front office. He burst in, ready to crack her jaw.

Instead of Ida waiting for him, he was greeted by a chubby Mexican girl smoking a cigarette over a newspaper at the front desk, a bowl of potato chips at her elbow. She looked like a Halloween pumpkin. "Can I help you?"

Wilson noticed the lights were out in the back rooms of the apartment. The place seemed spiffier than the last time he'd been there. The counter tops had all been redone in fresh green Formica, which proved Ida had some money, after all. He asked, "Where's Ida Long?"

The girl behind the registration desk was younger than Ida, but a goofy expression on her face made her look like just as big a nut.

She asked Bert again, "Is there something I can help you with?"

He was confused. "Who are you?"

"I'm Juanita. Ida's out of town this evening. How can I help you?"

Something was fishy here. The Ida he knew wouldn't leave just anyone with the cash drawer. She was tight with her dough and Bert wasn't sure she trusted her own husband. This girl was funny-looking and smelled like pancakes. What was he supposed to tell her? Maybe Ida forgot to let her know he was coming down here. These situations could be pretty strategic sometimes. If you said the wrong thing to the wrong person, it all went haywire. He had to be careful.

"My name's Bert Wilson, and I have some business with Ida. She just telephoned my house about half an hour ago and asked me to meet her here. That's all I know."

"Well, I haven't seen her since about four o'clock when she gave me the keys, so I'm not sure what to tell you. She probably called you from a pay phone and you misunderstood her. I have a terrible time hearing someone on those things."

"Well, when did you say she was here last? Four o'clock?"

"Half past, actually. She had to catch the bus to the city."

"Sure she did."

"Pardon me?"

If a large flatbed truck hadn't rolled past the motel, lighting the backroom, Wilson might not have seen the slight figure slip across the hall backlit by headlamps. It didn't take a genius to guess who it was.

"IDA!"

When she stumbled into a tin wastepaper basket, Wilson knew he had her. As the fat Mexican girl turned toward the back of the apartment, Wilson called again, "COME OUT RIGHT NOW, IDA, OR I'LL CALL THE COPS. I'M NOT FOOLING! I KNOW ABOUT YOU PULLING OUT THE WATER UNIT!"

He heard a drawer bang shut. When she didn't appear, he growled, "If you don't come out here right now and make good on what you owe me, I'll see you in court tomorrow! Don't think I won't!"

Ida came out of the shadows with her arms folded at the waist, looking rumpled as usual. "I didn't know it was you, Bertie. I thought you were someone else. I got to be awfully careful these days."

"Sure you do. Now, what happened to my water unit, and where's the money? You said you had it, or was that just another one your phony baloney stories?"

Ida smiled. "I got it right here." And she raised a .38 from her waist, pointing it straight at his forehead. Her eyes looked wild. "You're through blackmailing me, mister. I'm fed up with your evil. Juanita?"

"Yes, dear?"

"This is the fellow I told you about. He's stolen every cent I've earned on this place. Hand me that pen and paper, please." She pointed to a ring tablet next to the telephone.

"This is nuts, Ida," Wilson said, trying to keep the gun barrel away from his forehead. "I don't know what you think you're doing here, but I don't like it."

Juanita gave the paper and pen to Ida, who placed them in front of Wilson.

He bluffed a tough face, but was actually scared out of his wits. Who'd have thought it would come to this?

Ida told him, "Now, honey, what you're going to do is write out a note excusing me of all those debts you claim I got with you, and then you're going to sign it. Juanita'll be our witness."

"You're crazy!"

Ida frowned as she aimed the pistol at Wilson's nose. "Do as I say, Bertie, or I'll kill you right now. And don't think I won't, because I have no conscience about that, believe you me."

"You know, if you shoot me, you won't get this paper signed."

Ida laughed. "If I shoot you, you dumb cluck, I won't need it signed! You'll be carried out of here feet first and no one'll ever know what happened to you."

Wilson shot a glance at Juanita standing patiently back of the desk. "Are you going to let her do this?"

Juanita spoke out to Bert. "She told me what you did to her in that car. You're sick."

"What are you talking about?"

"That slave ride to Reno you took her on. Everything you did. It's disgusting."

Ida told her about that? Good grief! "Well, she's a goddamned liar! This is all a shakedown!"

"Don't curse in my motel," Ida growled. "It's nasty and I won't stand for it. Although come to think of it, what you did to me out in the desert was so filthy, I guess that's just the sort of fellow you are, Bertie."

"And you're a dirty little cheat. I must've been out of my mind to try helping you out when this is how you pay me back." He glanced past her to the fat Mexican girl. "I hope you're getting paid cash money tonight, because you won't see a dime, otherwise. If you don't believe me, ask Ida to tell you what she's got in her safe deposit box in Wyoming. When we went out there together, she told me all about how rich she is, but guess what? That bank she sent me to never heard of her!"

Ida stuck herself between Wilson and Juanita. "Safe deposit box? Wyoming? What are you talking about? I've been in San Francisco all week. You're nuttier than a fruit cake!"

"You're the one who's nutty, Ida, and I'll bet this girl knows it, too." Bert stared at Juanita. "Don't you, dear?"

"Quit talking to her," Ida warned, waving the pistol in Wilson's face. "I mean it. She don't have nothing to do with this."

"With what? This stupid plan of yours? I tell you, Ida, you've really gone the limit now. Your name won't be worth mud in this town tomorrow, no matter what that paper says."

Ida slammed her free hand down on the counter. "SIGN IT!"

Someone knocked at the front door, and a female voice called out, "Bert? Are you in there?"

Wilson shouted, "ZELMA, GET HELP!"

And Ida shot him.

Zelma screamed, "BERT!"

Wilson lay on the floor by the desk, a roaring pain in his upper chest. The back door slammed. Before he fainted, Wilson heard Zelma's wailing voice close by. "Hello? Operator? Get me the police!"

ELLISON HAD BEEN INVESTIGATING a burglary call only a couple of miles away at a motor park on Grant Avenue when the shooting came over the radio. He raced over to the El Sombrero, arriving about five minutes after Cochrane. An ambulance and two city patrol cars were parked in the crowded motel courtyard, people from both the El Sombrero and the Bluebonnet Motel milling about under the saggy palm trees and yellow porch lights, thrilled by the shooting. Wilson was awake and lying on a gurney in the ambulance, where a woman in a gabardine coat was mopping his brow with a borrowed handkerchief and giving him an earful over how he'd just risked his life over a cut-rate water conditioning unit. A patrol officer and one of the ambulance attendants stood just outside, waiting for Wilson to be driven to the hospital once Ellison was through with his preliminary questions.

Apparently, Ida Long had fled the scene and was probably long gone, but Ellison and Cochrane would still have to check out the bus station and the cab companies. Maybe they could get some line on her to find out where she was headed.

When Ellison walked into the motel office, Cochrane was grilling that fat Juanita girl about the .38 revolver Wilson had been shot with. The Mexican had a cigarette hanging off her lips. Cochrane asked her, "Do you know where Ida got the gun from?"

"The back room," the girl told him. She didn't appear too broken up by any of this and Ellison thought she had a tone to her gruff voice that wasn't flattering.

"Was it hers?"

"Well, it wasn't mine."

"Are you trying to be funny?"

"No."

"Did you know she was going to use it on Wilson?"

"Of course not," the Mexican girl answered. "She was just defending herself. She told me all about that fellow and he sounded dangerous."

"He threatened her?"

"Well, I heard what he was capable of, and I sure wouldn't go for a ride with him. He's a big creep."

Ellison left them and went back outdoors to see what Wilson had to say about all this. The ambulance attendant from Memorial Hospital told Ellison that Wilson was awake and reasonably lucid, despite the injection they'd given him for the pain. Apparently, the bullet had passed through his shoulder about four inches above his right lung, so the wound wasn't life-threatening. Serious, but not fatal. Wilson looked exhausted. His tie was loose and he slumped against the pillow on the gurney. Before Ellison began his questions, Wilson's wife decided to take the car and go on ahead to the hospital to fill out his paperwork. She kissed her husband good-bye and gave his hand a squeeze. Her eyes were teary and she looked more upset than he did. A good anesthetic made all the difference. Once she drove off, Wilson perked up and sounded reasonably eager to talk about what had just happened.

Ellison began by asking Wilson why he thought he'd gotten himself shot. "From what I've heard about Mrs. Long, she's a pretty shrewd business woman. She must've known she couldn't force you to do a stupid thing like releasing a note under a threat."

He managed a weak shrug. "I'd say she seemed desperate. Like I told your partner, I felt sorry for her. She's been doing the best she could to get the motel in shape, but she seemed desperate."

"How do you mean, desperate?"

"I don't know — like she was afraid." Wilson labored to get comfortable on the gurney. His hands were jittery, his voice shaky. The bandage on his upper chest had begun to ooze. He gave Ellison an abridged version of the ride he took with Ida out to Wyoming. "It's hard to explain. Most of the way there, I swear she was looking over her shoulder or something. It was strange."

Ellison scribbled that into his notepad. "Did she mention being afraid of anyone?"

"Well, no, but she seemed confused. I was always under the impression she really thought the money was available down there in San Francisco and she couldn't figure out what to do when it wasn't."

Ellison said, "So you think she actually did have the money, huh? At least somewhere?"

"Oh, I don't know," Wilson replied, his voice wheezing in the night air. A cool breeze had come up and the palm fronds scratched above the motel. "I mean, she acted pretty certain about it. Whatever that's worth. These things are tough to tell with her. Ida's got a way of making everything look on the level, and enough of it is that you can't be sure when something's not. I tell you, she's a damn good liar."

Ellison nodded. "I've gathered that much. There are a lot questions about her these days."

"There sure are." Wilson winced. "You really have to wonder, don't you?"

"Are you willing to sign a complaint against Mrs. Long about your water unit? We'll have a warrant filed tonight for the shooting, regardless."

Wilson stared out to where one of the patrol cars was rolling onto Rose Boulevard. His expression softened. "Look here, I know she just shot me and that's pretty serious, all right. I guess she might've killed me, too, if my wife hadn't knocked when she did. The thing is, though, I don't believe that's really what Ida had in mind when she called me down here tonight. I don't know if she had my money or not — well, I suppose she probably didn't, but that's no surprise, given everything she's done since taking over this rotten old motel. So I guess I don't really want to cause her any more trouble, but I would like to get back the money I loaned her and to be paid for my equipment. Beyond that, I don't know. Let me think about it, all right? She's had a hell of a time up here this year, and I'm not sure I want to make it any worse for her."

Now Ellison understood why Wilson seemed to loosen up after his wife drove off. He smiled. "You like her, huh?"

Wilson shrugged. "Yeah, I guess I do. Sounds funny, doesn't it, given that she just tried to murder me tonight. Like I said, I feel sorry for her. Ida's had some bum luck this year. It just seems to me she's not thinking straight anymore."

Ellison agreed. "Maybe if we can drag her into court on a charge of threatening bodily harm, we can get some answers. So far, we have a couple of people missing from this motel under mysterious circumstances and we haven't any real idea what's going on, and no way to force anyone to answer any questions."

Shifting his weight on the gurney, Wilson sat up. "I wonder, though, if that's the answer."

"What do you mean?"

"Look, I threatened to call the law on her already tonight, and that's when she brought out the gun. It could be that, for some reason, she's afraid to appear in court."

"Yeah, well, now she's done it," Ellison told him, "because that's probably where you're going to see her next."

A COLD WINDY RAIN drenched the Bay Area for most of that first month after Joe had returned to San Francisco. The weather was bleak and unrelenting and work stopped on the Embarcadero job. With time on his hands, he began riding a Muni bus up to North Beach in the afternoon and staying out way past dark. He wanted to forget about the motel and Ida. He hadn't telephoned up to Santa Rosa since he left and Ida hadn't called him, so he had no idea what was happening there and didn't care, either. He had no plans to go back. Besides, he was getting to enjoy the city, despite all the nuts and the traffic. Joe even thought about buying a car again, maybe a second-hand Ford Falcon that didn't take up much space on the street when it got crowded in the evening. Things sure had changed a lot since he last lived there after the War. From North Beach to the Tenderloin and the Outer Mission, it seemed he ran across loudmouthed Negroes and bearded bongo-thumping beatniks on every corner, shouting out slogans and obscenities he didn't even understand. For the first time in his life, Joe felt old and out of touch. As long as he could remember, he'd been chasing the world, trying to catch up on what seemed to matter to everyone, and now he'd been passed by and couldn't figure out how and when that had happened. But somehow none of that bothered him once he was riding the Muni up to the Embarcadero, where he could look out over the cold bay on a foggy morning and see ships docking at the busy piers, row upon row, and crowds of people from all over the world arriving at the city where Joe owned a house of his own.

His pals from the job liked going out on the town after knocking off work. San Francisco had more restaurants than Joe had ever seen, and thousands of bars, some of which he wouldn't stick his head in without a gas mask. One evening, he went up to North Beach with George Evans, Charley Snyder, and Les Ralston. The plan was to have a few drinks at some ritzy saloon on Broadway that George had read about in Herb Caen's column, then get an Italian dinner somewhere and go see a strip show. Joe hadn't been to a girlie show since the War and he had gotten in the mood for a bowl of minestrone soup and a plate of meatballs, too. He put on his coat and met the fellows at Market Street near Sixth, where they hired a cab. Getting out on the corner of Montgomery and Broadway into a gritty wind, George told them, "The guy who owns this place used to be a bullfighter. Paste that in your hat."

Charley asked, "Is his name Pancho?"

Les laughed. "No, I think it's Barnaby. Sounds like a fag, huh?"

They walked up the sidewalk to the gothic 𝕰𝖑 𝕸𝖆𝖙𝖆𝖉𝖔𝖗 sign, where Evans told Charley and Les to wait outside while he and Joe went in to see about getting a table. "These fellows get nervous if a crowd of regular people show up."

Charley said, "Just tell 'em Joe here's a cousin of Tyrone Power. That'll get us a table."

"I need a pack of cigarettes, anyhow," Les said. "Come on, Charley. Let's give these big shots a chance to fix us up."

"Sure."

"We'll be back in a minute."

While his pals went back down the sidewalk, Joe followed George Evans indoors where they were greeted by a lovely hostess. Evans cracked a big smile. "Get a load of this!"

There were bullfighting outfits tacked to the walls, garish matador paintings, a great ceiling-high mural of the Seville bullring, a big bull's head over the bar, and what looked to Joe like a giant blue parrot in a glass cage across the room cattycorner from the piano. The saloon was lively and loud with laughter and music, hot shots sitting all over the place. Was that Bing Crosby nuzzling a doll who looked like Ava Gardner? Maybe Gary Cooper would walk in and say hello to Joe. It was a hell of a crowd. Half the people in the joint were dressed like mannequins from a show window at I. Magnin's. Joe thought the whole scene was a riot and couldn't wait to sit down with a fancy drink. Then George came over to give him the bad news from the hostess. "We ain't got neckties and we ain't important. We're nobodys, which means no table and no service."

"Did you tell her about Tyrone Power?"

"Sure I did," Evans replied, "and she told me to go buy you a drink at the Mark where the really big shots hang out."

"To hell with 'em, then."

Joe followed Evans back out, where George told Les and Charley, "No dice, boys. I guess we're not good enough for this crowd. They think we're riff-raff."

"Is that so?"

"That's what they said."

Les flicked his cigarette down and rubbed it out on the doormat. "Yeah, well, I wouldn't drink here if they poured the booze down my throat. A place like this? Look around. Anyone can see it's a joint for queers."

Disgusted, they went up to Adolph's on Vallejo Street for beer and meatballs, and later on over to Bimbo's 365 Club on Columbus, where Joe got to see a naked girl swimming in a fish bowl. The next night, Joe went out by himself to see a movie at the Roxie Cinema and rode a cab up to Fack's on Bush Street for a cocktail and a couple hours of jazz. Another evening, Joe rode the Muni to a club called the Purple Onion at Columbus and Broadway where a frizzy-haired housewife told jokes about her husband, Fang, and a skinny fellow from New York said dirty things about Eisenhower and got booed off the stage. This wasn't his crowd and Joe felt odd sitting alone at a table with nobody to talk with, so he ordered a couple of cocktails and drank a little from both of them, pretending his date was stuck in the ladies' room.

Those days, Joe didn't really mind being alone. He enjoyed riding up to Fisherman's Wharf and eating a crabmeat sandwich in a salt breeze and watching flocks of seagulls annoy the tourists. Joe went to a boxing match at the Cow Palace and half a dozen ballgames at Candlestick Park to see Willie Mays blast a home run through the wind out into Del Courtney's band pit behind the fence in center field. Joe rode the bus a couple of times across the bay to Marin County to go sightseeing in Muir Woods and up to Mount Tamalpais, where Les Ralston told him a lot of guys got queer in the bushes. Joe didn't notice any of that, but when it wasn't foggy he could see clear out to the Farallones. Free of that stupid motel, Joe had plenty of time to knock around when he was off work. He even liked going out to the zoo every so often and flipping peanuts at the monkeys, or crashing into lovey-dovey teens with a bumper car at Playland-at-the-Beach.

One Sunday afternoon, Joe took the bus to Golden Gate Park and hired a boat at Stow Lake to float around on the water and relax a little. When he spotted a girl in another boat by herself having trouble getting anywhere, he rowed over to find that her boat was leaking and her shoes were swamped. Seeing she was about to sink, Joe helped her into his own boat and took her back to shore where she tiptoed out onto the grass and sat down to take off her shoes. She said her name was Pamela and offered Joe a corn muffin and some deviled eggs from a wicker picnic basket. Although Joe had brought his own lunch pail with a sandwich and a banana and a bottle of beer, he thanked her and ate a deviled egg with her under the shade of the cypress and eucalyptus trees. Lying back in the grass as Pamela gabbed on and on about how she and her mother used to come here for Bible study on Sundays, Joe fell asleep. When he woke up about an hour later, Pamela was gone and so was Joe's lunch pail.

Angry as hell, Joe ran around Golden Gate Park for a couple of hours looking for her and when she didn't turn up anywhere, he hired a cab to Mt. Davidson and hiked up through the woods, where he scratched *KILROY WAS HERE* with a soft rock on the giant one-hundred foot-high cement cross. A couple of days later on a rainy afternoon, his doorbell rang and Joe found three serious fellows in long topcoats on the stoop outside. When they identified themselves as cops, he almost jumped right out of his skin.

"I know what you fellows are here for," Joe said, his hands twitching.

"Yeah?"

"Well, I thought it'd wash off in the rain. I guess it didn't, after all."

"What didn't?"

"That 'Kilroy' on the big cross. I shouldn't have done it."

"Oh, so that was you, was it?" They laughed, and introduced themselves as Inspectors Cochrane and Ellison from Santa Rosa, and Detective Backman from the San Francisco Police Department. Ellison said, "Look, can we come in? It's cold out here."

"Sure." Joe stepped aside to let them indoors and went over to switch off the television. He had been watching a game show with the volume dialed low. The living room was cluttered with stacks of magazines piled here and there and a muddy carpet Joe hadn't run the vacuum cleaner over in weeks. The house stunk of fried onions and coffee. There was nothing Joe could do about that. After the cops hung their coats on the hallstand, two of them sat down on the sofa and the other took the lounge chair by the Philco set. Joe brought a chair for himself out of the kitchen and sat just inside the doorway.

Ellison drew a cigarette from his shirt pocket. "Mind if I smoke?"

"Go ahead." Joe hated smoking in the house, but he didn't want to sound argumentative.

Cochrane said, "You're a hard fellow to find, do you know that?"

Joe shrugged. "I've been right here all along."

"Well, we just spent a couple weeks looking for a Mr. Long, and apparently that's not your name, is it?"

"Nope."

"So how come you used a phony name up there in Santa Rosa?"

"Is there a law against it?"

"No, there sure isn't," Cochrane said, "but most honest people don't do that sort of thing."

"Well, I wouldn't live in that goddamn place under my own name. I worked there for a few months cleaning up that motel. It was a condemned joint. It wasn't fit for hogs to live in."

"Why'd you choose the name 'Long'?"

"It's easy to spell."

The cops laughed.

Then Joe told them about Ida's jitney accident, that leg cast she'd had to wear, and her big lawsuit. "Pretty soon, we started being pestered by insurance investigators almost every day. They'd sneak around, trying to prove Ida was only faking her injury, and a couple of times we caught them making pictures of us with a movie camera. Ida was positive they'd try and rig something up to keep her from getting that settlement for the accident, so we decided to go out of town until it was time to present her case to court. After all, a hundred thousand bucks is a lot of money."

Backman asked, "Did she get a lawyer?"

"Sure, she did. His name's Seymour Elrod, and he's in Belli's firm. Look it up, you'll get the whole goddamned story. It's pretty pathetic what insurance companies'll do to get out of paying."

Ellison said, "Well, Joe, what we're interested in right now is the whereabouts of your wife. I suppose you know what happened up at the motel two weeks ago, don't you?"

"It fell down?"

"Not exactly. Your wife shot Bert Wilson. There's a warrant out for her arrest."

Joe couldn't believe his ears. Ida shot him? Every time he was away from her, something crazy happened. "Did she kill him?"

"No, Wilson was lucky. The bullet hit him in the upper chest, close to his shoulder. He's sore, but he'll live. What we want to know is, where she is now. Can you help us?"

"Well, to tell you the truth, I haven't seen her in a while."

Cochrane asked, "Where do you think she might've gone?"

"I don't know."

"Does your wife have any living relatives you're familiar with?"

"Nope, they're all passed away." He hoped they wouldn't ask about Ocean City. If they did, he'd crack up.

Ellison asked, "How long have you been married, Joe?"

"About six years."

"Where'd you meet Ida?"

Now Joe told the biggest lie of his life simply because he didn't know what else to do. "She was working as a nurse at one of those rest homes down in San Jose when my Uncle Bill got sick. This was his house, by the way. I inherited it when he died about three years ago. Anyhow, I was down there visiting him and that's when I met Ida. We hit it off right away and the next thing I knew, we were setting up housekeeping. It all went pretty swell until her jitney accident, then I don't know what the hell happened."

"Well, you seem to be a decent sort of guy, and I'll be very honest with you: we're investigating the possibility of a murder, maybe two of them, and you may be right in the middle of it, if there is something.

Now, there's a warrant out for your wife because of that shooting at the motel, and she could turn herself in for that, and since Wilson doesn't seem too concerned with what she did to him, maybe it won't amount to much. But we've got a situation with Mr. and Mrs. Knutsen missing, and I'm sure you know about that. It's been in all the papers."

"I don't read them any more."

"Well, we can try to turn your wife up one way or another to get this whole thing straight, but if she's afraid of this warrant or what it's all about, maybe we can get her to think a little more clearly. Because if she cooperates with us now, it'll go easy on her. If not, well, she's got the finger of a possible murder warrant pointed at her. You can see that, can't you?"

"I suppose so." Joe nodded, trying to sound calm with his stomach churning. "What's the use of running?"

"Well, if she'd find the smarts to come in, or at least telephone one of us and find out what this is all about, she won't have to worry. This business of hiding is a rough thing."

"If I knew where she was, I'd tell her to give you fellows a call, but I don't."

Backman said, "We're not going to argue with you, Joe, but we've got reason to think you've kept contact with her. So you just better sit down with your wife as soon as you can and tell her if she wants to cooperate, maybe we can clear up this murder investigation. Again, the problem is we've got the newspapers hot on our neck and if one of those reporters breaks something before we do, boy, they'll ride her day and night. The Knutsens' relatives are really working this thing up and they're crucifying your wife. Now, we know there are always two sides, but we can't do anything for her unless we can get your wife to come in and talk to us. All we have are statements from other people about the shooting and everything else up there, but nothing from her. We just want to get to the bottom of this."

"Well, I wish I could get to the bottom of it myself. Maybe Ida flipped her lid. There was a lot of pressure on her with the motel going to pot and those insurance fellows pestering and heckling us. But so far as anything happening to those two motel people, I don't know a damned thing about it and if any newspaper reporters come around here to take my picture, I'll throw 'em over the goddamned fence."

Ellison stared at Joe. "But you don't know anything about it?"

"That's what I'm telling you."

"Well, you can stick to that all you like and I can't change it."

"No, you can't. If she really shot that fellow, like you say, I guess she went nuts, and if I knew where she was, I'd turn her in myself."

Just talking about Ida shooting Wilson made Joe queasy. He could barely look them in the eye.

Cochrane spoke up. "Joe, how well do you know your wife?"

"Well, maybe I don't know her at all. Ida's a lot smarter than I am. She's pretty well educated. You'd be surprised at some of the things she knows. Most of it's way over my head. She reads those astrology books — " Joe pointed over to the jammed-up oak bookcase next to the television set and the stack of magazines piled there — "and she can tell you stuff you'd hardly believe. I don't know where Ida's gone, but I guarantee she's got this all worked out in her head. You can bet on that."

"Did you think she was capable of shooting someone?"

"I didn't think she knew which end of a gun shoots. But I told that sonofabitch not to put a water softener in there. We didn't have the money for it."

"So she did all that on credit?"

"You'd have to ask her bank about that. It wasn't my business. Ida handled the whole damned place herself. I'm not the richest guy in the world, and I've worked for everything I got. I told her I'd help clean it up and do some painting, but I knew it was a bad situation. All I got out of it was four months of hard work and a sore back. I'd say the lady who ran off to Brazil got the best of the deal."

Cochrane cut in again. "Getting back to that, Joe, everybody seems to have different opinions as to where these people went, the Knutsens. What would be your guess?"

"I don't have any idea. That lady told Ida she was going down to Brazil or someplace like that, and Lonnie said so, too. That's where he thought she went."

"Did Muriel ever tell you directly?"

"No, I never spoke to her at all. She seemed like a wheeler-dealer to me. I can only tell you that Ida said Muriel was flying to Brazil and once she got settled, she'd send back for Lonnie. I guess that's what she did because one day he was at the motel, and the next he wasn't. Unless his family came for him."

"Did your wife ever mention anything about going somewhere with Mrs. Knutsen? Was there any talk of that?"

"Ida talked about a lot of things. I don't believe she had the money for a trip like that."

"But she's got that big settlement coming, doesn't she?"

"Not any more," Joe told them. "I don't think there'll ever be any money coming through on that. It's all blown up now."

"You know, Joe, the reason we've come down here is because we thought maybe your wife's all upset and thinks we're going to throw her in jail or something and never let her out. But that's not the idea. Maybe she just lost her temper with this Wilson fellow, maybe he deserved it, too. Who knows? But we do have to get squared away about these missing persons. You understand that, don't you?"

"Sure I do."

"Because the Knutsens are some place or another. We know that."

"They've got to be."

"Well, I hope so." Ellison got up from the couch. "Okay, now, Joe, we're not accusing you of anything, but if you don't mind, we'd like to do some snooping here this afternoon. We don't have a warrant, and you're free to toss us out if you like, but my boss won't be happy if I go back without being able to tell him there wasn't much to see at Joe's house."

"Well, there's not."

"Do you mind if we have a look around?"

"You think Ida's hiding in a closet?"

"Is she?"

Joe stood, too. "I'm going to get a beer. Look wherever you like. The attic's got a pull-down in the hallway. Don't break your neck."

He went off to the kitchen and left the cops to poke around in his closets. What did they expect to find? He didn't have anything to hide. Ida must have gone insane. Good riddance if she shot that guy. Wilson was a dope to let her steal his gun. Wherever Ida had run off to, Joe hoped she'd stay. He didn't trust her not to draw him into her trouble. This was worse than Ocean City, because the cops were already here. Ida was his wife, but her drama had nothing to do with him. Unless she could put herself together, he was better off alone.

Instead of a beer from the refrigerator, Joe heated up a cup of coffee to keep his brain straight. The cops had tried to trip him up. They were good at that. Ask the same question eight different ways and anyone was bound to forget a detail or two. It scared him. What did they expect him to say? Ida slipped some bodies under the couch? He didn't know where those motel people had gone and he didn't care, either. That was Ida's business. Maybe she knew and maybe she didn't. They were out of his hair now.

Joe listened to one of the cops nosing around in the back bedroom. He heard another in his own room. Sure, he was nervous. Who wouldn't be? Ida had been down here a lot when he was fixing up the motel. Who knows what sort of deals she'd struck with banks or race-track gamblers or those astrology nuts she had over to the house. If one of them was involved somehow with this mess of hers, who could say Ida hadn't left some evidence of it in her vanity or dresser drawer or somewhere else Joe wouldn't notice? But one of these cops might, and just the thought made him sick to his stomach.

Joe sipped his coffee and listened to a siren wailing over on Mission. This neighborhood ought to have made a good home. The house was in good shape and the heater worked and he could walk to the bus stop. Then Ida had her jitney accident and suddenly he had insurance people crawling over his back fence and that nosy lady across the street peeping out her kitchen window at him half the night. Maybe she was part of the insurance investigation.

Out in the hallway, the cops pulled down the attic stairs and were going up. Joe hadn't gotten rid of his uncle's stuff. Ida had it all shoved into one corner to make room for her own junk: boxes of worn-out astrology magazines, a couple of her mother's leather suitcases, her hope chest, racks of clothes she never wore, bags of odds and ends she refused to let Joe take out to the incinerator. He heard the cops tramping around overhead now, digging into crap up there. What were they looking for?

After a while, one of them came into the kitchen and said they were going to have a look in the basement, if that was all right with him.

"Sure it is," Joe told him, getting up to rinse out his coffee cup. "The light's at the top of the stairs and you'll find another in the side room where Ida was going to put a little apartment rental."

The cop nodded and left.

Joe heard them go downstairs. He hoped they didn't scuff up the new floor too badly. Ida had some fellow from Novato install it about six weeks ago and the dago plumber she hired to fix a leaky drainpipe dropped a wrench and put a dent in it. Joe ran water from the sink into his coffee cup and dried it off on a dish towel and wandered back out into the front room where he could hear the cops fussing about downstairs. He felt cold.

When they came back up from the basement, Joe was out on the back porch chasing off a neighbor's cat that had soiled Ida's flower planter. He threw a dead beer can at the cat as it scrambled over his fence. Then he heard Ellison in the kitchen behind him.

"We're done here."

Joe came back indoors. "Anyone hiding down there?"

The San Francisco cop asked, "How much are you thinking about renting that room out for?"

"I don't know that I am now," he told him. "It was Ida's plan, not mine. Who wants a stranger in his basement?"

"Well, it could be a nice fit for someone once it's trimmed out."

"If you say so."

Cochrane followed into the kitchen. "This is where you'll be for a while now, is that right?"

"Sure," Joe nodded. "I've got a job starting up next week in the Sunset District. I'm not going anywhere, so don't come see me at work."

"We won't."

Ellison said, "Thanks for your time, Joe."

"Yeah."

Then they left and Joe took a nap.

He had a nightmare that Ida had paid Lonnie and Muriel Knutsen to live up in the attic while she went down to Brazil and bought a coffee plantation that Joe was supposed to run for her. When he told Ida she was nuts, she shot him in the stomach and drove off in his old Studebaker. Then his dad appeared and asked what Joe was complaining about. Then he woke up.

Joe had always respected Ida's privacy. She had certain dresser drawers and a medicine chest he never snooped. Joe wouldn't touch her mail and hardly ever asked where she went during the day. This is what it had led to: cops dropping up to see him. Enough of that.

Joe pulled her drawers out of the oak dresser and emptied them onto the bedroom floor. He found a hundred dollars, a package of rubbers, a bill from a chiropractor in Millbrae, a Rosicrucian notice from Oceanside, and a Bay Meadows racing form dated last July. Joe put the money into his wallet. In the bathroom, he counted out her medications and read each label and emptied her little bottles into the toilet. He tore through her closet, sticking his hand into pockets and deep into each shoe and opened her old purses and threw her hats across the room. She had clothes Joe had never seen: a white taffeta dress with red polka dots and a ruffled front, a mauve silk dress with a flower at the waist. He also found a dry-cleaning plastic bag containing a full-length cape, new or unused, in Navy line with the initials "SH." It was made in Cleveland, and looked too tall for Ida. What the hell was that for? He tossed the bag back into the closet. Then he went out into the hall and pulled down the attic stairs.

Ida had collected a lot of crap. Most of it she stored up there. Joe switched on the light bulb and began digging into her boxes of treasures. There were more books on astrology, four Bibles, a Torah stuffed with Jewish lesson plans, a Book of Mormon, a bruised copy of *Science & Health*, and a stack of letters from a Catholic diocese in Milwaukee. He opened a box loaded with grade school textbooks and a copy of *High School Self-Taught*, another jammed solid with shoes, and a third holding more old dresses. Then he went over to her cedar hope chest. Up at Ocean City, Ida had kept this in her bedroom and asked that he keep out of it. When they came to Ellington Avenue, he helped her drag it up to the attic where she made him swear once again not to stick his nose in without her permission. Joe was not a curious person.

Ordinarily, he didn't care what secrets Ida kept. He wasn't interested enough. Today was different. He popped the latch and threw open the chest.

On top was more of what he had found elsewhere with Ida's belongings: an unpaid bill for $53 from the National Astrological Library, tucked together with a copy of the code of ethics from the American Federation of Astrologers, and a framed certificate of the Rosicrucian Fellowship that named Ida "Belovéd Adept," admitting her to the Fourth Degree of the Amenhotep Lodge. Tied by rubber band to that was a letter from Ida to the same organization, requesting information about the true nature of atoms and water, while noting her own *"intuitive qualities."* The typed reply to her correspondence described her as *"surely psychic,"* and advised Ida to study her astrology lessons Mondays, Wednesdays, Fridays, and wait for responses on Tuesdays, Thursdays, and Saturdays, but *"be sure to rest on Sundays. That way,"* the letter noted, *"you will get help on invisible planes."*

Stuffed beneath the astrology nonsense was an old photograph album. Joe took it out and leafed through faded images of dogs, cats, some postcards of Des Moines and Chicago and Knoxville, couples holding hands, a series of sailors, but no apparent photos of Ida herself. Under the album he found a water-silk taffeta volume, bound in white and gold: *"Baby First Years — From One to Seven"* and inside, a pile of congratulatory cards: *Blessings on your twins,* read the card from the Longfellow School Parent-Teacher Association. The list of gifts recorded in the baby book ran into the dozens.

Babies?

Joe had no idea what that meant until he opened a dusty envelope near the bottom of the hope chest, postdated February 23rd, 1949.

1. Frances Ida Corrigan: I am 19 years old; I live at 2109 Garfield Street, Louisville, Kentucky; I do practical nursing at St. Mary & Elizabeth Hospital.

2. The defendant and I are husband and wife. We were married in Jeffersonville, Indiana, October 16th, 1945.

3. Both the defendant and I are residents of Louisville, Jefferson County, Kentucky; we both have resided here continuously all of our lives.

4. I am the plaintiff.

5. The defendant Thomas Gallagher and I lived together as husband and wife from the time of our marriage until August 1948. The defendant has habitually behaved toward me for a period of not less than six months in such a cruel and inhuman manner as to indicate a settled aversion toward me and to permanently destroy my peace and happiness. The defendant has not supported me or the children in all our married life. We have lived off of charity the whole five and a half years we been together. He was a painter by trade but he wouldn't work half the time and what money he earned he would take out and buy whiskey and stay drunk all the time. We never had a decent place to live; we always had the cheapest places we could find. He would get third floor attic rooms for us or even in the alleys and in the rear of rooming houses. I had four children and two of the children died. I also had a miscarriage in 1947 when the defendant threw me down the stairs when I was three and a half months pregnant. We never had enough to eat in the house. I would be so bad off that I didn't have enough money to buy

a bar of soap to wash the clothes with or even wash
ourselves. Defendant never bothered to go out and get
the things we needed, he was content to let us starve
and do without. Defendant has been drinking whiskey
so very much that it was almost making him insane and
he got to the point where I was scared to death of
him. Every time he would come in drunk he would beat
on me. He has blackened my eyes time and time again
and beaten on me so that I had to go to the City Hospital for treatment. One time he knocked me down the
steps one week before my baby was born and the child
later died. I have gone to the prenatal clinic time
after time with blackened eyes from his beating me
and then there were times when I just wasn't able to
show myself on the street because of the way he had
beaten me up. Right now I can't focus my eyes on anything and the back of my neck pains me so and I have
such fearful headaches all the time, and it is from
nothing on earth but his mistreatment of me. The
defendant has gotten so wild when he was drinking
that I was afraid of him and one time he threatened
to cut me to pieces with a razor blade and I had him
locked up. Many a time in the middle of the night I
have had to bundle up my two babies and hurry out of
the house and wake up a neighbor to let me stay the
rest of the night with her because of the way the
defendant was carrying on. He had a vile vulgar mouth
too. He swore all the time and cursed me at the top of
his voice and would raise such a disturbance that the
neighbors would complain. Finally I got to the point
where I was too afraid of the defendant to live with

him and the two children were starving and our rent
was due and so I called the Juvenile Court and told
them I had no way of taking care of the children and
they put them in the Childrens' Center for me and I
went to work.

6. I do not feel that I was in any fault. I worked
as a practical nurse whenever I was able and I could
get a job. I would have a colored girl stay with the
children while I worked. I got a job at Our Ladies'
Home for Infants on Center Street and worked there
8 or 9 months and the defendant bothered me so on
the job and tried to get me fired, that finally they
became afraid of him themselves and told me they had
to let me go until I got rid of him, because they
couldn't afford to have him causing trouble all the
time. Then on other nursing jobs I would have to
leave on account of him causing so much disturbance
in coming around the place and calling me up on the
phone. Defendant did so very bad one time in the year
1946 and I taken out a warrant for him for insanity
and they dismissed him after a few days and said it
was just alcoholic trouble. Then my husband turned
around and served out a warrant for me for the same
thing, just to cause me trouble.

7. When I had anything at all to cook for the defendant I cooked. Half the time we didn't have anything.
I always looked after my children and I had help from
the neighbors when I was pregnant and couldn't work,
and the different charities helped me. I feel that
I did my duties as a wife. I washed and ironed and
cooked and kept house.

8. We have two living children now. They are Alice Anne 4 years old, and Helen Lucy 3 years old. They are in a Foster Home at this time out near South Creek. I want the children with me and I have a place for my children at this time if I am given the custody of them. The children are only in this home until I get their care, custody and control, if the court should find that I am the proper person to have them. I have bought them $45.00 worth of clothes since I have been working and away from my husband. I paid $40.00 one month for their board. The defendant is not a fit or proper person to have the care, custody or control of the infant children. He had never been a good father to them. He has never supported them since they were born and it has been up to me to see that they had food to eat and clothes to wear and that they were kept well and warm all the time.

9. I am in good health.

10. I earn $75.00 a month at the St. Mary & Elizabeth Hospital, or $60.00 a month if I take my meals and have my laundry done there, which I am doing at present. The defendant is not working as far as I know. I don't know anything about him now and I do not know where he is. The Juvenile Court cannot contact him to make him pay for the children.

11. My cause for divorce occurred and existed here in the State of Kentucky and within the past five years next before the commencement of this action.

Frances Ida Corrigan 2/22, 1949

Joe was so shocked, he accidentally let the chest lid slam shut on his hand. That was a divorce deposition. It said Ida had married at fifteen and gave birth four times. But wait a minute: that Longfellow card celebrated twins. The girls she mentioned here were three and four years old. So where were the twins? Or the other girls? Were they still alive? Where were they now? How could she not utter one word about any of this? Good grief, how many lies had she told him over the years? Had she been honest about anything? Her parents at Ocean City were named Macaulay. Her husband's name was Galla-gher, yet she wrote her own name on the deposition as Corrigan. So those people at Ocean City were probably not her real folks. Then why did she take their name? Did they adopt her? How had she wound up there? Who the hell was Ida, anyhow?

FORTY-EIGHT HOURS after the shooting at the El Sombrero motel, a warrant was drawn up for Ida Krueger on charges of assault with a deadly weapon, and law enforcement officers were notified throughout the area to arrest her on sight.

```
WANTED
ASSAULT WITH A DEADLY WEAPON.

Mrs. Joe Krueger, aka Ida Krueger, alias Long
Color: white
Age: 32 years
Height: 5'1
Sex: female
Weight: 130
```

```
The subject may walk with a limp, due to an injury to
the left leg. She cocks her head to one side and possibly
squints when reading. She has a bad temper, and is a pro-
verbial liar and confidence woman. Hair last dyed brown.
Gives occupation as astrologist or nurse and usually men-
tions she is a widow or that a member of her family had
died.
```

```
Last known address in this state was 490 Ellington
Ave. San Francisco.
```

When news circulated in Santa Rosa about the Wilson incident at the motel, information came out that Ida Long had borrowed some other money, too: a second five-thousand-dollar unsecured loan outstanding with Bank of America and another eleven-hundred-dollar unsecured note at Wells Fargo.

"I think we've got a bunco scheme operating here," Cochrane told Ellison on a rainy morning one week after their visit to see Joe. "The way the banks are describing Ida's transactions last month, it looks like she's been kiting funds."

"I doubt it."

"Oh yeah? Why not?"

"Well, think about it. Ida and Joe Krueger came to town, set themselves up under a phony name, and borrowed all the money they could get their hands on." Ellison opened a folder on Cochrane's desk. "If you look at these records, you'll see most of the money she took out of those banks went right back into improvements for that dumpy motel. She even bought a neon sign and some new furniture and hired a month's work of labor to renovate half of the units. You don't invest your money in the town where you got it if you're working some bunco deal."

"It's more complicated than that," Cochrane argued. "What if they were kiting those funds to get control of the motel and finance the improvements so they could sell it again? What if this whole case is about money, and nothing more? Maybe they came to town broke, or nearly broke, and saw the opportunity to get themselves set up in another career and needed to run this bunco scheme to get things rolling."

"Then we ought to go back down to the city and have another talk with Joe. Either he's stupid and doesn't know what's going on, or else he's putting up an awfully good front. You know, we forgot to ask him about his bus schedule last month — when he actually left town and such. I'd like to know when he was here and when he wasn't, because that'll tell us a whole lot about Ida's whereabouts at the same time."

"Speaking of that," Ellison said, his focus drifting briefly across the hall to a new stenographer named Stella, whose neat skirts were raising more than eyebrows, "I heard back from Romano this morning. He couldn't find any cab that had picked up Ida at the motel that night she shot Wilson, nor did anyone at the bus depot remember seeing her buy a ticket downtown. And, you know, she's the sort you wouldn't forget, either, with that squinty-eye and funny way of looking at you. And her limp, too. You'd think she'd be as easy to trail as an elephant in a roller rink, but it doesn't appear that anyone's seen her at all. "

"Want to hear my other theory about all this?" Cochrane asked, sipping from his coffee cup.

"Sure."

"All right, try this on for size," he said. "Muriel Knutsen sold her interest in the motel to Long for something less than five grand, right?"

"Yeah."

"So, let's say that Muriel and Joe Krueger had a scheme cooked up to run off together. First, they'd want to get as much money as possible, see? Then, they'd have to get rid of both the Major and Ida to cover their trail. Of course, Muriel takes off first, maybe even down to South America, just like she said she would. Then Joe ties up any loose ends here in town and plans to join her when it's safe. That's not impossible, is it?"

"No," Ellison agreed, "but what do we have to back any of that up with? I haven't heard anything about Joe and Mrs. Knutsen being friendly like that. I can't see him and Muriel flying away together. He doesn't seem the sort."

"Well, you might be right about that. San Francisco PD's keeping an eye on Krueger now, and they say he doesn't do much except go to work and come home again."

"A ball of fire, huh?"

Cochrane nodded. "Oh, apparently he gets out now and then, goes downtown to the movies, but he doesn't seem to meet anyone. I'm not sure the guy has any friends in the city other than those he works with."

"So, what if Mrs. Knutsen planted this whole tale about going down to Brazil with Ida to hide the fact that it was someone else she had in mind to go with all along, someone we don't know about at all? Then, if Mrs. Knutsen vanishes along with Mrs. Long, the whole story fits like a glove. Maybe that Dave fellow she mentioned in the telegram?"

"All right," Cochrane argued, "but why would Muriel disappear first, then the Major, then Ida Long, in just that order? Wouldn't buying the motel sort of knock a hole in the theory that Ida was heading off to South America with Mrs. Knutsen?"

"Maybe there was a change in plans. What do we know about the Longs, anyhow? Maybe Ida had some cash of her own salted away somewhere no one knew about, and she bought the motel to be her own property, not as a joint deal with her husband. Or maybe she had some of the money to buy the motel, but not quite enough, and that's why she took out those loans from the bank and worked that deal with Wilson. I went down to Bank of America where Muriel had her account, and found out that on the day she disappeared, Muriel purchased fifteen hundred dollars of traveler's checks."

"Well, that's helpful," Cochrane said. "If she's cashed any of those checks, we might be able to get a line on wherever she's gone since leaving town."

"Exactly."

"I want to talk to the owners of that motel next door. The Mexican girl told me Ida tried to buy the Bluebonnet before she got interested in Muriel's lot. It'd be worth it to hear what they have to say about that."

After lunch, Ellison and Cochrane drove over to the Bluebonnet Motel to speak to the Crandalls about Ida's disappearance. By then, the parking lot was flooded from the morning rainfall. Cochrane parked under the awning by the front door. Waiting on the threshold was Mabel Crandall, a smile on her face. She invited them into her living room behind the front office, where they sat on a yellow fabric sofa with a walnut coffee table covered with fishing magazines. Her husband, Del, joined them a few minutes later, and Ellison asked them both about the Longs buying the motel next door.

Mabel said, "Joe asked me over to see him a couple of months ago, very upset about something. He told me Ida had purchased Muriel's motel against his wishes and that he hated being here and asked if we might be able to manage it for him whenever Ida wasn't around. We only had a few business dealings with her. She was in and out of here morning, noon, and night, and was a perfect pest, and a born liar, too. She'd forget what she told you and tell you something else a few days later. She was an awful person."

Cochrane asked, "Well, what do you know about the Longs? Where they came from, for instance, and why they were up here in the first place?"

Del Crandall told the cops that he understood Ida had been managing a convalescent home in San Jose, but that she and her husband had gotten interested in the idea of a strawberry farm outside of town. Then Ida got to know Muriel Knutsen and found out the motel was for sale and that did it.

He told the officers, "She'd come over here a couple times a day talking my ear off about the motel business and what all went into operating one. She was sort of a sour individual, if I can be honest. She seldom smiled or had much to say about herself or her husband, and he pretty much kept to himself. Joe never came over here at all, that I can recall."

Mabel Crandall cut in. "Ida was crazy about astrology and took a lock of my hair and did a reading and foretold my future, which she said was bright as the sun so long as I followed my heart and paid close attention to the money side of things." She turned to her husband. "Isn't it so, Del?"

"Well, I don't know about that," her husband said, "because she didn't cut my hair or anything, but she did seem awfully interested in Muriel's motel. Ida figured that since Muriel's business wasn't going great guns, she ought to be able to get it for a cheap enough price, much more so with our place just next door, which has been doing fair enough. But we run this business together and it costs a lot to operate. You can't do it alone, and you can't really afford to employ anyone, either. It's tough going, let me tell you."

Ellison said, "But she had that Juanita running the front desk. How do you suppose Ida managed that? I doubt the girl was working for free."

Del Crandall told him, "Well, that's the sad part. Ida gets one of two different kinds of people to help her. Either they are down and out, and are willing to do almost anything for a few dollars, or she learns a person's weakness, finds out what they really want in life, and tells them she'll help them fulfill that desire. I don't care to guess how she persuaded that poor Mexican to work for her, but you can bet it wasn't all on the up and up."

"Yes, that's Ida, all right," Mabel agreed. "She knew that our greatest desire was to sell this motel and buy a home in Florida where we've been vacationing every year since my mother moved to Fort Lauderdale. So she told my husband and me that she had a fantastic amount of money due from a lawsuit and made us a terrific offer. It's just cruel. She's a conniver, but she couldn't take it if you gave it back to her. Last month she evicted one of her tenants, a nice lady who used to teach grade school here in town. Ida threw her out because poor Tildie wouldn't help clean up one of the back cabins. Well, for goodness sakes,

Tildie's arthritis is so bad she can barely hold a fork. At any rate, I took her in and when Ida saw her coming out of her new room over here, she accused me of stealing her tenant. I just laughed in her face, and Ida hated for people to laugh at her. Her face got contorted. She slapped her hands together like crashing cymbals. Then she withdrew her offer for our motel. That's just how she is, and anybody who's known her for more than half a day will tell you the same thing."

Cochrane asked, "Did you ever notice Joe Long being friendly with Mrs. Knutsen?"

"No, only Ida got chummy with her," Crandall said. "In fact, I remember Muriel telling us both one evening how she and Mrs. Long were planning a trip to South America. She said there were some terrific business investments down in Brazil and they had it all worked out to go there together and look it over."

"Although," Mabel added, "Ida told me one afternoon that Muriel had an old friend from college to go down there with her. I suppose that was to give me the idea that maybe Muriel used Ida Long's name as a way to disguise the identity of her true companion, whoever that might be."

"But she meant Ida," Ellison said. "Isn't that right?"

"Well, I guess so." Mabel nodded. "That's what we've thought all along."

A few days passed with nothing new, then a lawyer for Muriel's family up in Seattle telephoned the sheriff's office to say that her mother had just received a letter supposedly written by Muriel, mailed from Tijuana. It was typewritten, signature and all, not unusual since that's how Muriel handled most of the correspondence to her family and the typeface seemed similar to that from Muriel's portable typewriter. But there were the same sort of discrepancies as with the telegram that troubled her family.

Dear Mother:

Hope your feeling fine. Lonnie, Dave and I are alright. Dave said not to worry. I bought a new car a Cadillac. I been in a little trouble but I always work out my own troubles and affairs all my life. I am fifty-seven now and its about time my family keeps their nose out of my affairs. If anyone asks you where I am you don't know and if anyone asks you any questions you don't know. And I am writing to you under a different name thats if you want to hear from me.

Now mother don't worry about me and take good care of yourself. Tell the children not to worry also. I've sold most of my properties outright. You know Agnes has always been jealous of me even when I had the Turkey Farm she said I should knit sweaters for them I never did forget that. I'm sending Lonnie's pension checks to you to hold onto them until we get settled. I'm also if you meddle I'm having my utility bill sent also. Well, never mind I'll write to Westport and them send them. As I sold the cabins. The ground couldn't be sold.

I have a habit and it's very costly and don't ask me to explain that's half of my trouble. Lonnie wants to write to Bill and tell him we are alright. This is all for now. Love to all from

Muriel, Lonnie, and Dave.

"First off," the lawyer told Ellison, "Muriel's family claims that she usually began her letters to her mother, 'Dear Mom.' The text also refers to Muriel as fifty-seven years old, when she is, in fact, fifty-eight, and her mother would obviously know that. The mention of the West-port property being sold came as a surprise, too, since there was no record of such a transaction. The letter was signed, 'Muriel, Lonnie, and Dave' though no reference was made to any 'Dave' elsewhere, and, just as with that telegram, no one in her family has any idea who 'Dave' might possibly be. They also pointed out that Muriel usually signed her letters, 'Mimi,' but not this one."

Ellison asked what the family thought of the rest of the letter. Did it sound like Muriel?

The lawyer told him it certainly did not. "However, they do agree that if Muriel didn't write the letter, then it must've been someone who knew her pretty well, though her family claims the grammar and misspellings were not characteristic of Muriel. They tell me she was a stickler for that sort of thing. The fact is, no one up here believes she wrote it. None of it makes sense. They say it's a fake, and that really has them worried."

"Is there anything else they have to back that up with?"

"Well, Muriel was known as a pretty astute business woman over the past decade, yet we just discovered that she hadn't filed her income tax report for last year, and we doubt very much that something so important would've slipped her mind, unless her life has gone terribly off track somehow."

"We agree."

"Also, the Major apparently has a standing order with the Rexhall Pharmacy down there in Santa Rosa for a prescription that's pretty important for treating his disease. They tell me it's been refilled on a constant basis for the past several years and mailed to wherever he's been living. Well, the last refill on record now was back in December and no request has been put in for a refill."

"Maybe he's been getting his refills somewhere else. He's been shuffled around a bit this past year."

"Sure, but according to that same pharmacy, these last few years he's been all over the state by their records and hasn't yet missed his refills. So he obviously likes having them do it, or it's easier for him somehow, except these past few months, when they just haven't heard a thing. And he'd know they have him on record. Why not just cancel their refills if he's having them done elsewhere?"

"I guess that's a question for the Major to answer, isn't it?"

"Exactly my point."

"Wherever he is."

"Maybe we're wasting our time with all this," Cochrane told Ellison later that morning in a coffee shop on Fourth Street. "What if everybody turns up fine and dandy and all this fuss finishes with a minor charge against Ida Long for plugging Wilson with his own gun?"

Ellison tapped his cigarette onto the ashtray by his coffee cup. "I doubt that's the case. To me, what's strangest is the Major vanishing like he did, especially with him being that sick. Of everyone connected to this thing, he's the least important. The Major's got no money and he and Mrs. Knutsen were already divorced, so there's no legal tie there at all. Add to that the fact that he was ready to go back to the rest home when Mrs. Knutsen was all set to go to South America, and it just makes no sense."

"All right, so let's say we're talking murder here. Where does he fit in? Are we calling him a victim or a suspect?"

Ellison laughed. "A fellow who can't even dress himself? What would he have to gain? No amount of money on earth is going to help him now. The way everyone's been describing him, sounds to me like the Major's got one foot on a banana peel and the other in the grave."

"So he's a victim, then. If he's that bad off, why get rid of him? Why not just dump him in the rest home and say adios?"

Ellison said, "Maybe he knew something the killer didn't want coming to light."

"Like what?"

Ellison shrugged. "I have no idea, but apparently Mrs. Knutsen's sisters are planning to come down here in a couple of weeks. They aren't too happy that we can't tell them much more than we did a month ago, and if we can't get a line on either Muriel or Ida, we're going to hear bombs falling."

Cochrane stirred more sugar into his coffee. "Well, maybe we'll get lucky."

They did.

A week later, fifteen hundred dollars in traveler's checks purchased by Muriel Knutsen were found to have been cashed at the Emporium in San Francisco on the same evening Muriel was supposed to have left for Brazil, and another three hundred dollars' worth at a hardware store in Petaluma one week later. The signatures seemed genuine. Ellison had them sent to the FBI for confirmation along with samples of Muriel's handwriting for comparison. If Muriel had signed them, maybe she hadn't gone to Brazil, after all. At least not when she told everyone she was going. And if somebody had forged her signature, they had a different sort of problem, but one that could offer a concrete lead.

Then Detective Backman telephoned Ellison the next day from San Francisco. "I've got a tasty carrot for you boys. Either Krueger lied to us, or his wife's been taking him for a ride."

"How's that?"

"Well, my partner and I took a run through Ida's employment records down at the convalescent home yesterday, and saw that she'd listed her birthplace as Louisville, Kentucky. It said that she'd been married back there to a fellow named Thomas Gallagher and had a couple of kids."

"Okay, so she had a life before Joe. What of it?"

"Well, we made a few phone calls and apparently Ida turned up on the doorstep of Gallagher's sister in Lexington not ten days ago, telling them she's been living out in California these days and married to some rich fellow who owns a string of fancy apartment buildings. She handed out some pretty swell gifts to everyone, then offered to take her niece to St. Louis for a weekend to see another relative, before heading back to California again. Well, the kicker is, sweet aunt Ida apparently dropped the girl off in front of a movie house for a matinée and left her there, no money, no nothing. The girl had to call home to get a train ticket back to Lexington."

"You're joking."

"Not at all."

Ellison laughed. "Well, how do you like that? While we've been staking out nursing homes and race tracks all over this state, she's on a road trip, spending money like a low-rent Rockefeller."

"She's a case, all right."

Then Backman said, "But does any of this add up? I mean, she runs off from a cheap assault charge on Wilson, after investing a lot of time and money into fixing up some dump of a motel — "

Ellison interrupted. "Whose money, though?"

"Well, at least her time, right? At any rate, she heads back home just so she can show off how much money she's got, then takes off with a niece she hardly knows and then dumps the poor girl in St. Louis and runs off again. How come? Why Lexington, and why now?"

"Beats me."

Backman said, "We also found out Gallagher's been dead for several years now and we have no idea where Ida's kids are. Apparently she put them up for adoption. Whether she knows where they wound up, nobody's sure. His people back there tell us this was the first they've seen her in almost twelve years."

"Did they have any idea where she's been all this time? After she left Louisville?"

"Nope, all they heard was that she'd gone out west."

"Well, Joe said he married Ida about six years ago," Ellison told Backman, "so we've got a gap there, because he told us he met her in the city where she was working as a nurse. He didn't say anything about Ida being married before or having any children."

"Maybe he lied. Maybe he didn't want you to know where she came from."

"Why would he do that?"

"Well, that's a good question, isn't it?"

"Yeah, like where's Ida?"

HELEN KESSEL LIVED ALONE on a quiet lane that bordered one of the last orange groves near Pasadena. She owned a narrow old frame house in a two-acre stand of mature oak and walnut trees with a bedroom and a sewing parlor upstairs and a nice sunny kitchen downstairs with a front room that looked out onto her yard of grass and flowers. She was sixty-two years old and worked in her vegetable garden and had a daughter who taught ceramics up in Fresno.

One hot afternoon in late July, Helen's doorbell rang. A slight woman with brown hair tied up in a bun stood out on the porch. She looked to be in her early thirties and wore a plain yellow cotton dress soiled with dust and perspiration. The woman carried three white nylon purses in one hand and a black one in her other. She was not unkempt, but neither was she neat. Helen presumed she was all worn out from the heat.

The woman asked Helen for a cold drink of water, and when Helen went back to the kitchen to fetch a glass, the stranger trailed her into the house as if she had been invited, but she had not. Who would do such a thing? Helen might have told the woman to go wait outdoors had she not noticed her limp and how tired she looked. Instead, she said, simply, "You may have a seat in the front room, if you like. I'll bring your glass of water."

"Thank you," the woman replied, and went back to sit in Helen's easy chair by a side table on which Helen kept a tiny dish of chocolates. She tilted her head to one side and rested it on her hand after propping her arm on the table. Afraid the woman was about to fall asleep, Helen hurried with the water.

"Here you are, dear."

"Thank you so much." She took the glass and drank half, and told Helen, "It's awfully hot out. I've positively been on my feet since breakfast and that's not easy when you've had the troubles I've suffered with polio in my leg. I'm not complaining, but sometimes I wonder if God's lost sight of me these days."

"You ought to wear a sunbonnet," Helen suggested, taking a seat on the sofa across the room. "I won't go outdoors in this weather without one. I had sunstroke once and had to be revived by the postman."

Helen felt vaguely uncomfortable and hoped the woman would leave soon. Why had she answered the door? Her daughter told her she was too friendly. One day a stranger would slit her throat if she didn't look out. Best to keep that smile behind a locked door.

As the woman drank her water to the bottom of the glass, Helen noticed her nose was peeling from sunburn and her face had a rosy heat flush. The woman remarked, "The kindness of strangers is a blessing from heaven. I can't thank you enough for rescuing me."

Helen nodded kindly. "It's no trouble at all. I'd hoped to plant carrots today, but it warmed up so much I had to come indoors."

"Oh, I adore back gardens. When I'm home, my husband has to drag me out of the rows or I'd be digging by moonlight." She laughed. "He thinks I'm crazy, but I've always loved to feel my fingers in moist soil, don't you?"

"Yes, I suppose I do."

"Would you care to show me your garden?"

Helen was startled. A stranger hadn't even offered her name and now she wanted the grand tour? She must have sunstroke. "Oh, I'd love to, but you see I really don't have time. I need to go out soon to the market."

Her guest nodded. "Well, you've been more than generous. And I thank you again."

"It's no trouble at all."

The woman pulled one of the white purses up onto her lap. "Honey, I'd like to repay you, if I could, with one of these purses I knitted myself just this week. They're worth twenty dollars, but I'd be pleased to let you have one of them for ten as a discount because of the kindness you've shown me."

The woman held the purse out to Helen, who took it reluctantly. She had no need of another purse, especially this one that didn't look homemade at all. It was too pretty and Helen did quite a bit of crochet and was certain the nylon purses were machine-stitched. "Well, that's very generous of you. However, I couldn't possibly take it. I presume you're selling them and I'd feel awful depriving you of a profit for a simple glass of water. Besides, I doubt I have that much money in the house today." She added that last part in case the woman had something naughty on her mind.

Her guest said, "Well, you've been so kind to me, I wouldn't find it a hardship to sell you one for eight dollars. That's not much for all the work I put into making my purses, but I believe in being generous."

Now Helen wondered if the woman was a con artist, and wished she would leave. This was all too much. She handed the purse back. "You know, dear, I just don't keep any money here and that's the truth."

"Do you live alone?"

"Pardon?"

The woman held the white purse on her lap. "Since my husband Edgar passed on, I've had to fend for myself and housekeeping is such a chore I can hardly keep up with it any more. My eyes are so terrible these days, it's all I can do to make out the bills that need to be paid. It's not right to be alone."

She squinted as if to emphasize her affliction.

"Well, my daughter lives with me," Helen lied, "and I'm blessed to have her. She pays our bills and helps out with the dishes and I don't need to ask twice." Helen glanced over at the wall clock beside the fire mantle and told another lie. "In fact, she'll be home soon and we're going to the market downtown, like I said."

"Oh, you are blessed. My little girl lives in Florida and operates a beauty parlor and her husband has a fishing business in the Gulf. We all went to Mexico once and had a grand time of it. They've invited me out for Christmas next year and I hope to go if I can afford a plane ticket, but I'll travel by bus, if need be."

Trying to stay calm, Helen remarked, "That's sounds like a fine idea. If I weren't so busy, I'd travel, too. There's just so much to do here, I can't seem to make the time."

"I'll bet you do a lot of canning, don't you? My mother loved to can peaches and apricots, jams, jellies, and tomatoes."

"Yes, we do canning twice a year in the spring and summer, although my Caroline thinks we ought to consider winter now, too, for Christmas presents."

"Do you have a cellar? We stored our preserves in a cellar when I was a girl."

Now why would the woman want to know that? Her tone was odd and Helen noticed her eyes had steadied to a determined gaze. "Yes, we do," Helen replied, "but we don't hold them down there. It's not safe to use the stairs any more, so we store them elsewhere."

"Do you keep a lot of food in the house?" The woman drew a deep breath through her nostrils. "Mmm, I can smell your kitchen from here. Why, I'll bet you cook every day of the week." She sniffed again. "Am I smelling hot peppers? I've always loved hot peppers."

"You know, I really ought to get ready for the market," Helen told her. "My daughter'll be home any minute now and I'll need to change clothes."

She stood to let the woman see her time was up.

"Yes, I suppose I ought to move along myself. I've sold five purses today and I won't sell another sitting in this easy chair."

"Would you care to take some chocolates with you?" Helen offered, hoping to see her guest out the door, hippity-hop. "You may have as many as you like."

"Why, thank you, honey!" She leaned over and scooped the entire dish into her palm. "Can't go far on an empty stomach."

"No, you can't."

The woman got up, too, favoring her bad leg, and dropped the chocolates into her black purse. She said, "I'd really like to see where you store your preserves, dear. Canning's been a great enthusiasm of mine."

"Well, I'm sorry," Helen said, firmly now, "but I just don't have the time."

She felt scared and wanted to run this woman out of her house. She didn't trust her at all. There was something peculiar and rude about the questions she was asking. Why couldn't she just go?

Helen led the way to the front door and opened it. She watched the woman limp forward and thought she was exaggerating now, a phony baloney. That's just what she is, Helen decided, a phony baloney.

Near the door, her guest said, "I sold four purses to your neighbors earlier this afternoon and they were pleased to have them. You've been so kind to me, I've decided to let you have one for two dollars. It cost me twice that to stitch them together, but I absolutely won't put a price tag on hospitality. That's just how I'm made."

"Miss, I've told you I don't have the money, and I've already got a purse that suits me fine." Helen stepped aside to let the woman out onto the porch. "Now, if you'll excuse me, I really do need to get changed."

Her uninvited guest paused on the door threshold, as if debating whether to step outdoors or not. Helen felt a panic coming on as she worried about what to do should the woman refuse to leave. Why did she have to put up with this? What was the world coming to when you weren't safe offering a cold glass of water to a stranger on a hot day?

The woman looked her in the eye, longer than Helen would have considered polite. Her jaw was firm, her expression set. But then she said, "Well, dear, I won't keep you any longer. I weighed one hundred and five pounds after my bath this morning, and it's another mile to the bus stop, so I better be on my way." She walked out onto the porch and looked off down the driveway. "It's cooler now, don't you think?"

Helen leaned out past the screen door. "Yes, I suppose it is. Please be careful on my stairs."

The strange woman smiled back at Helen. "God bless you, honey."

That evening, Helen telephoned each of her neighbors on the road nearby and asked if any had bought a purse from the woman she described to them. Not one had seen her at all. On a pleasant Thursday afternoon one month later, Helen rode the bus into downtown Pasadena to shop for baskets and bought a newspaper to read over lunch. When she saw the headline in bold on the front page and a photograph of her peculiar guest underneath, she nearly fainted.

WALLY HUSTON WAS BACK IN TOWN. He had chased Peggy out to Wisconsin because he had thought if he didn't, she would find another fellow to marry. Peggy was going to college at Wauke-gan and wanted someone with substance. Things were changing these days and if you didn't keep up, you could fall behind. So Wally took a room in a new apartment building six blocks from the home Peggy shared with her mother, and made deliveries for a new auto garage until one muggy evening in early August when he found Peggy in her backyard swing arm-in-arm with her old high school sweetheart, Ray Snyder. Once her two rivals finished slugging each other, Peggy sent Ray indoors for a cold compress and told Wally she would rather kill herself than see him again. The next day, he packed up and drove back to California.

The first person Wally telephoned on the warm blue summer afternoon his bus pulled into Santa Rosa was Mabel Crandall. She offered him a room and meals at the Bluebonnet in exchange for doing handyman duty around the motel. Wally also got a temporary job at the county fairgrounds, repairing and painting the old wooden bleachers in the rodeo ring and doing some finish carpentry at a new exhibition hall. He had no intention of falling behind, and when the next girl Wally made a play for showed some interest, he expected to be ready.

So Wally was at the motel one bright sunny morning a couple of weeks later when he heard a knock on his door and found Mabel there, apron on and her hair bound in a net.

"Oh, you're up," she said, looking concerned. She adored Wally, though he didn't care to know why. She was older than Peggy's mother. "We missed you at breakfast and I was afraid you'd overslept your alarm. I know you don't want to be late for work."

Wally told her, "No, ma'am. I didn't oversleep. I'm just feeling a little under the weather this morning. Maybe it was that enchilada I ate at Carlitos last night."

"Honey, I have something for that, if you'd like. It's a bromo seltzer my husband swears by whenever I cook chili con carne. Delbert has a terribly weak stomach and plugs up the toilet if his food disagrees with him."

"Well, I ain't that bad off," Wally said, embarrassed to be talking about toilets with his landlady, "but I wouldn't mind trying your bromo, if it's not too much trouble."

"Oh, not at all. I've got guests waiting for the Greyhound, so I need to go say good-bye to them now, but I'll be right back. They're sisters to my former neighbor next door. They've been staying with us all week, hoping to find out something regarding the whereabouts of the Knutsens. The police just won't listen to them any more. It's a terrible situation."

"The Knutsens who owned the Rose City?"

"Yes, but they sold their interest in the motel to a woman named Ida Long, and now both of them seem to have disappeared and no one has the least idea what happened to them."

"I met Mrs. Long after she took over that place." Wally chuckled as he thought about that long rainy night in the city, how mad Peggy was when they finally got home. "She was kind of an oddball, wasn't she?"

"That woman was more than an oddball. We had a few business dealings with her and she was something, let me tell you. She'd forget what she said one day and tell you another thing a week later. She was a con artist and I didn't trust her for the time of day. "

Wally shrugged. "Except for being kind of a cheapskate, I thought she was all right. I did a job for her at a house she's got down in San Francisco. She needed a big hole dug in her basement for a garbage disposal or some such thing."

"What sort of hole?"

"Big enough for a catch basin, maybe five by five."

"Good grief, when was that?"

"Oh, last winter, I suppose. Me and Peggy drove down there with her and the Major, who had a doctor's appointment at the hospital. It took a couple of hours to dig and we didn't get back up here until after midnight. I think she only paid me about fifteen bucks. It wasn't worth it."

"And when did you say that was?"

"I don't know. January, I think."

"Wait right here, don't go anywhere."

"Sure."

Once Mabel left, Wally made a quick visit to the toilet. He remembered that evening, all right. Peggy had called him stupid all the way up to Santa Rosa until he finally slammed her in the mouth. Then she didn't talk to him for a month. After that, nothing was really the same between them.

Mabel came back across the motel parking lot to Wally's cabin with two middle-aged women, both of whom were wearing blue and gray shirtwaist dresses and pillbox hats. Their faces were sober and weary, and Wally wondered what Mabel had in mind dragging them down to his motel room. He still needed that bromo and hoped this wouldn't take long.

Although his front room was littered with old magazines and paper plates and empty beer cans, Wally invited everyone indoors and had them sit at the kitchen table after he cleared it off. Mabel performed the introductions, then let the sisters tell Wally what they thought had happened to Muriel.

"Frankly, we think she's been murdered," said Agnes, speaking up. "If she were able to get in touch with us, she would. And Lonnie's certainly nowhere that we know of. I feel they were both murdered. So does Ruth. Don't you, dear?"

Her sister nodded. "Yes, I'm certain of it."

"Well, I don't know nothing about that," Wally told them, worried about his role in all this. If there was some crime involved here, that could mean big trouble. Was he liable? "I just dug the hole I was hired for and went home again."

"What hole was that?" Agnes asked.

Wally recounted the car drive down to Ellington Avenue with Ida Long, the Major, and Peggy. He told them about digging the hole while Ida looked on, how she kept asking him to make it bigger, and then about driving the Major over to Mt. Zion Hospital and how Ida took the Major in and told Wally to take the car back to Santa Rosa. "She paid me fifteen bucks for the digging, but I ought to have charged her twice that because I had to knock through a layer of cement to get into the dirt. It was a pain in the ass. Excuse my language."

Agnes turned to her sister. "Dear, I think we ought to call the police and have this young man tell them what he just told us."

"They'd have to listen now," Ruth agreed.

"You're telling the truth, aren't you?" Agnes asked Wally. She spoke like one of the nuns at St. Anthony's who used to paddle him for misspellings. "This is very serious to us. The police already think we're a big bother, and we don't have any use for tall tales."

"Well, it's just like I told it," Wally replied. "I don't know anything else."

"I'll go telephone the police," Mabel said, getting up off the couch.

"How about that bromo, too?" Wally asked, his stomach really boiling now.

Within the hour, Ellison wheeled a blue Ford sedan into Mabel's parking lot next to a dusty fan palm and shut off the motor as Cochrane got out. This section of town was as ratty as ever. Ellison had heard talk recently about some businessmen from Corte Madera buying up half the street and bulldozing all the existing buildings, then putting up a new shopping center and a Holiday Inn with a big swimming pool and a convention hall next door. Maybe a couple of new movie theaters, too. Not a bad idea.

Taking out his notepad, Cochrane told him, "These ladies bug me. I was counting on them being on the bus by now. Do you have any idea how many times they've called this week?"

Ellison lit a cigarette as he got out of the car. "No, tell me again."

"Eighteen, that's how many."

They met Mabel at the Bluebonnet front office. It was hot and windy out now and Cochrane had to hold his hat down to keep it from blowing off his head. The dusty palm trees shook like flamingos above the motel.

Mabel said, "It's just remarkable that Wally happened to be here to tell us about that basement. The girls were ready to get on the bus back to Seattle. Who's to say we would've ever known, otherwise?"

Ellison asked, "Where is he?"

"Down in Cabin Five. Agnes and Ruth are gone, but they'll telephone from the first stop."

Cochrane smiled. "Swell."

They found Wally rooting through his refrigerator for some cream. He had taken a shower and changed into his work clothes and put on a pot of coffee. While Mabel went back to the office, Ellison and Cochrane introduced themselves and made Huston tell his story again, prodding him for more details while Cochrane took notes. Ellison asked who drove the Lincoln down to the city.

Pouring himself a cup of coffee, Wally sat down at the kitchen table and told them, "Well, since neither Mrs. Long nor the Major could drive a car, I did. Then, after the job, I asked Mrs. Long how she planned on getting back from the hospital and she said they'd take a taxi to the bus depot and come home that way. I parked her car in the driveway and left the keys with that Mexican girl at the front desk."

"Do you know when Mrs. Long got back? Was it that night, or the next morning?"

"No, I don't know, because I went home with Peggy, afterward. I wasn't living at the motel then, so I don't have any idea about that at all."

"Did you see Mr. Long down there?"

"No," Wally said, "but I remember the Mexican girl told me he was asleep in his room when I got back. That's why I gave her the keys. He was supposed to pay me an extra five dollars. I never saw it."

"How big a hole did you dig in the basement?" Ellison asked him.

"Oh, I'd say roughly five feet deep and square. Maybe a little bigger than that. She told me it needed to be at least that size for the plumbing and disposal unit to fit right."

"Do you think you could draw me a picture describing where you dug the hole? Where exactly it was in the basement?"

"Sure, do you have a pencil?"

Ellison took a pen from his jacket. "Try this."

"How about some paper?"

Cochrane tore off a sheet from his notepad. "Here."

"All right, let me see." Wally sketched a rough outline of the basement. "These are the stairs and here's the old garage door." He drew quickly. "And this is about where she wanted the hole dug. That's it."

He slid the pen and paper over to Ellison.

Cochrane asked, "Where was the Major during that time?"

"Mrs. Long had him sitting in the next room in a chair. He was in pretty bad shape and couldn't do much else but sit. It was a kind of small room, as I remember. Nothing in there but a couple chairs and a carpet. Peggy waited with him. Mrs. Long said she was converting the room into an apartment. It needed a lot of work. I heard what those ladies were saying, but as far as I was concerned, I was digging a plumbing hole, not a grave. It wasn't too big if she was going to put in a catch basin. How was I supposed to know what she really had in mind?"

"Don't worry about that," Ellison said, fiddling with a dry cigarette. He wished those ladies hadn't given Wally an idea. "When exactly did you dig the hole? What day of the month?"

"Well, let me think." He sipped from his coffee cup. "This might sound funny, but I actually remember it was on a Monday, now that you bring it up. I remember because I was between jobs at the time and Mrs. Long read my horoscope on the ride down to the city and told me that tomorrow, Tuesday, would be my lucky day to get another job. And, sure enough, I got hired to work on an addition at that titty lounge down in Novato, the Blue Fandango."

"Do you remember the date?"

"No, but if you show me a calendar, I can figure it out for you."

"I'll bet they've got one up at the office," Cochrane said, getting up from the table. "I'll be right back."

After he left, Ellison asked, "Do you mind if I smoke?"

"No, go ahead."

"Do you have an ashtray?"

"Hold on." Wally got up and went over to the table by the lamp stand. "Every room in this motel's got one and Mabel doesn't smoke. Funny, huh?" He grabbed an ashtray and gave it to Ellison, who set it on the kitchen table. The glass ashtray mimicked amber, but probably cost a quarter.

Ellison took out a match and lit his cigarette. He smoked Salems because his brother-in-law got them wholesale. Cochrane had an allergy and wouldn't let him smoke in the car, so Ellison had one now.

Sitting down again, Wally asked, "You think Mrs. Long killed the Major and put him in that hole I dug?"

Ellison exhaled a lungful of smoke. "I wouldn't know. We're just asking questions."

"She sure had the nerve."

"What's that mean?"

"Oh, I don't know. She's just the sort that seems to do whatever suits her and to hell with anyone else. I was afraid she wasn't going to pay me when I was done. She had me slaving in that hole for a couple of hours and I still had to argue her out of fifteen bucks. She's a case, if you ask me."

Cochrane came back with the calendar and dropped it in front of Wally. "Have a look."

Wally flipped the months back to January. "Let me see now." He skimmed his fingers down the dates. "Okay, it was the fifteenth."

"You're sure?" Cochrane asked.

"Yeah, I'm sure," Wally told them. "I know because me and Peggy went over to Napa for her aunt's birthday that Saturday after New Year's and came back in the middle of the week. Then she nagged about my work until Mrs. Long got me off the hook that following Monday by hiring me to dig up her basement and, like I said, I got the titty bar job on Tuesday. So, it's right here on the calendar: Monday, the fifteenth."

Ellison snuffed his cigarette out in the ashtray and got up from the kitchen table. "Well, thanks, Wally. You've been a big help. Get some breakfast. We'll be in touch."

"I suppose you fellows are going to dig up the basement, huh?"

"How about staying in town for a few days, Wally?" Cochrane said as he followed Ellison to the motel door. "We'd appreciate it."

Back out in the hot wind at the Ford, Ellison told Cochrane, "You know what this means, right?"

"Yeah, if Wally dug a grave in the middle of January, it probably wasn't for Muriel. She'd already been missing for a month. But the Major was last seen on the 15th, and nobody's heard anything from either of them since."

Ellison said, "Do you suppose the Major watched his own grave being dug?"

"That's a nice thought."

"But why kill him? What possible advantage would there be in disposing of a guy like that who could hardly get around on his own and already had a bed waiting for him in a convalescent home? Who would do something like that to a cripple?"

Cochrane tucked the notepad into his jacket. "Beats me."

"Or are we missing something here?" Ellison fired up the motor. "Maybe somehow the Major was mixed up in Mrs. Knutsen's disappearance, maybe he knew something about it that nobody wanted to get out."

Cochrane rolled down the passenger window. "Well, there's only one place we're going to find out about that."

Then he grabbed hold of his hat as Ellison shot the Ford out into the dusty boulevard.

HAD JOE KRUEGER KNOWN the roof was about to fall on his head, he might have gone out for a good long walk that evening. But while Cochrane and Ellison were obtaining a search warrant for the Ellington basement from a judge in San Francisco, Joe was busy reading a magazine article about tunneling under the Berlin Wall. He wasn't sure he'd be able to do that. The Japs tunneled everywhere in the Pacific and Joe'd crawled down into one at Leyte and had a panic attack.

That idea Ida had about renting out the downstairs apartment was something Joe began to reconsider. He enjoyed his privacy, but finding just the right fellow to eat supper with now and again, or share the television for a couple of hours, wouldn't be so bad. Joe had no expectation that Ida would be home anytime soon. Maybe she was dead. Strange men telephoned to the house every so often asking for her and hung up without giving their names. Who knows what sort of people she did business with? Joe gave up long ago trying to make sense of Ida. Once he saw that divorce deposition, he realized he didn't know anything about her at all. Another husband? Kids? Kentucky? Good grief. He certainly loved her way back when she took him into her life, but she was a nut. He was sure of that now. If she walked into the house tonight, he had questions for her that he knew she couldn't answer. Her behavior was incomprehensible. This Ida could not be the girl he had married. It wasn't possible.

Joe had a long day looming on the job tomorrow and eventually he put the magazine away and switched off the living room lights and went back to the bedroom. He took off his shoes and shirt and did his business in the toilet and brushed his teeth and combed his hair. He always combed his hair before going to bed. When Joe was a kid, his mother combed his hair at bedtime and got down on her knees beside him as they recited a prayer together. *"O God, through whose beauty we exist, bring us in safety to the morning hours. Amen."*

As Joe turned out the bedroom light a little while later, he decided he would call his dad tomorrow and let him know he was quit of Ida for good. He thought that would make him happy. His dad had never trusted Ida.

ELLINGTON AVENUE was dark and foggy, damp like a lot of evenings in the Bay Area. There was a chill in the street when Cochrane and Ellison parked across from Joe's house. Detective Backman found a spot down on the corner behind a patrol car carrying two uniformed SFPD officers. Another car driven by assistant district attorneys Meryl Hightower of San Francisco County and Cary Ellwood from Santa Rosa pulled to the curb on Whipple. A truck carrying a couple of men from the Department of Public Works arrived and parked nearby.

Securing a search warrant had taken all day, but they finally got one signed by the Superior Court and, just before nine o'clock, Detective Backman knocked on Joe's front door.

"Are you sure he's here?" Cochrane joked, buttoning up his collar. The steps behind him were crowded now. Two more patrolmen stood down on the sidewalk.

Backman nodded. "We've kept our eye on him since he got home. He hasn't gone anywhere."

A light switched on indoors.

"I think we woke him up," Ellison said, snuffing out his cigarette on the porch railing.

"It's past my bedtime, too," Cochrane added.

The front door opened and Joe Krueger's face peered out at them. "Do you fellows know what time it is?"

"Yeah, Joe," Backman told him, "it's time for you to give us another tour of your house, starting with the basement."

Ellison held up the search warrant. "How about being a good host and letting us in?"

"You fellows are crazy."

But Joe stepped aside to let them indoors. He had the living room table lamp switched on, and another light glowed in his bedroom. Other than that, the house was dark and cold.

"Do you ever turn the heat on, Joe?" Cochrane asked, glancing around.

Joe shook his head. "Costs too much. It's cheaper to wear a sweater."

Ellison laughed.

The two assistant district attorneys wiped their shoes on the mat and came inside. Behind them followed four uniformed patrolmen. A couple of them went back to the kitchen and stood by the door.

"How about showing us the basement, Joe?" Backman said, pausing in the hallway.

"You still think Ida's hiding down there?"

"We're going to take a look, Joe," Ellison answered. "So why don't you open it up for us?"

"You're the boss." Joe stepped past Backman and opened the basement door, then reached past the jam to switch on the downstairs lights.

"Go ahead, Joe," Ellison said. "Lead the way."

"All right."

They proceeded down the narrow stairs, one by one: Joe, Backman, Ellison, Cochrane, then the attorneys, and one of the patrolmen. It was dank and colder than upstairs. The basement had seen some improvements since the police had last visited, though the rooms were still poorly insulated. They noticed the wooden tongue-and-groove floor had a nice polished sheen to it.

Cochrane asked Joe, "Do you have any idea what we're looking for tonight?"

"I don't have a clue. Why don't you tell me?"

"Well, Joe, we have reason to believe there might be a body under here, so we're going to dig up your new floor and have a look."

Joe looked him in the eye. "I hope you're joking. What body? Who told you that?"

"Never mind who told us." Ellison glanced at Wally's sketch again and pointed to a spot just a few feet from the basement stairs and the west wall. "We're going to dig a hole right there. If you have any idea what we might find, now's the time to let us know."

"Well, I don't, so dig away if that's what you want to do. Let me know what turns up."

Ellison called out to one of the patrolmen. "Adams, bring 'em down!"

Joe sat on the living room couch, listening to the electric saw cut through his new basement floor. He thought his head was about to explode. He knew about the holes Ida had hired out to be dug because of the patches on the old concrete. She'd told him they were for plumbing, and whether he believed her or not didn't matter. He sure wasn't going to dig up his own floor just to see if she was telling the truth. He had Ida's basement at Ocean City firm in his mind, that moist smell of new concrete and freshly dug earth. Was she crazy enough to do this all over again? In his house now? His hands were shaking because he knew the answer.

The cop at the door had his eye on Joe. There were a slew of them outdoors now. Joe heard one fidgeting in the kitchen by the back door and another out in the yard. His basement was packed solid. The city workmen had electric flood lamps set up down there and Joe hoped they wouldn't burn his house to the ground. He heard a commotion out on the sidewalk. His neighbors were collecting right outside the front gate. He felt humiliated and got up off the sofa to switch on the radio, turning up the volume so he couldn't hear what people were saying out there. Joe refused to look at the cop by the door.

Under the glare of portable flood lamps, one of the Public Works men cut out a four-foot section of the floor with the power saw while his partner kicked the broken fragments away. That took ten minutes. Nobody left the basement. When the job was finished, everyone saw a layer of cement underneath with a distinct outline where the original concrete had been broken. The cement had a grayish hue different from the surrounding floor with clearly defined borders.

Ellison looked at the others. "Wally's hole?"

Cochrane nodded. "I'd say so."

Detective Backman said, "Let's break it up."

Ellison turned to the assistant district attorneys, Hightower and Ellwood. "Do you agree?"

"Yeah, break it up."

So Cochrane and Ellison took off their jackets and laid them off to one side, then rolled up their shirtsleeves. They grabbed a couple of sledgehammers brought downstairs by the workmen and began demolishing the concrete floor. Each blow rattled the flood lamps and shook dust from the ceiling above. Both attorneys retreated to the small adjoining room. Backman stood watch from the stairs. The clanging of the sledgehammers on concrete echoed out to the sidewalk. After laboring for an hour, they reduced that part of the cement floor to chunks of rubble. The room smelled wet and moldy. Both Ellison and Cochrane were soaked in sweat.

Upstairs, Joe's radio set played a jazz station while the cops took a short rest, Ellison leaning against the wall by the basement stairs, Cochrane next to a support post beside the flood lamps.

"You think Joe knows who we're looking for down here?" Cochrane said, wiping his brow with a handkerchief.

Backman said, "Well, if he doesn't, he's got to be one of the dumbest fellows around."

"Maybe Ida did all this while Joe was up working at the motel," Cochrane suggested. "What if it was all taken care of before he got back? Remember, Wally told us that Mexican girl said Joe was in bed up at the motel that night, so we don't have anybody placing him here at the time."

Ellison disagreed. "If there's a body down here, believe me, he's in on it."

One of the uniformed patrolmen brought down a jug of water and the cops drank it to the bottom. Then Cochrane and Ellison put the sledgehammers aside and grabbed a pair of shovels. Backman helped them rake off the concrete rubble to expose the dirt undersurface. The attorneys came back out of the small room to watch. Cochrane and Ellison divided the area into halves and began digging slowly. Five minutes passed and Ellison hadn't shoveled more than a few scoops off his section of the dirt rectangle before he uncovered the heel of a shoe.

"Well, what do we have here?"

Backman brought one of the flood lamps closer. Cochrane joined him, as did both attorneys. Ellison put the shovel aside and got down on his knees and began scraping with a penknife until he had the whole muddy shoe and a human ankle exposed.

Cochrane smiled. "Who wants to tell our pal upstairs?"

"Let's see what we've got here, first." Ellison turned to one of the Public Works guys. "Is there a hand trowel?"

"Hold on a second."

Attorney Hightower said, "We ought to call Tuttle."

Backman agreed. "Yeah, this is the coroner's job."

"Well, let me dig it out a little more," Ellison said, as a city workman handed him a trowel. Cochrane knelt beside Ellison. Backman held the flood lamp just overhead and Ellison began carving dirt away from the foot, digging down inch by inch until he was looking at the cuff of a pants leg caked in dirt.

They all stared for a minute. Both of the city workers eased forward for a closer look. Attorney Ellwood took a snapshot of the foot.

Finally, Cochrane said, "This has to be the Major."

Ellison nodded. "Probably."

Backman told Hightower. "Okay, let's call Tuttle."

Ellison laid the trowel aside, then said to Cochrane, "How about you go up and get Joe? Let's see what he has to say now."

Joe Krueger had been in the bathroom when the foot came out of the dirt. He had a headache and sour stomach. He drank a glass of Alka-Seltzer and sat on the toilet and thought about how nobody had ever told him that tomorrow would be a constant surprise.

When Joe flushed the toilet and came out of the bathroom, Inspector Cochrane was standing there in the hall, waiting for him. His coat was off, tie loosened, his shirt stained from sweat. He looked anxious.

Joe frowned. "Yeah?"

Cochrane said, "Follow me. There's something we'd like to show you."

"What's that?"

"You'll see."

Somebody was using the kitchen telephone, and Joe couldn't quite hear what the fellow was saying. He was talking too fast. Anyhow, weren't they supposed to ask before using his phone? Joe felt caught in a whirlwind. What did they want from him? He didn't do anything. Goddamned Ida. This was worse than New Guinea. At least out there he knew where the bombs were coming from.

Cochrane led Joe downstairs into the cold damp basement where concrete rubble was piled up on the near wall and a ring of flood lamps illuminated a dark shoe that jutted up from a rough patch of dirt. Good God! Joe stared at it. The shoe was attached to a filthy trouser leg. Ida had really done it now. They were both cooked.

Ellison spoke up first. "So, what do you have to say about this?"

Well, what could he say with that shoe staring back at him?

"I didn't know we had a permanent guest."

One of the city workers laughed.

Cochrane growled, "This isn't funny, Joe. You have a dead body in your basement."

"I can see that, but it's just as big a surprise to me as it is to you. And that's the truth."

Backman nudged over a chunk of concrete with his toe. "Come off it, Joe. How does someone have a body buried in his own basement and not have a clue how it got there?"

Joe's legs felt wobbly. He was scared half out of his wits. "Look, fellows, I know I'm in a bind here. I can see that. So this may sound nuts to you, but I swear I don't know a thing about this. I was away from here most of the winter. If somebody buried this guy in my base-ment, they did it without me knowing about it. That's all I can tell you. Besides, if I did it, why would I just sit here waiting for you to come get me? Don't you think I'd guess someone might look down here one day? You fellows were already out here once snooping around. Why would I sit on my ass waiting for you dig up my basement if I knew a body was down here? There's places around this country where nobody could ever find me if I didn't want them to, and I can tell you for damn sure, if I had someone buried here, I'd have been long gone before tonight."

Backman asked, "So when you saw us come down here to start dig-ging, you weren't curious at all?"

Joe's lips quivered as he lied. "Nope, I never gave it a thought. Why would I?"

"You weren't even sore about us tearing up your basement?"

"I figured to bill you for damages."

Ellison asked, "What about your wife?"

"What about her?"

"Where is she?"

"I bet I've told you fellows a hundred times, I don't know. And if you ask me another hundred, I'll give you the same answer, because I don't know. What else can I say?"

Cochrane asked, "Where's Mrs. Knutsen?"

"Ask Ida. Maybe she knows, but I don't."

"Has your wife contacted you?"

"I told you I haven't heard from her in months."

Detective Backman said, "You don't seem to know much at all, do you, Joe?"

"Look, fellows, it won't do any good to keep asking me these questions when all I can do is give you the same answers. Maybe you ought to start thinking about who really stuck this guy in my basement, because I don't know a goddamn thing about it."

A voice shouted down from the front room. "Tuttle's here!"

The upstairs of the house on Ellington became a riot of footsteps and voices as a dozen people filed indoors from the dark street. Dust shook from the basement ceiling as the upper floor trembled. A patrolman came down the stairs to let Backman know the coroner wanted the area around the body cleared out to preserve evidence. Ellison and Cochrane left Joe with the patrolman for a minute and crossed the basement into the small room for a brief strategy session. Once the coroner set up, there had to be some management of access to the basement. Joe Krueger had to be watched, too, whether he volunteered more information or not. Also, there had to be some consideration given to the possibility that the body did not belong to the Major, but if it did, where might Muriel Knutsen be buried, if she were down here, too. Ellison said to Cochrane, "Why don't you take Joe upstairs, see if his memory improves with a change of scenery."

"He thinks he's a tough nut."

"Well, he's being stupid now. We got him and he knows it. Lying won't get rid of that body out there."

Backman stuck his head in the narrow doorway. "The reporters want to come down. Television's here, too. Out on the sidewalk."

"Don't let them in unless Tuttle says so."

Backman nodded. "All right."

Meanwhile, the attorneys returned to the basement again, discussing jurisdiction pertaining to venue and evidence. When the coroner's assistants started unloading equipment near the body, Cochrane escorted Joe back upstairs to his bedroom to stew in his juices for a while.

Then Coroner Tuttle came down the stairs. He was dressed like a scruffy old college professor in a tweed coat and glasses. His expression was grim. He ordered everyone out of the basement except for his assistants, a couple of reporters with their photographers, the two attorneys, a single uniformed city patrol officer, Backman and Ellison. After the police flood lamps were repositioned to illuminate a wide area surrounding the body, Tuttle put on a pair of gloves and began his excavation. It was a tedious procedure. The body had apparently been buried upside down, as if shoved face first into the hole. One foot wore a shoe, and the other was bare. The legs were thick with dirt. Tuttle and his men needed more than an hour to dig down to the waist. The stench was terrible. When they reached the arms, Backman looked behind him where one of the photographers was setting his flash for another image. Next to the photographer was a young Mexican in suit and tie, scribbling into a notepad. Backman tapped Ellison on the shoulder. "Who's the kid?"

"Saludes. He's from our paper. Good young reporter."

"Has he covered any homicides? I don't want him puking on my new shoes when we bring the body out."

"I'll mention it to him."

Ellison drew a cigarette from his shirt pocket and fiddled with it, but didn't light up. Both attorneys held handkerchiefs over their noses against the stench. The photographers snapped pictures every so often, while the reporters jockeyed for better positions and took notes. The room felt cramped like a cave. Upstairs, people moved about, but were mostly quiet. Outdoors sounded like a circus as the neighborhood crowd grew with word about the discovery of a body in Krueger's basement.

After an hour or so, the coroner and his men had dug to the bottom of the basement grave and Tuttle climbed down for a close look at the body. It had gone head first into the narrow hole and lay on the nape of the neck, both torso and legs torqued oddly above the head.

"Look here, boys," Tuttle called out. "This is what did it. Strangulation."

Ellison peered into the hole. "What's that around his neck?"

"Well, I'd say it's his belt."

"For christsakes."

"I'd guess it's from his trousers." Tuttle brushed more dirt off the waist. "See? The loops are empty."

"I'll be damned," Backman said, kneeling beside the hole. "What a way to go."

The photographers' cameras flashed over and over, and one of the reporters dashed upstairs to call his city editor. Neither of the assistant D.A.s spoke.

"It's going to be difficult to make a positive identification. The body's too badly decomposed." Tuttle grasped the skull and carefully scraped tufts of dirt out of the victim's hair, then brought one of the lamps close to the head. "But I'm seeing burr holes here consistent with prior neurological treatments for Parkinson's disease, which we know Mr. Knutsen suffered from. Therefore, I believe we can make at least a tentative identification tonight. There does appear also to be enough flesh remaining on this poor fellow's hands to obtain fingerprints, so we'll try to do that in the morning and send them off to the FBI tomorrow afternoon. Boys?" Tuttle looked up at his assistants. "What do you say we bring him up?"

Joe stood under the trapdoor in the hallway, listening to Cochrane and a couple of uniformed officers scuttle about in the attic overhead. Another street cop waited by the front door and kept anyone out of the house who didn't have authorization to be inside. He was also instructed to prevent Joe from taking a walk. A small crowd had gathered at the top of the basement steps: some newsmen, cops, others whose identity and purpose there Joe couldn't determine. Every so often one of them would look over at him as if waiting for Joe to confess that he'd put that body in the hole. Well, they were all nuts. He felt as if this was some stunt, a stupid prank the fellows from work had cooked up to get his goat. Back in New Guinea, guys slipped bugs in a fellow's coffee cup now and then or gave somebody a hot foot. That always got a few laughs. This wasn't funny at all. What if someone got the idea of going up to Ocean City? Sure, there was a hotel sitting over the basement there now, but couldn't they get a search warrant to dig it all up if they really wanted to? He bet so. And if they did, it'd be the gas chamber for sure. Suddenly Joe became truly terrified and wished he could call his dad for help. He thought about Caryl Chessman in that green room at San Quentin and felt sick to his stomach again. Ida was gone and the cops were going to get him for that body in the basement. He was doomed.

Joe watched the coroner come up the basement stairs and hurry out the front door. It sounded like there were a hundred people outside now. Fog had dampened Ellington Avenue and cold seeped into his house. He heard the cops talking just overhead in the attic.

"Says here she owes some astrological society fifty-three bucks."

"She's in the red to a lot of people."

"I wonder how many of them she planned to pay back."

Joe went down the hall into his bedroom, where he found another cop hunting through the closet. His dresser drawers were pulled open, too, his things messed up. "What the hell are you doing?"

"Sir?"

"They tell you to come back here?"

"Yes, sir."

"What for?"

"You'll have to ask Detective Backman, sir."

"Goddamnit."

Joe retreated to the hallway. The cops didn't have the right. Who did they think they were? Gestapo? He almost bumped into Ellison coming up through the basement door.

The inspector stepped back. "Just the person I want to see."

Joe glared. "What the hell do you think you fellows are doing back there in my bedroom?"

"We have a search warrant for the whole house, Joe. That's how it is. We're just doing our job. You brought all this on yourself."

"I didn't do anything of the sort."

Ellison said, "Listen up, Joe. The Major had his own belt cinched around his neck. How do you like that? The coroner says his larynx was crushed. What sort of person would do that to a sick old man?"

This was becoming worse by the second. Ida must have gone psychopathic. Joe said, "Why would anyone want to kill the Major? He was a real nice fellow. Hey, I fed the sonofabitch half the time when he was staying with us up there at the motel and we'd talk about things. Did you know he was gassed at the Argonne, then went to college and wound up running a big newspaper? He led a hell of a life, I tell you."

"Why don't you tell us what really happened, Joe? Make it easy on yourself."

"I didn't kill him."

"Well, maybe your wife did it, huh? Do you think that's possible?"

"How should I know?"

"Joe, we've already got a warrant drawn up for your arrest. It says suspicion of murder. That's a mighty big fall. You could sniff the gas for this. What do you bet Ida knew we'd catch you in the house with the body? If you're telling the truth, and didn't know about the Major taking the long snooze down there, and your wife's the one who cracked his neck, but didn't want you involved, doesn't it stand to reason that she'd warn you? Even if only to let you know what we might dig up down there? I guess she didn't call you, after all, did she, Joe? Did she give you a call?"

"No."

"Look out, fellows." A voice spoke behind Ellison at the basement stairs. "Coming up!"

Ellison moved back to the hallway wall as the coroner's assistants lifted a stretcher carrying the dead body out of the basement. The corpse was wrapped tightly, but a sickening odor wafted into the upstairs of Joe's house. A patrolman at the door told them a city ambulance was waiting at the curb. Noise from the crowd outside rose as the stretcher moved out into the night air amid the glare of television lights. The front door closed again.

"Well, Joe, there you have it," Ellison said. "While you're sitting on your appointment at San Quentin, your wife'll be off somewhere living the life of Riley."

"Shut up."

"Don't drag your feet, Joe. You're going to jail tonight. The only question is how long you'll be there. We can make it a hell of a lot easier on you if you'll give us a break here. Quit stalling and tell us something we can use to help you out of this jam. Nobody's going to believe this basement could get dug up without you noticing a thing about it."

"I didn't say that."

"Didn't say what?"

"That I didn't notice the digging."

"Oh yeah?"

"Sure, I noticed," Joe said, his stomach doing somersaults. He had to tell them something now or they'd pin this whole business on him. "When I was down one night from that goddamned motel, there was a fellow here named Kendall that Ida had hired from Novato to put in her wood floor, and I went downstairs as he was getting started and saw the old patches where the original cement floor had been fixed. I noticed because this fellow wanted to break it all up to lay the new cement and I told him not to, said we couldn't afford it if he did, and he fought me on it for a while, until he finally agreed to skim something like three-quarter inches of new concrete right over the old stuff. He said the aggregate wouldn't hold as well, but I knew Ida wouldn't care, so he and I shot the lines together, and he did the floor. That was that. I went back up to the motel the next day to burn a pile of trash and when I came down here again later that week, the job was all finished."

"You said, old patches? More than one?"

"Yeah, one where you guys just dug and another one over by the garage door."

"Gordie!" Ellison called up into attic after Cochrane, then turned to Joe. "Are you telling me we ought to dig another hole?"

"That's up to you guys," Joe replied. "I'm just telling you I saw a patch there before we re-covered the floor."

Cochrane leaned down from atop the attic stairs. "What do you have?"

"Joe says there's probably another patch under the cement over by the garage door."

Descending the attic stairs, Cochrane asked Joe, "Did you dig a hole there?"

"I didn't say anything about a hole. All I'm telling you guys is that I saw a patch on the old cement."

Cochrane asked Ellison, "What do you think?"

"I guess we ought to go see what we've got." He flexed his biceps. "Another hour with that sledgehammer and I'll be Mr. Universe."

"Why don't you tell Backman? I'll send someone out to let Tuttle know what we're doing." Cochrane turned to Joe. "You're coming down with us."

Joe felt cold and tired. "What for?"

"To tell us where to dig."

"I need to use the toilet."

"All right, but make it quick."

Joe went to the bathroom and shut the door and thought about who to call when they took him to jail. Not his dad. Maybe George Evans from work. He drank a lot and bragged about his arrests for brawling at North Beach. He certainly knew how to post bail. Maybe he had a lawyer, too. Joe needed a lawyer. He zipped his pants up and met Cochrane in the front room where the curtains had been drawn open and Joe could see out to the street. Radio reporters were broadcasting from his driveway and the old coroner was standing in the lights of a television camera. Beyond Joe's white picket fence were more people than he'd ever seen on Ellington, a lot of them children, mostly Joe's neighbors and that sort who rubberneck at car smash-ups, a crowd of gossips and snoops. He hated them all.

Joe Krueger followed Cochrane back down into the dank basement. Before he reached the middle of the stairs, flashbulbs popped in his face. The reporters rushed forward, shouting his name. "MR. KRUEGER! MR. KRUEGER! HOW'D THE BODY GET IN YOUR BASEMENT? DID YOU KNOW IT WAS THERE? WHERE'S MRS. KNUTSEN?"

"What is this?" He shouted at the cops and tried covering his face. "Get them out of here! Those sonsabitches! Get 'em out of here!"

"WHERE'S YOUR WIFE, JOE? DOES SHE KNOW ABOUT THIS?"

Backman tried to make them quit. "All right, boys, that's enough! Knock it off!"

"COME ON, JOE! GIVE US THE STORY! WHY'D YOU DO IT?"

"All right, that's it!" Backman shouted. "Everyone, upstairs! Now! Out!"

"COME ON, JERRY, WE GOT A RIGHT TO BE HERE. THIS IS NEWS."

"You boys are interfering in an active investigation. We're not done down here yet. You can wait upstairs. We'll call you when we finish. Now get the hell out! Officer Duggan? Show 'em out of here."

Joe had slipped over to the far corner of the basement by the old garage door, away from the flood lamps. He stood there until those idiots from the press left the basement. One of the lawyers came back down with a large briefcase. The room was a wreck. All the wood flooring had been ripped to pieces and piled aside, exposing a gray surface of concrete where that fellow Ida hired had laid down the slab. Half the basement was rubble now, except for a big hole near the stairs where the body had been dug out. That was nothing but a dark pit. Joe listened to a lot of pushing and shoving at the top of the stairs. His house had been taken over by lunatics. A putrid odor hung in the damp air. Joe tried not to puke.

Ellison came over to see him. Cochrane had grabbed a sledgehammer, and one of the Public Works guys held a digging bar. Ellison said to Joe, "Okay, show us where it is."

Humiliated, Joe pointed to a spot roughly ten feet from the garage door. "Right about here."

"You're sure?"

"That's what I remember, because our plumber found an old beer barrel hidden in the dirt there and covered over with concrete. My uncle said this used to be a bootlegger joint."

Hanging his coat on a wooden chair he'd brought out from the other room, Cochrane asked Joe, "What do you think we're going to find now?"

"How should I know? You fellows seem to have all the answers."

Ellison pointed to the city worker. "Okay, let's get at it."

Joe stepped back into the corner to watch as the cops slugged away with the sledgehammers and the young city workman chipped off chunks of concrete with his digging bar. The noise echoed through the walls. Dust flew all over and Joe covered his mouth with his sleeve. One of the attorneys sat down at the bottom of the basement stairs and scribbled into his legal tablet. A photographer leaned his camera out over the steps and set off a flashbulb. The reporters scuffled for a better position.

The digging here didn't require as much time as on the other side of the basement. After fifteen minutes or so, they cracked through the newer concrete and located a discolored patch in the old cement floor. The other worker brought over a rake that Ellison used to clear away the rubble.

"Good guess, Joe," Cochrane said, wiping sweat off his brow. Everyone looked exhausted. Joe glanced at his watch. It was past midnight. The realization that he would be sleeping in jail tonight gave him heartburn.

Backman studied the patch. "It's pretty amateurish."

Ellison looked over at Joe. "Did you do this?"

"Hell, no."

"Do you know who did?"

"Nope," he told them. "Like I said, I was up at the motel when she had this dug out."

"And what was it for again?"

"She said a waterline broke."

"Well — " Ellison handed the rake back to the Public Works guy and nodded to Cochrane, "let's take a look."

They only needed a few minutes to break through the thin concrete patch. After that, Ellison and Cochrane switched to shovels and roughly six inches down into the earth, they struck something firm.

The top of a steamer trunk.

Ellison grabbed a rag and wiped the dirt off its leather surface. The trunk was sort of blue, but deteriorated and badly scuffed. Suddenly everyone in the basement was staring at Joe. All he could get out of his mouth was, "This might sound nuts to you fellows, but I've never seen that trunk before in my life."

A camera bulb flashed and Backman called up from the bottom of the stairs, "Someone get Tuttle!"

Hearing that, the reporters and photographers scrambled down into the basement and Joe went to hide in the small room. He would have buried himself if it were possible. This wasn't a jam you talked your way out of. Ida had lied and lied and lied. Then she cut out and left him to face the music alone in his own goddamned house. This was worse than Ocean City. At least then she had a plan get them both off the hook. He supposed this time she didn't need his help. She was free as a bird and he was about to take a nosedive into the gas chamber.

Joe heard the news photographers snapping away and peeked around the corner. Tuttle had come back down into the basement. Under his instructions, the city workmen grabbed the shovels and unearthed a broad perimeter around the old trunk, which was resting on end. When they finished, Cochrane and Ellison climbed down into the new hole and inserted boards on the bottom of the trunk to prevent it from bursting. Next, they tied a heavy rope around it. Then they took a couple of trowels and sliced away at the dirt pinching the trunk. With help from the workmen tugging up above, they managed to haul it out of the hole.

"There's no doubt about it," Backman told one of the attorneys. "She's in there."

Tuttle put his gloves back on and took charge again. "I'm going to open it now."

The crowd in the basement drew near the trunk. Flashbulbs popped. Joe left the small room. He thought he was about to have a blackout as he watched Tuttle pop the latches.

The trunk fell open and the coroner stared inside for a few moments. Then he pulled something out and identified it for the basement audience. "A woman's comb."

A hush fell over the room.

"And a pair of women's panties."

Joe heard the coroner unzip a canvas mattress bag inside the trunk.

A moment later, Tuttle announced plainly, "I have a body here."

The coroner reached over and grabbed a portable lamp and repositioned it next to the trunk. "Because of the decomposition, it's difficult to tell if this is a man or a woman, but I believe it is a female because of the general size of the body, the contour of the body, the fact that we've found a woman's comb and women's panties."

Joe heard Ellison murmur to Cochrane, "What do you want to bet that's Mrs. Knutsen?"

Tuttle added, "She's wrapped in some sort of rubber sheet. I'm removing it now."

The photographers flashed one photo after another. Word about the body spread to the upstairs and noise increased at the top of the steps.

As Tuttle gently peeled back the sheet encasing the body, he raised his voice. "All right, I can see she's clad in a white blouse . . . and a blue skirt . . . a panty girdle . . . stockings, but no shoes . . . I see a gold wedding band on the left hand . . . a diamond ring . . . and what appears to be a pearl necklace of flat gold pieces . . . The body of this woman has black hair."

Joe went back into the small room and threw up in a corner.

Half a dozen more city newspaper reporters stuffed themselves into the crowded basement. Nobody could get up the stairs now. If a fire broke out, Ellison thought, they'd all be cooked. He stuck the cigarette he'd been fiddling with back into his shirt pocket. Cochrane wrote himself a note about the wedding band and gold necklace. He would telephone Muriel's mother and sisters tomorrow morning. Detective Backman asked Tuttle, "How long would you say she's been in there?"

He shrugged. "Longer than that fellow we just exhumed, I'm sure of it. Judging by the state of decomposition, I'd guess several months."

"Half a year?" Ellison asked, leaning close to Tuttle. He kept his voice low, preferring not to have a crowd of newsmen deciding the case for him.

"Could be. That'll take a little time to determine precisely."

Backman asked, "And cause of death? Any thoughts?"

"Well, let me see here." The coroner summoned his assistants. "Boys, let's get her out of the trunk."

A flashbulb went off. Cochrane finished scribbling another note and joined Ellison near the trunk. Keeping the remains in the rubber sheet, Tuttle guided the corpse out of the trunk and onto a stretcher his assistants had brought downstairs. A fresh rancid smell bloomed into the damp basement. Most of the newsmen pressed handkerchiefs to their noses. The cops had almost become accustomed to the nasty odor. Once the woman's body was out of the trunk, another round of flashbulbs went off and Tuttle asked for a flood lamp to be positioned over the stretcher. Then he began a brief, but closer examination.

Tuttle worked quietly for a few minutes. Nobody else said a word. The basement air was stuffy and rude.

Then Tuttle said, "Well, decomposition has eroded enough flesh that I can see three small bones in her neck that have been badly fractured, indicating strangulation again as a likely cause of death." He looked over his shoulder at Detective Backman. "There's no belt here, no other obvious ligature instrument, so we may have to assume the strangulation was done manually."

Ellison leaned forward. "Could a woman have done it?"

Cochrane smiled.

Tuttle hesitated. "This is an extremely unusual method of killing for a woman to commit, chiefly because of the sheer physical strength required. It's my thought that a murder such as this would need someone with very powerful hands."

"Impossible for a woman?"

"No, not impossible."

Ellison motioned for Cochrane to join him over in a corner of the basement next to the garage door. They left Backman with the swell of reporters as more flashbulbs ignited. Tuttle continued his preliminary examination of the woman's body. A radio newsman at the top of the steps began describing the scene below. Assistant D.A.s Ellwood and Hightower headed upstairs.

Putting his back to the basement crowd, Ellison said to Cochrane, "Someone dug the hole for the trunk and did a pretty damned good job of it. Notice how clean the sides are? It looks as if they were cut to fit the trunk. And the cement job, too. Who's going to believe Ida did this all by herself? That's not a one-person job for someone like her. Not on your life."

Cochrane nodded. "I agree. No way in the world she strangled Mrs. Knutsen, dug the hole, jammed the body into the trunk, mixed the cement, put the trunk in the hole, then finished it off. Alone. There was someone else here, I'd bet on it."

"Remember Joe told us that if he knew there were bodies buried down here, he'd have taken off?"

"Yeah, but I don't believe it. He just didn't think we'd go to the trouble of digging them up. Or that we'd even suspect they might be hidden under his basement. After all, we did need Wally's statement about the catch basin to get us down here tonight."

Ellison shrugged. "Fair enough, but what I'm saying is, if it were me with bodies in my basement, and I thought the cops were getting close, I'd get the hell out. Like he said, we'd already been here once and the basement was the only place we hadn't really looked."

Cochrane replied, "Well, maybe he figured that running away would draw even more attention to him. Or maybe he was too scared to run. Either that or he was waiting for Ida to come back from wherever she told him she'd gone, and then the two of them could hightail it together. Not everyone thinks logically when they've killed someone."

Ellison said, "Well, if he goes somewhere, sure, maybe we think he's running. But if he runs, maybe we don't grab him, either, and by the time we dig up the basement, he's down in Argentina."

Cochrane watched Tuttle fold the rubber sheet back over the body once again. Backman began clearing a path through the crowd of reporters. Ellison drew the cigarette out of his shirt again. "Let's see what Joe has to say about this."

They looked back into the small room where they found Joe Krueger sitting quietly on a wooden chair, looking scared and disconsolate. The room was narrow and bleak. Joe fit perfectly.

"If he's a murderer," Ellison told Cochrane, "I'm Pinocchio."

As the two cops came in, Cochrane spoke first. "You're going to need a good lawyer, Joe."

Joe looked up, weary of this whole business. He knew he was fixed, no matter what. "I don't have any money for one. I'm not guilty, anyhow. No matter what they book me on or convict me of, I'm still not guilty of a goddamn thing."

Ellison lit his cigarette. "That's what you told us."

"And it's the goddamn truth."

Cochrane said, "Well, we've been giving this some thought, Joe, and what we've come up with is the idea that there's absolutely no chance at all someone could've murdered the Knutsens and buried them down here without knowing your house well enough to pick just the right place to hide the bodies, and not just from us, but you, too. Now, you say you didn't know they were under the floor, which doesn't make much sense to us, but if it's true, that means your wife killed them, and that leaves us wondering how she could've done it on her own, because those are pretty big holes and the Knutsens aren't midgets. Just dragging their bodies into those graves is too much job for one little lady with a bum leg. We figure she had help, probably digging the hole for Mrs. Knutsen, then putting her in it and covering up with the cement."

What could he say? Joe nodded. "If Ida killed those people, then she had to have help, all right, but I have no idea who it could be."

Cochrane said, "So you agree that Ida could've killed them?"

That brought him back to life. Joe knew he had to steer them off somehow or this could lead up to Ocean City and then he was really cooked. "Hell, no! Ida didn't kill anybody. She's gone nuts over that motel, all right, and I'll admit there's a lot of funny business going on, but she's not the sort to kill anybody."

Ellison said, "Well, she shot Wilson."

Wilson again, that bastard. Joe almost wished he'd shot the guy himself.

He told them, "That was his own goddamn fault. I told the sonofabitch to keep off our property, but he didn't listen. Now that I think about it, he's probably the one you ought to be talking to. Who's to say he wasn't trying to frame us? He couldn't keep his eyes off my wife, I can tell you that. He wanted her in the worst way. If it ever got out what he did to her on that trip out to Nevada, he'd be finished and he knows it. What better reason to go after us. You know, those two people in my basement aren't the only ones that disappeared. Ida's gone, too, and I'd be willing to wager she's not coming back, either. She's probably lying at the bottom of a canyon somewhere. I'll bet Wilson killed her to shut her mouth about what he did to her in Reno, and then he killed the Knutsens so it'd look like we did it."

Ellison smiled as he took a drag off his cigarette. "That's an interesting theory, Joe."

"You ought to look at that fat Mexican girl who worked for Ida, too. What do you want to bet she knows something about all this? Hell, she and Wilson could be in it together."

"You got it all thought out, don't you?"

"I didn't kill anyone."

"Well, Joe, I guess that'll be up to a jury to decide. In a few minutes here, we're going to take you downtown to the Hall of Justice where you'll be booked for murder on the fact of these bodies we just found in your house."

Joe felt pale, his voice hoarse from denials. "That's a hell of a thing to do."

"Well, it's the law, Joe," Cochrane told him, nodding toward a couple of uniformed patrolmen waiting just outside the small room. "We're also broadcasting an all-points bulletin tonight for your wife on suspicion of murder. The FBI's involved now, too, for a charge of unlawful flight to avoid prosecution filed in Federal court this morning."

Joe stiffened when he noticed one of the patrolmen holding a pair of handcuffs. He told Cochrane, "Go right ahead. I hope you do get her, because she's the only one who can get me off the hook now. But I still don't think we'll ever see her again."

"Well, either way you want to go," Ellison said. "Whether we find her or not, the fact is, you have a big problem, pal."

Joe Krueger stared hopelessly at the dirt floor. "I know it."

CHARLES AND IRENE BOLLINGER spent every waking hour of their lives in the service of the Lord Jehovah. They believed devoutly in the reward of spiritual life with Christ Jesus in heaven for those elected few whose virtue and obedience would allow them to avoid the great tribulation and inherit the Kingdom of God with the One Hundred and Forty-Four Thousand. When Charles was not earning his living painting houses in Encinitas, he and Irene distributed copies of *The Watchtower* on the sun-washed streets of downtown San Diego. Faith and fortitude held the Bollingers steadfast, year after year, despite the constant slurs and indifference of their fellow human beings. Well aware that boredom and frustration were Satan's triumph, Charles and Irene patiently canvassed the city sidewalks with Jehovah God's invigorating message.

Early one Wednesday morning in mid-September, fresh from breakfast at a delightful bakery, they noticed a truly forlorn woman staring into the ladies apparel window of a big department store on Broadway. Her simple print dress was shabby and wrinkled, stockings sagging, shoes scuffed and worn. She had ratty hair and wore dark glasses and appeared hungry and sore. The Bollingers approached her with the unbridled joy of Christ in their hearts. What mission were they on, after all, if not the salvation of this poor bedraggled soul?

They introduced themselves by the flashy show-window and elicited a grateful smile from that woeful child of God.

"Oh dear, this is so wonderful to meet you," she told them, "because I study the Bible myself. When I was a girl, I used to believe the reflection of love that smiles upon God's face came from me alone. Isn't that amazing? And it's straight from the Bible, too. You can absolutely look it up. I'd quote the chapter and verse to you, but I've been sick for a month and my thinking cap's fallen off."

Charles said, "We noticed you from across the street, and thought you might need our help. There's no disgrace in having troubles. Even our Lord Jesus had His obstacles."

"Of course He did," the woman agreed. "I won't deny my worries."

"Would you care to buy one of our books?" Irene offered, feeling neglectful of her mission that morning. "They're only a dollar each and I can't think of anything I'd rather use as a road map to the divine."

"Well, I don't have a dollar. I just walked here from 44th Street where my car broke down. I had surgery last month for cataracts and had to be in the county hospital six weeks waiting for another surgery that I'm embarrassed to tell you about. It's been the awfullest time. My landlady tried to kick me and my little Mary out of our apartment when we didn't have enough money to pay our rent. We slept in my car for three nights until the neighbors saw us and asked her to let us back in. But that's only until Friday unless I can find a job, and I won't ask for charity, because that's not how I'm made."

Bollinger and his wife were deeply stricken with sympathy over the sad woman's plight. They knew the Lord looks over the least of His children and asks us to do the same. So Charles and Irene invited her to have supper with them. "We'd be honored if you'd accept, and it'll be no trouble at all for us to come pick you up, Mrs — ?"

"June Smith, and I'd be delighted. You're so very kind. My daughter and I haven't eaten a decent meal in weeks."

"Oh, honey, it's our pleasure," Irene enthused, feeling almost intoxicated. How often had she truly put the Lord's mercy into practice? "What time shall we come get you?"

"Why, anytime after four o'clock ought to be fine, if that's convenient for you. Mary's at the park with one of her little friends from the apartments and I've asked her to be home by three."

Shading his eyes from the sun, Charles said, "We need to go now, but we'd be pleased to help you with bus fare back to your apartment, if you like. It's a long haul to 44th Street from here."

"Oh, I feel like such a bother."

Irene dug into her purse for some change. "Here, darling. Please take it." She passed a handful of coins to her new friend. "Nothing would make us happier this morning."

"Are you sure?" June said, sorting through the coins. They added up to just over a dollar. "This is such a blessing."

"Yes, indeed," Charles replied. "And for us, too. We'll see you later today. Do you know the exact address of your apartment?"

"Yes, I do. It's number 4235 at the Mar Vista, but I'll wait for you on the sidewalk so you won't have to worry about parking. It can be very busy during the daytime. What are you driving?"

"We own a green Nash sedan. I'll honk when we see you."

"And please take this," Irene added, handing June a copy of the Watchtower. "I want you to have it. A gift from one disciple to another."

"Why, thank you very much."

Walking off, Charles and Irene Bollinger floated on a cloud. For years they had preached how charity of acts and spirit transformed the heart and prepared the soul for its glorious reward at the foot of Jehovah God. Now, at last, they were truly witnesses to that exhilaration of divine generosity the Lord Himself taught His apostles two thousand years ago on the long dusty road to Jerusalem.

Charles rolled the Nash out of his garage about half past three and drove across town in a pleasantly mild breeze off the Pacific. He found the address with no trouble at all and saw June Smith sitting just up the street from the Mar Vista apartments on a small sandstone wall painted coral and aquamarine. She wore the same dark glasses and simple print dress that was threadworn and dowdy and did little to evict the poverty of her appearance.

Bollinger brought the auto around in a U-turn and ran it up against the curb near June in front of the Lilac Court bungalows. Then he got out and greeted her with a warm smile. "My, this is a nice little neighborhood."

June smiled. "Yes, it's very pleasant."

Charles walked over to help the poor woman get to her feet. She felt unsteady as she rose. Who could tell what afflictions she suffered?

He asked, "Is your daughter inside?"

"No, she's decided to stay overnight with one of her friends next door and I agreed because it's so tough on her being just twelve years old, and us moving about like we've had to these days. Do you have children?"

"Not yet, we don't," Bollinger confessed, reluctantly. "Irene's chosen to place that desire in the hands of the Lord, and if He sees fit, we will. If not, then we both understand that our path to His glory lies elsewhere."

"I'm sure that's true. Heaven has cloth of many hues that God alone assigns," said June, touching Bollinger's hand ever so lightly. "I have no dispute with His judgment. Shall we go?"

Irene had cooked a pot roast with sweet potatoes and corn, and they dined together in a simple whitewashed room whose picture window offered a vista of swaying palm trees and telephone wires down the street and a purple ocean sunset out beyond the harbor. Charles recited grace for the table, and passed the serving bowls to Irene and their guest, who ate with the hunger of the deprived. She offered no pride for bashfulness. Plate to mouth and a drink of water, plate to mouth and a drink of water. Charles was more pleased than he was capable of expressing. Christ truly dwelled in his heart and home this night.

"Do you read the Bible often?" Irene asked her guest, as she placed a slice of warm cherry pie before her.

June dabbed her lips with a napkin. "Why, sweetheart, I'd be lost without it. Most evenings my daughter and I take turns reciting the Psalms before bedtime. They help me forget my own pitiful worries and let me sleep with His blesséd assurance."

"You have such a dedicated outlook," Charles remarked. "I can't say that I've ever met a more courageous person, particularly one who's endured all that you have these past few weeks."

"Well, I don't blame anyone for my misfortunes. The Bible teaches that a scapegoat will bring us into a wilderness of our own making. If my husband hadn't lost his shirt in the oil game, I might not have found this strength I have today for surviving and keeping my daughter safe and well."

"Do you belong to a church?" Irene asked, clearing off the supper dishes. "We find fellowship so rewarding these days."

"Most churches I've been affiliated with don't take Bible study as seriously as I do, and that troubles me. How else can we expect to know the Lord, I always ask, if we won't bother to see what He has to tell us?"

"That's so true," Charles agreed.

Irene asked, kindly, "How long ago did you lose your husband, if you don't mind my asking? I know it's a very private thing."

"Three years ago, last month," June told her, a trace of sorrow in her voice. She raked her fork over the slice of pie. "He fell from an oil derrick and was instantly killed. I've never known quite how to explain his passing to my daughter, why he can't be with us in our travels, and why he's not here any longer to comfort us at night. He hadn't paid into his life insurance policy for more than a year before he died, and without his income or the money from his insurance, we lost our home, and have found ourselves in dire straits ever since. Do you think that's cruel to hold him up as the root of our troubles? My own health has been awful since my accident last year and I can't afford insurance, either. What we need more than anything is a place to live and a job I can take that might earn me enough to feed my little girl."

"You know, we have many friends in town," Charles told her. "Don't we, dear?"

Irene nodded. "Yes, of course."

"And I'd be terribly surprised if one of them didn't need some help around the house, isn't that right?"

"Certainly," Irene agreed, brightening now. "In fact, I can think of two names right off the top of my head, women from our Kingdom Hall who've mentioned how nice it would be to find someone who might come in and help with the family housekeeping during the day. Would that interest you at all?"

June's smile blossomed. "Oh, I'd feel blessed to have any sort of work. I'd be grateful for the opportunity."

"Well, let me place a telephone call or two and see what we can find." Irene rose from the table. "I just know you're going to make someone very happy." She hurried out to the living room and closed the door.

"Isn't your wife remarkable?" June commented to Bollinger. "She's trying to help me out of a terrible fix and we didn't even know each other until this morning. I read the astrology pages in the newspaper and there wasn't a word about any of this."

"Well, you'd be more likely to find it in the Bible," Charles said, after swallowing his last bite of pie. "We read the daily papers, like everyone else, but we don't rely on them for offering us any pearls of wisdom. God doesn't labor for the *San Diego Union*, or the *L.A. Times*. If He did, we believe there'd be less smut and more encouragement. Who needs to read about sex and murder every morning?"

June put aside her fork, and dabbed her lips once more with the napkin. "No one needs to tell me how awful this world's become. Why, hardly a soul today seems to have any respect for their neighbors. And I don't just mean those living next door, but everyone we pass by ought to receive the Lord's blessing from each of us in our daily lives. Yet they don't, and I haven't any good answers about why not. Cruelty is a big mystery to me, and I've given it a lot of thought. Truly, I don't believe in killing and I don't believe in dishonesty, because the Bible says those are sins, and I trust in that book more than I trust the morning paper at breakfast. I'd rather boil an egg."

When June excused herself to visit the toilet, Charles brought his dessert plate to the kitchen and stared out into the late summer twilight lit by streetlamps. He felt more buoyant than he had in months. This chance meeting with June was becoming a terrific opportunity for him to bat some ideas of his back and forth with someone other than Irene, who preferred prayer over reading the Bible with real discussion as he did. When his wife came out of the living room, Charles told her, "Darling, I just had a great thought."

"Why, so have I," Irene interrupted. "Margaret Dumont has agreed to our idea of a housekeeper, and June's going to need a place to stay and we have the back room. Of course, we can talk it over, but I really think we ought to ask her to stay with us while she gets herself sorted out. Don't you agree?"

Charles felt absolutely gleeful. "Yes, I think that's a terrific idea. She's just the kind who'll keep us on our toes, and it'll be wonderful having a child here, too."

"Maybe she'll join our church and let us introduce her to all our friends."

"I certainly hope so."

They heard June coming out of the bathroom, humming "When Irish Eyes Are Smiling."

As their guest returned to the dining room, Charles spoke up. "June? We've made a decision." He stopped for dramatic effect, something he loved to do.

June blinked. "Yes?"

Bollinger wrapped his arm around his wife. "Irene and I would like very much to have you and your daughter live here with us until you get back on your feet. We think it would be terrific. Just the right thing to do. What do you say?"

She blushed, patting her heart. "Well, I'm lost for words."

"Will you do it? You can't say no."

"Well, I do need a job," June stated, matter of factly. "I've never been a freeloader. I absolutely want to pull my own weight."

Irene beamed. "Then you'll be glad to know I just got off the phone with my friend Margaret who said she's in desperate need of a housekeeper. I told her all about you and she seemed very interested."

"I hope you told her I'll scrub floors if she'll let me. I've never been too proud to earn a dollar with a little sweat and elbow grease."

"We can drive you over there tomorrow for an interview, if you like," Irene said, taking her husband's hand. "Isn't it marvelous how this is all working out? We're so blessed to have run across each other this morning."

"It really is wonderful, isn't it?" Charles agreed with a huge grin.

"Yes, indeed," said June, smiling, too. "Just wonderful!"

June telephoned after lunch the next day to ask for directions back to the Bollingers' home. She told them that her daughter was out with the neighbor who volunteered to take a group of little girls to the zoo while June had her interview. Charles suggested that he just drive back and pick them both up, and June agreed, but said she had to speak with her daughter regarding what time she needed to be back from the zoo. June told Charles she would call back within the hour. Meanwhile,

Irene was busy cleaning up the back room for their new guests, vacu-uming, changing the linen, creating space in the closet and dresser drawers. It had been years since Charles had seen her so enthusiastic and he helped her by washing the bedroom windows and polishing the mirror atop the walnut highboy dresser. When they finished, a pleasant weariness fell over them and they sat side by side on the bed, admiring the job they had done. Charles kissed Irene and she smiled and kissed him back and took his hand and led him out of the back bedroom into their own and did something with him she hadn't done in months. Afterward, they retired to the living room to listen to records and wait for June to call back.

She never did.

The afternoon went by and shade covered the Bollingers' patio and a breeze off the ocean cooled the house. By suppertime, they began worrying that something had gone wrong, and Charles thought he might take a drive over to June's apartment. "What if she forgot our number?"

"But she called once already," Irene pointed out, "and I'm sure she wrote it down."

"Maybe she lost the slip of paper and she's been waiting for us to telephone her."

"Well, we don't have her number. I'm sure she knows that."

"Let's try information," Charles suggested.

There was no listing for a June Smith at that address on 44th Street, so Charles decided that June hadn't telephoned from her apartment at all, but either from a pay phone or her neighbor's home where June's daughter had been staying. In either case, since they wouldn't be able to call back, not knowing the neighbor's name, they decided to wait until June called them.

The Bollingers ate supper and stayed up to watch *Sing Along With Mitch* on television before accepting that June wasn't going to call that night. At eleven o'clock, they turned out the lights and went to bed, somewhat deflated in spirit after all the work they had put in that day, yet confident their new friend would telephone first thing in the morning.

After breakfast, Charles passed the morning paper over to Irene and went out to water his garden in the backyard. He had expected to sit out there today with June, discussing the merits of New Testament study and the question of sin in the modern world, particularly as it addressed worldwide communism and the atomic bomb. Instead, he fiddled with his azaleas, pruned Irene's white roses, and watched a long jet contrail from the Naval base unravel over the ocean. Then he went indoors and telephoned the office of the Mar Vista apartments.

"Hello? This is Charles Bollinger and I'm a friend of one of your tenants, a woman by the name of June Smith."

"I don't know anyone by that name."

"Well, she's been living there for three months. Are you sure you don't know her?"

"Could you please describe her for me?"

"Well, she's about five feet tall with brown hair. She has somewhat of a limp and has been wearing dark glasses on account of an operation she just had for cataracts."

The woman thought for a few moments, then told Bollinger, "I know who you're talking about, but she just moved into her apartment on Saturday. I know because I spoke with our weekend office manager, Mr. Pratschner, after he'd given her the keys."

"And she hasn't been there any longer that you know of? Apparently she just got out of the hospital."

"No, I'm sure I'd have remembered."

"Well, thank you very much."

Bollinger hung up the telephone and went back into the bedroom to tell Irene what he'd found out. The entire situation was becoming very suspicious and he didn't really know what to think of it. When he told Irene about his conversation with the landlady at the Mar Vista, she put up a pout. "Why would you believe that apartment woman over June? Maybe she misunderstood what you meant by how long June's lived there, not just this month, but all year long."

"Darling, she said she'd never seen her before last weekend. Why would she lie?"

An hour later, Charles answered the doorbell and found June herself waiting out on the front porch. Still in dark glasses and a dowdy dress, she said that she had taken a taxicab from her apartment after walking her daughter over to the neighbors'. Bollinger invited her inside, curious to hear her explanation regarding what the landlady at the Mar Vista had told him. After waiting for June to sit down on the living room sofa, Charles began as innocuously as possible, not wanting to upset his guest. "We missed you yesterday."

"Yes, I'm just so sorry about that." She brushed the hair off her brow. "It was the funniest situation. I was out for a walk in the morning, admiring the flowers in all the yards along the street, when suddenly I tumbled right off the curb! Can you imagine? I almost broke my neck."

Irene came out of the bedroom when she heard their voices. "How awful! Were you hurt very badly?"

"No, but I was so dizzy I completely forgot about coming over here. Then my daughter went off to the zoo with our neighbor without letting me know about it. They didn't get her back home until eight o'clock and I positively gave them a piece of my mind."

"We were told a Mr. Pratschner just gave you the keys to that apartment on Saturday night," Bollinger remarked, trying to be diplomatic while testing the discrepancies in June's story. "That you hadn't lived there before."

June frowned. "Well, I find that very interesting because he offered a bottle of beer to my Mary not ten days after I had my surgery. She told me right there in my hospital room in front of the doctor and my nurse, Miss Cathcart. You can call her up. She'll remember because I asked her to telephone the police and absolutely have him investigated. I've no doubt he would tell a lie like he did about me when he's hoping I'll forget what he tried to do."

"That's hideous!" Irene exclaimed, sitting down in a cane chair across the room.

Ignoring her, Charles told June, "Well, come to think of it, actually I heard it from the woman at the desk of Mar Vista. She told me Mr. Pratschner gave you the keys, but that you hadn't lived at the apartment until this past weekend."

"You know, I never saw her, either, so I can't comment on that, but we did live in the back, not that apartment we have now. I suppose she didn't know us from Adam and that's all right by me, too. I'm to blame, of course. I've never been trustful of people, not since my husband died and left us indigent. Did I tell you he bet his life insurance on the horses at Santa Anita and lost every penny? I've been ashamed to admit it and you're the first to hear the truth because he died two weeks and two days afterward, and never thought to tell me what he done. I suppose he was humiliated."

"We hate to sound distrustful," Irene remarked. "It's a terrible habit. All of us have our petty faults, don't we?"

"Well, I certainly have my share of faults," June admitted, sounding humble and contrite. "But I won't worry you any longer, because I don't have it in me to push my nose in where I'm not wanted."

She rose from the sofa, a look of abject defeat on her brow.

"Don't say that," Irene cut in, frantically. "We've only wanted to help and this is all so confusing. After all, we don't know these people at your apartment and the things they told us were so difficult to believe."

"We just wanted to be sure," Charles added, "for your little girl's sake."

"Well, I found a new offer in the newspaper this morning. A man from Point Loma needs to have his car driven over to Arizona for a hundred dollars, and I agreed. My cousin Norma lives outside of Flagstaff and she's been begging me for ages to come see her, and that's what we're going to do. There's a spare room over her garage where we're welcome to stay as long as we like, but we won't put her out if it's more than a month and I know there are situations I can find there to help keep us fed and clothed, so we won't be any more trouble to you."

Irene sighed. "Won't you take Margaret's telephone number, just in case? She's very kind and I'm sure she'd love to see you if you happen to come back."

June agreed. "Thank you, dear."

Then Charles asked, "May we give her your number, so she could give you a call, let you know where she lives in case you get back into town and need a ride? That'd be helpful, I think."

"Why, absolutely." June took a pen from Irene and scribbled a telephone number onto a slip of paper and gave it to Bollinger. "This one'll be good until the day after tomorrow at the latest."

Once June had left, Irene placed a call to Margaret Dumont and told her about June's change of plans, while Charles went out for a few hours. Later on that afternoon, after bidding on a house-painting job near Oceanside, Charles Bollinger came home and decided to telephone June once again to see if she might have anything to say that could resolve some of his misgivings about her. He dialed the number she'd given him that morning and a young woman answered. "Hello?"

"Yes, I'm looking for June Smith. Is she there?"

"Who?"

"June Smith."

"I'm afraid you have the wrong number."

"Oh, I'm sorry."

Bollinger hung up, presuming he had dialed incorrectly. He checked the number and tried again. The same voice picked up. Confused, Charles read the number back to the young woman, who confirmed he hadn't made a mistake dialing. "But there's no June Smith here," she told him. "I've had this same number for two years."

Bollinger hung up. There couldn't have been any mistake recording the number, since June herself had written it down for him. He went out back into the garden where Irene was watering her daisies and recounted his telephone debacle.

Irene said, "Maybe she just wrote her number down wrong. Mother used to do things like that. She was absentminded, though she claimed her trouble was having too much on her mind. I'll bet if June saw how she'd written her phone number, she'd have a good laugh on herself."

"I'm thinking about driving over there."

"Don't do that. You've already accused her of deceiving us once already. What'll she think if you bring it up again? Where's the virtue in suspicion? Besides, I really need you to dash out to the store. We're out of milk and powdered sugar. Could you go now?"

Once Charles had driven off to the market, Irene finished watering her flowers and went back indoors to telephone her friend Sonja, whose husband refused to join the Kingdom Hall, despite constant reminders from his wife that Christ had a timetable. Irene had the morning *San Diego Union* spread out on the kitchen table in front of her and doodled with a pen, drawing glasses and moustaches across faces in the paper while she chatted on the phone. Irene had no need for the daily news and rarely noticed even the most sensational or inflammatory headlines. This world concerned her less than Jehovah God's plan for what was yet to come. So that dour woman on the front page attracted none of her interest until she finished scribbling a pair of black glasses onto her face. Then she read the story beneath the photograph regarding a woman named Ida Krueger, wanted by the law for questioning in the case of Major and Mrs. Lonnie Knutsen, whose bodies had been uncovered in the basement of Krueger's home on Ellington Avenue in San Francisco. She hung up the phone from her conversation with Sonja and stared at the photograph of Mrs. Krueger.

When Charles returned from the store, Irene called him to the kitchen. "Darling, come here! Tell me who this reminds you of."

He stared at the photograph for a few moments. "It's impossible."

"It's June Smith, isn't it? Don't you agree? Clear as a bell. My goodness, she was right here in our own home!"

"I don't know. There's a certain resemblance, I admit, but I can't believe it's the same woman." He skimmed the headline story. "What would she be doing here? It doesn't add up."

"She's hiding, that's what. She's ducking the law by pretending to be someone else. That's why her story had us so confused, because it was all a lie. We were such fools, dear, and to think we fed her and found her a job. I think we ought to do something."

"We really ought to step back and consider this very carefully. Remember your Uncle Jonathan and that business with the shoplifters? They made a laughingstock out of him. Are you ready for that? Besides, weren't you the one telling me to show more faith in her?"

"I want to call the FBI right now. She shouldn't be free to walk the streets."

"Well, I almost feel sorry for her. I think she's sick. To do what she's accused of, she can't be in her right mind."

After almost an hour of arguing back and forth, Charles relented and agreed to place the call. He told the agent on the telephone, "I hope we're wrong, you understand, but I thought it would be the best thing to do."

Two FBI agents came out to the house just before supper and brought photographs of Ida Krueger and asked the Bollingers to repeat their story. Once all the details were filled in, the agents asked if

Charles might be willing to accompany them to the apartment where June Smith was staying in order to positively identify her as the woman who had visited them. Charles agreed and rode across to East San Diego in the back of one of the FBI automobiles.

It was late now and streetlights glimmered from the hills to the oceanfront and a cool sea breeze fluttered through the palms. Charles sat quietly during the ride over to the Mar Vista apartments. Guilt at betraying a Christian woman nagged him, even though he had read the litany of crimes June Smith was accused of. Was he handing her over to justice, or the Pharisees?

The FBI agents parked down at the end of the block from the Mar Vista and Bollinger got out with them. The street was quiet, and most of the apartments at the Lilac Court and Mar Vista were dark. Nobody was on the sidewalks. Another pair of FBI agents fanned out toward the Mar Vista, one heading for the back alley and another just down the block from June Smith's apartment. The agent with Bollinger told him, "We'll go up first and knock on the door to see if she's home. If she is, we'll bring her out and you can nod if she's the woman you met. Shake your head if she's not. Got that?"

"Yes, sir."

Another car pulled up farther down the block and parked. Two more men got out. Then a San Diego police cruiser arrived as well, and parked behind that vehicle. Both officers remained in the automobile. Two FBI agents went to the Mar Vista and knocked on June Smith's door. The lights were out in the apartment and no one answered. Bollinger crossed the street. The agents knocked again. When nothing happened, one of them produced a key and unlocked the door and called out, "Krueger, are you there?"

Bollinger drew close enough to the Mar Vista to hear a door slam shut in the alley and the sound of hurried footsteps. When he rushed in that direction, he saw June Smith blocked by agents and a uniformed

San Diego police officer. She was carrying a bag and wearing a red blouse and capris, which she was still tugging up to her waist. Bollinger heard her tell the FBI agent who took her bag, "I don't know anything about those people in San Francisco."

TRIAL

O N THE DAY the bodies were found, Ida Krueger's horoscope read:
"Those living under your roof are not in a very good mood."

Joe Krueger sat in San Francisco county jail for a month before Ida
was arrested. After just two days he felt claustrophobic and depressed.
His cell was small and bare and the jailhouse was so noisy he could
hardly sleep. On Wakde Island, he'd shared a tent with three other
fellows, one of them a rude and sloppy drunk from Nacogdoches who
wouldn't shut up and spent most of his nights going in and out of the
tent to piss in the dirt. Another fellow from Illinois sang in his sleep
and farted like a bassoon. There was no such thing as peace and quiet.
Even at Watsonville, alone after dark in his field shack, Joe had to
listen to Mexicans chattering away in the dark or scrapping over some
señorita. But at least there he could get up and walk outdoors if he
liked. County jail was the worst place Joe had been, and there weren't
even any Japs.

His union hired him a lawyer, some fellow George Evans knew
from North Beach. The attorney's name was Clyde Hagan and he
believed Joe was innocent. Or that's what he said. In a hearing before
Superior Judge Arlen J. Knack, Hagan tried to get Joe released on a
writ of habeas corpus, telling the Judge that Joe had no idea he had a
pair of bodies buried in his basement.

"The fact is, your Honor, my client was merely an innocent by-stander
in this sordid affair, no more criminal than a spectator at an automobile accident. His responsibility in this case is more geographical than

rational. My client is terribly sorry for what happened, he truly is, but he's being penalized only for the reason that he was proximate to the bodies."

"But Mr. Hagan, I'm sure you can see that a home is different than a public street. Those people were not exhumed from the sidewalk in front of Mr. Krueger's yard. They were buried almost underfoot. It's simply unreasonable to assume that your client had no knowledge of their whereabouts until the San Francisco Police Department pulled up the floor. Therefore, the writ is denied and Mr. Krueger will be held over for trial."

Next, at the conclusion of a four-hour session in which a dozen persons were called to the witness stand, none of whom were Joe's friends, a grand jury returned indictments charging Joe and Ida with the murders of Lonnie and Muriel Knutsen. So he had to remain in jail until the judicial system decided what to do with him. He wasn't too optimistic. Ida had left him in one hell of a jam and the more he thought about it, the more Joe became convinced she had probably been insane all along. George Evans and Les Ralston came by a couple times each week to see how he was getting by. Joe appreciated that. He was afraid to call his dad. Joe couldn't be sure his father wouldn't have a heart attack when he heard what his son was charged with. How do you tell your dad that the girl who married you also just railroaded you into jail for murder? Joe felt scared and humiliated. He sat in his cell day after day, trying to figure out what his biggest mistake had been — trusting Ida or leaving the reunion too late that night. Sometimes the stupid things we do in life are so obvious it's easy to see where we fell off the track, and we can always tell ourselves afterward we sure won't make that mistake again. But now and then, it's not so clear how we got ourselves into trouble, because the choices we made, those unfortunate turns we took, weren't as apparent at any given moment — maybe each individual decision was even benign — and it's not until the roof falls in on us that we even realize what's gone on, and by then it's usually too late. When that happens, we try retracing our steps to see if we can make sense of how it all went wrong, and even then we might not be sure it could all have been avoided.

JOE HEARD ABOUT IDA'S ARREST from one of his jailers, who brought the news along with a boiled egg and a slice of toast at five o'clock in the morning. Joe had been dreaming about driving a truck through the apple orchards next door to his dad's house and seeing a girl he used to know from high school riding horseback with no clothes on. Her name was Molly and she was a tart who got knocked up her sophomore year. In Joe's dream, she let him stare at her melons, but wouldn't let him get out of the truck to grab hold of them. Then she threw a dirt clod at his head and rode away and Joe thought about taking his pants off and driving after her, but the jailer woke him up about Ida and that was that.

An hour later, Hagan showed up and told Joe the newspaper fellows were coming and he'd better get himself presentable. George Evans ran one of Joe's old suits over to the jailhouse with a spiffy pair of shoes and a nice red tie and helped Joe comb his hair and look sharp for the cameras. It was a rotten business, being paraded in front of the press like he was that morning, flashbulbs popping, people yelling at him, Hagan hustling him along to a crowded room filled with cops and fellows in gray suits who didn't look friendly.

The newspaper fellows bombarded Joe with questions as he passed.

"Are you glad they caught her, Joe? What do you think about it?"

"I'm glad she's found, because there wasn't use at all for her to run."

"What're you going to say to her?"

"Well, I'm going to help her as much as I can. I hope she comes forward and gets this straightened out."

"Suppose she were to try to throw the blame on you?"

"Well, I don't think that'll happen. We always got along pretty swell."

"Could she have committed those murders and hidden the bodies without your knowing about it?"

"Anything's possible."

"Will you ask to see her?"

"If the police'll let me, sure."

"Do you still love her?"

"Why not?"

Then Joe saw Ida brought out between two court matrons and somehow he felt a whole lot better. Maybe because he knew he wasn't alone anymore. Maybe because all at once the attention in the room shifted away from him. Maybe because he hoped Ida would tell them he hadn't anything to do with those bodies in the basement and they'd let him go. She ought to do that, he decided, if she really loved him.

Ida had a moony smile on her face as she walked up to the row of newspaper men. She was wearing a yellow checked frock she used to do housework in up at Ocean City. Her hair was frazzled and limp. She looked tired but feisty and took after her assailants just as the questions began. Everyone was shouting at her, but she seemed ready for them.

"Why'd you do it, Ida? Tell us your side of the story!"

"Well, for starters, I didn't do anything, and neither did Joe, and that's the absolute truth. These fellows beat me up with wet towels and put chains on me and brought me back here without saying one word about any of this and I'm going to get Jake Erhlich to straighten it out, because it's a pack of lies, I tell you, a big fat pack of lies. Why, I didn't even know anyone was looking for me! Me and Joe are in the phone book for all the world to see and I'm not ducking out of anything. I went out for groceries one afternoon and wound up in Oceanside because that's where I do my Rosicrucian studies and I don't read the papers. You fellows believe everything the FBI tells you to believe, but they didn't say a thing about the fellow who's been blackmailing me for twenty years, did they? And he positively is, too, for thousands of dollars and he's the one you ought to be talking to about this business, and I can't say any more until Jake Ehrlich says I can."

"Where did Mrs. Knutsen go? What happened to Mr. Knutsen after she left?"

"You'd have to be God to answer that one, and you can't even prove to me that a triangle has three points."

"Do you have any idea what those bodies were doing in your basement?"

"How do I know how they got there? I'm not Houdini. Why don't you ask the neighbors? They seem to know everything about me, except that I'm a vocational nurse and a good one. I've treated FBI agents, congressmen, and actors. I know many fine people. I know Jimmy Durante. And I had a job lined up in San Diego."

"Who's this fellow you're talking about, Ida? Who's the blackmailer?"

"I've paid him thousands of dollars over the past few years. That's where my husband's bank account went. He positively committed the murders. Neither my husband nor I had anything to do with those motel people, but I could have easily been killed by that man at any time. I don't know his name, but I can pick his picture out anytime."

"But what about those people from the motel, Ida? How'd you get mixed up in that business?"

"Let me tell you about that. It was a filthy place. Absolutely. Full of dope — lots of little pills of morphine and twenty-four packages of something called Dimorale. I turned them all over to the authorities with hypo needles. People kept coming in for fixes, and I said, 'I'll fix you with my cane or shoe.' If I'd knowed about the dope, I'd never have bought the place."

"So, then why were you running, Ida? Where've you been hiding out? How come you shot Bert Wilson?"

"Hiding out? Shooting someone? Nonsense! Why, I didn't know the police were looking for me, and I never held a gun in my life, and I didn't know Joe had been arrested until someone told me just a few days ago. You boys just wait. The truth'll come out in court. Then you'll really see something. Absolutely you will. I got nothing to hide. I can smile and sleep and eat, even though the law treated me like an animal and needled me from one end of the state to another. You talk about the land of the free, and what kind of land is the land of the free when people can go into a person's own home and tear it all up? They took me by the house this morning and, Lord have mercy, there was black over my electrified kitchen and I'm a real good housekeeper and it was a perfect wreck, and I demand justice for what they done and I'm going to get damages. You call this the land of the free and talk about Russia, well, you'll have to prove to me that Russia is worse."

A crowd of photographers shoved forward. "Give us a smile, Ida! Come on! Say cheese!"

"Don't be smart! You might get your camera broken! I seen those terrible pictures you people put in the papers. They make me look all wrinkly and scraggly and snaggly."

Then Ida looked over at Joe and blew him a kiss and smiled like she was still his wife before marching out of the room.

AFTER BREAKFAST THE NEXT MORNING, Hagan told Joe, "They've got a good, strong case, Joe, and those bodies aren't going anywhere. I can try to argue that you didn't have a part of putting them in the dirt, but that just means Ida's going to sniff the gas. If you want me to take it that direction, say so now before I put myself up as her attorney, too. We can have two trials, that way, and hopefully the jury won't tie you both with the same rope."

Joe argued, "Why the hell can't Ida just tell them she killed those two and I didn't have anything to do with it? They caught her fair and square and she knows it. She even tried to kill that Wilson fellow. Can't they get her to tell the truth about all this without having a trial?"

"Sure, they can," Hagan told Joe, taking out a yellow tablet and scribbling something into it. "Now, she's not on trial for the shooting incident, so don't waste your time worrying about that, but if the D.A. can get her to plead guilty to the two murders and tell them you had no prior knowledge or involvement with the disposition of the Knutsens, well, quite possibly you'll get off and go back to your life again."

"So, there you go! She'll do it and that'll be that."

"But Joe — "

"No buts about it. I'll talk to Ida and let her know she's got to tell the truth because I'm her husband and it isn't right to let me rot in jail the rest of my life over something I didn't have any part in. I bet she loves me enough to do that. You just watch. She'll put them straight."

"Well, all right, we'll try that, but what worries me, Joe, is if we get a jury that decides Ida's guilty, then they're pretty likely to ride you along with her. And we probably won't get a second chance. Sure, there are always appeals, but you can't go into something like this expecting it. You have to try to win right out of the gate and there's a good solid case against both of you. I can't lie to you, Joe. Bodies in your basement. That doesn't look good. In fact, it looks guilty. If they think you had anything to do with that at all — "

"Well, I didn't."

"And I believe you, but if a jury decides common sense tells them you can't have a body in your basement without knowing about it, then you're stuck."

"I know that."

"So, why do you think she did it, Joe? From what I hear about Bert Wilson, I can see why she'd take a shot at him, but what was her angle with the Knutsens? It doesn't seem as if she had anything against them personally. Why kill them?"

Joe felt lightheaded and jittery again. He'd worked like hell the past few weeks to put the Knutsens out of his mind, and now here Hagan was throwing them back in his face.

"She's nuts, that's why," Joe said, feeling defeated by the whole story. He should've seen this coming after Ocean City, that she'd snap her cap again. Nobody does this sort of thing just once. It's not in human nature to steal just one apple from a neighbor's tree, especially when you don't get caught.

He told Hagan, "Ida was money crazy, and I guess that's the best way to think about all this. For instance, one day a neighbor of ours down the street sold Ida a dachshund pup for thirteen dollars cash after Ida told her the puppy was for a crippled seven-year-old boy who lived on a horse ranch down the Peninsula. She made that up on the spot. The next day she sold the dog to another fellow up on Mission for fifty dollars who wanted a little doggy for his kids. Ida'll do anything for money, I tell you. That's all you need to know. She's just crazy for it."

EVERYONE HAD AN OPINION about what happened at Ellington and most of it was idiotic. Joe read the morning newspapers every day and saw his whole life going to hell. Reporters from the *Chronicle* and the *Examiner* and *Oakland Tribune* somehow tracked down Stebbins and Hastings and got them on record about the murders. Stebbins told them how he and Joe had been best pals in the Pacific — heroes, actually — but that "you can never know about some fellows. Things happen and now and then they just snap. I can't quite figure it. It's not like Krueger at all. I've been wondering what could've come over him to do a thing like this. I've been wondering if his mind is quite all right."

Hastings was still a pal, though, and told every last one of them, "I just don't think Joe is capable of such a thing. I don't believe a word of it. I've known Joe for twenty years and I'll never believe it unless he swore on a Bible that he did it. You'll never make me believe he did anything wrong."

Then Joe read something a friend of Major Knutsen's wrote: *"Lonnie was a man of many interests. He was a mineralogist of no small knowledge, a very informal astronomer, and even an ardent archaeologist. I remember we took a picture of him once, standing by a huge dinosaur bone we'd found, and we teased him, saying we couldn't tell which was the bone. He used to lecture us on various subjects and he made everything sound like a great adventure. One summer he decided it would be a good experience for us to build our own cabin in the mountains, so he bought some land and the three of us spent most of the summer far back in the Blue Mountains, building what we thought of as a passable cabin. One of the highlights of my life was the trip he took us on through California, Arizona, and into old Mexico, paying all expenses. Can you imagine the high adventure of this to two young fellows like us? Most people have only heard of him as a murder victim. To me, the Major was a wonderful, wonderful man."*

After that, Joe quit reading the newspapers entirely. Hagan tried to get him released on bail, and struck out again and again. While Ida slept like a baby upstairs, Joe barely got a couple of hours a night. George and Les smuggled in girlie magazines and some phenobarbital that Joe took for a week until he got sick to his stomach and needed his cell hosed out. Then he quit worrying about sleep and began thinking about what he might do if he ever got out of jail. He came up with lots of plans: taking work in the oil fields down at Bakersfield or with home construction out in Colorado; re-enlisting in the Army Air Corps; going back to school to learn electronics; finding a hobo camp somewhere and tramping around the country; moving back in with his dad and taking out the garbage. Bakersfield seemed like the best bet. That's if he got out of jail.

Of course, Joe's real problem was that he knew now Ida was a nut. Whatever Ida thought about doing, that's what she went ahead and did, and Joe never had much luck talking her out of it. So how the hell was he supposed to get her to confess to these killings? He mulled it over in jail for two days. She was going to be tough to crack, all right. Meanwhile, the fellow who brought him supper told Joe that Ida was behaving like she was the star of the jailhouse. He said Ida was upstairs telling reporters and her fellow inmates how all the charges were a big mistake that was going to be rectified by Jake Ehrlich once he took over her case.

"She's a card, all right, that little lady of yours. Why, she's already got a book of newspaper clippings of herself. You ought to see it. It's really something. She's been telling everyone she starred in pictures down in Hollywood when she was a kid."

"Oh yeah? She said that?"

"Sure, she did. Ain't it so?"

"No."

"How do you know?"

"Because she never told me before."

"Well, my wife never told me she laid every sailor in a bar on Montgomery Street one night, until I caught her with the milkman who said he recognized her by the mole on her coochie. You can't trust women at all, Joe. Believe me, I know."

B OTH JOE AND IDA pleaded innocent. Hagan wanted to keep them away from the gas chamber, and that's where they'd go if a jury found them guilty of capital murder. Ida insisted she hadn't done anything wrong at all and had no idea what she was on trial for and wouldn't allow Hagan to tell anyone she did a thing to those motel people. Hagan told Joe he was going to plead insanity for Ida.

"If I don't persuade a jury that she was incapable of forming specific intent, your wife's going to sniff the gas, and that's the simple fact of the matter. De Kaplany got off on that and I think we can work that angle for Ida, too."

Joe had followed the de Kaplany case and didn't quite get the legal meaning of insanity, but if anyone was nuts, it had to be that fellow. Geza de Kaplany was a staff anesthesiologist at Doctor's Hospital in San Jose and a refugee from Communist Hungary who suspected his twenty-five-year old wife, Hajna, of having an affair, so he tied her naked to his bed with electric wire one August afternoon, taped her mouth shut, slashed her with a butcher knife, then clinically applied nitric, hydrochloric, and sulphuric acid to her face, breasts and genitals as punishment for her transgressions. Hajna was a stunning beauty, utterly gorgeous, with a striking elegance that almost defied description. The tormented doctor had written a note for her that translated into English as:

If you want to live
(1) Do not shout
(2) Do what I tell you
(3) Or else you will die

Of course, the pitiable creature, disfigured and tortured by acid, did, in fact, scream, and her shrieks were heard all throughout the apartment complex. When the police arrived and confronted a hideous stench within de Kaplany's bedroom, the esteemed doctor himself acted utterly unperturbed by what he had done to his lovely wife. When they took him away, he put across the smug aura of someone who had just answered the $64,000 question. The arresting officers were sure he'd lost his mind. That ended up being de Kaplany's defense: insanity — a brief, afternoon-long sojourn into a lunacy instigated by his traitorous wife, a princess with a whore's appetite for sex. The theory was offered that de Kaplany had a second, inner personality by the name of Pierre La Roche and that Hajna's infidelity aroused La Roche, not de Kaplany, to mutilate and murder the poor beauty. The jury bought it. De Kaplany's attorney refused to put the doctor on the witness stand, certain that if he testified in open court, his aristocratic Eastern European bearing and arrogance would betray him to the common folks in the jury box and they'd shoot him to the gas chamber where he probably belonged. Instead, he was judged not guilty by reason of insanity and committed to the California Medical Facility for the term of life imprisonment.

Hagan told Joe that if a fellow that evil could get off with a straitjacket, then he was confident Ida could, too. He'd plead her insane and get Joe off by arguing that he had nothing to do with the murders and couldn't have prevented his mentally ill wife from committing them, anyhow. Hagan thought he had a strong case. Joe wasn't so sure. Ida was pretty slick, but Joe had a feeling she'd gone too far. Bilking a handful of banks and a motel owner out of a few thousand was one thing, killing people was another. Joe had known a couple of fellows on Wakde Island who laughed about killing Jap prisoners after dark when they'd been posted to guard them. At first, their story went that some of the Japs had made a break for it. Then they admitted to getting too drunk to watch over them any longer and deciding to take care of the problem with trench knives. But killing wasn't the point. Both fellows bragged about the gold teeth they'd snatched and what they'd got from them on furlough in Australia. Nobody in Joe's outfit thought killing captured Japs was out of the ordinary, though doing it for a couple weeks of beer and dames seemed crazy somehow. One day Joe came to realize that not everyone thinks alike, or sees things the same way. People have reasons for what they do that have no relation to reason or common sense. They just do what they do because to them it's the most natural thing in the world.

O N THE FIRST MORNING of the trial in downtown San Francisco, dressed in a new brown suit George Evans had bought for him, Joe Krueger was escorted into court by Hagan and a bailiff by the name of Cornelius, who'd been at Leyte. Joe hadn't seen so many people in one room since induction at March Field, and he hated crowds. The huge room itself was paneled in dark wood and smelled like furniture polish and farts. He heard his name shouted about a hundred times, but acted like Helen Keller when Hagan and a bailiff led him across the courtroom. Joe hated attention. If he had any say, the trial would be held in a basement. His stupid wife was the one who wanted the circus. Newspapermen, TV reporters, and press photographers flew together like a bee swarm once Ida came into court escorted by a matron who looked like Mamie Eisenhower. Ida was wearing a pale blue sundress and a scuffed pair of shoes, but strutting about like Cinderella. While Hagan hustled Joe to a seat at the defense table and told him to keep his mouth closed, Ida started all over again with her rant about wet towels and chains and never shut up.

Straight off, as Joe went to sit down, Ida began yapping with the reporters. "Hello, boys! How's business? Gee, you got your hands full here today! Wait till you hear what they're going to try with me. I tell you, it's the craziest thing!"

"Hey, Ida, give us a pose, will you? Yeah, that's it! Big smile now! Sure, there you go!"

Joe thought he was about to throw up.

Just then, Ida shot over to the prosecution's table and swept everything off onto the floor, shouting, "Free papers for everyone!"

Next thing Joe knew, both bailiffs had Ida restrained and were
pushing her into her chair. Hagan tried calming her down, but Ida
struggled until they had her situated between Joe and Hagan, and Joe
put his hand on her arm. "That's enough, honey. You're acting nuts
and it's not doing us any good."

"Why, sure it is, Joey. You just mind your own business, honey, and
leave what's mine to me. Can you do that?"

Then Judge Newmark struck his gavel and this was what followed.

DAY ONE

OPENING ARGUMENT FOR THE DEFENSE

MR. HAGAN: May it please the Court, Prosecutor
Manning, and ladies and gentlemen of the jury: at
this time it is my privilege to outline to you in
a short sketch, as it were, the things that the
defense will show through the evidence that we
will introduce and through the inferences that we
can create from the evidence that has already been
introduced. The evidence will show that along in,
sometime in the later fifties or the early sixties, I guess it was, Ida Krueger was driving in
a jitney bus on Mission, and there was some sort
of an auto accident, and she was injured. She was
hospitalized and under treatment of doctors. And,
of course, the testimony will show, that she and
her husband, Joe Krueger, were somewhat belea-
guered in their home by investigators, checking on
Ida's physical capacity, for the insurance company.
They were also bothered considerably by bill col-
lectors because Joe, a hard-working man, who paid
his bills regularly, would, when paid, bring home
his money to Ida, and Ida ran the financial end of
the family. Joe had little knowledge of what went

on with their finances, as Ida handled them completely. But apparently, the evidence will show,
they were having financial difficulties, and Ida
wanted to leave San Francisco and go up to Santa
Rosa. And they did go to Santa Rosa. And up there,
the evidence will show, that Ida represented to Joe
that she was going to buy the Rose City Motor Court
motel that adjoined the Bluebonnet Motel where they
were living. Joe was not in favor of it, didn't
want any part of it, but said he would stand by her
and help clean the place up and then he was going
to leave because he didn't like Santa Rosa and he
didn't like the idea of the motel to begin with.
The evidence will show the tragedies that occurred
to the Knutsens and the discovery of the bodies in
the basement of the home on Ellington Avenue, lead-
ing to the subsequent arrest of Joe. Subsequently
Ida was discovered in San Diego, and I took over
that defense, too. The evidence will show that Joe
Krueger had no knowledge of these affairs, that he
had no knowledge that the tragedies had occurred,
he had no knowledge that the bodies were in the
basement, that he cooperated with the authorities
whenever they checked with him, and that he was
as surprised and shocked as anyone else when the
bodies were discovered.

Every crime is a union of intent and act. An
insane person, having no free will, cannot commit a
crime. The evidence will show that in the course of
that hearing, the Court on its own motion recogniz-
ing that Ida Krueger has a mental problem, had her

referred for psychological, psychiatric examina-
tions, and her abilities, her thinking and logic
and so forth were found to be impaired and a borderline mental case. The evidence will show that
she is given to hallucinations or impaired reason-
ing processes that are far from normal, that she
was psychotic or a borderline psychotic, that she
was subject to these psychoses; that this evidence
will prove that this mental situation that she has,
long preceded and long antedated the charges presented to you here in this Court, long before she
had any reason to dissemble or mask, or attempt
to mask, her true mental state. The evidence will
show that her mental capacity is not such that she
could form and hold in mind the premeditation and
the specific intent necessary to commit the capital
crime of first degree murder.

And the evidence, as I have said before, will
show that Joe Krueger had no knowledge and had no
participation in these things. And when the evidence is all in, and after argument, I will ask you
to acquit Joe Krueger and to find Ida Krueger not
guilty of first degree murder. Thank you.

DAY THREE

THE CLERK: Will you state your name and address.

THE WITNESS: Agnes Webber. I live in Yakima, Washington.

PROSECUTOR MANNING: Q. Mrs. Webber, could you give us the conversation that you had on January 1st?

A. Well, when I called up someone answered the phone and asked me if this was Muriel's sister Agnes and I said it was, and then I immediately started and asked how come that the phone had been disconnected in a motel, and this lady said that Muriel had left her in charge of Lonnie and the motel, and she said, "You know, Muriel sold the motel." And I said, "No, we had no idea." And she said, "Yes, she sold it, and she has gone on a trip."

Q. Did she say where?

A. She said to South America.

Q. Did she indicate in this conversation when she had last heard from Muriel?

A. I asked her when she saw Muriel last and when Muriel had left, and she said, "Well, Muriel was here on the 14th of December, I am sure. So, she must have left on the 16th."

Q. And did she say whether or not she had heard from Muriel since that time?

A. Yes. When I said we were all very worried about Muriel, she told me, "There is no need to worry. I received a card from Muriel from Mexico, and she said she was fine. She has had a little trouble getting to Mexico City, but that she was leaving on the plane immediately for South America."

Q. Did she indicate where in South America?

A. Brazil.

Q. Did you ask her to whom Muriel sold the motel?

A. Yes, I did, and she said, "I don't know." And I said, "Did you meet the woman or the person?" She said, "No, Muriel had her friends here, but she didn't introduce me to them."

Q. Did you ask her who you were talking to at any time?

A. Yes, I believe she told me that at the first of the conversation.

Q. What did she say?

A. Well, she said her name was Erma Long. E-r-m-a.

Q. That is the name she gave?

A. Yes.

Q. Now, did you indicate to Mrs. Long that you knew anything about her, that is, Mrs. Long?

A. No.

Q. And she indicated to you that she didn't know who the owners of the motel were, in this conversation?

A. Right.

Q. I show you here a telegram and ask you if you had occasion to receive a telegram allegedly from your sister Muriel Knutsen on or about February 28th, 1962?

A. Yes, that is the one.

Q. And I notice it's addressed to Agatha Weber.

A. Yes, we wondered about that.

Q. Your name is Webber, W-E-B-B-E-R?

A. Yes.

Q. And have you ever been known as Agatha?

A. No, Muriel called me Aggie, but my name is Agnes.

Q. I notice this telegram is signed Muriel, Lonnie, and Dave. Did you ever hear of a man named Dave?

A. No.

Q. Generally, in correspondence that you have had with Muriel over the years, how did she sign her name?

A. Most always just "Mimi," or, when she was with Lonnie, it was "Mimi and Lon."

Q. Now, did she bring up some other subject in relation to Muriel at this time?

A. She said something about Muriel having dope on her dresser. She named three: novocaine, cocaine, and morphine. Well, then, I told her that Muriel was a registered nurse and that she had a right to have it there, that she used it very likely for Lonnie — he had had an operation, you know. And she said she called the police in and they destroyed this; and I said, "The police would never do a thing like that, because that would be evidence." And she didn't have anything else to say.

Q. Now, at any time during this conversation did you say anything else to Mrs. Long?

A. Well, I asked her about Lonnie, and she said, "I will let you speak to the Major, so you will see he is all right." And when Lonnie came on the phone he —

Q. You recognized Major Knutsen?

A. Yes, he has a peculiar voice.

Q. What, if anything, did he say?

A. Well, he said, "Hello, Aggie." Very clearly. And then he seemed agitated and anxious and in a hurry to tell me something.

Q. What did he say?

A. He said, "I am afraid we won't see Muriel again."

Q. What happened when he finished saying that?

A. Well, this lady come back on the phone immediately and said, "Lonnie is very agitated because we didn't hear from Muriel at Christmas time, and no letters or anything, and the Major is just very agitated."

Q. Did you ask this Mrs. Long with whom Muriel had gone allegedly with on the trip?

A. Yes, I did. I asked her whom she had gone with and how she had gone, and she said she didn't know anything about it, that she hadn't met Muriel's friends, and didn't know anything about how Muriel had gone.

Q. What did you say to this?

A. I said it was funny that Muriel did change her plans, and that she hadn't meant to go in such a

hurry. I also told her it seemed queer that she
had left Lonnie there. She had intended him to go
to a home in San Diego and therefore it was funny
that she had gone in the manner she had.

Q. Now, what else did you say at this time about
Muriel, if anything?

A. I told her that I thought the woman that bought
the motel biffed her in the head and took everything she had. That is just what I said. I don't
know why I ever said it, but I did.

DAY SEVEN

THE CLERK: Will you state your name and address.

THE WITNESS: My name is Seymour Elrod and I live in Burlingame.

MR. HAGAN: Q. Mr. Elrod, you are an attorney, licensed to practice in the State of California?

A. I am, sir. The law firm of Belli, Ashe, and Gerry.

Q. And in the course of your practice, did you gain the acquaintanceship of Mr. and Mrs. Krueger?

A. Yes, I did. I first met Mrs. Krueger personally in October or November of 1961. She retained our office to represent her in litigation arising out of an accident, which occurred, I believe, on March 22nd, 1961.

Q. In your experience with the practice of law, Mr. Elrod, has it brought you in contact with people afflicted with mental disturbances?

A. Oh, yes.

Q. What observance were you able to make of her conduct?

A. I was always concerned with her sanity. I observed her to be extremely erratic in her behavior. She was extremely undependable on keeping appointments. In speech, she never seemed to be able to talk on a point to a question. She was the most difficult client to communicate with.

Q. And you weren't concerned at all, were you, about any head injury at this time?

A. I believe she had sustained a blow to the skull. And in that situation we always concern ourselves with a head injury.

DEFENDANT IDA KRUEGER: It hit my head up against that steel bar like that and broke all of my teeth across my gums, and twisted my neck; and the ambulance driver grabbed me by the coat and I almost went through the whole front windshield. And he put that little electric thing on me for physiotherapy.

MR. HAGAN: Q. Isn't it a fact, Mr. Elrod, that none of the medical reports that you either discussed or had occasion to examine indicated that she ever suffered any injury or damage to her brain or her skull?

A. Well, brain damage, no. There's no indication of brain damage, and I so testified when I stated that there is no indication of damage to the central nervous system.

Q. Or to her skull?

A. I believe the X-rays were negative for fracture of the skull.

DAY ELEVEN

THE CLERK: Will you state your name and address.

THE WITNESS: Juanita Lopez, and I live in Cotati.

Q. Did you have occasion to make a trip to Westport, Washington, with the defendants, Joe and Ida Krueger?

A. Yes, I did.

Q. Where did you go?

A. To the Dock Cabin Court.

Q. Had you ever been there before?

A. No, sir.

Q. And how did you find this motel?

A. Mrs. Long knew where it was.

Q. Did she direct you there?

A. Yes.

DEFENDANT IDA KRUEGER: You are lying.

THE WITNESS: I wished I was.

DEFENDANT IDA KRUEGER: You are.

MR. MANNING: Your Honor.

THE COURT: Now, Mrs. Krueger, I am going to insist that you refrain from such outbursts. I don't want to be sharp with you. It is not my desire to be that way.

MR. MANNING: Q. Now, did Mrs. Long or Mr. Long tell you for what purpose you were going to Washington

before you left on the way up, or anything of that
nature?

A. She said this lady, Mrs. Knutsen, was a dopehead and she had sold her this motel and gave her
all the papers to go up there and get anything out
of that she had bought.

Q. All right. Now, when you got to the motel in
Washington, what if anything did you do?

A. Well, when we got there, Mr. Long pulled the
car in front there and Mrs. Long got out and said,
"Well, here we are, Nita."

Q. Did you see anyone else about the premises at
this time?

A. No, sir.

Q. Was it open for business?

A. No.

Q. All right. What happened then?

A. So, we went inside and Mrs. Long said, "We
got to hurry and load the stuff up. Put all this
linen in the Lincoln." I said, "All right." So,
we loaded the Lincoln with linen, blankets, bedspreads, and electric heaters and irons and wall
panels.

Q. Now, how long were you there?

A. Well, we must have got there about 11:30 in the
morning, and we worked it over till about three
o'clock in the afternoon. Then, we went into Westport to have something to eat and went over to a
little town called Aberdeen where Mr. Long bought
some tools at the Sears Roebuck store.

Q. What kind of tools were these?

A. Well, he bought a couple of wrenches, one of these crescent wrenches, and a wrecking bar. And then we went back to the motel. I said, "Boy, it's going to take some really hard work here." It was really cold, and then it was getting dark. But Mrs. Long said, "Nita, we're going to have to work all night if the van is coming at 8:30 in the morning. We have to get everything out of here." So, we stayed and packed silverware and took one big bed down in that place, and then I told her it was getting along about to 10:30. I said, "Gee, I am sleepy and so cold. I'm going into the car and go to sleep." I tried to sleep, but it was too cold. So, I stayed out about twenty minutes. We had only kerosene lamps and candles besides the flashlight Mr. Long gave us.

Q. Did you work all night?

A. I worked all night. That is the truth. That was the coldest night I ever spent.

Q. Now, Miss Lopez, around February 27th or 28th, did you see Mrs. Long again in Santa Rosa?

A. Yes, I did.

Q. Where did you see her at that time?

A. She came up by cab and told me to meet her at the motel. She said, "Juanita, let's go for a ride in the City." I said all right, because I thought we were coming to the house again. She said, "Well, let's just go for a ride." I pointed us to San Jose and kept driving that way because I thought she said she had a motel down there, and I said, "Are we going to San Jose?" And she said, "No, just keep on driving." So, I kept on driving until we got way down there, and it was getting late, about 7:00, 7:30, I guess. But that was still lickety-split, because we were really going.

Q. How far did you drive?

A. Well, that was my point when I said, "Where are we going, Ida?" And she said, "We are going to Los Angeles." And I said, "Oh, no, we are not going to Los Angeles. Next service station I come to, I am going to stop." So, she sat there for a while not saying anything, and then we found a Shell service station sitting by the highway and a little grocery store in the back. There was a street running that way and I imagine there were some houses, and I guess we'd run into town if we had gone further.

Q. When you got to the service station, what did you do?

A. Well, I told her, I said, "I am going to get me a bag of peanuts." She said, "You're hungry?" And I said, "A little bit." So I went in the store there and I bought some peanuts and gum and when I come on out and sat in the car, she said, "I am going to make a phone call." Then she went to the tele-phone booth in the store and stayed there about thirty-five minutes, I guess.

Q. Did she have anything when she went into the phone booth besides the change?

A. Just her purse.

Q. Did she buy anything in the store?

A. Bought some writing material.

Q. What kind of writing material?

A. Tablet and envelopes.

Q. What happened after she came out?

A. Well, she just got in the car and said, "All right, let's go back home, honey." So, we came back up the highway to San Francisco.

Q. And when you got to San Francisco, what occurred?

A. I parked the car on the side of her house. But before that, she told me to let her out and for me to drive around the block. So, I said, "Okay." And I drove around the block and I parked it out around the side. She had the garage door open, so I went and tried to help her move this wooden box in the driveway, right at the edge of the garage. It was heavy and full of dirt and kind of wet as if it was raining on it, and she said, "We have to get all this dirt inside because my husband didn't want it out here." When we tried to move it, at first we couldn't and I said, "We better get some help for this because it's too heavy." And she said, "No, we don't need help. I'm stronger than you think." Well, I told her, "If we had a shovel we could pick this all up." So, she got a shovel from the garage and gave it to me, and we finally took both sides and shuffled it, you know, wiggled it back and forth until we got it inside the garage.

Q. At this time, did you notice anything about the basement garage?

A. Well, there was a lot of building material in the garage and two or three garbage cans with a lot of dirt in them sitting next to it, right

inside the garage door, and there was a half a sack
of cement, one of these green patio tables were
there, and a lot of building things, like they
were repairing. When I came in there I stepped on
a rock. I didn't look down. I just, you know, I
kicked it and I happened to look at it because it
was a rock sticking out of the cement, rock cement.
Q. And did you notice the color of this cement,
whether that was rough?
A. Yes, it was white.
Q. And where was this rough area that you noticed
at this time?
A. It was about the middle of the garage.
Q. Now, did you notice anything else about the
garage on this particular occasion?
A. Well, I didn't notice too much at the time. She
said, "This used to be a garage, but we are going
to fix it up as a basement apartment." Of course,
we was also going to bring some things down from
upstairs to load in the car and bring to Santa
Rosa. So, I told her, "Let's move this old table."
Q. What kind of a table was this?
A. It was an outdoor table like you have picnics, a
bench thing, on each side. And so I started to go
on the side of it — on that side to grab it. She
said, "Nita, don't you go over there - don't you
go over there." So, I stopped.
Q. What corner of the basement was this?
A. Right-handed side, as you are going into the
garage.
Q. She told you not to go over there?

A. Yes. And then she said, "Nita, let's push it
over this way." I said, "Okay."

Q. Did you notice anything unusual about that area
at this time?

A. Well, in that corner was a pile of dirt about
that high (indicating), I guess, and it was a
square, and I didn't pay no attention to it. I just
thought they were piling something, didn't make
sense to me.

Q. Was the dirt higher than the surrounding floor?

A. It was just about like that. (Indicating.)

Q. About twelve inches?

A. I would say.

Q. All right. What happened after you moved the
table and the dirt?

A. Well, we went back upstairs and Ida looked
through her mail. Then we drank some coffee in the
living room.

Q. And did you notice anything unusual about the
living room at that time?

A. Well, she had a blanket across the window, and
it had heavy drapes on it. At first, she wanted
to turn no lights on, and she had a flashlight.
I said, "Turn the lights on." She said, "No,
keep still. You're going to wake the old people
up. They're sleeping in the back room." I said,
"Isn't this your house?" She said, "Yes, of course
it is, but they're my tenants." I said, "Well,
turn something on. Are we going to sit in the
dark?" She said, "Well, I guess I can turn this
light on." So, she turned on a big table lamp and

she sat down in the chair and I sat down and I
picked up a paper and looked at it and drank my
coffee.

Q. Now, did you stay there that night?

A. Yes, we did. She told me to sleep on the couch,
and she laid on the floor in front of the heater
and slept.

Q. You drove back to Santa Rosa the next morning?

A. Yes.

Q. Do you think Mrs. Krueger lied to you about anything in the time you were driving her around and
working at the motel?

A. Sure, everything she ever told me was nothing
but a lie. I trusted her. I thought she was telling the truth because she used to tell me, "I'm
an honest person, Nita." I believed her, too; I
thought she was all right.

Q. You just followed along, isn't that true?

A. Yeah, because she was fun to be with at times.

Q. But you knew you had no right to dismantle that
motel in Westport, Washington, didn't you?

A. Well, she had all the papers, she said that Mrs.
Knutsen had gave her all the papers, and she had
seen the District Attorneys. She said that nobody
in either state could stop her from taking anything
because it belonged to her, and she bought it and
paid for it.

Q. Then she later on told you that that was not
true, is that right?

A. No, she didn't. She used to always make me
believe that it was hers.

Q. Are you testifying here to release yourself of any responsibility in these crimes, these murders?

A. No, I don't know nothing about these murders.

Q. You don't know anything about them?

A. No, sir.

Q. Let me ask you one more question. Did you have anything at all at any time to do with the murder of Muriel or Lonnie Knutsen?

A. I did not.

DEFENDANT IDA KRUEGER: You're lying. You should take a lie test and be given a dose of sodium phenetole to make you tell the truth. Let the cards fall where they may.

THE WITNESS: So long, Judas.

DEFENDANT IDA KRUEGER: You're a big fat liar.

THE WITNESS: I wish I was.

(Next witness)

THE CLERK: Will you state your name and address.

THE WITNESS: Adolfo Paoli. I live in Gilroy, California.

MR. MANNING: Q. Mr. Paoli, what is your business or occupation?

A. I am the manager of the Western Union, Salinas office.

Q. Now, I show you a telegram here and I am going to ask if you can tell me from what office it was sent.

A. It's from Salinas.

Q. That is your office?

A. Right.

Q. Tell me when it was sent?

A. February 28th.

Q. Now, tell us what your recollection is as to the origin of that telegram?

A. The message was phoned into our office from a coin box in the vicinity of Salinas, California, and was received in Yakima, Washington, that same evening.

Q. Is this a regular telegram?

A. It's a night letter.

DAY FOURTEEN

THE CLERK: Will you state your name and address.

THE WITNESS: Bert Wilson. I live in Santa Rosa.

MR. HAGAN: Q. Mr. Wilson, what is your business or occupation?

A. I am the owner of a water conditioning company, Wildew Enterprises.

Q. And how long have you had this business?

A. About eight or nine years.

Q. Are you acquainted with the defendants as they sit here now, Joe Krueger and Ida Krueger?

A. I have good cause to be acquainted with them. Ida tried to kill me.

DEFENDANT IDA KRUEGER: You are lying. You took me off to Wyoming and said you were an FBI man. Yes, he did. He said he was an FBI man, and he did something else to me, too. He ought to be treated with sodium pentothal and five psychiatrists to make him tell the truth.

MR. HAGAN: Q. Mr. Wilson, how did you first meet Mrs. Krueger?

A. It was about the third or fourth of March, 1962, where we discussed her need for water conditioning equipment.

Q. Now, let me show you Defendant's Exhibit for
identification, No. C, in evidence, and ask you if
you can recognize this?

A. Yes, that is a cashier check for $300 made out
to me.

Q. Will you explain the transaction, please?

A. She was to pay me $2,000 for the water condi-
tioner, and I just assumed that she was going to
pay me the total amount. So she told the girl in
the window to make a check for cash to Wildew Water
Conditioning Company for $300. And I says, "That
isn't the amount that we agreed on. You were to pay
me for all of it now." She says, "No, this is pay
for the inconvenience and you running me around."
I got quite involved trying to help Mrs. Long and
it did consume quite a bit of my time, so I says,
"Well, what about the water conditioner?" She says,
"I will pay you that tomorrow when I go to my bank
in San Francisco."

Q. So she insisted you take this $300 just for the
inconvenience she had put you through?

A. I told her I would take it off the total price,
off the purchase of equipment, but as it worked
out, everything she did was just diabolic. Everything was just laid out perfect, that no matter
when she went any place it was set up ahead of
time, just like she set me up. Everything was perfectly set up.

Q. Did you make that trip with her to the city?

A. Yes, I did drive her later that week down to San
Francisco to take her to her bank because she said

that she had a loan pending for $20,000 and she had
to check and see if it was ready. She explained to
me that you should establish yourself in several
places like the Jewish people do, establish yourself and your credit by borrowing from everybody
you can.

DEFENDANT IDA KRUEGER: You told me to do that.

MR. HAGAN: Q. And did she give you the money she
owed on the water conditioner on that visit?

A. No, she told me her loan wasn't ready yet,
but that she had $8,000 in a lock box in Sacra-
mento, and if I drove her there I could have my
$2,000 that afternoon, so that's where we went.
We stopped to have lunch at a drive-up restaurant just outside of town, and I called my wife
and told her what I was doing. Then Ida admitted
to me there was no lock box there, but that she
wanted to see how far I would go to get my money
because it was really in a bank out in Pine Meadows, Wyoming.

Q. And you were at lunch for how long?

A. About a half an hour, and then we left Sacramento and drove to Salt Lake and took a plane to
Cheyenne.

MR. HAGAN: Q. You went from Sacramento by car to
Salt Lake City?

A. Well, we did stop off at a club on the highway by Reno and had coffee at the snack bar there
and gambled a bit. I had some pie and coffee and
then we went on to Salt Lake and then I was finally
able to talk her into a plane.

DEFENDANT IDA KRUEGER: We stopped off in the desert. He was going ninety miles an hour.

MR. HAGAN: Q. Mr. Wilson, do you drink, by any chance?

A. I drink to be social, yes.

DEFENDANT IDA KRUEGER: He drinks something awful. He's alcoholic.

MR. HAGAN: Q. Were you drinking on this day?

A. Only coffee in Reno.

Q. What money did you use for the trip's expenses?

A. I had money of my own and also when we first pulled into the Richfield station I was going to fill the tank and Ida insisted I don't use my credit card because it would leave a trail. She said people could tie you into anything if you left a trail.

DEFENDANT IDA KRUEGER: That's what you suggested so your wife wouldn't know about it. I love my own husband more than anything. My husband's shoelaces in his shoes are too good for that creep.

THE WITNESS: So she gave me a $50 bill out of her pocket, which was probably one of my fifties. I took it gladly because I figured that we'd keep a record. She told me to keep a close record of all the expenditures and that she would settle up with me when we got back.

MR. HAGAN: Q. You didn't stop in any motels?

A. Not on the way. We did stop, like I said, at a couple of gambling houses along the line. I do like to gamble a little.

Q. What time of the day or night was it that you arrived in Cheyenne?

A. Late in the afternoon because we called from
the airport. I says to Ida, "As quickly as we get
into the airport, you get to the telephone and call
the bank and tell them we're coming so we can get
in and get right back out again." Then she made a
feeble attempt, actually, to reach the bank. She
got the wrong number and kept stalling and it got
too late so that the bank wouldn't answer, and
there was nothing left to do but spend the night.

Q. So you stayed in Wyoming until Monday?

A. I did, but she didn't.

DEFENDANT IDA KRUEGER: You bet I didn't, after
what you did in the desert. I don't forget an
experience like that. Never in my life did I ever
have such dirty, filthy things done to me. It's
undescribable.

MR. HAGAN: Q. Where did you stay?

A. We checked at the Ranger Motel in Pine Meadows that night, and after we ate supper at a diner
across the highway, I went to my room, and I guess
I passed out and went to sleep.

Q. You don't mean passing out from drinking?

A. No, I don't drink to excess. Ever. Then it was
about two o'clock that she came banging on the door
and said she had some coffee and a magazine for me,
but I had already retired.

DEFENDANT IDA KRUEGER: He asked me to bring it for
him.

THE WITNESS: A. I guess I had left the TV on, and
there was just the one remaining station on, and
she said she brought me some coffee and a magazine

about outer space, but I told her that I was tired,
and then she asked if I minded if she could come in,
and I said, "Well, probably better if you don't."

DEFENDANT IDA KRUEGER: He was so drunk he didn't
know what to say.

THE WITNESS: A. Then I guess she went back to her
room and I didn't see her after that. The next
morning I got up about seven o'clock and knocked
on her door. I figured I would take her over and
buy her breakfast. But there was no answer, so
I went to the manager of the place, and he came
down and after consistent banging at the door, she
didn't answer, so he opened the door, and found
the bed had never been slept in. After that, I just
went bowling and filled in the day waiting for her
to come back, and when she didn't show, I went to
her bank, where they told me no one had ever heard
of her. After that, I made arrangements to fly back
to Salt Lake City to get my car, and from there to
come on back home.

DEFENDANT IDA KRUEGER: You're still smiling about
what you did to me out in the desert.

THE WITNESS: A. I'm smiling because of the fact
that I feel I'm safe. You're down there and I'm up
here.

DEFENDANT IDA KRUEGER: You mean when you look at
me you can't forget the dirty things you did out
in the desert.

MR. HAGAN: Q. Mr. Wilson, I take it that this was
a logical and probable sequence of your business
relationships with Mrs. Krueger that you should

take a trip from San Francisco to Sacramento to
Reno to Salt Lake to Pine Meadows?

A. Well, the chain of events that happened before
led up to it, and I mean everything that she had
done, she plotted everything perfect to where I
fell into it perfect, everything that she did, even
setting up the banks, the businessmen in town, me
along with it. I fell right into her pattern all
the way. She planned it all down the line. She
didn't miss one cue, and I was detecting for a
mistake, detecting for something that would foul
her up to indicate to me that I was getting in too
deep, that there was something wrong, and I never
sensed it once. I have never known anybody more
normal about financial dealings. I mean it takes a
shrewd mind to overcome me, but she plays a better
game than I ever did.

DAY EIGHTEEN

THE CLERK: Will you state your name and address.

THE WITNESS: Joe Krueger, 490 Ellington Avenue, San Francisco.

MR. MANNING: Q. What is the state of your wife's health so far as you've known it?

A. Before this trouble, she's been going to the doctor every day, pretty near, for, well, a couple years, I guess. She told me she had leukemia, and had to go and have blood transfusions and all that kind of stuff.

Q. Did she ever tell you what it was costing for the treatments?

A. She told me it cost $80 for blood, about once a week.

Q. Now was she subsequently injured in an auto accident?

A. Yes, it happened in March of '61.

Q. Did you talk with any of the lawyers or claim adjusters or anything in reference to this accident?

A. No, she was handling it herself, and so I let her go.

Q. When did you leave San Francisco to go to Santa Rosa?

A. Sometime in November of '61.

Q. Why did you select Santa Rosa?

A. Just didn't have any other place to go.

Q. Whose idea was it to go up there?

A. Well, it was both of us, I guess, because Ida wanted to get out of town on account of the insurance adjusters were coming around there all the time.

DEFENDANT IDA KRUEGER: I can tell you why. Because it's warm, dopey.

MR. MANNING: Q. And where did you stay when you first went to Santa Rosa?

A. Bluebonnet Motel.

Q. Did you ever meet Muriel Knutsen?

A. Nope, never did.

Q. Well, did you have any feelings, misgivings, or otherwise about taking over the management of her motel?

A. Sure.

Q. Did you voice them to Ida?

A. I told her I wouldn't have anything to do with the dirty joint, but I would help clean it up if she wanted to run it.

Q. Now did you see Major Knutsen around there?

A. We took care of old Lonnie until about the middle of January sometime.

Q. Now, Joe, you heard the testimony in this case here in reference to the finding of these bodies in the basement of your home at 490 Ellington Avenue. Do you know how they got there?

A. I do not.

Q. Do you know anything about them?

A. Nope.

Q. There has been evidence here of the various statements that you have given to the police authorities who came to interview you at your home, and also to investigate into the causes of these deaths, and the statements that you made to those officers, are they true?

A. They are true as I know.

Q. Now, about this man Bert Wilson, did you meet him or know him in Santa Rosa?

A. Yeah, he kept coming down around the place where I was working. I guess he wanted to sell a water softener, or thought he did.

Q. Did you know he was making trips out of Santa Rosa with your wife?

A. No, I didn't.

Q. When did you first learn of that?

A. Well, about the time they were gone I learned it through his wife. She said they had taken off. That's all I knew until I heard from them when they came back.

Q. What were your feelings about this matter?

A. Well, I didn't like that, but there was nothing I could do about it.

Q. Did you seek any legal action against Mr. Wilson?

A. Not at that time. I just thought I better let it slide, and I did.

Q. Tell me about this automobile accident that Ida had been in March of '61, what was the nature of her injuries, do you know?

A. Well, she got her head bumped, smashed her teeth all out, got a knee jammed up, got her back hurt, and different things.

Q. Now, Mr. Krueger, just prior to your leaving to go to Santa Rosa you had outstanding against you and your wife at that time a great number of bills, did you not?

A. Quite a few.

DEFENDANT IDA KRUEGER: I taken the money and paid the doctor bills with it when I should have taken and paid the house bills with it. Just don't blame Joe, because that Bertie's nothing but a crook. Believe me. He absolutely is a crook, and he's a blackmailer. That's what he is. And tells me he would kill me and do away with me. "Oh, you're little," he said, "I could do away with you like nothing."

MR. MANNING: Q. The fact of the matter is, Mr. Krueger, when you left San Francisco to go to Santa Rosa, that you would say that you were in very poor financial condition, wouldn't you?

A. Sure we were.

Q. Do you know whether or not your wife had ever met Muriel Knutsen before going to Santa Rosa?

A. No, I don't.

Q. The fact of the matter is that you and your wife were planning to take over the Rose City Motor Court, weren't you?

A. I knew nothing about the motor court.

Q. You never had any discussion about it?

A. No, sir.

Q. Now, you knew, I take it, did you not, that your
wife was going over to the Rose City Motor Court
occasionally?

A. She went over there a time or two.

Q. Did you see her go?

A. Yes. She was over there working, she told me.

Q. She told you she was working?

A. Yes. She worked over there a few days.

Q. Was that when Mrs. Knutsen was there?

A. That was.

Q. And did she tell you how much Mrs. Knutsen was
paying her?

A. Very little.

Q. And you weren't interested to see what her
employer looked like?

A. No.

Q. And what was your wife doing for Mrs. Knutsen
at this time?

A. She was helping clean out a cabin so they could
get it rented.

Q. You didn't have enough interest at that time to
go over and help your wife clean anything out?

A. Nope.

Q. Mr. Krueger, at that time you hadn't gotten the
deed yet, had you?

A. I never seen the deed till here.

Q. Mr. Krueger, I take it you say that when you
first went over there to clean out the motel, you
indicated that you didn't know that your wife had
allegedly bought this place from Muriel Knutsen?

A. That's right, I didn't.

Q. And you, as far as you knew, your wife was merely going to manage it?

A. That's right.

Q. And the apartment that you were cleaning out was Muriel Knutsen's, wasn't it?

A. That's right.

Q. And you were very busy emptying her personal belongings and letters and things of that kind, and burning them in the back, is that true?

A. It looked like a bunch of junk to me.

Q. You realized there were a lot of personal letters there addressed to Muriel?

A. I never read them.

Q. And it was all coming out of her trunk?

A. There was no trunk.

Q. And you people were planning at that time to move into Muriel's quarters, is that correct, where she had been living?

A. Sure.

Q. And Lonnie was still there?

A. Yes.

Q. Did you think Mrs. Knutsen was going to come back and get Lonnie?

A. That's what Ida told me.

Q. How much did Ida pay you to clean up the motel?

A. Nothing.

Q. You mean to say you gave up your job in San Francisco and spent long hours painting and cleaning up the motel and didn't expect to get five cents?

A. That's right.

Q. And your only regular income at the time was a weekly $55 unemployment check?

A. Yes.

Q. And were you still paying for Ida's leukemia treatments?

A. Yes.

Q. You mean you gave her $80 a week while all you were getting was $55?

A. Right.

Q. Where did the money come from?

A. Out of my pocket.

Q. How did it get there?

A. I put it there.

Q. From where?

A. Out of this hand (holding up his right one).

Q. Where did you get the money to put in that hand?

A. Different places.

Q. Like what?

A. Where do you get your money?

Q. Is that your best answer?

A. That's right.

Q. Mr. Krueger, going back to what you told the inspectors on July 16th, before the bodies were found in your basement. Do you remember that you did talk to her about taking the place over before she bought it?

A. No, I don't think so.

Q. What was Ida doing in helping Mrs. Knutsen clean up?

A. What do they usually do when they clean up a place?

Q. Was she helping scrub it?

A. Certainly.

Q. Change the beds?

A. Haul out garbage.

Q. Help paint?

A. No, they weren't doing any painting.

Q. And then Lonnie was still there?

A. That's right.

Q. What did your wife say was going to happen with Lonnie Knutsen?

A. She said that Muriel was coming back after him.

Q. And did she tell you when you first went over there where Muriel was supposed to be?

A. She said the woman was going to Brazil.

Q. Did she ever tell you she was going to Mexico City?

A. Yes, she was going to Brazil by way of Mexico City.

Q. And then she was going to come back and get Lonnie?

A. That's what I heard.

Q. Now, Joe, regarding the basement at 490 Ellington Avenue, did you notice when you were standing on the corner where Mr. Knutsen was found that the thickness of that concrete wasn't very great?

A. No, I didn't.

Q. Joe, did you try to contact your wife after she allegedly shot Bert Wilson?

A. No.

Q. Had you heard from her?

A. No.

374 | MONTE SCHULZ

Q. Where did you think she was at this time?

A. I didn't care.

Q. So, you never did really look around for her?

A. Everybody else was, so why should I?

Q. And you indicated to the police that if you heard anything about your wife you would let them know?

A. I said if I saw her I would let them know.

Q. When you went to Santa Rosa, did you use the name of Long?

A. That's right.

Q. Why did you choose that name?

A. It's easy to write.

Q. And why did you take an alias in Santa Rosa?

A. Because I wouldn't want to live up there under my own name.

Q. You didn't like Santa Rosa?

A. Nope.

Q. Did you ever have any conversations with your wife regarding Muriel leaving?

A. Never did. Because I didn't know the woman.

Q. Who told you that Muriel went to Brazil?

A. Ida.

Q. So you are testifying that you had no knowledge of your own as to when she left?

A. That's right.

DEFENDANT IDA KRUEGER: Quiet. The master's got a headache.

THE COURT: You know, Mrs. Krueger, if you would stop talking over there my headache would go away.

DEFENDANT IDA KRUEGER: Have you really got a headache, your Honor?

THE COURT: Because you are talking so much. Just be quiet for a second.

IDA KRUEGER: Put a cold rag on it. I'll put a cool rag on your head. (turning to the audience) He's got a headache, an awful headache.

MR. MANNING: This is part of the pattern, the bizarre conduct of the defendant. This is part of the defense.

THE COURT: That might come out when the doctors testify.

DEFENDANT IDA KRUEGER: What doctors are you talking about?

MR. MANNING: It is hearsay and self-serving to this individual.

DEFENDANT IDA KRUEGER: Everything to you is hearsay.

DAY TWENTY-TWO

THE CLERK: Will you state your name and address.

THE WITNESS: Dr. Norman Chandler. I reside in St. Helena.

MR. HAGAN: Dr. Chandler, we have used this term schizophrenic quite a bit today. I'm wondering if you could relate to the jury what schizophrenic is, in your opinion?

A. In general, schizophrenia means a split of the psyche, a split in the patient's mental state at the beginning; and then follows a withdrawal from reality, a disintegration of behavior patterns, so that actions inappropriate to the situation frequently are displayed.

Q. Would you say, Dr. Chandler, that a person who is schizophrenic generally is anti-social?

A. Not necessarily. Some years ago it was felt that all schizophrenics derived from introverted persons, but subsequently we have gotten away from that notion. Many schizophrenics are far from anti-social.

Q. Now, in other words, the fact that a person may be a schizophrenic doesn't mean that the person couldn't carry on the ordinary functions of life, perform the requisite purposes and intents to do so, isn't that true?

A. Yes, that is true.

Q. And I take it when they get on the streetcar in the morning they know where they are going, when they get to their office they perform their duties in a workmanlike fashion, when they go home and get on the bus at night or the streetcar they know where they are going, is that correct?

A. That is correct.

Q. Where would you put Mrs. Krueger?

A: I think she belongs in an institution.

Q. Do you think that Mrs. Krueger can get up in the morning, dress herself?

A. Yes, she can.

Q. Do you think that she can, if she wishes, take a Greyhound bus and go to Santa Rosa?

A. I'm sure she could, probably farther, if you give her a chance.

Q. Do you think that she can carry on business affairs?

A. Yes, I imagine she could.

Q. Do you think she could buy a motel and operate a motel?

A. Well, that's a matter of taste. You mean on one day, or make a success of it? I think she could carry on business transactions.

DEFENDANT IDA KRUEGER: I don't think you should put that doctor on the spot, I'm telling you.

MR. HAGAN: Q. All right, now. Doctor, were you able to form an opinion as to the mental condition

of the defendant, Mrs. Krueger, as of December 1961
and January 1962, to form a specific intent to
kill?

A. I was so able, yes, sir. I found her to be what
I would call a diabolical liar on the grounds that
she shows cunning, ingenuity, cruelty, wickedness,
cold calculations, evil conduct and intent, like a
devil. When she was informed that I had examined
her, she went into a tirade. In effect, she complained that, "He never gave me a psycho." And that
nobody ever gave her a psycho.

DEFENDANT IDA KRUEGER: No, I never had no encepha-
logram test or no spinal. That's what they did in
the mental institution, gave me a what-you-call-it,
and I asked you that, absolutely.

THE WITNESS: A. She knows what she's talking about
because she's had plenty of psychos.

DEFENDANT IDA KRUEGER: You may say you are a
doctor, but I don't know if you are one or not.

MR. HAGAN: Q. I take it anything you may have
observed today has in no way altered your opinion?
A. No, it fits the picture of a very clever, cunning woman, who knows how to sell herself to a bank
when she needs money, how to sell herself in early
interviews. In this fashion, I have seen a number
of plays and a number of TV shows where there are
many wonderful efforts on the part of certain
actors and actresses to portray an insane person,
as they know him. And those people are able to do
that, and it's only for money. And here we have
a woman who realizes that she faces either life

imprisonment or death, in her words to me, who certainly with the brain God gave her is able to do as good or a better job than some of the actors and actresses.

MR HAGAN: Q. During this trial, much mention has been made of schizophrenia; can you tell me from your experience whether or not the defendant has this disease?

A. The answer is, no, she hasn't it. And in very short form, this is a story, but it is the answer to your question: God or nature, when they made certain individuals, had to decide in the course of making that particular individual that this is a pretty sensitive mind, and we had better put a shield or fence or insulation around her so as to protect her from this environment. Once having put that fence around, the diagram answers a lot of questions, because if one feels an emotion and this fence is around her, she has a hard time getting any emotion out. In other words, we refer to her as flattened in emotions and being apathetic or lacking in emotion, because no matter what she feels, she can't get it through the fence. And if the other type of emotion comes from the outside world, a stimulus is given for anger or fear or for anything else, she has trouble getting it through the fence. So, she is a poker face, flat, phlegmatic, no reactions, or ability to show an emotional display.

DEFENDANT IDA KRUEGER: You are calling the Mother of God a poker face. You ought to be ashamed of yourself.

THE WITNESS: A. This has all confirmed my ideas about her, because she can turn this faucet on, hot or cold, and with bizarre stuff or not, in the way a true schizophrenic can't. Now, we come to the intellect side, a kind of fence. A brilliant mind may reside there, but because there is a fence, this type doesn't look out through the fence at the outside world and people around them or engage in studies with them or transactions with them and move here and there and all the rest of it. The mind is turned inward, introspectively, toward the self, inside the fence. So, there is philosophizing, analyzing, romanticizing, writing poetry, inventing what-not-all, and always inside. And then on the will side, she is the one who is in her room all the time, not out in the car, not traveling. She is not getting interested in this or that or the other thing. She never spontaneously wants to invite anybody to go anywhere. She is always in her room. That is my conception of a schizophrenic type of person, and this woman is anything but, when we look at the exact opposites. All the way along, the only time a schizophrenic would ever act as Mrs. Krueger does would be out of a long period being in certain rigid attitudes and never a smile and all that, there might be a momentary explosion where emotional tension got so great you blew out one of the rungs in the fence, but as a going proposition, day after day, a schizo is just sunk. She can't do that sort of thing. So, testing her by everything that fifty years has told me about a schizophrenic, it isn't there.

DEFENDANT IDA KRUEGER: I am the Mother of God, and you can't deny it, no one can. I am the Mother of God. You try to give me some riddles, and I said, "Come and fly pink butterfly. God comes right down and smiles on the rainbows and clouds, and the little clouds smile back, and God smiles on the sun, and the sun is God, for He reflects through your window when you feel how nice and warm it is, and I am the Mother of God."

THE WITNESS: A. You see, that is the main thing, the size of it. She doesn't care particularly much for the truth. She cares for the statement or the story of a situation, which will serve her best in her own mind. Whether it actually serves her or not doesn't matter for the moment.

MR. HAGAN: Q. How would you treat a person like that?

A. The first thing I would do is pray, because I found that the psychopath, the sociopath, the person who for some reason never had woven into his or her nature the patterns that make him a good member of society, and care for society's rights, and know what is wrong and right, and what is just and unjust, and what is the law, and the other one. They grow up not having had that and not giving much of a damn about the whole deal.

DEFENDANT IDA KRUEGER: You shouldn't cuss the Mother of God, and I am the Mother of God.

THE WITNESS: A. In other words, an unfortunately large number of people have concepts that allow them to engage in sins or crimes against person,

property, morals, and still they are by no measure
of a psychiatrist insane or psychotic or necessarily seriously demented disorders. Otherwise, we
might as well send over the keys and open up San
Quentin and let them all out. Of course, they are
not normal by our standards. They are people that
wander away because they haven't social concepts,
and no desire to do the right thing by a husband
or by a son, or not to disgrace them and take anybody for a ride for money, or go into a bank where
I have to fill out a form. Maybe that is why I am
here. I am envious. When I go to the bank I have
to make out a list. I can't walk out with $5,000
without going through a lot of shenanigans. So, I
am against it.

Q. You used the term "normal"?

A. No, she is not normal. She is naughty.

DAY TWENTY-SEVEN

THE CLERK: Would you raise your right hand and be sworn?

THE WITNESS IDA KRUEGER: I don't swear. I am a Rosicrucian.

THE CLERK: Raise your right hand, anyway.

THE WITNESS: It is near my heart, and I take the Rosicrucian oath, and I am entitled to that. The Lord is my light and salvation. Why should I be afraid? The Lord is my light and my friend, and whom should I fear?

MR. MANNING: That is not an oath, your Honor.

THE COURT: My Clerk says it is all right if she makes an affirmation.

MR. HAGAN: You agree, Ida, that you are going to tell the truth and nothing but the truth, is that right?

A. I only know what I know. What I don't know, I can't tell you.

Q. But you are going to tell the truth because you recognize that this is a court of law and you have to tell the truth, isn't that right?

A. Of course. I always tell the truth. That's how I'm made.

Q. Now, Ida, the bodies of the Knutsens, Mrs.
Muriel Knutsen and Lonnie Knutsen, were found in
the basement of your home at 490 Ellington Avenue,
do you know how they got there?

A. I don't even know they are deceased. For all I
know, they are in Brazil. You asked me to tell the
truth and I am telling you just how I feel.

Q. You saw Mr. Wilson on the stand here in court
the other day?

A. I most certainly did. I will never forget him, I
can tell you that.

Q. Where did you first meet Mr. Wilson?

A. About five years ago. He was bowling in San
Francisco.

Q. That is when you were living at 490 Ellington
Avenue?

A. Yes.

Q. And that was long before you ever went to Santa
Rosa?

A. Yes.

Q. Now, how much money have you given Mr. Wilson
over these past few years?

A. I guess over $40,000.

Q. Tell us how that happened.

A. Well, I will have to tell you in my own way.

Q. Go ahead.

A. First of all, we went to Santa Rosa in the
beginning 'cause I was hurt in the jitney accident and I was thrown out of that car and crushed
my teeth and my gums and still have no feeling on
one of my arms and one foot yet. Well, anyway, we

went up there because the insurance people kept
a-bothering us so much. And that's where I seen
Bertie one day downtown to a five-and-ten store.
He said, "Hi, what are you doing up here?" I said,
"Well, I was hurt in a jitney accident." Well he
says, "Where do you live?" And I said, "It's none
of your business." But then he says, "You know
you can get a good buy in a place for the equity."
And I says, "What do you mean? Is this another
one of your shady deals that you have been pulling on me for years? You know I am getting tired
of this business and I am simply going to tell my
husband." So he said, "You go see it in the paper.
Look it up." So there was a little ad in the paper
for the equity in a motel for $3,000. And he said,
"I know this woman." And he introduced me to her.
I never seen the lady before in my life, and her
husband appeared and it's just a coincidence, but
he belonged to the Rosicrucian Order like I do.
And all she wanted was $3,000, so she could go to
Brazil, and I gave her $3,000 for her equity and
she was supposed to have it notarized and mail to
me.
Q. The deed?
A. Yes, but I never got it till after the first
part of January and I thought she taken off with my
money. Oh, that place was simply filthy. In fact,
I don't know how I'm going to clean up the place,
because here I am out $3,000, and Bertie says,
"Well, I can fix that." And he showed me a card
that he was an FBI man. Then he told some people

that I brought a gun on him. Heaven's sakes, even
if I disliked a person I wouldn't do that and I
don't know where they found the gun, but you won't
find no fingerprints of mine on the gun, and who
put it down there I don't know that. I have never
even seen one.

MR. MANNING: Q. When you came to Santa Rosa, you
registered under the name of Long, did you not?
A. Here's what I told you before and I'll tell you
again: we only went up there and registered the
name because of the insurance company.
Q. And wasn't it a fact that when you went to
Santa Rosa both you and Mr. Krueger were in bad
financial condition?
A. I don't know it's such a fact, and I don't know
what you mean: a bad financial condition.
Q. Now, while you were at the motel you met Muriel
Knutsen, did you not, in December of 1961?
A. How do you think I met her?
Q. And this was prior to the time you acquired the
motel, isn't it, 1961?
A. This is April 18th, 1935.
Q. Were you at the Emporium on the evening of
December 15th, 1961, with Muriel Knutsen?
A. No.
Q. Are you aware that two of her traveler's checks
were cashed on that night in the Emporium?
A. Well, I can't help what was cashed for her. I
can tell you about myself, but I wasn't even in
San Francisco. Why don't you go to Brazil and ask
her.

Q. The fact of the matter, Mrs. Krueger, is that
you were there when she cashed that $100 traveler's
check and you got the $100 and had it applied on
your account, isn't that correct?

A. No, because I wasn't even there.

Q. Isn't it a fact that you gave Mrs. Knutsen a
story about the fact that you were a very wealthy
woman, just like you told many other people, that
you were rich and that you would pay her plane fare
from Mexico City to Brazil?

A. That is a tale of someone else's.

Q. Did you tell Mrs. Knutsen, when you were discussing buying or discussing the acquisition of the
motel, that you and your husband had just bought
nine acres of good land in Santa Rosa and were
going to get into strawberries?

A. I don't know anything about any such thing.

Q. Didn't you tell Mr. Crandall that you and your
husband were going to help José Hernandez build
a house for him on one side of the ranch and then
you and your husband were going to build one on the
other side of the ranch?

A. Who is José?

Q. He's not a friend of yours?

A. No, I don't even know José.

Q. Mr. Hernandez — Joseph Hernandez?

A. I don't know him.

Q. You never saw him?

A. Well, I don't remember him.

Q. You don't know he is a good friend of your husband's, that you visit socially back and forth?

A. That's your tale. I don't remember.

Q. In your conversations with Muriel Knutsen, did you ever tell her that you were in a serious accident four years ago?

A. I don't know of even talking to that woman. I told you once, I'll tell you twice, I'll tell you the third time — do you know how to count straight? I don't know that woman, only what I told you I knowed, and that is all the dealings I had with her. And she's in wherever you call it, Cucamonga, somewhere.

Q. Did you tell Mrs. Knutsen during your discussions for purchasing this motel that you had gotten a $100,000 settlement and were well fixed for a venture to South America?

A. Maybe you can answer that question, because I don't know anything about it.

Q. Isn't it a fact, Mrs. Krueger, that you got Muriel Knutsen into your home that night on Ellington Avenue and that you killed her?

A. She's in Brazil. You're nuttier than a fruitcake at Christmas time.

Q. Is there any question in your mind that Muriel Knutsen was the body found in the trunk in your basement?

A. I haven't seen any such thing.

Q. Do you want a picture of that?

A. Yes, I'd like to see a picture of it. And produce the person. Oh, yes, I would. I told the doctor that I was willing to take sodium pentothal. You thought you would find me telling the

truth, that's why you wouldn't do it. I was perfectly willing to do so, because I'm telling the
truth. I have been incarsonated here and none of my
letters has ever gone out, and the way I have been
treated here is something funny. I have been beat
up with wet towels and chained up, and everything.
The SPAC has a law for the animals; you beat your
animals, and they put you in jail for it. I think
people should know the truth about this. They're
not going to give me pills and dope me up and
take me down here. Uh-uh, because I didn't take
anything for a long time. And under the Seventh
Amendment of the United States, whether you listen
or not, I have those rights to speak to an attorney
of my own.

THE COURT: Very well.

DEFENDANT IDA KRUEGER: And I want the press to
print it. Now, that is his attorney, not mine.
Because I have things here that has never been
investigated, and the FBI should be called in here
and thoroughly investigatc. You have never heard
the truth. Because I can't get through to him, and
he don't get through to me. That's it.

MR. MANNING: I'm going to object to this procedure.

DEFENDANT IDA KRUEGER: No, you are not objecting.
Sit down and be quiet. I know my rights because
I'm the Mother of God.

MR. MANNING: Q. Isn't it a fact that you killed
Muriel Knutsen with your husband to get title to
that motel and to get title to those traveler's
checks?

A. You know, you're the biggest liar God ever put
breath in.

Q. Isn't it a fact, Mrs. Krueger, the reason you
were burning Mrs. Muriel Knutsen's things on the
17th of December was that you knew Muriel Knutsen
had been murdered in your house and left here in
San Francisco?

A. I have told you now for the fourth time she's
in Brazil and it's up to you and the FBI men to go
and bring her back, and not me.

Q. Did you have any discussions with your husband,
Joe Krueger, prior to your acquiring the equity or
whatever you want to call it, of Muriel Knutsen's
ownership of this motel?

A. No, because he would have flipped his lid. I
bought it in all good faith through Bert Wilson.
I thought it was a good buy and I even went and
borrowed from the banks, which he cleaned me out
of, and that place was so filthy I wouldn't even
let a dog of mine live in it. There was whiskey
bottles and papers of all different things, and
also dope in there, which was turned over to the
Sheriff's Department. There was stuff in a white
envelope like this here, and I tasted it and it
was awful bitter, and it had "s-n-o-w" on the
outside. And I give that and some little baby
spoons all burnt black and a lot of hypo syringes
and different size, and some needles, and I also
give them some stuff, it had Demerol, and it's
about that size in vials and there were twenty-
four in a box and nine boxes of that. I also give

them a baby bottle full of stuff that had little
grooves in them, and also some little bitty tiny
white pills, I don't know what they was, don't
ask me, but people with prescriptions don't
have that much. And I was seriously hurt and I
never had that. Don't tell me you get that with
prescriptions.

Q. But after this, Joe started doing a lot of work
around there, didn't he?

A. He had to clean the place. I had to ask him. He
said, "What did you do with the money?" He said,
"Do you have money?" I said, "Yes." "Where did you
get it?" And I told him.

Q. You told Joe where you got the money? Where did
you tell him it was?

A. I told him I had it in my lock box.

Q. And he wasn't surprised when you had $5,000 in
a safe deposit box that he knew nothing about?

A. Are you surprised if your wife has something
you don't know about?

Q. I'm asking you if he expressed surprise.

A. I'm asking you a question, too. Can you answer
that?

Q. And Major Knutsen was still there at the motel?

A. Yes. And I couldn't handle him myself because
I was on polio crutches at that time, and I could
barely get around.

Q. You had a cast on your leg?

A. I had polio crutches on. Did you hear me? I am
a person who was pronounced insane, but I think I
have more brains than you.

THE COURT: Now, I am going to ask the audience to be quiet. This is a very important case and if you don't be quiet I will ask that the audience be excused. I want quietness. It is hard enough listening to this witness without listening to the audience as well.

Q. Now, on or about January 15th, or thereabouts, in the year of 1962 do you recall seeing a man named Walter Huston?

A. I don't even know a Huston.

Q. Do you know a Peggy Milton?

A. No, I don't.

Q. Did you at any time request Mr. Huston to drive you to your home at 490 Ellington Avenue?

A. I don't know the man, much less drive me somewhere.

Q. Do you deny coming to San Francisco with Lonnie Knutsen and Peggy Milton and Walter Huston and going to your basement at 490 Ellington Avenue?

A. Of course I do. That man has gone to Brazil with his ex-wife. I have been telling you that and I am telling you for the last time.

Q. Did you put Mr. Knutsen in the back room at that time?

A. How could I put anyone anywhere when I can't put myself on my own feet?

Q. Now, isn't it a fact that you requested Mr. Huston to dig a hole in the exact spot and in the same hole that the body of Lonnie Knutsen was later found?

A. I don't know anything about it and I don't know about a hole.

Q. Didn't you then, after this hole was dug, direct
Mr. Huston to take you to Mt. Zion Hospital with
Lonnie?

A. Nope.

Q. Would you say that Major Knutsen was a pretty
sick man at this time?

A. He could get along better than I could.

Q. He had no problem getting out of the chair?

A. If he was helped.

Q. He couldn't lift his hands, could he, above his
chest?

A. He could lift them pretty good.

Q. He couldn't feed himself?

A. He could feed himself if you put it in front of
him.

Q. Didn't you get rid of Lonnie Knutsen with your
husband because he was causing too much investigation by the family, too many people coming from
the Sheriff's office questioning about the disappearance of Muriel Knutsen? Isn't that why you got
rid of him?

A. I don't know anything about it, and before we
go any further, you and I are going to meet one
another halfway peacefully, and if you don't, I'm
telling you, I'll meet you halfway in Tel-Aviv. You
call this a good free country where people treat
people worse than animals? I tell you, the United
States is pitiful. You act worse than animals, and
put people in insane asylums and they act more
sane than you people who call yourselves human
beings. It's true, every one of you knows it to be

a fact, and you go try to civilize other countries
when your own country is not civilized. You're
worse than the Nazis. At least they do line them
up and shoot them. They don't kill them by degrees.
THE COURT: With all this yelling, I am telling you,
you are not doing any good in your case.
A: What case? They have no case on me. I mean,
after all, you take a person and throw her through
the automobile and crush all her teeth and gums
and put her in a hospital, have no feeling in her
hands and feet. Don't you understand English? If
you don't I can talk Greek to you.
[Unreportable remarks by defendant Ida Krueger]
MR. MANNING: Well, I don't even know what she is
talking about, either, your Honor.
THE WITNESS: You don't know when I am speaking in
English, either.
THE COURT: Mrs. Krueger, please try to behave
yourself.
A. My name is not Mrs. Krueger. My name is the
Mother of God.
MR. MANNING: Q. Do you know your husband who sits
over at the table with Mr. Hagan?
A. That's my father.
Q. How many times did your husband Joe come down
to San Francisco with you?
A. Are you in Jupiter 240 degrees and Uranus 120?
That's 360 degrees.
Q. From your cabin, No. 3, at the Bluebonnet, the
office and the motel of the Rose City Motor Court
was very visible, wasn't it?

A. I don't know what you mean, "visible."

Q. You could see from the front door the office area where Muriel Knutsen and Lonnie were living at that time, isn't that true?

A. You would have to have invisible eyes, if you did, because I'm partly blind, anyway.

Q. Well, your husband has no trouble with his eyes, does he?

A. No, but he doesn't even know the woman, he never saw the woman.

Q. But Joe, you say, was around the Bluebonnet, was he not?

A. Where do you think he would be? In the moon?

Q. Mrs. Krueger, you are sure that the night Major Knutsen disappeared, or left, or whatever you want to call it, that you were with your husband that night?

A. Where do you think I was, for heaven's sake?

Q. Were you with him at 490 Ellington Avenue, San Francisco?

A. We were at the El Sombrero until sometime —

Q. You never left Santa Rosa on the day or the night that Lonnie disappeared?

A. Oh, shut up. You shut up until I'm finished talking. And you respect the Mother of God.

THE COURT: Now, Mrs. Krueger, listen; I told you yesterday that you are not doing your case any good.

THE WITNESS: I'm telling the truth. I'm rightful to tell what's here. I can't remember names, and that's why I asked him, and I asked him something

because if you don't remember you can't say something. I mean, after all, yesterday I even went
upstairs with such a severe headache, and if it
wasn't for the girls putting hot packs and giving
me aspirins, and I was laying still, I couldn't
even think straight. Because I don't remember a
lot of things. I went once one time and got lost
and was in Hawaii. It's not a funny situation. You
needn't laugh.

MR. MANNING: I think under the circumstances I will
conclude the cross-examination.

A. You ought to be ashamed of yourself. You are not
a man. You're a gangster.

MR. HAGAN: Your Honor, at this time I'll ask
that we take an adjournment. This woman has been
through such a strain and I think we should adjourn
until tomorrow morning, I don't think that she can
stand any more of this.

THE COURT: I agree. Do you, Mr. Manning?

MR. MANNING: Your Honor, I wouldn't want to say
what I think.

THE WITNESS: "When Irish eyes are smiling — "

THE COURT: I think we'll adjourn until tomorrow
morning at 10:00 o'clock.

THE WITNESS: (Singing) " — it's like the morning
spring. When Irish eyes are smiling they'll surely
steal your heart away."

DAY THIRTY-ONE
ARGUMENT FOR THE DEFENSE

MR. HAGAN: Ladies and gentlemen of the jury: our
long arduous task is rapidly coming to a close.
These two people, Joe and Ida Krueger, as they sit
here now, are presumed innocent of these charges
that have been made here, and that presumption
goes with them when you retire into the jury room
to deliberate, and that presumption is just as
much a reality in the evidence of this case as
the clerk's desk is. They are presumed innocent.
Because the experience of mankind has taught us
that the two things most difficult to separate and
define and take apart are the utterly innocent and
the utterly guilty. It happens quite often that
innocent people are convicted; we have cases all
the time; I have books on it. I think the evidence
will illustrate to you that Joe Krueger has nothing whatever to do with this. There are suspicious
circumstances as to his wife, but more about that
as we go into the details. Believe me, if they had
a witness that could show you Joe was in San Francisco on the last days of either of the decedents,
he would have been here, and the fact that there

aren't any witnesses like that, proves that Joe
Krueger had nothing to do with the actual murder of
these decedents.

All the Perry Mason novels, for the most part,
are based upon some trick of circumstantial evidence, something that seems to be so, but after
full and exhaustive investigation they find it is
not so. Like a magician on the stand, we saw a
woman in half. We know he couldn't have done it,
but it seems like he did. We see him shoot pistols
into people, tear chicken's heads off, and the
chicken comes walking out of another place. They
take a five-dollar bill and burn it with a match
and open an orange and find it. Circumstantial evidence. You know it didn't happen, because there
it is. So, all the safeguards that the experience
of humanity can devise to apply to give to you as
rules of reason in seeking out the truth through
circumstantial evidence. The newspapers claim it's
a murder case. And it might be a murder case; we
don't think it is. But is it at all reasonable
to suppose that a man who is involved in murder
with the bodies buried in his basement is going
to wait around there after he gets word like that
until they come and arrest him? Joe was there from
the time he left Santa Rosa. He was living at 490
Ellington and gave the authorities carte blanche
to go through, do anything they wanted, including
the last time they came out with picks and shovels to take the basement apart. Joe has told you
he knew nothing about what was in the basement, he

didn't know anything about these murders, he never
met Mrs. Knutsen, never saw her, didn't know her.

Obviously, Ida physically couldn't kill Mrs.
Knutsen by herself. That poor woman was bigger
than she was, a health faddist, kept herself in
good condition. So Ida would have had a problem
trying to seize her and wrestle her down and choke
her, and there's no evidence at all of any physical assault by Ida Krueger. We know Lonnie was
murdered. I reasonably believe that those are the
bodies of those two people. The big question is:
who did it? Who truly did it? Now, just because
this poor demented creature winds up with some of
the property that Mrs. Knutsen had is no indication
that she did the acts.

DEFENDANT IDA KRUEGER: What's he talking about?
They have gone to Brazil, for heaven's sake.

MR. HAGAN: Well, an imaginary doubt would mean
that you imagined the Martians flew in here and
seized the Knutsens and buried them and put them
in the basement. You could imagine. There is no
basis in reason for it. That is an imaginary doubt.
They want you to think that Ida transported the
Major through the public streets of San Francisco
out there to that home and murdered him. How would
she do it? If she called a taxi, the taxi would
remember the man. All taxicabs have manifests, all
which are in access to the District Attorney. They
are public records.

Now, the man that stands out most startlingly
in this entire investigation is Mr. Bert Wilson.

Apparently this poor simple man was being led by
the nose by Ida, a half-demented creature. This
woman, she's no bargain to be around, as you can
see. But I'm sure it's like how people are born:
no one chooses to be born ugly: ugly of spirit,
ugly of mind, or ugly of body. They are born that
way. Do you think she's normal?

Joe Krueger has no knowledge of these things and
he was just as much shocked as anyone else when
that body was discovered in the basement of his
home, and he told you in that statement about the
welfare cases they had who would come into that
motel. It's a run-down, junky motel on the outskirts of the town, with its marginal and destitute
tenants.

DEFENDANT IDA KRUEGER: Bertie did all of it. I
told you the truth, and he also taken me across
the country and he said, "I could kill you, and
nobody would ever find out. If you don't get out
of Santa Rosa, I will kill you myself." That is a
funny thing, too, how he said I had a gun, because
I never saw no gun. That is a funny thing to me or
anybody else.

MR. HAGAN: Murder in the first degree requires,
like any crime, a union of act and intent. Now, the
situation here is that there is evidence of two
murders, but what proof is there that Ida Krueger
did it? Where is the evidence of anyone seeing the
defendants strangle the Knutsens and putting them
in a grave? None at all, and these are the kind of
prosecutions that work out the terrible hardships

that sometimes are found in the law. There is no
evidence that links Ida to these acts. She is
related to the Knutsens in steps of property, and
that sort of thing, but that is not murder; that is
not murder.

DEFENDANT IDA KRUEGER: I have done nothing to no
one. I have only been taken for a sleigh ride, and
Bertie has been doing that to me for years, and
you know what he threatened to do, he did to me out
on the desert, and he even told the people that
he was going to pretend to find someone's husband,
and he was lying.

MR. HAGAN: If the evidence looks suspicious, you
must return a verdict in favor of the defendants.
As far as Joe is concerned, you acquit him just
like that. As far as Ida is concerned, I don't see
anything where she could possibly be held for first
degree murder, or even for second degree murder,
because there is no evidence here that she was in
physical combat with either one of the defendants,
that she assaulted them, that she attacked them, or
that she physically could have attacked them. This
is not a murder case, ladies and gentlemen.

I feel that Ida Krueger is a borderline mental
deficient. I agree heartily with Dr. Chandler that
she belongs in an institution and should have been
put in one, years ago. I believe that she is dangerous to herself and to society. I feel that is
a problem that has to be led in that way, but it
doesn't make her a murderess. We have in our law
under Section 26 of the Penal Code, a statement:

"That all persons are capable of committing crimes except those belonging to the following classes: one, children under the age of fourteen in the absence of clear proof at the time of committing the act charged against them, that they know it is wrongfulness; two, idiots; three, lunatics." How could you better classify Ida Krueger?

The prosecution will tell you that you must be cold, you must be dispassionate, you must have no pity, that you must be like icicles, you must be god-like. That is not quite my code. I feel the kinder, the more human, the more sympathetic a person is, the higher he grows in the scale of being. I feel that there is something god-like in being kind and sympathetic and merciful and that the man who has lost the sense of brotherly love and kindness and mercy in his heart is not much better than the beasts in the field. Secure in my belief and confidence in you, I will now conclude in the hope that I have answered every question necessary to gain an acquittal for Joe Krueger and a release for Ida Krueger.

DAY THIRTY-THREE

ARGUMENT ON BEHALF OF THE PEOPLE

MR. MANNING: First of all, I certainly want to
thank you for the attention that you have paid to
the evidence that has been presented during this
trial.

DEFENDANT IDA KRUEGER: I thank you, too. Go out
and call me Jake Ehrlich. And someone bring me
some bubble gum, please?

MR. MANNING: Now, as you know, the two defendants, Joe and Ida Krueger, have been charged by
an Indictment in this case that they jointly are
responsible for murdering a woman by the name
of Muriel Knutsen and her former husband, Lonnie
Knutsen, and that this final murder took place on
or about January 15th, 1962. Even though I believe,
and I will certainly hope to demonstrate, that
the murders took place here in San Francisco at
490 Ellington Avenue, we are not required under
the law of this state to actually prove that that
took place. I believe the evidence amply demonstrates that these defendants are guilty of murder,
and only one degree of murder, and that is first
degree.

DEFENDANT IDA KRUEGER: Speak for yourself. People who live in plate-glass houses should speak for themselves. Why won't the FBI go to Brazil and find these people? I never seen anyone.

MR. MANNING: You will be instructed, ladies and gentlemen, that murder is the unlawful killing of a human being with malice.

DEFENDANT IDA KRUEGER: You bet it is, and because God said so. You stand up in the way of sin, but this is a law of the Lord, and it is His law to premeditate day and night; and He shall be like a tree planted by rivers of water that bring forth His fruit and His seed; and whatsoever He shall doeth shall prosper. But the ungodly is not so, but is like the chaff that the wind drives away.

MR. MANNING: This was not any spur-of-the-moment thing; this was during the days in Santa Rosa; and it was planned until Muriel was brought down here and done away with in the basement at 490 Ellington Avenue. I further believe the evidence demonstrates in this case, that the element of robbery is involved as to Muriel Knutsen; that she had the deed, she had the traveler's checks; and the next time they appear, those same traveler's checks are in the possession of these defendants.

If they committed this murder for the purpose of robbing Muriel Knutsen of her property, it's first degree murder. And this, ladies and gentlemen, under our law is true, whether they even intended to murder. If they only intended to rob her and a person is killed intentionally, unintentionally,

even accidentally, it is still murder in the first
degree.

DEFENDANT IDA KRUEGER: Why don't you go to confes-
sion once and ask God to forgive your soul. You're
worse than the devil.

MR. MANNING: There's nothing strange about it. Robbery is the mere taking of somebody's personal
property from their possession or immediate presence without their consent through the use of force
or fear. In other words, you either can take it from
them by overpowering them or you can take it by putting them in fear, as in the use of a gun in a store
or something of that nature. That is all robbery is.
In this case, if you find from this evidence that
there was an unlawful agreement tacitly understood
between these two defendants to commit robbery or
to commit murder, then both are equally responsible
whether or not both actually committed the crime of
murder, and whether or not both were even present at
the time that the crime was carried out.

Now, Dr. Chandler, who has been practicing since
1913 and who has specialized in the field of psy-
chiatry practically since that time, gave Ida
Krueger the accepted tests for mental and nervous
disorders, and agreed that she had no mental dis-
order. In fact, he said that she in some respects
is a sociopath, a prevaricator. I think that if
someone has a real delusion that that person was
the Mother of God, then that person would act that
way, she wouldn't act the way we are now observing
her act.

DEFENDANT IDA KRUEGER: When you people taken and killed Jesus Christ and put him in the Cross, and Pontius Pilate even washed his hands of the whole situation, and I would like for him to tell me how can you come to the state to hypnotize yourself. I'd like to know. I would like to know if I could hypnotize myself more than I did here. I would like him to answer that question.

MR. MANNING: She has too many symptoms, she tries to play the part too well, but she —

DEFENDANT IDA KRUEGER: I'm no actor. I don't have anything to do. I never worked for no acting theaters, and I'm not interested in them, furthermore.

MR. MANNING: Our court-appointed psychiatrist agreed she could form any intent she wanted. Normal? They said, no, not normal: anti-social, someone who just doesn't want to comply with the rules of life, the norm expected of a good citizen; someone who wants to take the law into her own hands, wants to act as she wants to act. But this is not mental; this is why we have people in prison for the same reason.

DEFENDANT IDA KRUEGER: Speak for yourself. What about that Doctor DePicasso who threw acid in his poor wife's eyes, and they let him go, and I sit here and I don't know nothing. No, nothing — absolutely.

MR. MANNING: Well, a very strange thing happens at the time they arrive in Santa Rosa. They don't paint themselves as people having a difficult time. They don't paint themselves as people looking for a

job. What do they tell Mr. Crandall when they register? They say that they are well set financially.

DEFENDANT IDA KRUEGER: You never questioned any of
them witnesses, and every one of them is lying, and
I have about fifty people who —

MR. MANNING: This is the first story they tell. And
it gets better. They have come to Santa Rosa because
they have a friend named José who has a 40-acre
ranch a little bit down the road, and that they came
up there to help José, or Joe is going to help José
build a house on it, and they are going to raise
strawberries with José. This is the story they are
giving under the name of Long in Santa Rosa. Now,
with that in mind, can you imagine the buildup
given to Muriel Knutsen, who has had a lifetime
dream, apparently, of leaving the United States and
going to Brazil? Mrs. Knutsen had acquired a motel,
and there is no question that this is not a first
class motel. Nobody is trying to paint it as such.
It may be third class, whatever you want to call it.
It's run down, it's in need of work, and she has got
it and she's trying to make both ends meet with it.
When she got this motel, not only did she have this
problem, but she had the responsibility of feeding,
cleaning, bathing, and clothing Lonnie Knutsen. So
you see, it really wasn't too difficult for someone with a conniving, clever mind to work on Muriel.
And how do we know what happens? Because we have
a letter, the last document ever written by Muriel
Knutsen on this earth to anyone. And it is dated
December 14th, '61. She writes this to her mother:

"Dear Mom and all: It looks like my dreams are about to come true. I have a wonderful chance to go to Brazil with another Rosicrucian woman. She's rich and will pay my plane fare from Mexico City to South Brazil and back to San Diego. When she read the literature I had from Eden, the subtropical health settlement, she wanted to go there as soon as possible. She and her husband just bought nine acres of good land here and he is now getting it put into strawberries and not able to leave at this time. So she is helping me with expenses and will have plenty left to invest when we get there. She will lend me $10,000 and take the Rose City Court as security. She has got the pioneering spirit, was in a serious accident four years ago and got a $100,000 settlement, and is well fixed for adventure to South America. We plan to leave in a few days."

Then, on the 15th, Muriel Knutsen makes the greatest mistake of her life. She gets the deed notarized. This was the coup de grace. Now the Kruegers are ready. Everything has been done that needs to be done. The deed is notarized, transferring title to this motel to Ida Long, the traveler's checks have been purchased. All that's left is to get her to San Francisco to 490 Ellington Avenue. Now, this is not a particularly difficult thing to do. Mrs. Knutsen is certainly not, from what we can see, a stranger to business affairs. She knows that before any notarized deed is going to be turned over, there's going to

be some money coming up. So what can you imagine,
having heard the stories given by Mrs. Krueger to
Bert Wilson on the trip to Wyoming, what was told
to Mrs. Knutsen? What lock box was Mrs. Long going
to produce the $10,000 out of? And we know they
go to the Emporium on the night of the 15th, and
I take it Muriel has got the deed to the motel
and her traveler's checks and the only thing that
remains to be done is to get her to Ellington
Avenue. Well, I would say that she was probably delayed and persuaded to stay overnight by
some excuse, the banks are closed, "I can't get
my money. The lock box is secured. We'll get it
tomorrow."

DEFENDANT IDA KRUEGER: Nicodemus, shut up and be
quiet! You've had your say. It's our turn now.
What am I doing here, anyway? I've been to a mental
institution, but that's no sin.

MR. MANNING: In any event, we know that this was
the last transaction or business of any kind that
Muriel Knutsen ever made, the last that anyone
ever saw or heard from her until she ends up in
the cement on Ellington Avenue. This woman was
not, at the time she was recovered from that trunk,
clothed for bed. She had her regular clothes on,
skirt, blouse, underthings. She had obviously no
indication at the time she was attacked that this
was going to happen. This was done, ladies and
gentlemen, for only one reason: to get that deed.
The Kruegers were desperate. They were broke. They
had nowhere else to turn, and Muriel was a victim.

Now, we have heard of her physical condition, and
there is no question that Muriel was no weight
lifter. Muriel was five foot one, she weighed
around, I take it, 125, 130 pounds. Apparently she
had been a very active woman in her life. From
what we know she could repair roofs, help paint,
work around the place, etcetera. So it wasn't a
job for one person. This woman was capable, I am
sure, of fighting back; but not against two, not
if you are taken by surprise. And as the doctors'
reports show, she lived very shortly after the
initial attack.

In the grand scheme of this case, you are going
to have the activities of the Longs, and you are
going to have the activities of the Kruegers, kept
separate and distinct; and when the activities of
the Longs in Santa Rosa are completed and all the
money is borrowed and the Knutsens are disposed
of and the motel is finally sold for this alleged
price that they put in the Examiner, of $72,000, or
for any profit that they could get, there weren't
going to be any Longs; there were just going to
be the Kruegers on Ellington Avenue, whom nobody
knew in Santa Rosa as having lived at this motel
and having owned it. Now, at about this time comes
the itinerant construction worker, Mr. Huston. He
is approached by Mrs. Krueger to dig a hole in her
basement in San Francisco. Mr. Lonnie Knutsen is
helped into the car and then comes Mr. Huston and
Peggy Milton and Mrs. Krueger. When they get to
San Francisco, they go into the garage and Lonnie

Knutsen is put in the back room. Obviously, at this time, the grave of Muriel Knutsen has been sealed with concrete. So, Mr. Huston prepares the grave, unbeknownst to him, of Lonnie Knutsen, and he is given directions and size and shape, four by four, follow the line, and then it is going to be a catch basin. He digs, and she keeps telling him to make it deeper and wider, and to neaten it out, and that is it. The next thing we know, the Major is taken to Mount Zion Hospital, and she takes him to the emergency entrance, and this is the last anybody saw of Mr. Knutsen.

So, it is clear that they also planned this thing with the understanding that when they are caught she is going to play the "mental," and he is going to play the "lack of knowledge." She is up to it over her head. She has nothing else to go on. He believes he has a chance with his denials, but not when he has to fabricate a defense to fit him. This is the oldest thing in the world. When you have no defense, you find a scapegoat, but it doesn't fit and it can't fit because it is not the truth.

MR. HAGAN: Your Honor, I think we will have to stop proceedings. The defendant is either asleep or drugged.

MR. MANNING: I'm going to ask that any remark like that go out.

THE COURT: That may go out of the record.

MR. HAGAN: I don't know. She has never been asleep in the courtroom before since we have been here.

(A short recess is taken.)

MR. MANNING: So we go out there, and as Coroner Tuttle told you, we go into the basement, Mr. Krueger is there. Oh, no, he doesn't want to look at the search warrant, he couldn't care less. He didn't realize at that time that we were going to tear up any floor or any concrete. He had been talked to by law enforcement officers for months. I guess he thought we were going to go up to the attic again. Instead, we go to remove the new wood floor, and then the new concrete, and what do we find in the corner of the basement? We find this rough patch, and from under that finally was recovered the body of Lonnie. With this information, and now believing that Muriel is also there, we bring Mr. Krueger downstairs. And we asked him that very night, "Mr. Krueger, you have seen this, are there any other places in your basement where there were any holes, to your knowledge?" And Mr. Krueger, in our presence, points to a space right by the pole, and he tells us, "Yes, in that area you will find a round barrel hole that had been used apparently in prohibition days for a still of some sort." Now, we want to save tearing up this whole place. So, what happens? We tried to take a statement from Mr. Krueger at that time, and he denied any knowledge of all the patches. He knows nothing about the one in the corner; he knows nothing about the one in the middle; he knows nothing about any of them. And yet now he wants you to believe, oh, just a slip-up, "I remember very well my wife told me about the first one." But why didn't he admit them

to begin with? Now, what's the problem here? If he
knows about one, why not about two? Well, there's
two reasons: first of all, of course, he knows that
there are two people missing, and there has been a
lot of investigation about it.

DEFENDANT IDA KRUEGER: Bertie tells me he wants
my body and pulls his pants down — "and you will
do what I want you to do." That is a pretty dirty
thing, pretty dirty boy, I will tell you.

MR. MANNING: Ladies and gentlemen, when you review
this entire case and the evidence, you can only
come to one reasonable conclusion, and that is
that both of these defendants are equally responsible and guilty of the crime of first degree murder
as against Muriel and Lonnie Knutsen. They are
the only ones who will profit by their murder and
the only ones who profited financially from this
record; and when you have reviewed this evidence, I
am going to ask that you find both of them guilty
of the charge in that degree. Thank you very much
for your attention.

DAY THIRTY-EIGHT
READING OF VERDICTS

THE COURT: Now, Mr. Foreman, I understand you have arrived at a verdict, and before you present the verdicts to the clerk, I am going to ask you, have you arrived at a verdict on both defendants and on both counts?

THE FOREMAN: Yes, we have.

THE COURT: Very well. Would you please present the verdicts to the clerk?

(Thereupon the verdicts were presented to the clerk, who, in turn, presented them to the Court.)

THE COURT: (After having examined the verdicts and returned them to the clerk) Very well, record the verdict.

THE CLERK: The People of the State of California against Joe and Ida Krueger.

"We the jury, find the defendant, Joe Krueger, guilty of the crime of felony, to wit, murder (Muriel Knutsen), as charged in Count 1 of the indictment and determine the degree to be first degree," and signed, "Antonio G. Chela, Foreman."

"We the jury, find the defendant, Joe Krueger, guilty of the crime of felony, to wit, murder

(Lonnie Knutsen), as charged in Count 2 of the indictment and determine the degree to be first degree," and signed, "Antonio G. Chela, Foreman." "We the jury, find the defendant, Ida Krueger, guilty of the crime of felony, to wit, murder (Muriel Knutsen), as charged in Count 1 of the indictment, and determine the degree to be first degree," signed, "Antonio G. Chela, Foreman." "We the jury, find the defendant, Ida Krueger, guilty of the crime of felony, to wit, murder (Lonnie Knutsen), as charged in Count 2 of the indictment, and determine the degree to be first degree," signed, "Antonio G. Chela, Foreman."

THE CLERK: Unanimous verdict as to all four counts, as to each defendant.

DAY FORTY-FOUR
JUDGE NEWMARK RENDERING PENALTY VERDICTS

THE COURT: Ida, I'm going to speak for the first
time in this case. I'm going to ask you to listen
to me. I'm going to express my feelings and my
thoughts about this case for the first time. Now,
I might say that my mind has been tortured ever
since this verdict was rendered, and I am not
trying to be dramatic about this, but I am not
ashamed to say that I have asked for divine guid-
ance to direct me to render the proper decision in
this case. I don't think any personal problem that
I have ever had has given me more concern than this
decision today. And I realize that the easy way
would be to say, "Well, the jury has spoken, it's
their responsibility." But it is also mine. I think
only cowards avoid responsibility. And I might
say that no greater decision have I had to rule on
since I have been on the Bench.
DEFENDANT IDA KRUEGER: Thank God you have a
conscience.
THE COURT: Now, I realize that it is not my duty
to impose a death penalty; it is my duty to determine if there are any extenuating circumstances

why I should set aside the jury's verdict of
death.

DEFENDANT IDA KRUEGER: I'll tell you, because I'm
not guilty, that's why.

THE COURT: I have read all of the Supreme Court
cases concerning the death penalty and I have found
no formula to guide me. It is my duty as a Judge to
independently weigh and consider the testimony and
all the ramifications of it, and to determine in my
own mind if the evidence warrants the death penalty.
Now, it seems to me to impose the death penalty in a
circumstantial case, it should be done with extreme
caution. The evidence against Ida is much stronger than the evidence against Joe. So, should the
punishment be equal? I think sound judgment would
indicate it should be, but after many a sleepless
night I have come to the conclusion that the planning, the execution, the guiding criminal mind, was
that of Ida Krueger, and not of Joe Krueger.

DEFENDANT IDA KRUEGER: I have never in my life ever
thought any such thing.

THE COURT: In my opinion, he would not commit this
crime without her.

DEFENDANT IDA KRUEGER: He never has done nothing.
I don't believe that man is any more guilty than I
am. Bertie took him for a sleigh ride. He's been
taken to the cleaners.

THE COURT: She was the prime mover. Unfortunately,
as I see this case, Joe's loyalty to his wife —

DEFENDANT IDA KRUEGER: He's a good man. And I love
him very, very much. My husband to me is like

a father, a father I never had. And a brother I always wanted, and a husband combined in one, and a mother, too, that I never had.

THE COURT: — is somewhat greater than his loyalty to justice. Now, should a man die for such loyalty? I think not. Here's a man who's never been in any trouble in his life, a frugal man, who meets Ida, becomes enamored with her, and married her because he was lonely. But from that time on his troubles began. In my opinion, he fell under her spell, just as were all the other victims in this case.

DEFENDANT IDA KRUEGER: What spell do you mean, Judge?

THE COURT: In that sense, he was just as much a victim as all the other victims in this case. Now, I think it will be conceded by all that the motive of this crime was robbery. So, who was to benefit by this robbery? In my opinion, only Ida Krueger. This is also impressive in my mind: after the verdict was rendered by the jury, without any planning on her part, without any thought processes going through her mind, without steady thinking of the situation whatsoever, she went into a hysterical outburst, and she yelled and screamed at the top of her voice that Joe had nothing to do with this crime. She said that at the time she was in the basement, Joe was never there. I think what she was telling us, or trying to emphasize, is that her participation was greater than his.

DEFENDANT IDA KRUEGER: He's the kindest man in the world. Why don't you send him home? I'm ready to face death because no one can kill me, because I am the Mother of God. If I die, I'll go on Easter morning.

THE COURT: It seems the evil doing was Ida's. So, in my opinion, in Joe's case it seems to me the proper punishment, considering all of the evidence and considering his past life, is a certain but lenient prison sentence commensurate with the errors in judgment he made along the way here, yet mindful of a rehabilitation I feel reasonably confident he's capable of achieving.

So now we come to Ida's case.

DEFENDANT IDA KRUEGER: And I'm not guilty, either. That is the truth, so help me God.

THE COURT: The problem in her case is quite different. There are no extenuating circumstances that I can find which should prompt me to reduce her sentence. I can find more to the contrary to uphold the jury's verdict.

DEFENDANT IDA KRUEGER: I haven't done anything. I have never taken no one's life and God is my Judge. You ought to go get Bertie and Juanita and ask them some questions.

THE COURT: It is my opinion that Ida's wrath can be easily aroused. She has no respect for law or order. She's demonstrating this right at this very moment in this courtroom. She will always be a constant menace to society.

DEFENDANT IDA KRUEGER: I have never hurt no one in my life.

THE COURT: Her disregard for the rights of others has been amply displayed right in this courtroom.

As far as rehabilitation is concerned, I feel that
she is beyond that. She has been a troublemaker all
her life. She will be a troublemaker the rest of
her life.

DEFENDANT IDA KRUEGER: I have been a sick person.

THE COURT: For her, life has never had any meaning.
I therefore deny any motion to reduce the penalty
in Ida Krueger's case.

Now, to formally pronounce judgment: Joe Krueger, I
sentence you to seven years in prison, to be served
in a minimum-security facility, subject to parole.
You may not be responsible for these crimes in the
same manner as your wife, but I cannot hold you
blameless, either. It's my hope that you'll see what
choices you made that brought you before this court
and be able to avoid those errors in the future.
And to you, Ida Krueger —

DEFENDANT IDA KRUEGER: The same thing.

THE COURT: I say this —

DEFENDANT IDA KRUEGER: God is my judge. I haven't
done one thing, I really haven't. I really haven't
done one thing.

THE COURT: I have to read this death sentence,
and I might say that I am reading it with a heavy
heart.

DEFENDANT IDA KRUEGER: Well, I haven't done anything and I'm not going to take it, absolutely.

THE COURT: Ida Krueger, you having heretofore been
convicted in this Court of the crimes of murder,
in two counts, and a jury having found in each
case, that you shall suffer the penalty of death —

DEFENDANT IDA KRUEGER: Help me! Somebody help me! Stanley! Get Pete and do something!

THE COURT: It is therefore the judgment of this Court, in Count 1 and Count 2 of the Indictment herein, that you, Ida Krueger, be executed and put to death in the manner prescribed by the laws of the State of California, by the administering of a lethal gas in the State Prison in the State of California, that shall be legally designated. And may God have mercy on your soul.

DEFENDANT IDA KRUEGER: And may God have mercy on everyone's.

J OE SHOULD'VE KNOWN it would all play out like that. The trial flew by day after day and he hadn't the vaguest idea what it was all about. Witnesses Joe had never heard of paraded into court and testified about things Joe didn't understand. One cop after another — a few Joe recognized, others he didn't — and a private dick from Washington State, explained investigations regarding Joe and Ida's affairs months before Joe had even known people had their eyes on him. Three bankers from Santa Rosa and another from San Francisco claimed Ida swindled them by borrowing loans under false pretenses. Store owners and clerks from Sears and the Emporium said Ida cheated them by kiting checks. A couple of fellows from Marin testified that Ida owed them money for work done both at the El Sombrero and down on Ellington. Insurance fellows in the city told about Ida's jitney accident and how they felt confident she had faked her injuries. That liar who laid the T&G floor for Ida got up on the stand and claimed Joe and Ida blocked him from chunking up the old cement. Nosy neighbors on Ellington testified that Ida lied about where she came from, children she claimed to have given birth to, churches she attended or didn't, family she had in another state, according to her ever-changing story. For her own part, Ida behaved like a nut and disrupted the proceedings and tried to have herself declared insane, and what did it get either of them? Joe knew Ida was guilty and Hagan knew she was guilty and so did everyone else. Yet she came into court every morning asking for bagels, lox, cream cheese, and bubble gum; giving a different juror the evil eye each day; faking an epileptic fit one afternoon; falling asleep in her chair on another; banging her shoe on the table; grabbing chalk from the blackboard; sweeping papers off the bench; making faces at the TV cameras and press photographers; disregarding Judge Newmark's daily admonitions to keep quiet; and lying, lying, lying about everything under the sun. Yet she also made dozens of clever drawings and wrote touching little poems for the press and courtroom spectators. Hagan called for a mistrial at least once a week. Meanwhile, Ida yelled and laughed, and argued and never quit interrupting whoever had the floor. Joe wished he'd had a gunny sack over his head so they wouldn't be associated together. It probably wouldn't have made any difference. When he was on the witness stand himself, he felt like a fool. They asked him the same goddamn questions over and over again, trying to trip him up, make him look guilty. He was lucky the Judge felt sorry for him, or he'd have gotten the gas chamber, too. Seven years in prison wasn't on his mind when he first drove into Ocean City that night, but he had to admit things could've been a lot worse.

Hagan clapped him on the back when the Judge left the bench for good. After that, it seemed to Joe like everything came loose at the seams. The courtroom was flooded with people, spectators rising to mingle with witnesses and jurors, reporters pouring in from the corridors. Hagan ran off with the prosecutors and Joe stood by himself for a few minutes, listening to the postmortem on the trial from everyone within ear shot. He felt sick to his stomach. Just behind him, he heard Muriel's sister Agnes and her mother Mrs. Claiborne talking to a crowd of reporters.

"Oh, I really expected life for him and the chair for her. I thought it might be life imprisonment, but the evidence was so conclusive, the finding of the bodies in the basement. I couldn't see how they could be found anything else but guilty."

"Agnes, are you satisfied with the death sentence?"

"Well, I'm on the spot. When you think about the death sentence intellectually, you think that maybe it should be abolished. But it's pretty hard to believe that way when it's your own people."

Mrs. Claiborne added, "It's what they deserve. I'm satisfied, but it won't bring my daughter back."

"What do you think about Ida claiming to be the Mother of God?"

"Oh, for goodness sakes, I didn't think she believed in God one iota. She has a lot of nerve. I'll give her credit for that. Her outbursts in court were very unusual. The Judge shouldn't have allowed it. But I'm glad it's over. Everything was done in a fair way. I hoped she wouldn't get life. She shouldn't be let loose to do more of that kind of work. She justly got what she deserved."

When Joe glanced in their direction, he saw Mrs. Claiborne glaring at him, a smug self-satisfied expression on her face.

A reporter got his attention. "Did you have anything to do with the murders, Joe? You can say it straight now."

"What?" His head was swimming.

"Did you kill those people?"

"No, I didn't."

"What about Ida? Did she murder the Knutsens?"

"Go ask her yourself."

"Did you expect Ida to be found legally sane?"

"Yeah, I guess so. But I think she's nuts."

Then a lanky bailiff Joe hadn't met before grabbed his arm and led him out of the courtroom.

In the hallway, he found Ida spouting off as usual, two bailiffs, a deputy, and a matron named Eloise close at her side, all five utterly surrounded by an enormous crowd of reporters and hangers-on. She looked mad as a hornet and her voice rang across the corridor.

"I'm not afraid to die, but I can take you out there to the house and show you exactly what happened. They had a whole keg of nails and long pipes and little white pills. They held a gun to my face. What could I do? They were going to shoot her to the moon."

"Who was that, Ida? Who was going to shoot her to the moon?"

"Bertie and Nita, you nincompoops! They did it. They took her into my basement and did away with her to blackmail me. What was I supposed to do?"

"Were you with them at Ellington?"

"I was there, sure. Where else? They said they would kill me if I didn't do it. They said they'd fix me up good and they gave me some little white pills that made my eyes go like this — " She wagged her hands in front of her eyes like windshield wipers. "They're both wicked, those two! Bertie, he put the trunk in the hole with ropes. He had somebody in the trunk. I was doped. Those little white pills. And they had a gun."

"Did Muriel yell when she died?"

"I don't know. She was in the trunk all the time."

"Do you think you got a fair trial, Ida?"

"Well, it was a lousy play. I never even knew the characters. And Nicodemus was ornery and bloodthirsty since the day I got here. And his so-called witnesses were the damnedest bunch of strays you've ever seen. Same with that jury over there. Look at them staring at their own feet and hanging their heads because they have guilt in their hearts and can't look no one in the eye. This was what I call a number one kangaroo court. I hope they see my face as long as they live. How can they convict someone who don't know nothing? They must've got paid off. I can sleep tonight, and that's more than I can say of some people. But if they kill me, they'll have something to think about on Easter Sunday.

"You're not afraid of the gas chamber?"

"Oh, Mother McCreedy, it's just cyanide pellets one, two, three — bing, bing, bing, and you're off. I am the Mother of God, and I haven't done nothing wrong. I never saw no bodies, but let me just tell you something: a pretty angel at the gate gave me seven keys to seven rooms. Each was in beautiful colors. There were fountains and I could smell rosebuds. I went through all seven rooms, like I was a little child. And something hot flashed over me and I could smell roses and everyone was chanting, la-la-la. Everyone was happy. It was like a fog. I could hear an echo. And there was a little bridge, sort of golden. A lady took me by the hand and wouldn't let me cross over. She said I was worthy, but I was too young. I'd have to wait awhile. My little brother was killed when he was seven years old. He was carrying my violin and I couldn't help him. A big truck hit him. God is my judge, but man is not. Man can kill me, but God takes my soul. I'm not afraid of nothing. I know I'm not guilty. Life is a revolving door. I have nothing to confess."

"What about Joe? Do you think he should've gotten the same sentence?"

"Oh, that poor fellow's so confused," she said, smiling. "I do believe he's as sick as I am."

For a moment there, Joe Krueger thought he might just walk past Ida and leave all of this behind. Then one of the reporters noticed him, and the tide swelled in his direction, parting for Ida to greet him once more. Joe's bailiff let him go, so he could embrace Ida if he wanted. He didn't know how he felt, but then Ida pushed close to him and held out her arms.

"Hi, honey."

She smiled, and somehow he did, too. Ida slipped her hands around his waist and cuddled up to him just as any wife would do and laid her head against his chest. Maybe out of habit or something else he didn't know about, Joe hugged her tightly and smelled that same old lemon scent in her hair. She put her face up and kissed him like none of this had ever happened.

"Do it again!" photographers urged. "Please, Ida, just one more! Kiss him again!"

Ida snapped back. "What kind of people are you? I'm going to write to Governor Brown."

"Are you going to miss your husband, Ida? What do you say?"

She smiled at Joe. "Sure, I'll miss my honey. I love him." She squeezed his hand once more, and then let go finally as the matron took her by the arm again.

"Bye, Joey," Ida told him, in her best little girl's voice. "I can write to you and you can write to me."

"Sure we can."

Unsure of what else to say, he told her to watch out for herself, and good-bye.

As Ida was led away, she blew Joe a last kiss. "I'll be seeing you, honey."

EPILOGUE

T HE DAY AFTER SENTENCING, once both Ida and Joe had been taken away from the city, a popular astrologer for one of the Bay Area's more prominent newspapers published this in her morning column:

> Ida Krueger is one of those rare persons
> who are born evil. She has a mean streak
> wider than the Milky Way. Her horoscope
> rivals only that of Bluebeard in its zest
> for murder. She has a great power of eva-
> siveness and cunning. She has one of the
> most intrinsically evil horoscopes I've
> ever seen. Most murderers have an evil
> opposition between two planets in their
> charts, but Ida has all three squares —
> all involving powerful planets. The stars
> have given her a malific energy, a product
> of an almost unbounding ego, an almost
> animal hatred, and a genius for destruc-
> tion. Ordinarily, she would have been a
> warm and affectionate person, but both
> her sun and moon have evil afflictions,
> which destroy any good inclinations. This
> perversion gives her a powerful ego in
> constant stormy relations with people,

and a great restlessness. Her impulsiveness and restlessness is manifested in the
many aliases and a constant urge to keep
traveling. Saturn is in close conjunction with her moon, causing a brooding and
jealous nature. She hates people strongly
with an illogical animal-like instinct.
Neptune, the planet of deception, adds
its rays to her moon, giving a feeling of
being above the law and a mystic faith in
herself. She feels she can get away with
anything. She's a daring person. The woman
is a gambler, but Jupiter square to Mars
in her horoscope means she'll be unsuccessful. Her judgment is confused. She
doesn't know when to quit. She has a perverse genius for deceit and destruction.
The stars doomed her from the start. Hers
wasn't a horoscope. It was a horror-scope.
If she believes in herself, she must have
a hard time living with herself.

Joe Krueger served three and a half years of his seven-year sentence at a minimum-security facility in the Central Valley. He hated
sleeping in a cell, but found most of the penitentiary experience more
rewarding than the Army Air Corps. Getting up early was a snap and
work detail was easier knowing he wouldn't be blown to bits. Sweep
up here and there, do a bunch of laundry, weed now and then, and
clean toilets. No big strain. Prison was mostly boring, but he had a
couple of pals to play cards with and commiserate over mistakes in life,
and when he was released, Joe promised to stay in touch. He didn't,

of course, and that was all right, too, because sometimes we just don't see far enough down the road to know where the next turn is. After getting rid of that goddamned house on Ellington Avenue, Joe wound up at Fresno, where he enrolled in night school to learn about electronics. For the first time in his life, he sat in class without dozing off and even asked questions every so often. Joe liked the idea of fixing radios or television sets, maybe getting work as an electrician. He knew he wasn't the smartest guy in the world, but if he could just earn a fair paycheck and keep out of trouble, he could figure out the rest.

Joe heard from Ida six times when he was in prison. She knitted him a couple of sweaters and wrote about all her new friends behind bars. If he hadn't known better, Joe might have thought she had taken off to a summer camp and forgotten to go home. It was Hagan who told Joe that Ida had dodged the gas chamber on a series of appeals and the threat of a new trial, and, just like always, set herself up to make good somehow, though Judge Newmark still gave her a life sentence, warning that she should never be considered safe to return to open society. At county jail, during the penalty phase of the trial, she'd scribbled a poem on the back of a newspaper that she'd handed out to the reporters to copy down:

As I sit here in this hot place called Hell
I wonder why I'm not doing so well.
I wonder why these people with keys,
Always want me on my knees?
I wonder why the women I know,
Are just as cold as snow?
I wonder why the air in here
Don't smell as fresh as the air out there?
What's the place called, beyond the gate?
Oh! I know, the free world where I met my fate.

Throughout the trial, Ida had put on a show and gotten her way, even finally evading the death sentence. Now and again, during his own time behind bars, Joe wondered if Ida had put on her act for him, too, if love was just as phony to her as the stories she told. We give our hearts away so easily, sometimes it seems as if people are just waiting out there for us. Whom can we trust? Ida was a big heartache for Joe, when he got right down to it. Whether she was nuts or not didn't really matter to him, any longer. She was behind him now, and he wasn't looking back. Truth was, he'd discovered who Ida was that night she smothered the Spagnolinis, yet he still took her away with him to San Francisco. How come? Was she so sweet and pretty that love disguised her rotten heart? Why the hell had she lied to him about her past? Why hadn't she told him about her kids and husband? For that matter, what had Ida really been digging a hole for in her basement that rainy night? Ever since the Knutsens were brought out of the ground, Joe thought about a dry cement patch in the boardinghouse basement six feet from where he'd buried Spagnolini. What if the Macaulays were lying in the dirt under that hotel next to Frank and Vera? Nobody saw their auto go over the cliff. He thought about her keeping him out of the basement that night. What if everything about Ida was just a big fat lie? What would that make him? Every so often, when she and Joe would fight, Ida would bake a batch of peanut butter cookies for him and set the plate on his bedstand to let him know she still expected to be his wife in the morning. He always ate the cookies and lay beside her again.

Joe stopped writing back to Ida by his second year or so in prison and quit thinking of her as his wife. In fact, he began to consider her a weed in his brain that needed eradicating. One day he put every-thing from her out of his cell and told the guards to get rid of it. He requested a stop on her mail and eventually he forgot the sound of her voice. That's when he began to make a plan for life after prison.

To help pay for night school and a small room above a downtown pool hall, Joe found part-time work at a tire repair shop. He'd work mornings and spend most afternoons at the library to do his homework in the stacks. He got a library card and checked out books on electrical circuitry and real estate. He wasn't sure whether he ought to repair homes or sell them. Maybe he would do both. Ambition wasn't a quality Joe possessed in spades. Nobody is born with an eye to setting the world on fire. The instinct for that comes later when the build-up of everything seems inadequate and nothing makes sense except to make improvements. Some are better at that than others. A few run the show for everyone else. Joe Krueger wouldn't be running any show, but he finally had the insight that obedience to the necessity of earning a good living, developing a healthy self-respect, and being a good citizen among his peers was attainable only if he pointed himself in the right direction.

His heart led again.

Joe met a young woman at the insurance office where he registered a used Dodge Dart he had bought for $500. She had a face like Debbie Reynolds and nice figure, too. Her name was Joyce Filbert.

"Like the nut," she told him, with a darling smile that glazed his eyes.

"You mean if I took you out I'd be dating a nut?"

"Yes," she laughed. "I suppose you would."

That Saturday night, Joe drove her to dinner and then to a movie house to see a western with John Wayne and Dean Martin. Joyce liked westerns. Her great-grandfather had come out from Illinois in a covered wagon and she told Joe how she often dreamed about being a pioneer wife on the prairie.

"I don't know," Joe replied, picturing Joyce hauling wooden buckets of water from a grassy river bank. "That seems like a lot of work."

"Oh, it's not the work that kills us, Joe. It's feeling that it doesn't serve any good purpose. But there's no better reason for work than knowing we're really making something hand-in-hand that belongs to each of us. My mother used to tell me that when we work together, it's half the struggle and twice the joy."

After that, Joe started seeing Joyce Filbert every other night until they both agreed they were in love and ought to look into a marriage license. Then Joe told her about Ida. He sat her down on his sofa and let her know he'd been in prison and what Ida had done to those motel people in Santa Rosa. Naturally, he left out the Spagnolinis and Ocean City. Joyce cried for two hours, but didn't tell him to go jump in the lake. The funny thing was that she wasn't worried about Joe having been in prison for capital murder. No, all she really wanted to know was when he planned to get his divorce from Ida. She wasn't curious about Ida or how Joe felt about her; Joyce just wanted Ida out of his life. So Joe found a lawyer across town and filed the papers for dissolution of his marriage.

Joyce baked him a lemon cake to celebrate.

They moved to Stockton a few months later and got married a week after his divorce was final.

Some of us are born, grow up, grow old, and die in the same life. Even when we change addresses or our last names, we live substantially as we always have, as we've always known. Others manage to look away. Joe Krueger woke up one morning with the thought that no one can be told how tomorrow will arrive. The sun moves across the sky and we hurry around and, if we're lucky enough, we lie down at dusk in the arms of someone who loves us so much we can't wait for morning.

That's how Joe felt six years after leaving prison.

He got himself hired by Allstate to sell life insurance. Joyce had suggested encyclopedias, but by then Joe had come to believe that everyone wanted forgiveness for mistakes and leaving something behind as recompense was the only sure thing you could do. They bought a ranch-style house on a shady street with a grassy front yard and a two-car garage and a flagstone patio out back. Soon, Joyce gave him two daughters, Catherine and Christina, born two years apart almost to the day in April. Joe bought a white Ford Falcon and joined a bowling league and became a member of the Elks club and went fishing on the delta with a group of fellows he met at a barbershop. He had more friends than at any time in his life and felt a certain satisfaction that followed from the knowledge that he was liked.

A couple of years or so after his little girls were born, Joe brought his new family out to Santa Fe to see his dad. He was proud of the new life he'd made for himself and wanted to show it off. Walter Krueger had retired and was plenty eager to meet Joyce and the kids and take them around the desert in his new Jeep. He told Joe how he'd always had faith in him and that he knew one day Joe would right his course and become the man everyone knew he could be. Driving home from New Mexico, Joe held Joyce's hand in the front seat and sang to his pretty daughters.

There are crossroads whose waymarkers are made obscure to us by virtue of our own deliberate calculations. We map out our lives by designs we believe are drawn in careful consideration of those consequences we deem most applicable to our wisest desires. Truth is, we choose only what we know and our judgment is flawed. Life is more random, more circumstantial, than we care to admit. If there is such a thing as Fate, its intervention occurs at instances, not as a tapestry by warp and weft. What's done cannot be undone, and redemption is a fable, but every now and then the fortunate are passed to a better way.

Twenty-four years after that rainy drive into Ocean City, Joe Krueger found himself at a roadside fruit stand on Highway 99 south of Fresno on a windy summer afternoon. He was driving home from an insurance trip to Bakersfield and had stopped to buy a bag of peaches for Joyce. Dust lifted across the road into a shelter of walnut trees surrounding the fruit stand. Half a dozen automobiles were parked in the dirt, and a pack of wide-eyed children ran about like rabbits. It was on a day such as this that Joe felt a kind of greatness for appreciating that small adventure each of us finds in family life. In the backseat of his Falcon was a pair of teddy bears he'd bought at a Five & Dime for his little girls. The clerk joked that Joe seemed kind of old for stuffed animals and Joe laughed because his heart was so full of the joy his children brought him. That feeling made him homesick and anxious to get back on the road again. If he drove fast enough and got a break with traffic, he could still tuck his beautiful girls in at bedtime. Then he and Joyce might watch TV for a little while, cuddling under the blanket until one of them fell asleep. If Joe were awake, he'd watch Joyce sleep and stroke her hair and whisper in her ear how lucky he was that she loved him and how dearly he loved her in this happy summer of his heart.

A whirlwind of small boys and girls ran ragged circles through the parking lot, raising dust amid that laughing nonsense. Joe stood patiently about fifteen feet away from the fruit bins, his eye on the ripe peaches he intended to buy for Joyce. A crowd of people waited in front of him, blocking his view of the cash register. The sun was hot and dry and some of the men wore hats. Joe used to wear a hat. There was a time he thought it gave him a jaunty look, but that was long ago, and he didn't worry so much anymore what people thought about his appearance. Joyce told Joe he had a solid build and a handsome smile and a lovely twinkle in his eye. Her opinion was all that mattered these days.

If it hadn't been for those kids sailing about, Joe might not have noticed her at all until it was too late. Her voice had been drowned out by their screeching laughter and noisy auto traffic out on the road. But the fact remained: Joe saw Ida before she saw him. That made all the difference in the world. Because if she'd caught sight of him first, what happened next wouldn't have mattered in the least. Ida was rounder than Joe remembered and her hair was bundled up under a net, but she wore the same sort of frumpy dress he'd seen her in so often, that plain blue cotton floral, and he knew instantly it was her. Holding a brown sack of fruit, she cheerfully completed her transaction with a slight Mexican lady at the cash register.

"Why, thank you, honey! I absolutely taken the biggest ones you had!"

How Ida came to be there in that moment, or where she was going, how she was even free again to go about in the world, Joe would never know. Nor did it really matter as he saw her knot the sack in her fist and turn in his direction. The crowd in front of him had separated enough that he stood out now, and as soon as she looked up, Ida would see him plain as day. But then one of those small boys in shorts skidded through the dusty gravel, tripped, and tumbled at Ida's feet. He skinned both his knees. Blood and dirt. He shrieked like a peacock. Ida gasped, and bent down to comfort the injured boy. She cupped his head and spoke to him in a kindly voice. And in that instant, Joe found his opportunity. He escaped the crowd of worried onlookers and rushed to his Ford, parked under a dusty walnut tree. His heart beating like crazy, he started the motor and backed out away from the fruit stand, nearly hitting another automobile pulling in. One accident was enough. Feeling suddenly like the luckiest man on earth, Joe Krueger ran the Ford up onto the highway, heading north, and put his foot into the gas.

THE AUTHOR WISHES TO ACKNOWLEDGE THOSE WHO CHOSE TO FOLLOW THE STRANGE AND CURIOUS PATH OF THIS STORY FROM ITS BEGINNING.

MILES CORWIN, ERIN COX, MARIANNE DOUGHERTY, WYLENE DUNBAR, KAREN FORD, BARBARA GALLAGHER, GAR ANTHONY HAYWOOD, LUCAS HUNT, GARDNER MEIN, NEAL MITCHELL, LUKAS ORTIZ, BONY SALUDES, JANE ST. CLAIR, CAROL SHELLEY, PHILIP SPITZER, NICOLE STARCZAK, SID STEBEL, GEETS VINCENT, ROBERT WEVERKA.

THANKS GO TO THE LATE, GREAT BARNABY CONRAD, FOR HIS INSIGHTS INTO THE SAN FRANCISCO OF THE EARLY SIXTIES DURING WHICH PART OF THIS STORY OCCURS.

A HUGE DEBT OF GRATITUDE EXTENDS ESPECIALLY TO LYNN DUGGAN, WHOSE TIRELESS INVESTIGATIVE REACH LED FROM COAST TO COAST AND MANY PLACES IN BETWEEN, AND WITHOUT WHOSE INVOLVEMENT THIS NOVEL WOULD CERTAINLY NOT BE THE SAME.

AS ALWAYS, A DEEP APPRECIATION OF GARY GROTH AND HIS ENTHUSIASM FOR GUIDING MY WORK INTO PRINT.

THE WRITER'S ART IS NOT EXCLUSIVELY THE DOMAIN OF SOLITUDES. THERE IS A BEAUTIFUL WORLD BEYOND THE PAGE, AND A FAMILY'S LOVE ENRICHES THIS DAY AFTER DAY. SO, THANK YOU, WESLEY, JOHN HENRY, AND NICOLE, ALWAYS IN MY HEART.